The Angelo she remem[...] a man's passion, and m[...] gotten her alone long e[...] that he wanted to make love to her. Beatrice had been tempted, but an awareness of all the women he had loved kept coming between them.

She could not help wondering if he truly loved her, or was she simply a challenge—the one woman, out of a multitude, he had not been able to bed?

In the end, she had taken the route of a romantic heroine, and had fled from him, thinking that if he truly loved her he would follow her to London.

When that did not happen, she told herself it was confirmation that his feelings were not as strong as she had hoped. But she could not deny that she had been in love with him when she left Italy.

Even now, five years later, she was curious as to who it was that lay beneath his spell.

No, Angelo Bartolini was not the sole reason Beatrice Fairweather was returning to Italy... but he was the foremost one.

Also available from MIRA Books and
ELAINE COFFMAN

THE FIFTH DAUGHTER
THE BRIDE OF BLACK DOUGLAS

Watch for the next historical romance from
ELAINE COFFMAN

THE HIGHLANDER

Coming November 2003

ELAINE COFFMAN

THE ITALIAN

MIRA®

ISBN 1-55166-946-3

THE ITALIAN

Visit us at www.mirabooks.com

Printed in U.S.A.

THE
ITALIAN

Open my heart and you will see,
Graved inside of it, "Italy."

**Robert Browning (1812-1889),
English poet.** *De Gustibus,* st. 2.

One

It was early. The streets of the city were dark. Turin was not yet awake. Beyond the river Po, the bony spine of the Alps was barely visible against a darkened sky. Overhead, the steadfast stars still powdered the heavens, for the sun had not yet come to bless the dewy earth with light.

Angelo made his way along the street that was once called *Decumanus Maximus*, the old Roman road. The long black coat seemed to muffle the tread of his boots upon the ancient paving stones.

He passed along the facade of the buildings that opened onto the square of Palazzo di Città, where the Roman forum and medieval markets had once stood. A sound reached his ears. He paused for a moment near the corner, where the base of the unfinished clock tower waited, its work stopped by the French under Napoleon and never resumed.

The steady clip of hoofbeats cut into the silence. His first thought was that he had been followed. He listened, not moving. He heard it again, and stepped into a doorway darkened by a low overhang. He pressed himself against the door, swallowed by darkness and his coat. His mouth was dry; in spite of his daring, his heart could still pound with fury. His breathing was heavy, almost painful. He drew in another breath and held it until his head began to throb.

The hoofbeats drew closer, and a horse-drawn cart came slowly into view. He heard a clattering and saw the jugs of milk. He exhaled in relief, but he did not dare to move out of the deep shadows. Things are not always what they seem. One move made prematurely could cost him his life.

He was suddenly aware of the tense numbness in his legs and stomach. Perspiration broke out across his forehead. He remained perfectly still. Only his eyes moved as they followed the progress of the cart, until it turned and disappeared into a narrow street.

He did not move. Neither when the cart had passed completely from sight, nor when the steady clip of hooves grew faint. He waited, still as uncut marble, until all was silence.

Slowly, he began to inch his way out of the protective darkness of the doorway. He continued on his way up the street. He kept close to the buildings, his ear finely tuned for the sound of footsteps or the ring of the hooves of another horse.

He was learning a lot about back entrances, side doors, secret passageways and the numerous ways of going to and fro without drawing too much attention. Intrigue was new to him, as were these clandestine meetings, and he was still conscious of the need to look ordinary and up to nothing.

This he found humorous, for the inconspicuous were always those who were up to something.

Nearing his destination, Angelo walked more briskly. The sky over the Alps was beginning to lighten. The mist creeping up from the river Po deepened around him and left a damp sheen on the ancient stones of Turin's streets and buildings.

There must be an easier way to do this, he thought,

feeling his bunched-up nerves slowly unknotting, like a raveling sleeve.

These secret rendezvous always made him uneasy, for he never knew if Metternich's spies had somehow learned about them. He knew what would happen if he were caught. If he had been marked as the next target, they would be relentless. They were men who had killed before, and for crimes less than his. Many of those killed were good friends—friends he laughed and drank coffee with one day, and then never saw again.

Some bodies were discovered later, floating downstream. The rest simply vanished. If he had anything to be thankful for concerning the Austrians, it was that Metternich was more concerned about what went on in Milan than in Turin—although Angelo knew that would not always hold true.

He turned the corner and headed down a narrow street. It was dirty and littered—definitely one that was not much used, except by a few resident rats. At the point where the street almost hit a dead end, he paused in front of a battered door.

He knocked softly, three times. He paused, then knocked twice more.

From the other side of the door came the sound of a shuffling gait. Metal scraped as the bolt was thrown.

The door opened slowly.

A cool draft passed over him, and Angelo stepped inside. The hallway was narrow and ended with a flight of stone steps that led to the cellar below.

He glanced at the young boy who had opened the door, and saw the face of the country he was fighting to give birth to. Just ahead was the flickering light of a branched candlestick that cast eerie shadows on faded and peeling walls. The printer's mute apprentice stepped into view.

He looked Angelo over carefully before motioning for him to follow.

Angelo fell in step behind him.

Halfway down the stairs, he was greeted by the familiar smell of printer's ink. A moment later, he entered the room and saw Lorenzo Spurgazzi hard at work setting type.

"*Ciao,* Lorenzo."

Lorenzo peered at him through fingerprint-marked glasses and his plain, round face brightened. "Hello, my friend. I was wondering if you were going to bring me some more work to do."

"I am your best customer, am I not?"

Lorenzo wiped his ink-stained hands on a rag. "Of course! Of course! You are my most excellent paying customer, so that makes you my best one."

Ah, Italia, Italia, it always comes back to money, thought Angelo. He gave Lorenzo the update he had written last night—an update on the Austrian situation in Lombardy and Piedmont.

"How soon can you have it ready?"

Lorenzo squinted as he glanced over the page.

Angelo plucked the spectacles from Lorenzo's nose and, quickly taking the handkerchief from his own pocket, began to clean them. When he finished he handed them back to Lorenzo. "See if this isn't better."

Lorenzo put the glasses on and his brows shot up like the slanting lines of a steep roof. "Much better," he said, looking as happy as a man in new corduroy. He glanced over the paper. "I can have them to-morrow…late. A hundred and fifty copies, as usual?"

Angelo nodded. "I will send Nicola to pick them up."

"He is a good man."

"And a good friend," Angelo said.

Lorenzo's gaze returned to the paper in his hand, and he read, "'Italians! Free and independent we shall seal the peace of brotherhood with our own hands.'"

He shook his head in a way that was both thoughtful and sad. "God willing, that will be true. You have a knack for expressing yourself and lighting a fire in the hearts of all those who read your notices."

"Unfortunately, my knack for setting fires extends into the Austrian camps, as well."

"You know you are plotting against the most powerful man in Europe. Metternich holds the fate of the world in his hands. His spies are everywhere. You must be very careful."

Angelo said with a grin, "Of course I will be careful. I am young and not yet married—therefore I have plans that do not include death or imprisonment."

Angelo left as he had come, quietly and quickly. Only this time, he took a different route through the dark streets of Turin. As he walked, the tension in his body began to subside.

He was glad the worst was over.

The thought had no more than entered his mind, when he rounded the corner and came face-to-face with a detachment of Austrian hussars. He knew by their slow pace that they were on patrol.

Either that, or they were looking for him.

He was about to continue, when one of the men, spotting him, shouted.

Angelo turned around and started to run up the

street he had just come down. He wasn't about to let it end like this.

When he reached the intersection, he turned down a side street.

Behind him, he heard shouts and the rub of sabers pulled out of scabbards. A loud whinny, and the horses broke into a run. The hussars were giving chase.

He could hear them close behind him, nipping at his heels. He ran harder. Now it was a matter of life or death—a contest between his cunning and their large number.

He raced down the street and turned at the next corner. He spied an overturned cart with a broken wheel and crouched behind it. He dared not look, but he listened. The Austrians did not turn up the street, but rode on by, passing not more than four arm's lengths from where he hid.

At the next intersection, one of the officers held up his hand and the detachment came to a stop. The soldier spoke to the soldier next to him. "I think we have missed him."

"Down a side street, do you think?"

"Of course. The Piedmontese do not come out in the open to fight. I will go back and take a closer look. He is on foot, but I wager he has a horse waiting somewhere."

After a few more words and several glances backward, the officer turned, and breaking away from the others, rode off in the opposite direction.

Without moving a muscle, Angelo remained where he was for some time, in case the hussars, not finding him, decided to double back. When the sky began to lighten, he crept out of his hiding place, and after a stretch of his tired muscles, he continued on his way through the city streets, until he reached a little-used carting road.

He had a small pistol in his pocket, but once the shot was discharged there would be no time to reload. He wished he had his saber, but it was waiting at the edge of town with his horse.

Surrounded by silence, he stopped concentrating solely on the danger he was in to focus on getting back to his horse. He preferred to make a clean getaway, without engaging anyone, but he knew it could easily go the other way. For this reason, he always had to be ready to kill—if it came to that. Violence was not Angelo's way, but when one was backed against a wall, animal instinct took over.

When he reached the edge of the city he saw, across the way, the dark mass of trees where his horse was tied. Yet he was cautious. He knew the hussars could be waiting and watching for him, hidden behind some building, waiting like the vultures they were.

He remained motionless for a while longer, and kept an ear cocked for the sound of horses, or voices, but he heard nothing. At last, he decided he could not remain there forever. The city would be coming to life soon.

With a look in each direction, he ran across the clearing.

He drew near to the place where his mount waited, and heard a soft whinny. He reached his horse and untied him. With the reins in his hand, he was about to mount, when there was a rustling in the brush to his right. From the corner of his eye, he saw the oily gleam of gold braid on a uniform, as the dark form of an Austrian officer stepped out of the cover of trees.

The officer glanced around as if looking for something. "Pity. I put off killing you some time ago because I hoped you would lead me to your compatriots."

"I am alone, as you can see."

"I can kill one as easily as a dozen."

"You could end up like Caesar."

The officer laughed and reached for his saber.

Angelo glanced quickly at his horse. His saber was in the scabbard on his saddle, but on the opposite side. Realizing he had no choice he dove under his horse. As he rolled to his feet on the other side, he grabbed the hilt of his saber and turned, giving his horse a slap to the rump as he faced his opponent. The officer lunged, and their sabers rang out with the clash of metal against metal.

Immediately, Angelo noticed two things: First, the Austrian did not have the thin, light saber, the *sciabola di terreno,* a superior saber designed for dueling by his Italian countrymen. Second, the officer was not schooled in the manner of Casanova, for he stood facing Angelo with a dagger in one hand and his saber in the other.

He presented a nice frontal target that a twelve-year-old could hit.

Casanova had been the first to toss aside the dagger and turn sideways at a ninety-degree angle, so only his side was presented to his opponent—providing a much thinner target allowing more flexibility.

Angelo assumed this stance and saw the confused look in the Austrian's eyes. The posture was obviously new to him.

He was surprised again when Angelo made the

first dramatic thrust, something that was impossible to do if you faced your opponent.

After only a few seconds, Angelo nicked the man in the shoulder and drew first blood. Honorably, he stopped and saluted the officer by bringing his saber up in front of his face. "I have no quarrel with you," he said, and turned away, intent upon mounting his horse to ride away.

"In spite of your fancy methods, you are still a dead man," the officer said, and lunged with the obvious intent of stabbing Angelo in the back.

Angelo whirled around, saw he had no choice and, with a sudden move, lunged and thrust again.

The officer glanced down at the red stain that slowly spread over his chest, and, with an expression of shock, dropped to his knees and fell forward.

Angelo did not have to check. He knew the man was dead—the saber had pierced his heart.

He mounted swiftly and rode back into Turin. In less than twenty minutes, he turned up the street where he resided, relieved to see the gates to his villa rising before him.

Angelo Bartolini rode through the open gates, his mind too focused on the events of that morning to take notice of a black cat that darted across his path.

Two

Beatrice had always known she would go back to Italy, when the regrets of the past overcame her fears and hesitations of the future, but it was not until she was living in Paris that she made the actual decision to return.

After thinking about it for only a few days, she dispatched a letter to her aunt and uncle who lived near Florence, telling them of the anticipated date of her arrival.

I shall take a diligence from Paris to Nice, and travel by boat from Nice to La Spezia. From there I shall travel to Pisa by coach, and then to Florence, and then to Villa Mirandola.

I cannot adequately convey my excitement at the thought of seeing all of you again, and renewing my affections for the family I have always held so dear.

I wrote you some time ago that I had moved to Paris to continue my study of painting, and it has proven to be a wise decision. I long to paint all the lovely places I saw during my last visit, and I especially look forward to painting all of your portraits. I hope you will indulge me in this. I have so much to tell you, and look forward to hearing everything you have to tell me.

Once she made the decision to return it took only a week to pack her belongings, including the supplies and canvases in her studio. Before she had time to think of what this trip would mean the day of her departure arrived, and she found herself settled in a rather pathetic diligence drawn by four horses.

Paris was bustling beneath awnings, where patrons crowded around tables at the outdoor cafés. Shops were open and horse-drawn carts clogged the streets, along with wagons and lumbering cabs that looked ready to collapse. With a heart that pounded with excitement, she watched out the window as they passed the Morgue on the Île de la Cité and the Pont Neuf bridge.

Beatrice always looked at life as an adventure— one that constantly provided her artist's eye with numerous opportunities to observe and to sketch. Not even the pathetic diligence escaped her well-trained eye, and she made a quick sketch of the postilion, who drove the team while sitting upon his own horse.

He was a colorful figure in enormous jackboots, who brandished a long whip that he cracked with much finesse. He reminded her somewhat of the stories she had heard about highwaymen, when she was a child.

But not even such a performance could breathe life into those horses.

Inside the coach there were six passengers—Beatrice, and a family of five. The children were small, well mannered and slept most of the time.

"Are you traveling to Nice?" she inquired of the mother.

"No, we are going to visit our family in Troyes. I fear the children would have me quite weary if we were going all the way to Nice. Is that your final destination?''

"No, I have quite a long journey ahead of me. I, too, am going to visit family. They live near Florence.''

"Such a long way, but you are young and have no children to supervise.''

No, Beatrice thought, *I have no children—but I might be married and the mother of several children by now if I had remained in Italy and had given free reign to all the passion between Angelo Bartolini and myself.*

She pushed such thoughts away, preferring not to think about them right now. *I have been sufficiently haunted by them in the past month,* she decided. *It is time I focused my thoughts on the trip at hand.*

Before too long, they were out of the congestion of the city and into the country, where the diligence bumped and bounced over rough roads, and the scenery was repetitious and rather plain. There was not a lot of traffic on the road, but Beatrice did notice that beggars seemed to pop up as prolifically as the dandelions that grew along the way.

They passed through many old towns with drawbridges, moats and tall towers. They traversed rickety old bridges, and passed an occasional chateau surrounded by farmland, as gradually the countryside grew more interesting.

When looking out the window became tiring, she passed the time sleeping, or talking to *Monsieur* and *Madame* La Pierre and the little La Pierres. At one point, when she noticed how tired *Madame* La Pierre was, she said, "Please, *madame,* let me hold little

Yvette for a while. There is a nice view out the window that I am sure she would enjoy."

"Oh, *mademoiselle,* you are overly generous, and I should decline out of manners' sake, but my arms ache something dreadful."

Beatrice opened her arms and took Yvette onto her lap. Yvette was an adorable little girl, two years old, with tightly wound blond curls, and the loveliest big blue eyes. She could talk, but her primary form of entertainment was sucking her thumb, which she would pop out to answer a question, or to point at something she saw along the roadside.

Beatrice played a few games with Yvette and taught her an English nursery rhyme. When she returned Yvette to her mother some time later the little girl soon fell asleep.

Beatrice took out her sketchbook and captured images of Yvette in various poses. She sketched the other family members as well, and fully intended to paint the scene while in Italy, but *Madame* La Pierre was so taken by the drawings that Beatrice gave them to her.

"Thank you! Thank you!" *Madame* La Pierre said. "I have never met an artist before. You have such talent. Have you ever considered taking it up professionally?"

Beatrice only smiled and said, "I have thought about it."

When they stopped that first night Beatrice bid the La Pierres adieu and wondered who her new traveling companions would be. Whomever they were, she prayed they would not be predisposed to talking for the entire journey, for such people were the bane of travelers and made a journey almost torturous.

If Beatrice tried very hard, she could find one good

thing to say about the inn where the diligence stopped that first night—that it gave her the opportunity to get out of the cramped coach and stretch her legs.

The food was abominable, the wine poison, the surroundings abysmal and she could not find adequate words in all the English language to describe the condition of the beds. All in all, she found it quite miraculous that by morning she had not contracted some dreadful illness, or at least a few fleabites. The only sign of efficiency that she witnessed was the presentation of the bill, which was long for a stop of only seven hours.

Although awakened at two in the morning and told to dress so they could be on their way, she actually looked forward to being in the diligence again, and was the first one inside that morning.

Her anticipation dwindled, however, when she realized there would now be eight adult passengers and two children crowded into the small space, and she found herself quite concerned and dreading the trip. Her concern turned to absolute horror when she saw a rather enormous woman approach the diligence. It occurred to her that this woman would require the space of at least two persons, perhaps more. When she thought of the four-day journey to Nice that lay ahead, Beatrice immediately ordered her luggage to be removed.

"But, *mademoiselle,* we have already loaded your luggage."

"Then, you should know precisely where it is, so you can just as easily unload it."

She had learned that reasoning with a Frenchman was about as effective as complaining about the weather. In the end, she was forced to pay them handsomely to remove her luggage. While they were earning their reward, she made arrangements to hire a private coach to take her the rest of the way to Nice.

It was an expensive choice, albeit a wise one, for the road to Nice led through the center of town, which gave Beatrice the opportunity to see what was happening there. It was market day, held in a square dominated by the presence of a gloomy cathedral that took up one side, looking grim and cold in the midst of such gaiety.

Although it was still early, the square bustled with vendors setting up their booths beneath canvas-covered stalls, where they hung merchandise that fluttered in a lazy breeze. Everywhere she looked, she saw fruit sellers, lace sellers, food vendors and the latest creations by the village shoe smiths. The farmers were there, too, grouped around baskets filled with eggs and bright, shiny vegetables.

Traveling by diligence or private coach, the journey from Paris to Lyons, a distance of about three hundred and sixty miles, was covered in five days. The coach she hired was a remarkable improvement over the diligence, and it was pulled by six horses instead of four. It also boasted two postilions.

She had to pay a great deal more to travel at a faster pace, which meant more frequent changes of horses, but she was assured they would make it in four days' time, without her being roused out of bed each morning at two o'clock and told to dress and be in the coach in half an hour, as was customary when traveling by diligence.

The road to Nice was a long one, and the journey tiresome, which made her question her sanity at such an undertaking. But it did afford her ample time to examine her reasons for making the trip in the first place.

One of the postilions asked her why she was going to Italy. "I have family there," she replied, "and I have not seen them for quite some time."

That was true, but seemed more so when she heard the words aloud. She asked herself the same question. *Why am I going back?*

True, there was the longing to reconnect with the only true family she had. Beatrice had four sisters, but the youngest, Maresa, was the only one she was close to. However, Maresa was happily married with three children, and had an orphanage to oversee.

Because Beatrice had lost her mother at an early age, her domineering father and three older sisters, who had inherited their father's disposition, raised her. There was never a sense of family or togetherness, for her father looked at being a parent the same way he viewed being a viscount—it was a duty.

The Bartolinis, on the other hand, were the epitome of familial love. They were a strong family, with each member having a distinct personality, and Beatrice was drawn to them from the moment they met, in spite of her shyness. In all the years between, she had never found anything to take the place of family, and something within her wanted, and needed, this family connection.

Beatrice wanted not only to get to know her family better, but also to capture each of them on canvas. Painting was her life now, and that meant she approached each day from a painter's perspective. Perhaps this was motivated purely by her desire to give something back to the family that had given so much to her. But she knew, if she were honest with herself, that part of the reason was that she wanted to document their existence. Perhaps one day when she settled in one place, she could line the walls of her home with the portraits of her loved ones, the way other families did.

It gave her a good feeling to think she would have the opportunity to paint each of them, one by one, which would afford her many occasions to not only study them in detail, but to spend time with them alone, in silent observation.

She closed her eyes and imagined each family member sitting before her, and made predictions as to what each would look like on canvas. It was peculiar that of all the family members she could recall in vivid detail, it was Angelo's canvas that remained blank.

"Ah, *mademoiselle*," the postilion said, "are you sure it is not the love of some handsome Italian man that draws you back?"

Well, that certainly took her aback, and she said, "Of course not. I have yet to meet the man for whom I would endure the torture of this travel."

The postilion laughed and winked at his compatriot. "You have not met the right man, *mademoiselle,* for if you had, you would be willing to walk on hot coals to be with him."

The French are ever a confident lot, she thought, and found her mind focusing rather vividly upon Angelo. Were there other reasons for this trip to Italy and was she simply ignoring them?

No, she decided honestly. He was one of the reasons. Not the only one. *Then, why is his canvas blank?* she asked herself. Perhaps it was because she did not know, as yet, how or where things would lie between them. As someone who dealt with emotions daily, she knew Angelo's reaction at seeing her

again, and the relationship that would be renewed
between them, either positive or negative, would
greatly influence the image she painted. One could
not paint a portrait void of emotion, for there would
be no life, no feeling.

Whenever she thought of Italy, she envisioned so
much—the study of art and history, the emotion of
pathos, the intricate embroidery of intrigue, the back-
drop for illicit love, the study of tribulation, patience
and the passage of time.

It was all there. Waiting.

The next three days passed, one after the other,
and soon they were stopping at a way station to make
their last change of horses before continuing on to
Nice.

Beatrice left the carriage during this time, to walk
around a bit and stretch her legs. When she returned
to the station house, she saw the two postilions ar-
guing with an old woman who looked on the point
of tears.

Beatrice watched for a while, and when she could
stand it no longer, she walked toward them. "What
is happening here?" she asked.

"Nothing—it's just a crazy old woman," one of
the postilions said.

"Oh, *mademoiselle,* I am not crazy, only desper-
ate. My son was gravely wounded in an accident, and
I left Genoa to come to Paris to be with him. Praise
God, he has recovered and I am on my way home.
On the way, my coach was set upon by robbers, and
I was left here, stranded, without any means of going
on. I begged these gentlemen to allow me to ride as
far as Nice, but they refuse."

Beatrice glanced at the old woman with her neat
gray hair held back in a knot by two combs, attired

in a black dress and heavy black stockings. No one this old should have to suffer such. "You may ride as far as Nice with us, and there I will arrange for your passage to Genoa."

The old woman crossed herself and took Beatrice's hand and kissed it. She began to speak in Italian, too rapidly for Beatrice to understand everything.

"Mademoiselle," one of the postilions said in a warning tone. "If I might..."

Beatrice glanced at the old woman's lone piece of luggage. "Load her bag, and let us be off."

Soon they were settled comfortably in the coach. "I am glad your son has recovered," Beatrice said. "Were you in Paris long?"

"Three months. And you? You do not speak French like a native."

Beatrice smiled. "I am English. I am going to Florence to visit my aunt and uncle."

"Oh, Florence, the loveliest of cities."

"Yes, isn't it?"

"You have been there, then?"

"Yes, although it has been almost five years since I was there."

"I can see the excitement in your face, and I hear it in your voice."

"I suppose it does show, for I am excited to go back. I don't know how to describe it. I feel as if I am old, and yet, each mile I travel is compensated with the subtraction of years and I will arrive younger and more carefree than when I embarked."

"Ah yes, I remember that feeling. Oh, to be seventy again." She spoke with a voice that rustled, dry as garlic.

"What a lovely thing to say, especially when all one hears about growing old is complaints."

"I, for one, venerate old age, because I find it quite extraordinary. Why would I want to repeat the past, when it is the future I find exciting."

Captivated by this old woman who seemed to have come out of nowhere, Beatrice began to think there was something almost magical about her sudden appearance in her life. "Forgive me for not introducing myself. I am Beatrice Fairweather."

"Giuseppa Timoni."

Soon the two of them fell into flowing conversation, and Beatrice found the time literally flying. Before long, she began to tell *Signora* Timoni more about herself.

"If I have any regrets from my previous visit, it was that I allowed my shyness and inexperience to guide me, rather than living as the Italians do. I love the way Italians, with their turbulent past, take everything in stride. They live each day to the fullest."

Signora Timoni nodded and said, "That is because the past has taught us there is little security in planning for the future. With us, everything is for the first time, whether it is the Tuscans eating their white beans, or the Neapolitans talking with their gestures."

Beatrice found such thoughts a bit overwhelming, and it gave her pause. She closed her eyes, and could almost feel the warmth of Italy reaching out to heat her chilled English blood and melt her hard, Anglo-Saxon crust.

"So tell me why you have not mentioned your young man? He is Italian, no?"

With her eyes closed, Beatrice meditated upon that for a moment. And when she opened her eyes, she was smiling. "Yes, he is Italian, although I am not so sure he is *my* young man."

"That must be why you put off talking about him. You were waiting until you had no more things to talk about."

"Or perhaps I was saving the best for last."

"You have not seen him for almost five years?"

"Yes. I find it hard to believe. His name is Angelo." She paused, surprised at how much emotion the sound of his name still elicited.

"Was it difficult leaving, and staying away from him?"

"Much more so than I ever dreamed it could be."

"And yet, you know it was for the best."

"Yes. I have no doubts about that. The first year was the most difficult. By the second year, I was feeling quite like an old woman who had lost her spectacles—confused, exposed to the world, uncertain of each step, swearing I saw things that were not there. Once, I was so lost in thought, I even paused to say good afternoon to a grandfather clock as I passed."

"Time did not help?"

"The third year," she said. "That is when I began to realize that time does heal wounds—but it does not make one forget. I saw time more as the eternal teacher, for it taught me the past is something one must learn from, or at least resolve, before it is possible to move on. I realized then that I could never completely put him out of my mind until I saw him again and answered the question that has always haunted me."

"You wanted to know if you did the right thing?"

Beatrice stared into those wise old eyes. "How do you know these things?"

"I was young once, and in love, like you. There is no memory like the memory of first love."

"And yet, I left Angelo and Italy in the bloom of young love. I did not realize until I reached England that I had left a part of myself behind, as well."

"You have said what you lost when you left. Now, you must ask yourself what you hope to find by returning."

"I am not sure I can do that."

"You should always take aim before you release the arrow."

Beatrice found her heart warmed by this woman's wise counsel. *Signora* Timoni was like the mother she had never had, and she felt comfortable confiding in her, as if she was meant to meet this woman at this point in her life, and share these truths with her. "I need to know he has forgotten me and gone on with his life, so that I may, in turn, go on with mine."

"And if he has not forgotten you?"

Beatrice put her hands upon her knees and held them there as she leaned back. "Well, then, I suppose I need to know that, too. Your questions have raised so many questions. How will it feel to see him again? Will my heart be still, or will it race at the sound of his voice, and stop completely with one look from his dark eyes?"

"It would seem you still love him, which makes me wonder—why did you leave him in the first place?"

"I knew you would get around to asking me that. It is a question I have asked myself time and again."

"With no answer?"

For a moment Beatrice sat there, as lost and forlorn as a shipwrecked creature who has at last found his foot upon dry land. "No, I have answers. At least now I do. They did not all come to me at once but, gradually over the years they began to infiltrate my consciousness. My first reasons were justifying ones. I was too young to know what love was, but then I remembered I was three and twenty—not exactly a nursling. And there was my shyness—an almost painful shyness—but that did not seem quite valid, because although I was shy around Angelo, he was also the first one to show me the way out of the maze of timidity I was lost in."

"Nothing is as bold as love," she said. "Ahh, *dolce amore*... How well I remember those days, before my hair turned gray and my hands became as stiff as iron. I remember my husband, who would wax the tips of his mustache with pitch. He was a simple man, a farmer, but he loved me well. Passion blazed between us, until we were both burned by it, and to this day, it warms me still."

Dolce amore...sweet love, Beatrice thought.

"If only I could have seen the truth in that back then, but I could not. I was too inexperienced at the ways of the heart. Faith! I had never even had a beau...had never even been kissed when I first came to Italy."

"No man could have called himself Italian if he had let you return in that same state."

Beatrice laughed outright. "Oh, he is Italian to the core but, I must say, he took his time about it. He paid me little notice at first and then later, when he did notice me, it was on the occasions when I did or said something so utterly foolish or ridiculous that I wanted to swim back to England, if it meant I could escape his laugh, or the mystery in those eyes."

"And now, the memories of those humiliations come to the front, do they not?"

"Oh yes, and I am recalling now the most vivid incident. It was a time after the grape harvest, when my cousin Serena and I were sitting on the edge of the vat where the crushed grapes awaited straining.

"'Don't sit too far back,' my cousin said. 'You might fall in, and the stain will never wash from your clothes.'

"My reply was a confident one, for I said, 'I have always had an exceptional sense of balance.' I would have exhibited it, too, if Angelo had not wandered into my view at that particular moment, and the sight of him so unsettled me that I lost my balance and flipped over, backwards, into the vat."

Beatrice paused. "I have never forgotten that sweet, sticky smell. After swallowing a good portion of the vat's contents, I decided to remain there, rather than humiliate myself further by clumsily climbing out in front of him. Unfortunately, Angelo, being the type that has a strong conviction of gentlemanly behavior, grabbed me by the arm and pulled me out. As he patiently picked grape seeds and grape rinds from my person, I began to feel sick. 'I don't feel very well,' I said.

"He told me I had probably swallowed too many grape seeds."

Signora Timoni was smiling. "Surely, that was the last of it."

"No, it was not. My teeth were blue for a week."

Angelo had taken her by the hand and led her out into the garden to stand behind the protective screen of a fragrant jasmine in full bloom....

Beatrice looked up now and saw that *Signora* Timoni had fallen asleep.

After a few minutes, she closed her own eyes. Before long, her mind drifted back to what Angelo had said that day, out behind the jasmine.

"You must understand, *cara,* that not all comparisons are made to injure. I am trying to understand you. You are puzzling to the extreme, and therefore exasperating. I have never met a woman like you. I find you very flowerlike. In the Alps we have a flower called a gentiana that blooms only in cold weather. It is a beautiful purple-blue flower, and often it blooms against a background of snow. I see you as that gentiana, only you are trying to be a rose. I keep asking myself why. Do you not see that it is only when you try to be a rose that you fail? Be what you are, Gentiana…grow where you are planted… bloom at your appointed time."

"Oh, does that mean I should return to England?" she asked.

He shook his head. "Your strong will always gets in the way of your intellect." He leaned closer and kissed her on the lips.

Beatrice had been so astonished that her mouth fell open. It was her first kiss, and she had been trying to relish the moment when he gave her a second one. Faith, she had felt as if she were blooming.

It was a wonderful memory that warmed her. Slowly, Beatrice lifted her hand to touch the tips of her fingers to her lips, surprised at the way her heart slammed against the wall of her chest.

Oh dear, she thought. If the thought of one kiss did this, what would happen when she saw him?

After that first kiss, there were many, many more. There were also times when she doubted someone with Angelo's looks, charm, polish and experience could possibly fall in love with someone like her. He was in possession of all the *savoir*'s—*savoir-faire, savoir-vivre*. She wondered if he saw her not as a love object, but as a challenge. He had said as much himself that day when they spoke in the garden, just before he kissed her.

The Angelo she remembered was a man, with a man's passion, and more than once he had gotten her alone long enough to make it known that he wanted to make love to her. Beatrice had been tempted, but an awareness of all the women he had loved kept coming between them.

Was she simply the one woman, out of a multitude, that he had not been able to bed?

In the end, she had taken the route of a romantic heroine, and had fled from him, thinking that if he truly loved her, he would follow her to London.

When that did not happen, she told herself it was confirmation that his feelings were not as strong as she had hoped. She could not deny that she had been in love with him when she left Italy. She simply had not known what to do about it. Her regret was that she had taken the path of least resistance. Why hadn't she been stronger? Why did she not stay and see where their love for one another would lead?

Even now, she was curious as to who it was that lay beneath his spell, and if he whispered to her in soft Italian that melted over her like kisses. Did another woman look at those penetrating, chocolate-brown eyes, the high cheekbones, and think just how pleasing his face was to look upon; how charismatically charming he really was?

No, Angelo Bartolini was not the sole reason for her return…but he was the foremost one.

At that moment, the carriage hit a bump, jostling

Beatrice from her reverie and *Signora* Timoni from her sleep.

"Nice," the postilion called out.

In ten minutes' time, the coach stopped at an inn, and Beatrice felt a stab of regret that *Signora* Timoni would not be accompanying her farther.

"I have so enjoyed our visit. I do wish you were continuing on to Florence."

"As I wish you were on your way to Genoa. I shall never forget you, sweet English lady."

"Nor I you."

Once they alighted from the coach, Beatrice arranged for *Signora* Timoni's passage to Genoa. "Fortunately for you, there is a boat leaving in two hours. I, on the other hand, must stay the night, for the next boat to La Spezia leaves at dawn. I have asked the postilion to drive you down to the quay, and to help you get onboard." She withdrew from her purse a small silk pouch that contained several coins. "I want you to take this."

"You have been far too kind already," *Signora* Timoni said.

Beatrice took her hand, put the pouch in her palm and closed the fingers over it. "I will rest better knowing you have enough money to see you home."

Signora Timoni kissed her on each cheek. "Be happy with your Angelo. Do not let time slip away."

"We are ready now, *signora*," the postilion said, having carried Beatrice's bags into the inn.

"Goodbye and Godspeed, *Signora* Timoni," Beatrice said, and then she watched the coach disappear along the road that led down to the sea.

Beatrice left for La Spezia at first light, and, entertained with the recollections of the previous day and the anticipation of seeing the Italian coastline,

she passed much of her time on deck. She spent the
night in Pisa, and left for Florence the next morning.

It was impossible to travel through the pleasant
Tuscan countryside from Pisa to Florence and be serene, for each turn of the wheel brought her closer
to her destination.

She sat with her window down so she could not
only see Tuscany, but also hear and smell it. Many
of the things Beatrice saw were familiar, and she
recalled having seen them during her previous trip,
but she did not remember so many little white
crosses along the roadside. It wasn't that the crosses
themselves were peculiar, for there were many such
crosses in England, and many towns, such as Charing
Cross, had derived their names from them.

However, these crosses were different, for some
had roosters perched on top, while others had tiny
spears, pieces of sponge, garlands of thorny vine, or
even a hammer and nails dangling from them. When
she asked the driver to stop at one of them, she observed a small coat and a box of dice.

"Why are all of these things hanging on the
crosses? What do they signify?" she asked.

The driver explained simply, "They are objects
connected with the death of the Savior, *signorina*—
the cock that crowed at Saint Peter's denial, the
spear, the sponge soaked in vinegar, the coat the soldiers threw dice for, the crown of thorns—they are
all here so we will remember, *signorina*."

Once back in the carriage, Beatrice was anxious
to arrive at her destination. She found it difficult to
sit still, when she wanted to fly on a winged horse—
but even that would not get her there fast enough.

She arrived in Florence at last, and after spending
the night in a lovely little inn near the banks of the

Arno, she arose early the next morning. Already she was experiencing the dry mouth, moist hands and rapid heartbeat of anticipation, and at the same time, she was also confident. She was no longer the shy, insecure woman who had left Italy. Now she faced her fears and sent them packing.

She admonished herself. "Stop trying to understand why you left. You left because it was the right thing to do at that time. You had not discovered who you were or what you wanted to do with your life. I daresay if you had married Angelo then, you would not have been able to hold him. He would have taken a mistress before six months was up. You had to become the gentian, Beatrice, before you could see yourself as someone Angelo could love."

Filled with expectancy and hope, she wondered if she would arrive and soon realize all this nostalgia wasn't all it was supposed to be. She did not know how she would feel the first time she saw him—or how he would feel when he saw her—but her luggage was loaded and the coach was ready. The villa and her future awaited her...with or without Angelo Bartolini.

She stepped into the coach and settled herself for the short ride to Villa Mirandola. As the coach lurched forward, she reminded herself that her leaving had not broken his heart.

No, but it would warm hers to find that she had, at least, cracked it in a place or two.

Three

Five years had passed since Napoleon had been defeated and the war ended, but the problems for Prince Metternich were just beginning.

While his valet dressed him, Metternich stood beneath a flattering portrait of himself painted in 1815, when he was appointed State Chancellor. He was reading an impassioned letter that had arrived that morning from Milan, sent by Count Karl von Schisler, head of the Hapsburg secret police in Italy. Von Schisler wrote:

My Prince, this was written by a young, idealistic liberal in Turin. His name is Angelo Bartolini. There are many with his political beliefs and doctrines, but none have his likeable personality, or the absolute integrity and sincerity that draw the Italian people to his side. He is described as warmhearted and genuine in his love for the peasants and the middle-class. He is called a true patriot—a man who will freely surrender anything for the common good, or sacrifice what is most dear to him for the benefit of others. He is an inspiration to the people, a man who came along at the right time. His biggest asset is that the people trust him. In reading this, it is my hope that you see what we are up against.

Furious, Metternich wadded up the letter and threw it across the room. "Imbecile...incompetent fool...he writes as if he is championing this Bartolini's cause. I do not want to know his virtues, or what the people think of him. I want to know his past, his darkest secrets and his fears. That will be the only way to stop him.''

Metternich stopped speaking so suddenly that his valet looked up in a questioning manner.

''Finish buttoning my coat. Shall I tell the emperor that my clumsy valet is the cause of my tardiness?''

As the valet set to work, Metternich drummed his fingers on the table beside him, aware now of a sudden change of heart, for he was thinking, *If we could win such a man over to our side, we would have Italy in our pocket.*

Prince Clemens Wenzel Nepomuk Lothar, Prince of Metternich-Winneburg, was precisely what his name conjured up. He was the most powerful and the most feared man in all of Europe. He was the foreign minister of Austria and the leader of foreign policy for the house of Hapsburg.

The Grand Seigneur was considered quite handsome, and he possessed all the finer attributes of a gentleman—education, fine manners, immense wealth; and he was quite brilliant diplomatically. He was, however, a product of a society that was removed from the poor peasants living and working like slaves in the cities and rural areas.

Metternich was beyond shrewd. He was serious, possessing a keen sense of reality. When he was against something, it was not due to lack of insight or foresight, but because he saw himself as the preserver—the one who would see to the preservation of the society he was born into and the emperor he served.

So far, that seemed to be working, for he presided over one of the most pervasive police states in history, a reign others described as "a large army of soldiers, a sitting army of bureaucrats, a kneeling army of priests and a creeping army of informers."

Prince Metternich was without equal in his talent for appearing as the prince of peace for Europe, while inwardly vowing to crush the revolutionary ideas of people and their hope for independence. His extreme brand of conservatism complemented perfectly his utter hatred for liberals and nationals.

He wanted Europe back the way it was before the war, with the lower class ruled by royalty. And why wouldn't he? He was a prince, after all.

But not the prince of peace.

In his magnificent home, Metternich paced the gleaming parquet floors in front of the tall windows of Metternich Palais. With his hands behind him, he gazed out at the towering spray of fountains in the spectacular gardens and watched as his carriage was brought around to the front.

"My Lord and Prince, your carriage awaits you," one of the servants announced.

Dressed in his most splendid clothes, Metternich turned on his heels and went downstairs. A few minutes later, he stepped into the carriage and headed for his appointment with Francis I, Emperor of Austria.

Metternich knew the king had never completely forgiven him for arranging the marriage of his daughter, Marie-Louise, to Napoleon, and because of this, Metternich was determined to win back the emperor's favor by handing him all of Italy, on the proverbial silver platter.

"Ah, my dear Prince," the emperor said as Metternich was ushered into his presence. "Come and bring me up to date on our little wayward Italian kingdom."

"Your Majesty," Metternich said, bowing deeply, "I am always happy to provide information to you on any subject."

"I understand the radicalism is becoming more of a threat to our conservative ideals. Is this something I should be concerned about?"

"I have everything under control, Your Majesty. It is nothing more than the patriotic babble of a few university students and liberal aristocrats who have nothing better to do. Naturally, since Austria has the two richest Italian territories of Lombardy and Venetia, these romantics and liberals are demanding their own government in all the Italian states. The movement started in the south, in Naples, and is spreading northward."

"Of course. Everyone knows there is no money in the south," Francis said.

"Your Majesty is very astute in seeing to the center of this."

"Still, I do not want anything to cause problems for us. I had to give up the title Emperor of the Holy Roman Empire, which had been in my family for a thousand years. I will not tolerate anything that threatens the Emperor of Austria."

"If Your Majesty would like, I can step up our security and increase the number of our troops in Italy, as a precaution and as a reminder to the Italians that we will not tolerate their middle-class dreams."

"I think reinforcing our protection in those areas

would be wise. Personally, I would find it comforting to know we have the power to enforce our rights."

Metternich bowed. "I shall see to it immediately, Your Majesty."

When Metternich arrived at his palace he immediately sent for his emissary, Baron Maximilian Werberg.

"I want you to leave for Milan immediately. I am writing a letter for von Schisler. You will deliver it to him personally, and see that he understands the seriousness of the matter. I want to know about a young radical named Angelo Bartolini, who seems to be stirring up trouble." Metternich thought about this faceless Italian patriot, who bothered him more than he let on. "Have you heard of him?"

"No, my Prince, the name is not familiar to me."

"Perhaps that is because he is active in Turin, although his radical writings often appear in Milan."

"I know the type," Werberg said. "They champion the cause of Italy's conscripted soldiers—men who returned after Napoleon's fall to discover they were no longer masters of their own house, but prisoners of peace."

"Precisely. Politically, the Italians think everything that is happening in Italy is wrong, especially in the north. They cry out that Piedmont and Lombardy suffer under what they term 'the brutally harsh efficiency of Austrian bureaucracy.' This alone is reason to use death and prison sentences as a matter of routine discouragement. It is for the good of Austria that I am forced to keep the Hapsburg spies everywhere."

"Most of the trouble began with the secret society they call the Carbonari," Werberg said.

"Yes, I know all about it and its members. Almost all of those we have assassinated or imprisoned are Carbonari members, foolishly loyal to their sacred oath."

"It is a small movement, my Prince."

"Insurgence in Italy might be small, but it is growing, and any united movement of patriotic resistance that sweeps all the way from Naples to the north is of grave concern. These radicals must be stopped. That is why I am sending you."

"I shall leave immediately, my Prince."

Metternich finished his letter to von Schisler, sprinkled it with fine sand and put his seal in wax. He handed it to Werberg. "Tell von Schisler to be in contact as soon as he has the desired information."

Werberg took the letter and bowed. "I will leave within the hour, my Prince."

Metternich nodded. He did not bother to watch Werberg's departure. Instead, he was recalling something Werberg had said: *"It is a small movement, my Prince...I know all about it and its members."*

Apparently, there were many who knew of this unrest, and of the call to freedom that rang from the throats of Italy's young aristocrats and educated liberals.

But only he saw them as a threat to the world.

Four

Angelo put on a little of his favorite scent, adjusted his cuffs and donned his jacket. He then began to arrange in his pockets his money clip, handkerchief and knife. He sounded the bell on his watch, checked it against the time on the mantel clock and, after adjusting the chain and fob, dropped it into his watch pocket.

He carried his coffee into his library and sorted through yesterday's mail. The letter from his father caught his eye, so he opened it and read. His father wanted him to come home. There were urgent matters to discuss about the family estate near Turin. Not one word about what those matters were, or how the Bartolinis' estate figured into things. It wasn't the best time for Angelo to leave Turin. There were urgent matters here, as well, but his father rarely asked anything of him. He would find the time to go to Tuscany.

Angelo put the letter in the drawer and locked it, then sat down to add a few figures and transfer them into his ledger. He wrote a letter to his parents telling them he would be home next week. The other letter was to his banker.

He moved to a large trestle table in front of the window, where he had been studying the design of the gardens at Villa Adriana, the old Bartolini estate near Turin.

Villa Adriana had been named after one of his father's grandmothers when she moved there as a young bride in 1440. No one had lived there since his father, Tito, married his mother, and Gisella had wanted to live at her family home, Villa Mirandola, in Tuscany. It had always been a dream of Angelo's to live in the ancient villa and to restore the vineyards, gardens and fountains to the magnificent state they had once enjoyed.

Naturally, his mind lingered on the idea that perhaps what his father wanted to talk to him about was that very thing, for Tito always said, *"When you are older, and wiser, I will give Villa Adriana to you."* Angelo was older. The part that concerned him was, did his father see him as wiser?

His father did not approve of Angelo's politically liberal views, or his involvement with the Carbonari, and for that reason, Angelo doubted his father was ready to give him Villa Adriana. Angelo knew he would have to be patient. His father would make that decision when he was ready; it was fruitless to expect Tito to budge until he was ready to do so. Angelo could not complain. His father had given him the Bartolini villa in Turin, and highly approved of the garden he had restored there.

Angelo worked for over two hours on his sketches for the addition of more vineyards at Villa Adriana, and when he finished, he picked up the newspaper from the corner of the desk, carried it to the chair next to the window and sat down.

He opened the paper, and the headlines seemed to jump off the page:

CAPTAIN EGON HOFLER FOUND MURDERED NEAR THE END OF VIA NUOVA ROAD

Angelo felt his mouth go dry. He had been trying to put the incident out of his mind, but here was a reminder in two-inch letters. Egon Hofler. Now the man who had tried to kill him had a name, and that brought it down to a more personal level.

He caught himself. This was not the time to go soft over what had happened. A man had tried to kill him, and he had defended himself. He recalled the faces of his friends who had gone missing at the hands of men like Egon Hofler. There was no room for feelings or fear in times like these, and truthfully, Angelo did not feel either. His strong will and belief in the aristocratic, the educated, the intellectual and in the enlightened university students informed his actions. He was part of the growing minority that wanted independence from the foreign influence of Austria and Prince Metternich.

He adamantly opposed and resisted Austrian rule, and hoped for the eventual unification of a free and independent Italy. Until Italy was free, he was committed. It wasn't the way he would have chosen to live his life. He had degrees in both botany and hydraulic engineering. He would rather be making intricate drawings of fountains and vineyard terracing, but for now, he was putting that behind him and focusing upon the secrets hidden in certain hearts.

He had killed a man—but he had prepared himself for such an act long ago, when he decided to devote himself to the cause. He had known it was only a matter of time. He would not be distracted by thoughts of the murder. Men who dwelled upon such made mistakes, and Angelo did not intend to make any. There was no room for footfalls of doubt dogging his conscience. He was devoted to taking risks for the good of the people. He had known the dangers. There was no turning back; there could be no regrets.

He read the article and learned the Austrians were looking for a suspect—one who was highly skilled in the art of fencing. There was a reward for information. There were plenty of men in Turin who were adept with a saber, so he did not worry overmuch, but neither was he too confident. Only time would prove the outcome. Until then, life went on.

He moved to another article, and then another, and soon the matter was out of his mind. As he read, he circled a few phrases, several paragraphs and one complete article, all of which were anti-liberal propaganda that sided with the authoritarian attitudes and views of the Austrian government. Now he had fodder for the article he was writing for Milan's liberal newspaper, *Il Conciliatore*.

He read that Lord Byron was in Bologna, without his illicit love, the married Countess Teresa Guiccioli, who was only nineteen. He considered for a moment the rumor he had heard only a few days ago concerning Byron—that the father and brother of the countess, both Carbonari, had persuaded Byron to become one of them. He hoped that was true.

He read an advertisement for a horse auction, and then, with a glance at the clock, realized he would have to stop, or be late for a meeting with his best friend, Nicola Fossa. After folding the paper, he made a few minor adjustments to his clothing and departed.

Turin's streets were crowded, and the voices of passersby were barely audible over the clatter of traffic and the shouts of drivers in their cabs. It was a

pleasant day. The sky overhead was clear and the
sun warm upon Angelo's face—something he noticed with pleasure, since only a month ago snow had
whirled about him, driven by a fiercely strong wind.

The rattle of curb chains and the clip of hooves
on stone streets interrupted his thoughts, and he
watched a patrol of the King of Sardinia's hussars
come down the street, in full dress uniform, horses
prancing, sabers gleaming, the plumes on their hel-
mets waving like flags with each movement.

About the same time, two diplomats from the Austrian Chancellery came around the corner. They
walked on each side of a tall, rather aloof man of
aristocratic bearing. Several chancellery police followed the trio.

Angelo had no idea who the man was, but thought
he must be someone important to require such escorts
and security. The diplomats said something to the
man they escorted, but they were too far away for
Angelo to hear. It was probably a moot point, anyway, since they would have spoken in German.

The three men watched Angelo with eyes as cold
and blue as Austrian crystals. As they drew closer,
one of the diplomats said something. This time they
were close enough for Angelo to hear the guttural
sounds of German.

Suddenly, two of the policemen rushed forward to
block Angelo's way. "Count Karl von Schisler
would have a word with you," said one of them.

Count Karl von Schisler... Angelo knew the
name. The count was the head of the Hapsburg secret
police in Italy. If Metternich had a wish, von Schisler
carried it out. Angelo took that a step further, realizing that if von Schisler knew who he was, so did
Metternich. He also realized he had been wrong to

think Metternich was more concerned about Milan than Turin: von Schisler's presence here indicated otherwise.

It was a chilling lesson for Angelo: he had underestimated Metternich. He swore to himself that he would not do so again.

The three men stopped in front of Angelo, and von Schisler said, in perfect Italian, "I wanted to meet the man who is responsible for stirring up so much trouble for us in Turin. I like to know who the opposition is, even though they are in the wrong."

"It is the duty of the opposition to oppose, is it not?"

"It is a duty that could prove harmful. You are a young man with your life ahead of you. I do not advise you to continue on the path you have chosen. To do so could be very bad for your health. Italy is under Austrian control and it will remain under Austrian control. Nothing you can do will change that."

"We are Italians, not Austrians. Italy belongs to the people."

"You are whatever I say you are—and I say you might be Italian but you belong to Austria. A slave does not choose his master."

"Italy is not a slave, but a country."

"Italy is an idea. One that will be conquered."

"You are wrong. We will not stop until Italy is united."

"United?" He made a scoffing sound, and the other men laughed. "You have nothing that unites you, save a common language, and it takes more than that to bring together a country."

"We seem to be at a stalemate, then. You want Italy, and so do we."

It was obvious the count was in a rage now. His

fair skin had turned scarlet, and Angelo could see through the blond hair that even his scalp was red. His anger had overpowered him and pushed him toward revenge, which was really the best place to have him, Angelo thought. Anger made a man do stupid things.

"Rome...all of Italy is synonymous with conquest. You were meant to be conquered. It is all you know."

"You underestimate us. The ax forgets, but the cut log does not."

Angelo's heart burned with indignation, and he itched to tell him the Italians had something else in common that he overlooked—an intense dislike of anything Austrian. He remembered, however, the words of Athenodorus as he took his leave from Caesar: *"Remember...whenever you are angry, to say or do nothing before you have repeated the four-and-twenty letters to yourself."*

With the wise words of the ancient Romans guiding him, Angelo nodded and said, "Thank you for your advice, Count von Schisler."

"Like a dog, you are allowed one bite. Bite again and you will be destroyed. We will be watching you, Bartolini. It is only a matter of time until you will make a mistake. That is inevitable. And when you do, we will be there, and I will personally see to it that will be your last mistake."

Angelo watched them turn in that stiff, formal way the Austrians had, and walk away. If he felt any triumph at all, it was in noticing that the red blotchiness from the count's face had traveled all the way to his fingers.

Angelo shoved his hands into his pockets and continued down the street, comfortable in the knowledge that his heart was wholly and completely Italian.

Nicola was waiting for Angelo at the prearranged place—one of the coffeehouses not far from *via* Po.

As soon as Angelo sat down, Nicola leaned forward. "Metternich has the head of the secret police in Turin," he whispered. "I ran into Giuseppe Mantra a few minutes ago. Ironically, he was on his way to your house. I told him you were meeting me here and that I would tell you."

"I know about von Schisler. I just spoke with him."

"You what?"

"I met him on the street. He was with some men from the chancellery. He wanted a few words with me."

"Blood of the Madonna! How did he know who you were?"

"I assume someone pointed me out to him," Angelo said. "I knew the time would come when they would know who I was. After all, they must eagerly wait for each edition of *Il Conciliatore,* so they can glean all the names and information they can."

"I know, but it is still shocking to hear such has happened."

"We were warned about such as this—therefore we must be prepared."

"I suppose something like this makes one prepared, doesn't it."

"As prepared as we can get," Angelo replied. "Did Giuseppe have any other information?"

"Giuseppe doubts von Schisler's presence here is a permanent thing, but more a move made to frighten us. He said our spies have gathered information that indicates Metternich is quite apprehensive, particularly about the situation that is developing here. He said you would be interested in knowing your name was discovered in some documents found on Metternich's desk. That confirms why von Schisler is here. You must be extremely careful, Angelo. You can bet your life that Metternich knows much more about you than your name." He paused. "Now, tell me what happened between you and von Schisler."

Angelo and Nicola ordered coffee as Angelo related what had transpired between him and von Schisler. Then the conversation turned to the purpose for their meeting today.

"I delivered my letter to Lorenzo. He is printing a hundred and fifty copies. They should be ready later today."

"I will go tonight to pick them up."

"You must exercise great care, Nicola."

"I always do."

"I mean you must be even more careful now," Angelo whispered as he leaned forward.

Nicola's expression said he sensed the warning in Angelo's tone. "What are you trying to tell me?"

Angelo finished off the contents of his cup. "Drink the rest of your coffee and we will walk through the *piazza.*"

"But it is market day. The *piazza* will be noisy."

"Exactly."

Nicola nodded and drank the last drop. Angelo paid the check, and the two of them walked toward the *piazza.* Soon they were among the vendors' stalls, speaking in hushed voices.

"Do you think we are being watched?"

"Without a doubt. Just because there is no smoke, does not mean there is no fire."

They stopped for a moment so Angelo could purchase the latest paper from Milan. "I had a little trouble after I left Lorenzo's."

"What kind of trouble?"

"The Austrian kind," Angelo said. "Did you read today's paper?"

"Yes, of course."

"You read the article about the captain found on *via* Nuova?"

"That was you?"

Angelo nodded.

"Madonna!" Nicola made the sign of the cross. "I cannot believe it was you. How did it happen? Did you mean to do it? No, forget I asked that. You are probably the finest swordsman in Turin. You wouldn't make a mistake like that."

"Thank you for your confidence. Unfortunately, the answer to your question is yes. He was out for blood. I decided it should be his."

"Was he alone?"

"He was one of those clever thinkers without a whit of talent for swordplay. He left the regiment to find me on his own...and when he did, he lunged, facing me in the old style. I nicked him and hoped he would be satisfied, but he was not."

"We can only pray they do not track this thing back to you. How do you feel?"

"I cannot let this unsettle me, although I do think about how far I have come. As a child, I was afraid to squash a grape."

Nicola, obviously trying to lighten things a bit said, "That was because your father placed grapes just beneath saints on the blessed hierarchy."

Angelo smiled at the reminder of Tito. "He still does."

They came to a vendor's stand, and Nicola said, "Let us stop here."

Angelo looked at the farmer's proud display of melons, tomatoes, beans, cabbages, zucchini, artichokes, pyramids of colorful fruit and even garden plants growing in little terra-cotta pots. "Have you taken up gardening?"

Nicola shook his head. "Hardly. I promised my grandmother I would bring her some seeds."

"Seeds?"

Nicola grinned and pointed to several varieties, telling the farmer how much he wanted of each.

They fell silent, watching the farmer's wife carefully deposit each little pyramid of seeds on a small square of paper, then carefully fold and wrap it before she tied it with string. Angelo felt warmed by the sight of this, and the assurance that things would go on as before, for he saw that even in these small ways the Italian people took pride in what they did.

"Why don't you come with me? She always asks about you."

Angelo decided a visit to *Nonna* Fossa might be a good way to get his mind off Metternich. "All right. It would be good to see her again."

They strolled across the *piazza,* enjoying the gay and happy noise of market day, made louder by the stone walls of the buildings and the lack of trees and shrubbery to absorb it.

They walked past the old ladies in their black dresses and thick black stockings, lined up on the benches like little black crows on a fence, watching the spectacle with sharp eyes that missed nothing— noting the exact number of items a neighbor bought, or the purchases of earrings by a young beauty, or the satisfied smile of a banker.

The face of Italy was here, with all its undisguised emotions. Every Italian learned early in life to read the message of the face. Words did not always match the expression and therefore could be dismissed. But the face mattered. It never lied. It was this quality of life that Angelo found lifted his spirits when they so needed just that.

The sight of the old ladies in black reminded Angelo of *Nonna* Fossa. "It has been a long time since I saw your grandmother. She is well, I hope."

"She is well enough to shame me into helping her with her garden. It always starts with seeds. Soon, I will be digging up the garden—and since you know so much about gardening, I thought…"

"I plan them, I don't dig them," Angelo said. "Besides, I intend to leave long before that starts."

"Deserter."

"When it comes to digging vegetable gardens, I am that," Angelo said.

"You love raising grapes," Nicola said.

"I love making wine, and that involves raising grapes—which reminds me, I had a letter from my father. He has asked me to come home."

"That is unusual," Nicola said. "Is anything wrong?"

"No, he wants to discuss some things about Villa Adriana, but I have no idea what. He hopes that by not telling me, it will heighten my intellectual curiosity and therefore send me hurrying to Tuscany."

Nicola smiled. "Well, does it?"

"Of course," Angelo said with a laugh. "My father wouldn't waste time saying such, if he did not know it would work."

"When are you leaving?"

"In a day or two," Angelo replied. The sooner the better, with von Schisler in Turin and the Austrian officer dead.

Five

"Blood of the Madonna! What is that horrible smell?"

Tito Bartolini came into the room, kissed his wife and said, "I have missed you, *amore mio,* but how can you breathe with such an odor in every room?"

Gisella dropped her rosary in her pocket and put down her embroidery. "I don't smell anything."

"I am gone five days and return to a house that smells like a bad perfumery, and you tell me you don't smell anything?"

Gisella took a deep breath and came to her feet. "No...well, perhaps a hint of turpentine—or is it varnish?—but nothing more."

"Turpentine? Varnish? Why would you smell turpentine or varnish? What have you been doing?"

"Nothing. Beatrice is here."

"Beatrice? I calculated her arrival to be next week."

"Your calculations were wrong."

"When did she arrive?"

"Two days ago."

"Do you find her much changed?"

Gisella smiled. "Oh yes. You will like what you see, Tito. She is quite grown up now."

"Still shy?"

"Not so much that she cannot speak out, but just

enough that I find it attractive. She is quite poised, and so very lovely, with the sweetest disposition. I know Teresa would be very proud of her. I find it sad that the girls never knew their mother.''

Tito patted her hand. ''Yes, they do. They are fortunate that Teresa was your twin. Whenever they look at you, they see her.''

''I suppose that is some compensation, but it isn't the same.''

''I know. Now tell me, what news of Maresa? Does Beatrice see her sister often?''

''No. When Beatrice was living in London, Maresa spent most of her time in Yorkshire. Tell me, my love, how was your trip? Are you tired?''

''No. I was blessed with good traveling conditions. It did not rain once, so the roads were quite dry. Have you heard anything from Angelo? I sent him that letter asking him to come home.''

''Yes, he wrote that he would be leaving right away, so I am expecting him to show up any day now.''

''Hmm,'' he said, and seemed to dismiss that part of the discussion, preferring to return to the peculiar odors inside the house. ''I am glad Beatrice is here, and I shall go and greet her directly, but first, I want to know about the turpentine and varnish.''

''I believe I can answer that, Uncle Tito.''

Tito turned around and saw his niece, Beatrice Fairweather. She wore a painter's smock smeared with rainbows of color. ''How good it is to see you. I was beginning to think you had forgotten all about us.''

''I could never forget Aunt Gisella or you, Uncle Tito,'' Beatrice said, her words showing she still possessed the same air of quiet reserve she had when she was there before, along with the hint of confidence and maturity that was as fresh as the streaks of paint on her smock.

The golden hair was no longer worn down, but braided and wound about her head in a more womanly fashion. It had always been her fair hair and pale English skin that reminded Tito of Venus, when she sprang full-grown from the foaming waters of the sea in Botticelli's painting, *The Birth of Venus*. It was a painting Tito saw frequently, for whenever visitors came to Villa Mirandola, they always wanted to go to Florence, and that meant a visit to the nearby Galleria degli Uffizi.

Now, he had the living image of Venus standing in the doorway, as bright and innocent as if she were fresh out of her shell.

"Shame on you for waiting so long to bless us with your presence. I cannot tell you how good it is to see you again. Had I known you were arriving sooner, I wouldn't have taken that trip. However, I must say, the surprise at finding you here is one of the nicest things about coming home."

She gazed affectionately at him. "I understand you have been to Venice."

"You know how I am always looking for good wine bottles. Come and give your favorite uncle a fond greeting."

"You are her only uncle," Gisella said.

His face brightened at that. "Well, I suppose I am. I hadn't thought of that."

Beatrice met him in the center of the room. He readied himself to embrace her and held out his arms, but Beatrice laughed and said, "A quick kiss on the cheek will have to suffice. I would not want to ruin your traveling clothes with my paints." She held up the skirt of her white smock to display the paint smears.

"Painting? Surely that hasn't become a job for a woman. What are you painting?" His tone turned humorous, as if he thought she were speaking in jest. "Of course. You are painting your room...or is it the inside of the villa?"

"I am doing a portrait of Aunt Gisella. We finished working a short time ago. I was cleaning up when I heard your voice."

"Oh, that," he said, reminded of his blustery entry.

"I suppose I have become accustomed to the smell of turpentine lingering about. I shall open more windows next time, Uncle. I promise."

"Well now, perhaps I shall grow accustomed to it, as you and Gisella seem to have— Now, tell me in truth, what is this business of painting Gisella's portrait? I knew you were painting, but I thought perhaps landscapes. Portraiture is most difficult. I had no idea you had progressed to that level. You never indicated such in your letters."

"I believe they call that modesty," Gisella said. "Beatrice has more than proven she is not only talented, but gifted. While in France, she studied with Elisabeth-Louise Vigèe-Lebrun, and not only at her home in Paris, but often at her country house in Louveciennes." Gisella slipped her arm through her husband's. "You should see her work, Tito. She is quite exceptional. Brilliant, I would say. I remember my mother's side of the family as being both creative and artistic. It must be something innate within her...a female trait..."

Tito gave her an amused look. "All the good traits are female ones, according to you."

"Are they?"

"Yes, but I seem to recall your uncle once built a stable door and painted it."

Gisella's laugh, like her presence, lightened the mood and feel of everything around her, until even the strong scent of turpentine was not so overpowering.

"I had forgotten about that."

"Another female trait," Tito said. "Did you also forget that he made such a mess of it, he had to hire a painter to redo it?"

"And the entire door collapsed a week later."

With a wink at Beatrice, Tito said, "I want to see some of your work, but first, I must clean some of this traveling dust off myself."

While Beatrice combed her hair for dinner, it occurred to her that already she was feeling a part of the family, and had since the moment of her arrival. Her aunt and uncle were warm, welcoming and so unbelievably affectionate. Each time she saw them, they greeted her with a kiss to each cheek. They were nothing like her stiff family in London, with their rigid codes and blood as cold as the clime. She compared herself to a flowering plant that had never blossomed. But that was about to change. She could bloom with this family. She knew she could.

She recalled how quick Uncle Tito had been to praise her accomplishments as an artist, which made her think about how different they were from her achievements in society. This did not occur by happenstance, but by choice.

She remembered with a shudder those years before her father's death, when she was forced to endure torturous hours at balls and was passed over by every man looking for a wife. As for taking fashion seriously, she failed miserably. Often referred to as dowdy or clinging to a style considered long out of fashion, she refused to wear the subtly seductive gowns of soft, clinging fabric that was almost transparent, with décolletage that was considered à la mode.

As for her father, she would have preferred to think of him as a white, hovering shape of fatherly devotion that still influenced her life, but he had been neither a guiding light, nor a gentle and loving man who wanted only the best for his daughter.

He gave nothing but financial support to his five daughters, and voiced disappointment in the youngest two—Beatrice and Maresa—and consequently never expected anything from them. The eldest three daughters married well, although not for love, and that was the extent of their success. It was a pleasure for Beatrice to know that she and Maresa were the only two to distinguish themselves because of what they did, rather than by whom they married.

The Viscount of Strathmore died not knowing that his youngest daughter, Maresa, would not only marry into a very wealthy family, and marry for love, but would go on to be the benefactress and charitable founder of a home for the orphaned children of those English men who lost their lives fighting Napoleon.

When their father died, Maresa inherited Hampton Manor, the Fairweather country estate in Yorkshire, and she gave it to the British government with the stipulation that it would be a home to those war orphans, and that its vast farmlands would not only support them, but pay for the education of both boys and girls.

As for Beatrice—the viscount would never know

that she no longer stuttered, or that she had developed what he had referred to as a "childish hobby," into a talent that enabled her to paint the portraits of many members of the French aristocracy.

As a child, what she expected from her father was criticism and a brusque manner, and in that she was never disappointed.

Because her mother died giving birth to Maresa, the brilliant haze of a mother's influence in Beatrice's life had been missing, just as it had been in Maresa's. Beatrice thought about that fateful day when Maresa was born. Although at the time only a small child, not quite three, and too young to remember with any great detail, she grew up knowing the story of the doctor advising her father that he could not save both his wife and the child, and how her father, certain that after four daughters he would, at last, have a male heir, had said those ill-fated words: *"Save my son."*

Their beautiful, Italian mother had died, and Maresa—because of the guilt their father felt each time he looked at her—was destined to live at Hampton Manor, while her four sisters resided in London with their father.

Many times since, Maresa and Beatrice, who were extremely close, found themselves discussing which of them had suffered the most: Maresa, abandoned and living in exile without her father and sisters in her life, or Beatrice, with unloving sisters and the presence of a father who cast a dark shadow of fear over her life. The good that came out of all of this was that, unlike their three elder sisters, Beatrice and Maresa were not shallow or unfulfilled or dependent upon people who offered friendship based upon the girls' beauty, wealth or social position.

Those people were, according to Uncle Tito, "Snobs, of the sour-grape variety."

Beatrice twirled in front of the mirror and looked at her reflection. She saw none of what she was looking for: the shyness she felt inside. That everyone could see what she could not was always a source of puzzlement to her.

As the years passed, she gradually began to feel more comfortable and at ease, and wondered if this was a sign she would eventually overcome her reserve. Or, was shyness something you were born with, like eye color, that did not change?

Angelo had been the inspiration, the one to open her eyes. She had her painting to thank for the progress she had made. The words, the thoughts, the feelings she could never express verbally were conveyed in the glittering richness of canvases that spoke a language of light, color and warm contours—all delivered with the stroke of a brush.

With a final pin to anchor her golden curls, she went to join her aunt and uncle for dinner. As she descended the stairs, she found herself wishing her cousin, Serena, were here, but Serena was visiting Uncle Tito's sister in Rome, which left Beatrice anticipating her return.

At the bottom of the staircase, she caught a glimpse of a painting of the Antonari family and stopped beneath it. She saw her grandparents, Constantine and Guilia, and, seated in front of them, the twelve-year-old twins: Beatrice's mother, Teresa, standing endearingly close to her twin sister, Gisella.

Behind her grandparents were their two sons, Antonio and Paolo—four children, young, beautiful and smiling as if they had their futures secured. Little did they realize then, that before the passage of too many years, Antonio and Paolo would die in an uprising against the French during the Napoleonic Wars, or that Teresa would die in a cold clime in far-off England, giving birth to her fifth daughter.

She studied her mother's face, so like Maresa's. She felt a smile lift the corners of her mouth as she recalled how often she had wished as a child that she had inherited the dark, glossy hair of their mother.

She remembered saying so to Maresa when she first came to live with them in London. "Oh, how I do wish I looked like Mother. You not only look like her, but you got the best of everything Italian in the family."

Maresa had replied, "But you inherited as much as I did. I have father's eyes and mother's hair. You have the opposite."

Beatrice had looked at her sister, with her lovely English blue eyes, her dark Italian hair and pale olive skin, and said, "How can you say that, Maresa, when all I have is this pale, blond hair, pitifully white skin and mud-brown eyes? Have you ever seen an Italian that looks as I do?"

Practical as ever, Maresa said, "No, but only because I don't remember seeing anyone Italian. We seem to have a shortage of them here in England."

Of the many things Beatrice had to thank her sister for, the most special was Maresa's daring to come to Italy to visit their mother's sister, Gisella—something Beatrice would have been terrified to do, especially during the war.

She gave the painting a final glance and went to join her family.

Uncle Tito was pouring a glass of wine when she entered the salon. He waved her forward in that odd way Italians have, by turning the fingers of the hand downward to motion someone forward, instead of the English way of turning the fingers up. "Come in, come in, and join us for a glass of Chianti before dinner."

"Thank you, Uncle, but I cannot. You see, I only drink Villa Mirandola wine."

His face took on a comical expression of animated delight. "Then, you are in luck, for I have it from the finest authorities that this is not only from Villa Mirandola, but from their private reserve." He passed the glass under his nose and inhaled deeply. "We bottled this two years ago...it was an outstanding year."

"In that case..."

Aunt Gisella was considering her. "You look a trifle pensive, Beatrice. Are you homesick for England, or missing your artist friends in France?"

"No, of course not. It is nothing like that. I was thinking, on my way down here, how very fortunate I was that Maresa had the fortitude to visit you during the war. Had she not, I fear I never would have mustered the courage to come. Even then, she had to practically beat me over the head with the idea. Leaving England to sail to Italy seemed completely off my map of possibilities."

"I don't believe that in the least," Uncle Tito said.

"Oh, it's true," Beatrice said. "In many ways, Maresa was fortunate in being banished to the country. She grew up much more independent and self-assured than I."

Uncle Tito pondered that for a moment. "Yes, I can see where you would feel that way about Maresa, but I withhold my judgment as far as you are concerned. It's true that Maresa is independent and self-assured, as is Serena. Maria! I was worried in the beginning that they might not get on, but you should have seen the two of them together. They never missed anything. And there was Angelo to give them ideas and offer knowledge about things we would have preferred them to know nothing about.''

At the mention of Angelo's name, Beatrice felt a sharpness in her chest. Her one and only visit to Italy might not have been a long one, and the memory had been dulled by the passage of time, but her mental image of Angelo was still as vivid as if they had met yesterday.

Her greatest joy and her biggest dread was facing Angelo again.

"Did Gisella tell you that Angelo lives in Turin? He is now Piedmontese and living in the Bartolinis' villa in the city.''

"Yes, she told me. I know you must be happy to have him in the city where your family lived. You said he lived in town, but I remember when I was here before that you mentioned a large estate near Turin.''

"Villa Adriana,'' Gisella replied. "Perhaps you shall see it. It is quite magnificent.''

"As lovely as Villa Mirandola?''

"I think it is lovelier.''

"Do you, now?'' Uncle Tito said. "Then, why were you so stubborn, insisting we live in your family home after we married?''

"Because I love it so when you indulge me, Tito,'' she said, and kissed him on the cheek.

It was one of the few times Beatrice had ever seen her uncle with a red face.

"Is Angelo taking advantage of Villa Adriana to design fountains and grow grapes? I remember he had studied such while at the university.''

"Unfortunately, he became involved in a University of Bologna group, one that stood for liberal ideals and the cut of one's coat, the shape of one's cravat."

Beatrice smiled at his lighthearted manner of reply, but she had heard from her aunt that he did not approve of Angelo's involvement with the liberal political groups. When Aunt Gisella reminded him that he would have done the same thing when he was Angelo's age, he said, "Of course, but I would not have been so fearful of losing my own life as I am of Angelo losing his."

All this talk about Angelo was unsettling for Beatrice. Not because she did not want to hear about him, but because he had touched her and awakened something within her—an almost magnetic attraction to him that the passage of time had not erased.

She was not foolish enough to think there could ever be anything between them. He was too carefree and fun loving, and unable to stay committed to any one woman for long. She shuddered to think how many women there must have been, in the years since she left.

"I know you are worried about his political involvement," Aunt Gisella said. "I worry for him, as well. Two days ago I heard that Count Francesco Garelli's son, Augusto, has been sentenced in Milan. They have ordered his hands chopped off before he is executed."

"*Amore mio,* you know that has long been the Austrians' favorite decree when it comes to punishing the Carbonari, just as you must know it is also their habit to commute the sentences to imprisonment in order to appear magnanimous. They foolishly think that will earn our respect, trust and blind obedience. I see no reason to think they will not do the same in Augusto's case.''

''I am not as convinced of that as you are, because I remember these are the same Austrians Angelo wrote us about when he was living in Milan—and thankful I am that he moved to Turin,'' she added, crossing herself. ''Do you not remember all the horrible things he mentioned?''

''Vaguely. It was something he said in reference to the Venetians and Lombardians, I believe—therefore nothing for you to worry about, since Angelo is in Piedmont and ruled not by the Austrian emperor, but a Savoy king.''

''Tito, you know Vittorio Emanuele is one of the reasons our young men are consorting to spread liberal ideas among the people. And we all know Metternich has him in his pocket, as he does all the rulers in Italy.''

''I know, just as I know Angelo will keep a cool head.''

''I know he will, but it isn't what's going on in *his* head I'm worried about. How long will the King of Sardinia tolerate these aristocratic young liberals before he calls on the Austrians to intervene? Angelo has given his heart and soul to this cause. Therefore I worry.''

''I am concerned for him, and will remain so, as long as he stays in Turin and out of Lombardy and Venice. Should he return to Milan, then I will worry.''

Beatrice was frowning. ''I don't understand, Uncle. Why would a distance of a few leagues make so much difference?''

''It isn't the distance, it's who sits on the throne. After Napoleon, Lombardy and Venetia were made into a new kingdom directly under Austrian rule, and that means the emperor, Francis I. Turin, Genoa…all of the Piedmont area was given to the Kingdom of Sardinia. Unfortunately, King Vittorio Emanuele is a weakling.''

''And Prince Metternich is a very strong and compelling man.''

Aunt Gisella, who had been gazing thoughtfully at her husband and niece, said, ''There are two things Angelo loves to verbalize—his desire for a free Italy and his dislike for those who oppose it.''

Uncle Tito cleared his throat. ''I know how outspoken and patriotic Angelo is, just as I know who it was in this family that taught him to be so.''

Beatrice almost laughed at the guilty look on her aunt's face.

Colossus, the family mastiff, came wandering into the room and pushed his wet nose against Beatrice's hand. ''Colossus, you devil, what are you doing?'' Uncle Tito said.

Beatrice looked down at the huge fawn-colored mastiff with the black face. His head tilted sideways, he was watching her intently, and she could not help thinking how effectively this gentle dog had put an end to any further discussion of Angelo. As he gave her hand a big lick, she laughed and said, ''I do think he likes me.''

''It's the linseed oil that he likes,'' Uncle Tito said. ''You better keep a tight lid on your paint box. Shall we go to dinner?''

With her aunt on one side and her uncle on the other, Beatrice walked with them to the dining room.

Throughout dinner, although she joined in the casual conversation, the memory of Angelo never left her. He had been the source of her thoughts for years, a man she held separate and distinct from any she had met before or since.

with conversation. She sighed to herself as though for ...
her. She had begun a note to her husband, correcting ...
a man she knew in name and almost knew from pay ...
just one other in group.

Six

Angelo walked up *via* Po.

Fat drops of rain splattered his long, black overcoat. Because of the rain, the widely spaced streetlamps provided nothing more than a dim illusion of light. He heard the sound of horses trotting over paving stones. Ahead of him, a calash approached with top up and lantern unlit.

As it drew even with him, the calash slowed and the door opened enough for a hand to reach out and send papers fluttering in his direction.

Angelo caught one, and watched the others fall to the paving stones, wet beneath his feet. The driver cracked the whip and the calash hurried on down the street.

He moved to the nearest street lamp and held the paper to the light.

Brothers, to arms! Austrian despots are holding the Piedmontese prisoners in their own country. It is time for Piedmont, for all of Italy, to reject the crown of foreign rule. The eyes of the spies are everywhere. Our brothers are being executed for daring to harbor the thought of a free and independent Italy. The time approaches when every Italian must heed the call of emancipation.

Long live liberty! In the name of freedom! Unite!

He folded the paper and put it in his pocket. He knew the proclamation was not local, or written by a Piedmontese liberal, and he wondered if it had come from Milan.

In the darkness ahead, he could hear the sound of curb chains and hoofs moving at a fast clip. Even before they moved into the dim light, he knew they were the king's cavalry of lancers, and they were riding too fast to be on patrol.

Both the king's troops and the Austrian patrols had increased in number since the body of the captain Angelo had killed had been found. Today's paper contained a lengthy article, obviously written by an Austrian. Angelo was glad he was leaving for Tuscany in the morning. He thought it best to remain out of sight for a while.

He stepped into the dark shadows of a doorway and watched the lancers ride on by. He could hear the shouts as they passed by the wet proclamations lying in the street. They picked up the pace and rode in the direction the calash had taken.

He remained where he was for a few minutes and thought about the men in the coach. Poor bastards. He hoped they were smart enough to get off the main road. Things would not go well for them if they were caught. If they weren't killed by the lancers, they could find themselves hanging in the square in less than three days' time.

He continued on his way, keeping to the dim side streets. He walked briskly until he reached his house and was safely inside. Only then did he allow himself to think about the party of lancers ferreting around the area along the river. He would have to avoid the river as much as possible when he went out later tonight.

The rain had stopped by the time he finished dinner and changed his clothes. He ordered his horse brought around. When he saw his coal-black horse led into the shadows of the *porte cochère,* the large covered entrance that led into the courtyard and stables, he went outside. He mounted and rode toward the home of Countess Caroline Cambiano, a liberal sympathizer who opened her home to the Carbonari for a meeting.

Once there, he learned that the Hapsburg secret police in Milan wanted to question him, and that spies in Turin were monitoring his movements for potential dissidence. His name had been added to the list of those suspected of publishing seditious proclamations.

Angelo looked at Giuseppe Mantra, thankful they had at least one spy working for them. "That isn't all," Angelo said. "I suspect they are intercepting my mail."

"It is highly probable. I will look into it. In the meantime, you might consider going out of town for a while."

"I have already made those plans. I leave tomorrow."

"Good. The fewer you tell, the less I will worry."

"No one knows save you, Nicola and my valet."

Giuseppe nodded and disappeared to mingle in the group of men. Angelo noticed he was careful not to spend much time conversing with any one person. And before long, he seemed to have disappeared altogether.

Angelo thought about what Giuseppe had said. It was a good thing he was leaving Turin. He knew the police wouldn't forget about him any more than he could put the memory of the blond Austrian out of his mind, but his absence should allow things to cool down a bit—at least, as far as the suspicions surrounding him were concerned.

He made the rounds and spoke with several members, but he did not have conversation on his mind. He stayed less than an hour, and after a short visit with Nicola, he said, "I must go now. I have an article to finish writing."

"I, too, must go. Fioriana is waiting for me. I told her I would stop by on my way home. I will ride as far as the bridge with you."

"You are spending a considerable amount of time with Fioriana. Is this something serious?"

"It is moving in that direction."

"Dear me, I don't know if I am prepared to be an uncle."

"I don't know if I am prepared to be a father."

"You would make a perfect father."

"That is what Fioriana tells me."

Once they were outside, Nicola put a detaining hand on Angelo's arm. "I have something for you. Giuseppe Mantra gave it to me earlier. He said to give it to you."

He handed Angelo a folded proclamation, the kind the king and the Austrians posted about town to display their pompous declarations. It was an offer of a large reward leading to the arrest of the person or persons responsible for the murder of Captain Egon Hofler, of the Austrian Imperial Hussars.

Angelo folded it and placed it in his pocket.

"Do you think it's a good idea to carry that? If you are caught…"

"I intend to throw it into the river, after I tear it into little pieces."

Nicola and Angelo parted company before they crossed the Po, and Angelo went on alone. He stopped in the middle of the bridge and tossed the pamphlet and the proclamation into the water below.

He continued across the bridge, guided by the street lamps' golden cast which glistened on the wet streets, a result of the fine drizzle that spread like a tent over the city. Turin, with its grid design, made navigating easy.

On this side of the river, the streets of Turin had few travelers at this time of night, although Angelo did hear the sound of cabriolet wheels rattling over paving stones a few blocks away.

Suddenly, gunshots erupted. He paused to listen, but there were no more sounds. Another assassination, he thought, and that meant even more of the king's dragoons would be out patrolling the streets.

He urged his horse forward and picked up his pace. He passed the colonnades, deserted and lonely in the rain, and turned the corner. Anxious to be home, his well-mannered horse eased into a smooth gait, and the sound of his iron shoes against the great flagstones rang in harmony. He passed several *piazzas,* each different in its own way, with statues, fountains or grassy parks ringed with benches where adults would sit to watch their children play.

Before long, he rode through the open iron gates of his villa and heard the gruff, bellowing bark of Tiberius. The sight of the great mastiff running out to meet him was always a warm welcome. Tiberius's eager greeting reminded him of that of Tiberius's father, Colossus, his dog at Villa Mirandola. How far in the past that part of his life seemed now.

Tiberius followed him into the house, where Angelo poured a glass of wine from the decanter on the hall table and carried it to the library. There he set to work, writing the last five pages of another article for *Il Conciliatore,* Tiberius falling asleep at his feet.

It was almost three o'clock in the morning when he finished. He asked his valet, Cesare, to take it to a fellow Carbonari member, Filippo Visconti, who would deliver it to the newspaper in Milan.

Now, that would certainly alienate the Austrians if they found it. It would also get a fine noose looped around his neck. He would have to delay his departure for yet another day.

The next morning, Angelo rode over to Nicola's house. He did not turn around, but if he had, he would have seen two men riding behind him.

"Good morning," Nicola said. "I thought you were leaving town early."

"I had a change of plans," Angelo said.

"What's happened?"

"Nothing yet, but it could. Let's go sight in our pistols. I'll explain why, later."

"I'll meet you out front in a minute," Nicola said. "I returned home not more than fifteen minutes ago. I intended to go out again, so I had the groom leave my horse saddled."

Angelo was mounted and waiting by the time Nicola rode up to join him. They did not talk about anything political until they were well out of the city.

"So, tell me why you canceled your trip," Nicola said.

"Not canceled, only delayed. If all goes well, I will be leaving tomorrow."

"What caused your delay?"

"I have decided it is time to get the munitions I've purchased out of my house. The Austrians are increasing the pressure on the citizens of Milan. House searches and arrests are becoming commonplace. And now that von Schisler has made his introduction to me, I think it only a matter of time before they come snooping after us in the same manner—that is, if they have not already started."

"I thought perhaps they had, after you told me about von Schisler," Nicola said.

"It is much more severe in Milan than here, right now. Believe me."

"I always do," Nicola said. "I'm glad you want the munitions moved. You have been overly generous with your time and your money. I don't know of anyone who has spent so much to purchase the munitions we need, or to help the families of the men killed by the Austrians. Sometimes I worry you are trying to shoulder too much of the responsibility. It isn't all up to you, you know."

"I know, if for no other reason than that my best friend is always ready to see I don't forget. How soon do you think you could get the guns out of my house?"

Nicola looked thoughtful. "I think I could arrange everything by tomorrow night."

"Good, but come after midnight. That time of night will be safe from the prying eyes of neighbors. I think I will leave for Tuscany in the morning, unless you feel I need to be there."

"Not if you tell me where everything is."

"Cesare knows."

"Fine. Tell him we will be there at midnight."

Angelo sighed. "It will be a relief to know they are gone."

"It will be a big relief to both of us," Nicola said.

They rode toward the river and into a clearing near an embankment. It was a place Angelo and Nicola frequented when they wanted to practice shooting targets or sight in a new gun.

They dismounted and tied the horses a short distance away. Between shots, they continued their discussion. "Do you have an idea where you will store the munitions after you take them from my house?" Angelo asked, taking careful aim.

"I've had that planned for some time," Nicola said. "I was only waiting for you to tell me when. I have spoken with the Carbonari in Lombardy. We will take everything to Milan, so it will be out of Turin completely."

"Be careful in Milan," Angelo advised. "You not only have the Hapsburg spies to contend with, but Cardinal Rusconi has his own personal spies poking around. They have arrested dozens of the so-called conspirators. Giuseppe Mantra said he is watching Lord Byron, who, by the way, furnishes money and arms to the Carbonari, much in the same manner as I am doing."

Nicola fired a shot and broke a small branch he declared he would hit. "I don't think they will do anything to Byron and risk having the English breathing down their necks."

Angelo nodded. "I agree."

"It would be nice to think our priests and cardinals were on our side, wouldn't it?" Nicola said.

"It is a reminder that we cannot have everything. It also reminds me that it is a blessing to have a friend like you—one that I can trust like a brother," Angelo said.

"You were my best friend even before you saved

my life. Now you are closer to me than any brother could ever be. After that night, I gave you my life-long allegiance.'' Nicola leaned over to pick up a dirt clod, which he tossed into the air.

Angelo broke it with his first shot. ''I only pushed you out of the way of a jealous lover. I don't deserve to be canonized. You make it sound like I did something heroic.''

''It was heroic—or have you forgotten? The bullet that almost made you bleed to death would have killed me.''

''But it didn't and we are both alive. I know you would have done the same for me.''

''No—I would have taken off running!''

The two of them shared a much-needed laugh, and arms around each other, in that close-knit way Italians have of showing brotherly love, they walked back to their horses.

Hidden behind the cover of dense foliage not very far away, two Austrian spies were watching.

''A tender sight,'' one of them said. Do you think they are *l'omosessuale?*''

''I think they are Italians. You know how they are, always expressing themselves with enthusiasm and fervor. To observe them evokes memories of childhood. Thankfully, we grew out of that sort of thing. Come on, they are mounting their horses.''

The two spies rode into town and went to see von Schisler.

''You followed them?'' von Schisler asked.

''Yes.''

''Well? What do you have to report?''

''Nothing,'' one of the spies said.

"You came to my office to report that you have nothing to report?"

The other spy spoke up. "We are reporting we observed them shooting targets."

"Shooting targets?"

"Yes."

"And why does one shoot targets?" von Schisler asked.

"To improve one's aim."

"And why would they do that?"

"Because they know they will be needing that finely tuned skill."

"Ah," von Schisler said. "So, you think they are planning something? A revolt, perhaps?"

"Of course. Italians are always scheming about something."

Von Schisler's face was turning red. "I knew a general once, who was a brilliant failure. He made the mistake of making assumptions based on generalities. I ask for spies and I am given idiots!"

Von Schisler put both hands on his desk and glared. The two spies, obviously nervous, stepped back.

"You have one more chance to prove yourselves," von Schisler said. "I want something I can use, something incriminating. Do not show your faces in here again, unless you have something I can use to arrest Bartolini. Now, get out of here."

Von Schisler watched the two leave. He knew his anger and his speech would change nothing, because these men were not the caliber of spy he needed. They could not find their way through an open door. He needed Austrian Hapsburg spies, not these local fools in the king's employ.

He sat down and wrote a letter to Metternich re-

questing the kind of Hapsburg spy they used in
Milan—someone with a penchant for detail who was
shrewd, calculating, conscientious and fanatically
loyal.

The next morning, Angelo asked for his horse to
be saddled and brought to the back of the villa; then
he put on his saber belt and a long overcoat to hold
out the rain.

It was still early and the streets deserted when he
left home. The wind and rain had stopped, at least
for the moment. He hoped his trip would be as fast
and easy as possible, or at least one with no com-
plications.

Once he was out of town, he kept off the main
roads. The sky grew lighter, and when he turned to
gaze back toward Turin, he could see the Alps looking as though they were dusted with sugar, outlined
sharply against a pale opal sky.

He thought of glaciers and chamois, and how the
Italians who lived there spoke mostly French, although they were Piedmontese. It always sent blood
coursing through his veins to see the Alps. He liked
it here in the north, where the air was cool and crisp
in the fall, the snow silent and deep in winter, and
the Alps Hannibal crossed always in sight. He passed
a cart driven by a farmer, and nodded. The farmer's
wife sat beside him, dressed in black, the scene oddly
reminiscent of a black-and-white engraving.

Angelo loved to ride, and exercised his horse
daily, but it was these longer jaunts that energized
him, although he kept a watchful eye—an occasional
brigand might be about.

He rode along planted fields, meadows and or-
chards, and traversed untouched plains where poplar,

sycamore, aspen and plane trees grew. Along the road, rows of birch and aspen marked the fields. They were old trees, tall and slender, a reminder that not everything in Italy was undergoing change. From time to time the bell tower of a church would pierce the sky, over the jagged tops of trees. He passed two peasants forking hay into a hayrick, and farther on, a young girl leading a cow.

Toward nightfall, he stopped at a small farm to purchase feed and water for his horse, and, after giving the farmer a few coins, a length of sausage and a tin of water for himself. He was shown to a stable where he could bed his horse and sleep in an empty stall.

The next morning, he was off before the rooster crowed, after leaving three more coins and helping himself to another measure of feed for his horse. The night before, Angelo had noticed the way the farmer studied his horse and inquired about an animal with such a bloodline, one that was obviously superior. He thought it best to remove the source of the farmer's temptation.

He rode on toward Genoa.

Seven

In Milan, von Schisler was sweating profusely, something he always did when in the company of Prince Metternich.

Across from him, Metternich paced the floor. He was not happy about the situation in Milan or Turin, and he was in a mood of extreme displeasure over having to come to Milan in order to prod von Schisler into taking action.

He turned to look at von Schisler, standing there like a great white whale, spineless as jelly. "We have enough pamphlets plastered over Milan to start a war," Metternich said. "We have talk of an uprising in Naples. We have a dead officer in Turin. We have munitions that have mysteriously disappeared in Novara. We have grumbling and assignations. And you stand there, looking pompous and clumsy, giving your long excuses without a flicker of cleverness or intelligence."

"I am sorry you find me incapable of leadership—"

"I find you incapable of everything, even expressing your incapability. The only thing you have done with lucidity and brilliance is to march in here with your benevolent attitude, like you were herding goats. We already have one pope. We do not need another one."

"I thought it best—"

"You are incapable of thought, just as you are incapable of learning from past mistakes. You have proven yourself incapable of understanding the enemy, and incapable of making the right predictions about what might happen in the future. If you cannot think like the enemy, you cannot defeat him. Unfortunately, you have the mind of a dead general."

"What do you want me to do?"

"I want you to think, von Schisler. I want you to follow up the enemy remorselessly until he is utterly destroyed." He paused and studied von Schisler's face, then turned away in disgust. "You are all smoke and no fire, and this is too important to be left to an idiot."

"I can do whatever it is that you want."

"I want you to find out what this Angelo Bartolini is involved with. His name keeps coming up. In the eyes of many, he is approaching sainthood. I want to know if he had anything to do with the murder in Turin."

"I do not think Bartolini is involved. I had a talk with him. And there is the fact that he is still in town. If he were guilty, he would have left immediately after the killing."

"You imbecile! Don't you know the safest place for the fly to sit is on the flyswatter? If you are unable to commit a crime, you cannot suspect others. We must have ears that hear everything, and eyes that see all. I do not know what effect these idealists with their liberal thought have had upon you, but, by God, they terrify me. Do you realize what we stand to lose if they gain the upper hand? They are becoming the bane of my existence and the malady of our times. They must be stopped. They must be extinguished."

"You want them killed, Prince?"

"Yes, you idiot! If that is what is necessary to achieve what we must accomplish, kill them. Kill anyone who gets in our way. What do you think this is—a game of spies and martyrs?"

"You want me to spy on Bartolini?"

"I want you to put spies on all of them, especially those active with the Carbonari. I want to know everything they do, where they go, who they see, how they spend their time. I want something to connect Bartolini with the captain's murder. I want reasons to imprison them—and to hang them. It matters not, as long as they are out of Austria's way."

"But you must have something, if you already suspect him."

"I suspect him because I know his kind. I hate him and his high principles. I detest everything he stands for. However, while you have been stuffing yourself with pasta in the company of that French tart, my other spies have been busy learning what they could about Captain Hofler's death. Consequently, I have discovered there was not much of a duel, judging from the small number of footprints found in the area and the lack of perspiration on the body, which would indicate our captain was involved with a superior swordsman. Because there was only one prick to the skin and the second blow was a perfectly placed fatal one, straight through the heart, the murderer has a proficiency with a rapier. The man who killed our captain was not an ordinary bumbling fool, but a man of supreme athletic skill and keen intelligence. If he is not of the nobility, he should be."

"Bartolini is not a nobleman."

"We do not know what Bartolini is, since he was

adopted. He could be the King of Prussia or Napoleon's illegitimate son, for all we know. These things I have learned while I have been waiting for you to get me answers. Now, get out of here and do not sleep until you know everything going on in Bartolini's mind.''

Von Schisler fell over his feet getting out of the room. His kind made Metternich sick. He hadn't the first idea what it took to be a spy, or a leader. He was fool enough to think a pig could become an elephant by shoving scallions up his nose.

Metternich moved to the window and stood rocking back and forth, his hands locked behind him. He saw von Schisler cross the *piazza* below. Metternich turned away, repulsed by the sight of him. How was it that he was surrounded by incompetents?

God, what he wouldn't do for even one man like this Bartolini.

Metternich did not know much about him, he only knew about his kind. What distinguished Bartolini from the masses was his ability to act according to his beliefs. He did not want power or fame, and that made him an even greater threat to Austria. He wanted justice. This was reason enough to hate him, for Metternich knew he stood for everything he had once stood for. He was everything Metternich was not. He was young and filled with the fire, and he possessed the truth and the honesty that Metternich had started out with but had lost somewhere along the way.

Metternich felt that each word Angelo spoke, each breath he drew was a personal affront to him, a mockery.

Oh, he had read Bartolini's impassioned pamphlets, the articles in *Il Conciliatore*. Metternich prided himself on being a shrewd judge of character, and he had seen Bartolini's kind before—a man with no regard for himself, a man who put love of his country and his countrymen before everything, even personal gain. Who was this Bartolini—this man with no past, of unknown birth?

It disturbed Metternich more to find a man with honor and integrity than one who was base and unjust. At least the latter he could deal with. *Ye Gods,* Metternich thought, *I have priests with far less honor.*

Angelo Bartolini was a sleeping dragon, and Metternich feared that before it was all over, something would happen to make him a national hero, a man with a mythic rendering, and at Metternich's expense.

No matter what a man's weakness, if he was willing to risk it all, including death, if he was willing to suffer along the path he had chosen, then he was a man who would be forever consecrated in the hearts of others.

Metternich saw Angelo Bartolini as someone deadly, because he reminded the Italians of what was once great about Rome.

Eight

After leaving Florence, Angelo turned his horse along the road that followed the curve of a stream. Several miles later, he left the valley and followed a little-used trail to the top of a steep hill, where he rode along the brow for a few more miles. With Florence half an hour's ride behind him, it would be another half hour before he rode through ancient iron gates that opened onto a winding road lined with cypress trees.

There, Villa Mirandola would be waiting, a crown on the top of a hill, surrounded by his father's grapevines and groves of olives with silver leaves.

When Angelo saw the road rising ahead of him, he set his horse to a trot, anxious to be home at last, after so long an absence. He was surprised at his calculations. Was it truly over a year since his last visit? The sound of hooves ringing hollow on the road reminded him that he was on Tuscan soil, a hard-baked mixture of limestone and clay, littered with stones of alberese and marl.

He wondered if his mother would be in the lemon house, taking advantage of the cooling afternoon breeze, or standing on the balustraded terrace, gazing out over the sweeping views and praying for his safety with her rosary in her hands, as his father wrote that she often did.

He turned through the familiar gates of home and waved at a few peasants working among the grapevines, then paused to talk with a few who worked close to the road. After a few minutes, he bid them goodbye and urged his horse into a gallop, eager to be home at last.

He knew his father would be in the fields, but would expect him to stop by the house, to see his mother. It was something his father had taught Angelo when he was a boy. "Honor your mother," he said, "and always see to her needs first."

When he arrived, hot and covered with dust, he ran up the steps and into the cool interior of the house. He was greeted almost immediately by the housekeeper Patricia, and after giving her a fond kiss, he set off to find his mother.

He followed the sound of conversation coming from the salon. His mother's voice he recognized immediately, but the other was foreign and unfamiliar. He paused a moment to listen. The woman's command of Italian was quite good, the accent fair, and her native language English.

His mother conversed with the woman as if she knew her quite well, and Angelo listened closely for some hint of recognition.

Who was she?

He stopped short of entering the room, debating whether he should enter and satisfy his curiosity, or direct his long legs to take him at a swift pace to his room and save greeting his mother for later, when he was cleaned up and more presentable.

His mother did not know the exact day or hour he was arriving, and his sudden appearance would catch her off guard. Once she checked him over and satisfied herself that he was as whole and hardy as the last time she had seen him, almost nine months before, she would want to know how his trip was, and how things were going for him in Turin. Then she would ask if he was keeping away from trouble with the Austrians.

And therein lay the difficulty.

She would want details. *What are you doing with these Carbonari friends of yours? Is it dangerous?* she would ask. *Have you seen your father yet? You are not in some sort of trouble. Did you know the man who was jailed in Milan?*

Although his mother knew he was a member of the Carbonari, she had only suspicions and no true idea of the political situation or the risks those with liberal ideals took with their resistance. Living in the Tuscan hills, one did not experience the atrocities suffered by those living in Turin and Milan.

Many of his friends from the University of Bologna were also active in what some thought of as a romantic political movement. His mother knew many of her friends had sons who were also involved, for most of the Carbonari came from the privileged class. They were educated. Many were aristocrats. All were united by courage, honor and fidelity to the sacred oath they had taken.

He had written to her once, and said, "I am not a hotheaded aficionado, marked by extreme, unreasoning enthusiasm for a cause. I do what I do to liberate Italy, or the idea of Italy, from the yoke of foreign rule."

True, there was no Italy now, only separate regions with a similar culture; different rulers; different currency, weights and measures; and different dialects of the same language. One day, it would be a country united, under one flag and one government.

But first, the Austrians had to be dealt with.

He heard the rattle of teacups, and decided to clean himself up before seeing her. He turned away and walked with great strides down the grand hallway toward the stairs.

He had one foot on the stairs when he heard his mother's voice. "Angelo?"

He paused.

"Is that truly you, or are you a ghost composed of all my yearnings to see my son after so long an absence?"

He turned and strode toward her, then took her in his arms. "I could never sneak past you as a child. I don't know why I thought I could get away with it now." He kissed her cheek. "How is it possible that I grow older, while you turn back the clock?"

She was looking him over. "Have you seen your father? You are not in some sort of trouble, are you? Did you know the man who was jailed in Milan?"

Humor tugged at his mouth. "You know Father always taught me to see to you first. As for the man jailed in Milan, I don't know him." He glanced up the stairs. "I thought I would clean a little of this traveler's dust off myself before greeting you."

"You aren't running from the Austrians, are you?"

Her comment caught him by surprise. "Why would you think that?"

"Yesterday, I learned that the only son of Countess Elena Carafa was hanged in Milan. I know he was a Carbonaro, like you. Now, I worry that your activities, like his, will bring you into fatal conflict with the Hapsburgs."

"I am careful, Mother."

"I would rather you were not involved."

"Too late for such sentiments now."

"I know the idea of Italian patriotism runs as warmly through your head as it does your blood, but I cannot bear the thought of your loyalty being the cause of something happening to you."

He looked heavenward with a teasing grin and said, "Alas, the curse of being an only son."

"Love is not measured by quantity any more than it is measured by descent from a common ancestor."

He looked at this remarkable woman, who along with her husband had taken him in—a gypsy baby abandoned at their doorstep.

"Have you forgotten about your guest?" he asked. "I heard you talking when I came in. That is why I decided to clean up before I presented myself. Who is it, by the way?"

Gisella opened her mouth and promptly closed it.

Angelo gave her a curious look. Was she in some sort of daze? "Do you know who you were talking to, or have you forgotten her name?"

His mother seemed to come around. "Of course I know who it is. Believe me, it is no one you would be interested in. She is an acquaintance from England, who lives with her husband in Florence. She comes to Villa Mirandola occasionally to visit and have tea."

"Then, I shall leave her to you, while I clean up. Afterward, I will go in search of my father. Hopefully, by the time we return, your visitor will be gone."

His mother smiled. "Tito is anxious to see you. It is difficult for him, you know, having his only son gone."

"It is only difficult because that leaves him with two women and no male to back him up."

Gisella patted his cheek. "Still the tease. You know your father needs no one to back him up. He is quite capable of being blustery when he feels it is called for."

"Where is my sister? It is awfully quiet."

"She is in Rome, visiting your aunt. She will be home soon, so enjoy the quiet while you can."

"I intend to." Angelo kissed his mother. "I will see you later. Give my regards to your English friend, and my apologies for not meeting her. And thank you for sparing me."

"Thank me later," she said as she walked away.

Angelo watched his mother leave. She was acting strangely, and something told him it was not just her reaction at seeing him after so long. Sometimes women could be as transparent as glass; other times, they went beyond complicated.

When Angelo came downstairs after changing clothes, he could hear that his mother was still entertaining her English friend, so he slipped out the back way and went to find Tito. He knew his father would be in the vineyards. He knew they were burning the branches they had pruned from the olive trees and the grapevines, for he had seen the smoke from a dozen small fires rising up in a thin gray column as he rode toward the villa.

Angelo thought it a fine thing that he still looked forward to seeing his father with much the same excitement he had felt as a child. Tito was someone stable and constant in his life, a man Angelo prayed he would some day resemble, for he feared it would be impossible for anyone to be Tito's equal.

As he suspected, Tito was cutting a few last twigs from an olive tree as Angelo walked up the road. His back was to Angelo, and Angelo signaled to the

workers to remain silent. He was almost close
enough to touch him, when Tito turned around.
When he saw Angelo, he was so shocked, that he
dropped his knife.

"My son," he said, and embraced Angelo. "You
have given me the shock of my life. How good it is
to see you. Is it possible that you have grown even
more handsome?"

"That is what the ladies tell me," Angelo said.

"Still noticing them, I gather."

"Always. I am my father's son, am I not?"

Tito laughed and patted Angelo on the back.
"When did you arrive?"

"Less than an hour ago. I stopped to clean up a
bit before coming to see you."

"Did you see your mother first?"

"Of course. That is the way you raised me. Do
you think I would forget?"

His father's eyes sparkled. "No, I am just surprised she let you go so soon."

"She was having tea with a married friend."

Tito seemed surprised. "A married friend?"

"She said the lady was English and living in Florence. I assumed she pointed out the fact that the lady
was married, so as to discourage me."

"Your mother knows that would not be the deter-
rent she would hope. But that is enough of that for
now. Come, let us take a walk—I have much I want
to discuss with you, and now seems the perfect
time."

"I have been eager to talk with you since receiving your cryptic letter."

"I knew curiosity would get you here in record
time."

"You mentioned something about Villa Adriana."

"I have what I hope is good news. How would you feel if I told you we are all moving to Villa Adriana for a time?"

"Moving? You mean the entire family? Including Serena?"

"Yes, but only for a year or so. Perhaps less. I want to restore the vineyards and plant more grapes. I cannot oversee the doing of it from here, due to the distance, and I cannot go up there alone for so long a time without your mother."

"I cannot think of anything I would like more than to have my family nearby. You know, I have been working on some drawings to restore the gardens, and I mapped out the vineyards. I saw several places where I thought it possible to extend the plantings."

"Confirmation indeed that this is the right time to consider such, then."

"When do you think we will leave?"

"I am hoping within two weeks' time. I have everything here attended to, and these workers have all been here so long, they know what to do.

"Let's walk back to the villa. I know your mother is in the midst of planning a grand dinner tonight, to celebrate the return of our son. I need to relieve myself of a little of Villa Mirandola's rich soil before we eat."

They started back up the rocky path that wound its way among the grapevines and olive groves. As they walked, Tito asked Angelo about the situation in Turin and Milan, and Angelo explained it all as best he could.

"Your mother does not understand," Tito said. "I think that is because she would rather have you here, where there is relatively little friction with the Austrians."

"That is because your Grand Duke Ferdinand is rather passive, and the people do not burn with the thought of a free and independent Italy."

"Gisella understands that much, and she never misses an opportunity to blame the Neapolitans."

"Because that is where the Carbonari started?"

Tito nodded.

"Only a woman could blame the Neapolitans for what the Austrians do," Angelo said.

"That does about sum it up, doesn't it?" Tito said, and the two of them laughed as they continued down the path toward home.

Inside the house, Gisella decided not to tell Beatrice that Angelo had arrived, just as she had not told Angelo that Beatrice was at Villa Mirandola. She had already spoken with the cook, and plans were set for a lovely dinner to celebrate a multitude of things. If the saints were with her, and Tito did not tell Angelo that Beatrice was here, then she would be able to surprise both of them at the same time.

To Gisella, it seemed the right thing to do—to allow each of them to see the other at the same moment, thus not giving the advantage to either one of them.

Only moments before, she had sent Beatrice up to change for dinner. "Wear something extra special tonight. We are celebrating."

"Celebrating what, Aunt?"

"I want it to be a surprise," Gisella replied, then said another prayer that the surprise would really work for both Angelo and Beatrice.

When Angelo and Tito arrived, Gisella sent Angelo up to change. When she was alone with Tito, she said, "You didn't tell him Beatrice was here, did you?"

"Of course not. Angelo said you were having tea with a married friend from England who lived in Florence. I didn't know what the true story was, so I decided to stay completely out of it. You women can certainly complicate things."

Gisella said, "Oh, thank you, Tito," and gave him a big kiss.

"I have only one question. How are you going to get both of them in to dinner without them seeing one another?"

"I told Angelo dinner was at eight. I told Beatrice it was at seven forty-five. That way he can walk in and, *voilà*, they see each other."

"And die of shock."

Gisella crossed herself. "You mustn't say such, even in jest."

"I hope you know what you are doing," he said.

"I do. And what about you?"

"What do you mean?"

"Did you tell Angelo you were giving Villa Adriana to him?"

"In a way," he said, and added, "I will go dress for dinner now."

"Not so fast. What do you mean, 'in a way'? Just how many ways are there to tell the truth?"

"There is the immediate way and the delayed way."

"And you call *women* complicated!"

Uncle Tito took Gisella in his arms. "My love, I have always called women an absolute necessity. What would men be without them?"

"Exactly," she replied, and went upstairs to dress.

Tito shook his head and followed the woman he had been following for most of his adult life.

At seven forty-five, Beatrice joined her aunt and uncle in the salon next to the dining room, wearing a gown of the latest French design, elegant and simple, of a deep burnished gold, and with a border made from a Persian scarf. The deep V-necked bodice was particularly French in its plunge.

Tito handed her a glass of Chianti. "For such a dress, I should open a bottle of champagne," he said. "My dear, you are exquisitely beautiful tonight."

"Thank you, Uncle," Beatrice said as she accepted the glass. "It has been a glorious week and I am feeling especially grand."

"You mustn't let Serena see that dress," Gisella said. "She will be completely captivated by it, especially with the lovely trim around the bottom."

"It is a Persian scarf. I found the pattern and colors too lovely to pass up, although I did pay more for it than I normally do."

"For such a dress, a woman has a perfect right to be extravagant," Gisella said.

"I agree, and promise to take both of you to the opera, if you promise to wear that dress," Tito said.

Beatrice was standing beside the piano. She took a sip of wine and listened to the compliments Uncle Tito paid Aunt Gisella, who looked beautiful in emerald-green satin.

Upstairs, Angelo made the last adjustment to his white cravat in the hall mirror before he went downstairs. As he drew near the salon, he heard the same voice from this afternoon, and decided the English lady from Florence must have stayed for dinner.

He walked into the room wearing only black, with a white shirt and fitted trousers. He had kissed his mother and was reaching for the glass of wine his father offered, when suddenly the sound of breaking glass interrupted the moment.

Angelo's head jerked around, and he saw danger standing by the piano. His first thought was, if this was his mother's married friend from Florence, she was very seductive. His blood was running red tonight.

"I am so sorry," she said.

"Don't worry, my dear," his mother said, hurrying to the woman's side. "I am thankful you did not spill it on your beautiful dress."

Angelo saw the narrow shoulders, the lovely bosom with the plunging neckline that was definitely French, and the golden hair. He liked what he saw so far.

His father led her away from the piano and handed her another glass of wine.

She smiled at him and said, "Are you certain you trust me with this?"

"Unequivocally," Tito said.

Angelo watched the exchange. She was lovely, whoever she was. Composed, dignified, with an incredible sense of bearing. Familiarity hovered in the air like a static charge but never settled upon him.

The room fell into an awkward silence.

Gisella brought her hand to her head. *"Madonna mia!* Don't tell me you don't recognize her."

The woman looked down at her feet.

Angelo knew many English women, but he knew only one shy one. "Hello, Mouse."

She watched him with eyes as bright and innocent as daisies. Her nod was almost undetectable. She said "Hello," and the word floated over him like silk.

"I am relieved you finally recognized her, although I hardly think it appropriate to call her Mouse. She is scarcely the same woman she was five years ago.''

"Oh, I can see that for myself,'' Angelo said as he studied Beatrice's slight form. ''Some things need no explanation.''

It was a rude shock to his system, seeing her thus, and like her, he was still trying to recover. A graceful woman was a deceptive being, capable of hiding much, for illusion was her element. He saw in Beatrice all of these things, for the woman he remembered was a mere illusion compared to the woman standing before him.

Gisella looked from one to the other. ''I must say, it certainly took you long enough to realize it.''

"I fear I would be easy to forget, Aunt, considering I did my very best to be invisible whenever Angelo was around.''

"Exquisitely shy, I recall.''

"I am still shy, but now I am also confident.''

"I see.'' He was aware of his mother standing silently beside him—something quite rare for her—with an enlightened look on her face. A look he would call amused interest danced in her eyes. ''You are curiously quiet,'' he said to her.

"I have suddenly realized one can learn a lot by remaining silent,'' Gisella said.

"You should not let Father hear you say that.''

"Too late now. I cannot believe that after all these years, I am finally witnessing my wife learning the great truth of silence,'' Tito said.

A gust of wind came through the open windows. Somewhere in the house a door slammed. Angelo's body gave a jerk, and he turned sharply in the direction of the sound. His pose was defensive as he gave the room close scrutiny.

"It was only the wind catching a door," Gisella said, looking at him with a suspicious eye, her face suddenly pale.

He saw the way Beatrice looked at him, as well. He saw the questions in their eyes. He knew they wanted to ask, *Why are you so tense?* He did not want to answer them right now. How could he? How could he tell them the truth—what it was like always to watch your back and to sleep with your pistol under your pillow, eyes half open?

Only his father seemed to not notice. "I am quite famished," he said. "What do you say we go in to dinner. I will escort your mother," he said to Angelo.

Angelo went to Beatrice and offered her his arm. "May I?"

"A pleasure," she said, and walked with him into the dining room.

Angelo was trying to decide if he would prefer to sit across from her to view her lovely face, or next to her so he could see just how low the décolletage of that gown really was.

His mother decided for him when she said, "Beatrice, you may sit there, and Angelo, please take the chair across from her."

The wine was poured, and Tito lifted his glass in a toast. "To family," he said, "and to the celebration of the return of two family members long absent."

"To family," everyone repeated, and each raised a glass.

The meal was served along with the conversation. Angelo noticed how Beatrice was queried frequently, and how easily she handled the press of questions, as well as being the object of so much attention.

He was a man of quick judgment and keen insight. In Beatrice he saw something genuine—a woman who was open but not overly eager to please. She presented the facts as they were, without a hint as to how she wished them to be accepted. This was something he rarely saw in a world of subterfuge, pretense and treachery, where lying was considered an art.

"Beatrice, you must tell Angelo about your life, your artistic endeavors, since your last visit here," Gisella said.

"I'm afraid it would seem quite calm and boring after the excitement and danger he lives with," she replied.

"Calm is precisely what I hoped to find when I returned," he said. "Mother said you are an artist now. I never knew your interests lay in that direction."

Her face reddened, but only slightly. "I always knew I wanted to be an artist, but prior to coming to Italy, it was never something I considered seriously. I began, as many artists do, with lessons, to discover if I had no talent, or to establish the fact that I did."

"That must have been a terrifying first step," Tito said.

Beatrice smiled. "Terrifying is a perfect description, Uncle. At that time in my life, I easily could have been intimidated into believing I could not draw a straight line. The English can be quite daunting, you know. Take Queen Elizabeth, for example. As a child I always loved to hear the story of her answer to her council when they opposed her on Mary Queen of Scots."

Angelo watched as she paused to take a sip of wine, and as she tilted the glass, her head came up and her eyes met his. He let his gaze drop lower, along her throat and down to the place where her dress plunged. *Yes,* he thought, *she has changed,* and wondered if Paris was responsible. When he glanced back at her face, she was no longer looking at him, but the flush of color to her face said she was aware of his attention.

"Well, don't keep us waiting," Gisella said. "What did Queen Elizabeth say?"

"Oppose me, and I will make you shorter by a head."

Everyone laughed, and Angelo added a sense of humor to the list of attributes he was compiling about this woman he had once loved—sobering reminder though it was. He wondered if he was getting old, for he had trouble reconciling the woman he remembered with the woman he saw and listened to now.

He stroked his chin, fighting the allure of this highly desirable creature. The attraction was still there, which surprised him, since he had thought things between them concluded long ago. He was suddenly curious as to why he felt attracted to her a second time, when it had never been his way to re-kindle a past romance.

His curiosity aroused now, he asked himself why. Was the attraction bona fide, one born of a desire to get even; a remnant of long-lost feelings; mere curiosity to see where her feelings lay; or one born of the need to know why she left in the first place?

He dropped his hand and gave his attention to what she was saying.

"A succession of painting tutors came and went for almost two years, until I began to feel I could teach *them* something. It is not pompous bragging, but something based upon fact. I knew my execution was more careful, and I had a truer feel for color and tone than most of those who taught me.''

"I don't think that is bragging, either," Tito said. "It is being confident, as I am confident last year's Chianti is far better than the year before."

"Is that when you began to paint on your own?" Gisella asked.

"No, it was when I knew I was ready to be taught by the masters. You must understand, however, that a woman has to be approaching the rank of genius, to convince one of the masters to take her to tutor, and even then, a woman can never expect the same advantages afforded to men."

"But there have been many excellent women artists, and quite famous ones," Uncle Tito said.

"Our own Artemisia, for one," Angelo added.

"True, but unfortunately I did not have a father who was a painter as did Artemisia Gentileschi, Angelica Kauffmann, or Mary Moser. Each was fortunate enough to have a family member as a mentor."

"So that meant there were no opportunities for you to have an introduction by any means other than your own talent and hard work," Gisella said.

"Yes, and not only for me, but for women artists in general."

Angelo heard himself ask, "Did you find they did not accept you, or that they did not take you seriously?"

"Both. More than once, I was advised to 'dabble in the arts' as a way to amuse myself. One teacher's advice was 'Paint if you must, but as a pastime. Never, ever, my dear, take it seriously.'"

"I keep thinking how this conversation would have exploded by now, if Serena were here," Tito said. "There is nothing that raises her ire like the repression of women. Hearing your stories makes me want to apologize to you for having not one whit of artistic ability.''

"If it makes you feel better, I do actually consider myself fortunate not to have had an artist figure in my immediate family. Women who did often found their works signed by their mentor, as well.''

"Now, that would send Serena through the roof,'' Gisella said, ''and it makes me furious, as well. I cannot believe anyone would tolerate such.''

Beatrice replied, ''It is tolerated because men are considered serious artists, while women are thought to be too fragile to pursue artistic endeavors.''

Angelo had been determined to listen but not to become involved in Beatrice's life. But he quickly became fascinated about her past, and incensed by the outrageous injustices against her, the obstacles she had faced and overcome.

There was a time in the past when he would have thought differently, but after dealing with the Austrians and the repression of the people, he was against injustice in any form against men or women. To involve himself with Beatrice again would be a big mistake, but he resented the injustices against her. There should not be one set of rules for men and another for women, any more than there should be one set for the rich and another for the poor.

Feeling the beginning throb of a headache, he lifted his glass and finished his wine, having decided that if he was going to get a headache, he would prefer the cause to be wine rather than women.

Dessert was served. Angelo had wine, instead. He was about to have another glass, when his father requested a bottle of champagne.

When the champagne had been poured, Tito stood

and turned toward Angelo. He lifted his glass in a manner remindful of a salute and said, "To my son, who has always pleased me immensely. I have never missed a day to give thanks to God for the blessing and privilege of raising you and the joy of seeing the man you have become. And so, it is to you, Angelo, that I raise my glass with a father's pride."

Angelo drank to the toast, and embraced his father, totally overwhelmed.

Before Angelo could respond, Tito withdrew a folded document from his pocket and handed it to him.

"I can think of no finer tribute than to say that I have, this day, signed the papers to transfer the land of my ancestors to you. With love, honor and gratitude, your mother and I give Villa Adriana to you. Although we do retain visitors' rights," he added with a wink.

Angelo was stunned. Although he had known he would probably inherit Villa Adriana, he had never dreamed it would come to him so soon, and certainly not when he was involved with the liberal movement. "I don't know what to say. It is something I have always dreamed of, but I never thought it would happen while I was still relatively young."

Tito laughed and said, "Twenty-eight *is* young… not 'relatively' so."

"Let us move into the salon," Gisella said.

As he had done before, Angelo walked with Beatrice. "I'm glad all of your difficulties in becoming an artist have had a happy ending."

"Oh, I am still working on that. I have the training. Now I must become the artist."

"What are your plans?"

"I have not made up my mind completely. I have

just concluded three years of study in Paris, where I received several offers for commissions to paint portraits. I have not decided if I will return to France and accept them, or remain in Italy for a time to paint.''

''I hope you choose the latter.''

She glanced at him with a surprised expression. ''I find that hard to believe.''

He stopped and turned toward her. ''Why do you find it hard to believe?''

''Are we going to ignore the past and pretend it never existed?''

''I don't know. Do you want to?''

''I prefer to be honest.''

''If I were honest with you right now, *cara,* it would embarrass you.''

''I don't embarrass as easily as I did back then.''

''Good.''

''I didn't tell you that for your benefit.''

''I know why you told me. I like the cut of your gown, by the way.''

''I noticed.''

''That is why you wore it, isn't it?''

''I wore it because I like it, and I will tell you now that all the times I wore it in Paris, I never once had a man look at me the way you did tonight.''

''That doesn't say much for French men, does it.''

''I did not say it as an affront to the French.''

''I know why you said it. I hear the lump in your lovely throat, and I see the homesickness in those amber eyes.'' He drew a finger down the side of her cheek and let it trail over her lower lip, until she slapped it away.

He laughed. ''That's better.'' He offered her his

arm again. "Now, we can go into the salon much more relaxed than we were in the dining room."

"I don't know," she said. "I find it's much easier to make war than peace."

As they walked into the salon and past the curious gazes of his parents, Angelo graced everyone with the gift of his laughter.

Nine

Beatrice lay in bed. It was the perfect setting. The evening was warm, the windows open, the room dark, but she could not sleep.

She tried squeezing her eyes shut, but they had a way of opening in spite of all she did. Thoughts of Angelo consumed her. She might as well face it. She had had high aspirations that she would be charming and gay and completely immune to anything connected with, or mindful of, Angelo.

Things had not gone according to her plan.

After much thought, she decided that was because she had made plans and prepared herself to meet the Angelo she had known before—and the man she'd seen tonight had been different.

That was an understatement. He was eons away from the jovial tease she had left a few years back. Yet, that did not seem to matter. The questions she wanted answers to had all been answered. Almost five years away from him had not changed her attraction to him, or her feelings. Her heart still pounded at the sight of him, and the slight huskiness to his voice still left her weak in the knees. She would have to be careful around him...very, very careful.

Go to sleep, she told herself. *Tomorrow you can worry about being careful.*

She closed her eyes and lay her forearm over them, thinking that if she kept her eyes closed long enough, she would go to sleep.

An hour later, she was still awake, and Beatrice was not a person to lie abed when her eyes were open and her mind was alive with thought. If you weren't going to sleep, what was the point in remaining in bed? All she was doing was thinking about Angelo, and that was the last thing she needed to do.

Whenever she could not sleep, she found painting to be the perfect antidote—and more productive than lying in bed, bored to her toes. She dressed quietly, in a simple dress without petticoats, and took great care not to make any noise as she went downstairs.

The painting she was doing of her aunt was almost finished. If the need for sleep did not overcome her, it might be possible to finish it tonight. She thought about the colors she might use, almost feeling the emotion reaching out to her from the warm earthy tones of Naples yellow, ocher and raw sienna, and the colors she was out of and would have to mix, Venetian red, burnt sienna, raw umber, ivory black. For her aunt's dress, the subtle hint of blue and green.

She could almost hear her first painting tutor, a small, fiery Italian with the medieval name Gerozzo Boccaccio: *"You must remember that it was Cennini who first wrote of seven natural colors. Four of them are mineral colors—black, red, yellow and green. Three are natural colors, and these you must encourage by artifice so you will have white (which he called bianca San Gianni), blues, ultramarine, azurite and gallorino. These are the colors that da Vinci later called primary colors."*

She continued on her way, wondering where Gerozzo was now.

In the room Aunt Gisella had designated as her studio, she set to work. The diluent she had mixed days ago, using the same formula handed down from the Renaissance—processed linseed oil, raw linseed oil and a hard-resin varnish made from Congo copal.

She blended the first color and tested it on the fleshy part of her hand, near the place where the forefinger and thumb joined. She did the same with the other colors, and, when she finished, gave a nod of satisfaction and began to paint.

As she worked, she would pause from time to time to study the richest areas of the painting, which were lighter and made more pure by setting them against larger, darker areas. Using this technique, she made the flesh tones of her aunt's skin appear luminous against the dark coils of fine black hair.

She did not know how long she worked, and the need for sleep did not penetrate her consciousness until she had finished and begun to soak her brushes. She stretched and brought her hand up to knead the knot at the back of her neck, then picked up another brush—

"I thought you went to bed hours ago. What are you doing up?"

She looked up to see Angelo framed in the doorway.

He was not a big man—although taller than average—but his body was that of a horseman, supple and light. She had already decided that the way he moved had not changed, for well she remembered the fine gestures, the fluid action of his body. She recalled watching him fence with his fencing master, and the erotic thoughts his movements had inspired.

At one time, he was nothing but one big smile.

And now, it seemed, he rarely smiled.

It was hard to believe this was the man who had once said, ''Ah, the women...they love me too much.'' She wondered if the man she had known and once loved was gone for good.

''I could not sleep, so I decided to finish Aunt Gisella's portrait.''

''I saw it earlier, when I came back downstairs. Remarkable likeness—the expression, the arch of her brow... I find it difficult to believe you did not know you had such talent. What other talents have you kept secret?''

''None, I'm afraid. I suppose I've been too busy developing this one. Or perhaps I am a one-talent woman.''

''Are you? That's odd, for I seem to recall several.''

''We all have our differences of opinion. What you look on with remorse is my reminiscence.''

He smiled, and she had a glimpse of the old Angelo, but the smile faded.

''I can reminisce. Take now, for instance, and how well I remember our last evening together. You kissed me like you could not bear to be away from me for even a moment. And then you left the next day to answer the call of distant England, and broke my heart in the doing of it.''

The memory of the evening was something she kept as one would keep a special gift, never using it but hiding it in a secret place where she could look at it and enjoy it again and again. The memory had always been the brightness in a world that was, for her, empty and dark—and now he was saying she had broken his heart. How did he always know what to say?

"I daresay I did not break your heart."

"And you are some sort of expert on broken hearts, I take it?"

"It was not easy for me to leave, in spite of what you think."

"Then, why did you leave?"

"I thought I explained it to you."

"You spoke in generalities. You did not speak of what was in your heart. If you had, I would have been in England waiting for you when you arrived."

His words stunned her.

I would have been in England waiting for you when you arrived...

She felt as if she were dreaming. Was he telling her that he would have done the very thing she had wished for, *if only* she had been more truthful with him? She brought her hand to her head, trying to remember precisely her words that night.

"Exactly what reasons did I give you that you label generalities?"

"You don't remember what you told me, do you? Well, I remember quite vividly. Allow me to refresh your memory. You were too young and inexperienced for a man like me. A man such as I was could never be content with one woman. You mentioned the difference in our religions, and in our cultures. You made mostly sweeping statements—a clutter of clichés, shallow appraisals, passive acceptance of preconceived notions, wrong information and gossip about me—and few revealing truths. All of which made me sound insincere and quite superficial."

"You make me seem callous."

"It was callous."

"I did not see it that way. My feelings were never frivolous or lighthearted, and I did have a care for your feelings. More than you could ever know."

"Now, why do I find that difficult to believe?"

"Then, we are perfectly matched, for I find it difficult to believe my leaving affected you in the least."

She untied her smock, folded it and laid it aside. She could not believe she was saying these things, speaking her mind and not being shy about it. Suddenly, she was articulate, when she had feared her words would come tripping over her tongue.

"Perhaps everything you say is true. Perhaps everything I did was prompted by my own insecurities and immature beliefs, but you, Angelo...can you not see that you were like a knight in shining armor to a plain, shy English girl? Is it so impossible to imagine that pitifully timid creature chose to ignore the truth in order to cling to the illusion that what happened between us was real?"

"It was real."

His words did not penetrate her consciousness, and she continued with her own vein of thinking. "Do you not know that I have relived it a thousand times?"

"And you think you were the only one?"

"It isn't the same thing. For you, our time together was a mad, lamentable experiment, something you would come to regret. It was a game. I was a challenge. I knew without a doubt that once you had me in your bed, that would be the end of it. But for me, it was a key that unlocked the prison I had placed myself in. My mind was closed and opportunity locked out, for I was tied to my solitary, rather reticent ways. A person without ambition is already dead. Can you not see that you were the spur that pricked the sides of ambitions that were quavering at best?''

He was smiling at her now. ''Are you trying, in a roundabout way, to give me credit for your talent?''

''No, I am not that foolish. What I am giving you credit for is showing me the dissatisfaction I felt with my life. I existed. I did not live. I was like a bird who returns to the same nest, year after year.''

''And yet you returned to England and the same familiar nest.''

''Before I reached Pisa, I wanted to come back to you.''

''Why didn't you? Why would it have been so difficult to turn around and return to Villa Mirandola?''

''I knew it would never work.''

''You were afraid to trust. That was your problem. You did not believe in me. You did not believe in us. You did not even believe in yourself. You refused to think I could be in love with you. I was not after a torrid affair. I had a past filled with those. You misplayed your cards and we both lost the game.''

''I'm sorry.''

''It doesn't matter now. Whatever your reasons, whatever our feelings were, it is over now.''

''You sound so certain.''

''Don't tell me you came back because you were having second thoughts.''

''I came back for a lot of reasons, so it's possible that one might be lumped in there with all the others.''

''Might be?''

She shrugged. ''There is no way of knowing for certain.''

"Oh, but there is," he said, and the next moment he was holding her in his arms.

Her startled eyes grew round, and her breathing stopped, as if air was trapped in her throat. She brought her hand up and placed it against his chest, but he captured her hand in his and drew it around him, then held it with his other hand, pulling her against him.

"Let's see if we can find the truth," he whispered.

He lowered his lips to hers and caught her in the middle of a response, her mouth open. She prepared herself for the fierce kiss she knew was coming, and found herself completely off guard when he kissed her with such tender passion that her knees threatened to buckle beneath her. It was an invitation—the kiss of a man who knew exactly what he was doing and how to kiss a woman to make her want more. And she did.

She was weak and she knew it. It had been so very long, and she loved him so much, fearing now that she still loved him with the same searing intensity, when he was merely curiously exploring to satisfy himself and answer a few questions.

When she was ready to shove him away, he outmaneuvered her again, breaking the kiss, brushing his lips lightly against her nose and saying "Welcome home, Gentiana."

To have him call her that, brought tears to her eyes and she had to turn away. He was a master at seduction, and he knew just how to play her to make her end up in his arms. She could have withstood anger or bitterness, but this mixture of teasing and understanding with just a hint of masculine forcefulness was undoing her.

As if knowing her discomfort, he took command

of the situation, and she recalled how he had always been quite good at doing that, too.

He walked around the room, looking at her finished canvases and those in progress. ''You told us at dinner how your life went in London. Tell me about Paris.''

She closed her eyes and took a deep breath, fearing she was drawing too close to him and knowing it was too soon.

''I mentioned that I painted and took instruction from various artists, but none of them was of the caliber I needed. That was when I decided to go to France. I wrote a letter to Elisabeth-Louise Vigèe-Lebrun in Paris. She invited me to visit her and show her some of my work. I did, and she agreed to teach me.''

''How long were you there?''

''Three years.''

''And now you are capable of this,'' he said, gesturing at her paintings. ''You must feel extraordinary, knowing you did something so remarkable all by yourself.''

''I am happy because I found something I love and excel at, but I cannot accept all the credit, because part of it belongs to you. And for that reason, I could never allow you to think I do not hold you in the highest esteem. Falling in love with you completed me. You gave me confidence by encouraging me to stand on my own two feet. I was so pitifully shy when I came here, but you were like a magnet that drew the real Beatrice out of her shell. I have always thought of loving you as a blessing. Please accept the truth of what I say, not because I want to appear magnanimous but because it is the truth.''

''I find that hard to believe.''

"Believe this, then—if there had been no love between us, I would have ended my visit here and returned to England, where I would still be in London, looking after my father's town house, empty, shy and unfulfilled."

"Well, I am glad I could be of service."

"Don't make it sound cold."

"When love ends, there is nothing left but ashes. Cold ashes."

She picked up a brush and began to dry it. "It didn't feel cold to me. When I arrived in England, I never knew love could feel so empty."

"We all react differently."

"And you? How do you see it?"

"I look upon it more as a bout of drunkenness. When it was over I had a headache, but after a while it was gone."

"Then, you didn't love me, not really."

"And you think you were different?"

"Do you really want me to tell you what I think? Yes, I think I loved you, and furthermore, I think love is exactly what they have always said it is. It means you have no common sense, and that you care about another person more than you care about yourself. It means there is a person who can walk into the room and make your world light up. It means you feel intense joy when you are with him and a terrible longing when the two of you are apart. It means... Oh, I don't know why I'm waxing poetic with a stone. You have no heart...only amorous feelings. You can't love a woman, you can only make love to her. There is a difference, you know."

"Ever the romantic."

"Personally, I think being romantic is much better than the reality of being in love." She threw down the brush she was holding. "Love! Bah! Who needs it?"

"You do, *cara,* and badly."

"If that is an offer, I decline."

Suddenly he started laughing—the wonderful laugh that she always adored hearing—and the next thing she knew, she was laughing, too.

When her sides ached, she leaned against the table weakly. "I cannot laugh any more. It hurts too much."

The sound of birds chirping prompted her to glance toward the window, where the first pastel tints of morning gave faint outline to the ragged silhouette of hills. "I do believe this is the first time I have ever stayed up all night, and yet, I do not feel sleepy in the least. I wonder if I will make it through the day, or suddenly sink like a stone."

"I think you have what it takes to remain awake."

She smiled at that. "I think I shall have a cup of tea. Would you care for some?"

"Remarkable."

"My, you are certainly looking at me strangely. Why? What did I do besides offer you a cup of tea?"

"Such a transformation is extraordinary. I am beginning to doubt my memory."

She laughed outright. "Oh, I fear your memory serves you correctly." Her gaze skimmed over his person. His clothes were much as she remembered—the fine linen shirt, black pants tucked into expensive leather boots. "I find you equally changed. You are not the man I remember, either."

"The music has gone out of all our lives. You are different. I am different. Italy is different. The whole world has changed and we along with it."

"I know. I saw so many changes while I was in

Paris, but I sense it is even greater here. There are times when I try to compare the Italy I remember with the Italy I see now. It appears dreamlike, and leaves me wondering if I will soon awake and see bizarre landscapes and distorted objects.''

He stepped closer to stand between her and the flickering light of the lamp. She gazed for a long while at him, and, in spite of the shadow in which he was standing, she saw, or fancied she saw, the expression on his face and in his eyes. It was again that expression of almost reverent ecstasy, which had so worked upon her the day before.

His was a face she would love to paint.

She picked up one of the clean brushes and stared at it in her hand. More than once she had told herself, in the days following her first visit here, that Angelo was like a hundred young men she knew in London, forever and always the same—jocular, carefree, irresponsible and, when it came to women, insincere.

It reinforced her feelings and validated that she had been right all those years ago to vow she would never allow herself to waste a thought upon him.

That had somehow changed upon her return, and from the first instant of seeing him again, she was under his spell and seized by a feeling of joyful pride that he would openly proclaim the depth of the love he had felt for her before she left.

Yet, there was also a tiny part of her that wondered if he was here only to see if he could succeed where he had failed before—in spite of what he said about feelings of love and a broken heart.

''What are you doing up so late?'' she asked, letting fall the hand that still held the paintbrush. Yet, as she spoke those words, an irrepressible delight and excitement brought a blush of color to her cheeks.

"What am I doing up so late?" he repeated, looking straight into her eyes. "You must know that thoughts of you rob me of my sleep. And now, I find myself miraculously in the place I wish most to be— in the room where you are."

At that moment a gust of wind whooshed down the chimney and sent a branch scraping against the window.

Even the elements seemed wild with excitement, and she wondered how she would handle things, now that he had said what her soul longed to hear— though she feared he said it only because he knew she desired it.

"I think it best that you forget what you said, just as I have forgotten it," she said.

"I could never forget anything you did or said. Not one word, not one gesture."

"Stop it. I do not know why you insist upon saying such." And clutching the paintbrush tightly in her hand, she turned to place it in the paint box with the others. But even as she did, her mind was going over what had transpired only moments before.

Though she could not recall her exact words to him, or his to her, she could recall the emotions, and that was enough to make her instinctively realize the brief conversation had served to place them on different terms, and in so doing had brought them closer. She was both euphoric and panic-stricken at the thought of this newfound intimacy. It was too soon. She was unprepared for this.

She knew she could not stand here all night staring down at her paint box, but she was apprehensive about turning to look at him again, afraid of what she might see in his beautiful, but ever seductive, brown eyes. She was filled both with indecision and nervous tension, and in the vision of her artist's imagination, there was nothing disagreeable or gloomy that she could grasp and hold like a weapon. To the contrary, there was something heady, bright and invigorating.

She turned back to face him.

"I believe I'll take that tea now," he said.

She did not trust him. Worse, she did not trust herself, and she found herself saying, "Wouldn't you rather go to bed?"

"With you? *Cara,* if that is an offer, I accept."

She smiled with relief and cuffed him on the arm, for this teasing, playful man she could handle. "Now, *that* is the Angelo I remember, and tea *is* all I'm offering."

"I have a feeling I could change your mind. Want to place a wager?"

"No, I am certain you could…if I gave you the opportunity."

He laughed softly, and a moment later they were making their way through the dimly lit interiors of the villa to the kitchen.

"I hope Patricia has a fire going," Beatrice said.

"Patricia is always up early, but by now, she is probably out gathering eggs."

The fire was lit, and a teakettle was warming, but Patricia was nowhere in sight. Beatrice set about gathering the tea things, and had everything prepared by the time the water began to boil. She removed it from the stove and poured it into the teapot.

She was leaning on one side of the chopping block and he on the other, while they waited for the tea to steep.

"Are you sleepy yet?" she asked.

"No. Are you?"

She shook her head. "I don't know why I'm not. I will probably start babbling before long. If I do, will you please tell me to go to my room?"

"I don't know. That depends on the babble. Perhaps it would be something I want to listen to."

"I doubt that," she said, and began to pour the tea. "I know you would have preferred your traditional coffee. I'm sorry I did not think to offer it to you."

"I have been known to take *una tazza di tè* from time to time."

Una tazza di tè...a cup of tea. She loved the language, and when he spoke, the words seemed to liquefy and pour over her like warm chocolate. He breathed the words, as if they were written on something glossy, sleek and smooth.

"Here is your cup of tea," she said, and handed it to him.

He took the cup, their fingers almost touching but not quite.

"How long will you be in Italy?" He carried the cup to the table and sat down.

She put a spoon of sugar in her tea and stirred, then joined him at the table. "I have plans but no time limits. I want to stay long enough to paint all the Bartolini portraits, if your parents don't grow weary of me first."

"You know that would never happen. They are happiest when we are all here. Mother was most distraught to learn Maresa and Percy would not be coming for Christmas."

"I know, but Maresa's baby is due in February and the doctor advised against taking a lengthy trip."

"This will make four, I think."

"Yes, two boys and a girl, so far. They came to

see me once, when I was in Paris. The children are
beautiful, and so well behaved. Percy is a commander now.''

"He will be Admiral, I am sure, before he leaves
the navy.''

"Maresa and I think so.''

"Sometimes it does not seem so long ago that she
was here. Other times, it seems a lifetime ago.'' He
carried his teacup to the counter.

She stood and picked up her cup.

"Here, let me have it.''

His fingers brushed against hers as he took the cup
and placed it on the counter next to his.

Her head jerked up and she met his steady gaze.
She could feel his hand slide over hers until he en-
circled her wrist. He tugged her forward, and when
she was close enough, he kissed her, long and lingering.

"I wish you were wearing the dress you wore to
dinner tonight.''

"I can't. You scorched it every time you looked
at me.''

"I wanted to do more than that, and you know
it.''

She lay her head against his chest, remembering
the way he had looked at her all evening. She wanted
him to look at her like that again.

"The right feeling. The wrong time. You are tired
and need to go to bed.''

She pulled back and smoothed the folds of her
skirt with her palms. Not because it was necessary,
but because she needed something to do with her
hands. She was having trouble understanding him.
One moment he was passionate and seductive, and

then he would turn casual, almost coy. It left her confused.

She closed her eyes, wishing he would kiss her again.

"I've enjoyed our visit, but it's time for you to go to bed," he said.

She took a step back. "I think I'll find a book in the library to take to my room. Reading always puts me to sleep. Good night."

"Good night."

She was almost to the door when he called after her, "I will come with you."

"Well, come on, then. What are you waiting for, an engraved invitation?"

"I know you better than that," he said, catching up to her, and the two of them walked down the hall.

They reached the library and each set off in a different direction. Beatrice had no idea what she wanted to read, so she pulled out one volume after another, hoping something would catch her eye. After twenty minutes or so, she withdrew a copy of *Madame* de Stael's book, *Corinne*. "I've found mine. How are you coming with your search?"

"Not so good."

"Are you looking for something in particular?"

"I thought I would like to read Byron's *Prisoner of Chillon*. I started it once but never finished it."

"Byron's books are on the top shelf. I know that, because I returned a book of poetry for your mother two days ago."

"You say that because you want me to climb up this ladder."

"No, it's the truth." She carried her book with her as she joined him. "Up there," she said, and pointed.

He located the ladder, one with wheels that followed a metal bar around the circumference of the room.

She watched his ascent. "Don't fall."

"I have an excellent sense of balance. I never fall."

"Oh, is that so?" She placed her book on the ledge, then planted her hands on each side of the ladder and, with a hard shove, began to push the ladder around the room.

"Wha— Hold on now! What are you doing?"

"I'm testing the validity of your words."

"Beatrice, I warn you."

"Haven't you found a book yet?"

He grabbed the corner of a shelf just as it whizzed by, and the ladder jerked to a halt.

Beatrice was laughing so hard she barely heard him speak.

"You know what happens to women who like to make pranks, don't you?"

Breathless, she answered, "No, I don't know."

He started down from the ladder. "You are about to find out."

She snatched up her book and made a dash for the door.

He cut her off before she reached it, and grabbed her with such force that the two of them went tumbling to the floor.

Angelo managed to twist his body before they hit the hard stone, so he landed on the bottom with Beatrice sprawled over him.

"Oh my," she said, and made a move to get up.

"Uh-uh, I'm not letting you off this easy," he said, and she felt his hand on her leg.

"Oh dear. Let me up."

"Not on your life." His hand inched higher.

"We made a frightful noise, Angelo. Someone is certain to come in here."

The sound of voices interspersed with footfalls could be heard coming down the stairs.

"Let me up. Someone is definitely coming." His hand was just below her knee now.

"A quick kiss and I will let you go."

"What kind of idiot are you? Your parents, or someone else, is almost upon us."

"One kiss now, or two later. What's it to be?" His hand was over her knee.

Uncle Tito's voice rang out. "I think it came from the library."

"Two later," she whispered, and found herself on her feet.

She had no more than tucked a stray curl in place when Angelo shoved *Corinne* into her hands.

An instant later, his parents walked into the room. They stopped immediately and looked at each of them.

"What on earth are you two doing in here this time of the morning?" Aunt Gisella asked.

"I was about to ask the same thing," Uncle Tito said.

Angelo found his tongue before Beatrice did. "Beatrice couldn't sleep and came down to finish your portrait. I was reading the paper in Father's study. It was almost daybreak when we ran into each other and decided to have a cup of tea."

"In the library?" Aunt Gisella asked.

"I don't see any teacups," Uncle Tito said, and glanced around the room.

"We had tea in the kitchen like civilized people. After we finished, we came here for a book," Angelo replied.

Tito looked down at Beatrice's book, then at Angelo. "Where's yours?"

"I had the misfortune to select Byron. He's on the top shelf."

"We have a ladder," Uncle Tito said. "Why didn't you use it?"

At that, Angelo and Beatrice burst out laughing. Tito and Gisella seemed puzzled, which only made the two young people laugh harder.

When Angelo got control of himself he said, "I did use the ladder, but I found it difficult to stay onboard."

Aunt Gisella looked from one to the other. Suddenly, a smile lifted the corners of her mouth. "You weren't pushing each other around like you and Serena used to do, were you?"

Before Angelo could say anything, Beatrice said, "I have my book, so I think I will go to my room now. Good morning, Aunt…Uncle…Angelo."

"Deserter," she heard him call after her.

Ten

In her room, Beatrice tried to read, but she found it difficult to concentrate on *Corinne*.

Thoughts of Angelo kept getting in the way.

She found herself completely captivated by him—for the second time in her life. She wondered if there was some sort of rule somewhere, some adage that said something like, *Twice in love, twice the marriage*. Well, perhaps something a bit more eloquent than that, but with a similar meaning.

As for Angelo, he was nothing like the man she saw earlier in the day, nor was he the man she remembered, but a combination of the two.

In the privacy of her room, she found herself leaping off the bed and dancing around the room with the flexible elasticity of movement one would expect from a ten-year-old child. When she caught a glimpse of her face in the mirror, she was as captivated as surprised at the fresh eagerness, the inner joy expressed in her smile and eyes.

She stopped smiling and looked at herself with a critical eye. Did he think her dowdy in her simple blue dress? Were her arms too round? Did he see the stray curls of loose hair as gracefully attractive, or were they just plain sloppy?

She thought about Angelo's boldness one minute and his seeming lack of interest the next, and how it left her confused. Was she still capable of setting him on fire? Or was he merely a creature of habit with such a long and illustrious history of seduction that it was second nature to him?

After a little more thought, she decided it was too early to tell.

It would do no good to attach frills or forebodings to what had happened today, but a deep flush of pleasure did come over her face when she remembered her promise of two kisses.

He will probably forget....

She read two sentences of *Corinne* before she fell asleep.

Later, when she awoke, she was not sure how long she had slept, but it was long enough that she was ravenously hungry, so she wasted no time in getting up.

Once dressed, she went downstairs to find everyone, but no one was about. She saw Patricia rubbing wax into the dining table with such a furious assault that Beatrice almost laughed outright, for it did seem as if Patricia had something personal against that table.

"Good afternoon, Patricia," she greeted warmly, unable to stop smiling. "Where is everyone?"

"I believe your aunt and uncle went for a walk in the vineyard. Angelo went riding. He mentioned doing a little target practice, I believe."

One good thing about being an artist was that one never had to worry about what to do with spare time. And as someone who loved everything about painting, right down to the stained clothes and smell of turpentine, Beatrice felt the day was never long enough to accomplish everything she so optimistically planned each morning when she awoke. Her

daily goal was to become a better artist than she was
the day before.

For the rest of the afternoon she worked in her
studio, measuring and cutting canvas and stretching
it across wooden frames. When she finished attaching
the canvas to the fourth frame, she decided that was
enough, and turned to other tasks.

She loved the time she spent there, for her studio
was her crucible, her trial and her proving ground. It
was the source of joy and disappointment, of pride
and humility, of vision and reality, and she saw herself as a scholar of humankind and nature, a devotee
to the consummate labor of painting.

She gazed at her aunt's portrait with a critical eye,
and asked herself why was it so important to capture
the woman's likeness and those of all the Bartolinis.
Was it proof of her existence?

Was it some sort of validation?

Or was it simply a way to keep herself and her
family immortal? Whenever she looked at family
portraits, she thought of them not as reproductions of
deceased beings, but as stamps of immortality. Portraits were a gift to all who came after—a gift to
posterity and the future.

Although she derived much pleasure from painting, it was not something she did only because she
enjoyed it. It was not a matter of choice but an emotional kind of persistence, a near obsession. Her creative passion was a divine sort of mandate—some
predestined drive planted within her spirit before
birth. She thought of that as miraculous.

Today, she also felt a bite of tension she had not
felt previously. It was not the restlessness that came
from an artist's frustrations, but a more personal

type. She found her mind had a tendency to stray from her usually disciplined devotion.

Once, she found herself examining her reflection in the window, smoothing her hair and giving herself the once-over from a side view.

Another time, she even went so far as to walk to the door and step out into the hallway. She looked in both directions and, seeing no one and nothing of interest, turned around and went back into her studio.

She found herself doing hasty, undetailed sketches of various angles of Angelo's head, as she often did as a preliminary study, prior to painting a portrait. She did not think much about it at that moment, but later she would reflect upon this and wonder if it was normal curiosity, or some indication that she was still in love with him.

"I thought I would find you here."

At the sound of Angelo's voice, she realized she had been completely lost in thoughts of him, and strove to pull herself back from the depths of concentration.

He was framed in the doorway, looking better than two sunsets trying to outdo each other.

She felt an inward flush, as if she had drawn too near to a fire. "I did not hear you come in."

"I doubt you would have heard a German opera in the next room. What were you thinking about with such detachment?"

"You might say I was absorbed with thoughts of my vocation."

"A lofty answer for one usually so down-to-earth."

"That is the way it is for those of us who exist in a world that lies somewhere between concept and reality. That is why I am confused most of the time."

"You are as changeable as spring. I keep remembering one woman and seeing another. You seem to adapt well to your surroundings, whatever they are. Take now, for instance. No one could possibly doubt you were an artist."

"When in Rome, do as the Romans."

He stepped farther into the room as if preparing to take a survey, picking up this object and that. He picked up a cake of color, turned it over in his hand a time or two and put it down. "Did you know there is more to it than 'When in Rome, do as the Romans'?"

"No, that is all I have ever heard quoted."

"'When in Rome, live as the Romans do: when elsewhere, live as they live elsewhere?'"

She laughed. "You made that up."

"No."

"Yes, you did."

"No, truly, I did not. Supposedly, it was the advice Saint Ambrose gave to Saint Augustine."

"Well, thank you for enlightening me. I always think it a day well done when I have learned something."

He stopped in front of his mother's portrait. "Each time I look at this, I see something I did not see before. It must have been difficult to capture her as you did."

She toyed with the buttons at the throat of her dress. "It is always difficult to paint women."

"Now, why do I have no trouble believing that?"

He turned away from the portrait and toward her. There was no mistaking that look. It was penetrating, as if he was trying to go beyond the conversation they were having, to a place where there were no restraints, no control, no boundaries.

"So, tell me, why is it difficult to paint women?"

A bit self-conscious now, her hand came back to the buttons at her throat. "Because the artist must remember to paint a woman younger than she is."

"Yet, you must be true to the subject."

She looked up and saw he had changed neither the direction of his gaze nor the intensity. Something told her not to let him gain control of the moment, and she lifted her head and met his eyes. "Yes, one must be true to the subject, but when striving for truth, there is a point the artist must not cross over— if he wants to sell the painting. Paint the truth, lose a friend."

"Is that an adage, or the truth born of experience?"

"I will ask some of my former friends."

His laugh broke the intensity of the previous moments. "The world of art has matured you. You are pleasingly honest."

"Do you really think so?"

"I do. When you were here before, you were as green as the hills."

"Well, I suppose that is better than being as old as them."

He laughed more readily this time, and she had the impression he was enjoying her company, or at least found it entertaining. "I don't remember you had such wit."

"You seem to remember a lot about me...some of it even flattering."

"You don't approve of flattery, do you?"

"I find it deceptive."

"When you know me better, you will find I don't resort to something as corrupting as flattery."

"Then, I have misjudged you, and ask your forgiveness."

He stepped closer, and she saw hair the color of Turkish coffee and eyes of the same dark hue. His white linen shirt was open at the throat and limp from his ride. His boots wore the dusty evidence of his walking about during target practice.

He stepped close enough to take her arms in his hands and pull her against him. He kissed her nose, her eyes, and whispered against her mouth, "You may ask anything of me you like."

Eleven

Angelo was sleeping soundly when he heard foot-steps in the hallway outside his room. He lay per-fectly still and listened. The footsteps drew closer. He eased the bedcover back, climbed out of bed qui-etly and reached for his gun. He saw the faintest trace of light coming through the crack under the door. He pointed the gun.

The door opened and he expelled a ragged breath. His father stood in the doorway with a candle in his hand.

"Aren't you the one who taught me never to sneak up on a man when he was asleep?"

Tito stepped into the room and shut the door. "I have a candle in my hand. Do I look like I am sneak-ing?"

Angelo put the gun down and raked his hair with his hand. His heart was still pumping furiously. "Madonna! What if I had shot you?"

"Then, we would not be having this conversa-tion."

Tito put the candle on the table beside Angelo's gun, and that was when Angelo noticed that his fa-ther was dressed.

"What time is it?"

"Three o'clock."

Angelo glanced toward the window and saw no

light coming in around the cracks in the shutters. "Where are you going at three o'clock in the morning?"

"We are going hunting."

"I hunted enough in Turin that hunting has ceased to be a sport for me."

"Hunting is a birthright, not a sport. Come on. Get dressed. We are going after some wild boar. They are eating my grapes."

"So that is why we are going."

"It is, but that is between you and me. For all others, we are going because the boar are eating the flowers and vegetables in your mother's garden. Now, get dressed like a dutiful son, and don't keep your father waiting."

Angelo dressed quickly. He gathered up his rifle, his pistol and his bag of ammunition, which he slung over his shoulder. "It's been a long time since we went hunting together. Is anyone else going with us?"

"Nando and Giacomo, but they are going to be too old if you do not hurry."

They went downstairs and saw Colossus standing there, wagging his tail, ready to accompany them. Tito gave him a loving pat. "Not this time," he said, and Colossus whined pitifully and went to the corner by the front door, where he dropped down into a pathetic heap. He lay his head on his paws and, with huge mournful eyes, watched each movement the two of them made.

"He knows the other dogs are going," Angelo said. "He is not going to be happy with you."

"He will forgive me, though, because he knows if he doesn't, I won't be so eager to overlook all of his transgressions."

The horses were saddled and waiting with Nando and Giacomo. Angelo greeted the two men he had known for most of his life, then called the two hunting dogs to his side, and mounted.

They rode off, with Tito, Nando and Giacomo reminiscing about previous boar hunts, and Angelo listening to the stories the three of them told, much as they had done when he was in his youth and had taught him how to track his first wild boar.

The sun was coming up by the time they reached the woods on the far side of the vineyards.

Not long afterward, the dogs began barking and Nando dismounted and checked for tracks. "Fresh ones," he said, "going this way."

They started off again, but when the brush grew too thick to ride, they dismounted. Angelo tied his horse with the others and continued with them on foot, soothed by the weight of his father's words and comforted by the wisdom that was always hidden in his stories. From his memories of boyhood, he recalled the sound of that same voice, telling him stories of Etruscans and gladiators, of Caesar, Leonardo and the glory of Rome.

His love for his father had been nurtured over the years, and now, as a man, he could not separate himself from the circumstances of his birth, and the man who had taken the orphaned child in his arms and called him son.

Tito was the one who had taught him to judge a man by his character and not his title or the fatness of his purse, and the one to take the cuttings of grapevines in his rough, brown hands and show him how to plant them so they would grow into another vine. He was the same man who had disciplined him when he needed it, and had held him in his arms and cried with him when he was in pain. He nourished Angelo's flourishing spirit with the incalculable resources of his own. He encouraged the principle of righteousness, and taught Angelo what it meant to be a man, and he did it without tearing Angelo's tender heart, or bruising his soul or holding him back when it was time to let him go.

Tito had filled his head with knowledge, loaded his arms with firewood and taught him the value of a day's work, and shown him the comfort of a book, a loyal dog and a warm fire at night. He had showed him how to love and honor a woman, how to shoulder his grief when it seemed too heavy to bear, and how to have pride in what he accomplished and not in what he had.

Angelo had grown into a man, humbled to stand in his father's shadow. His father was a strong thread that ran through the fabric of his life.

He had given him a past in order to build upon the future. Images of his father were all around him, and he knew the weight of love and the tenacity of belonging.

The sudden, loud baying of the dogs pulled his mind back to the present. They were deep into the woods now, and the dogs began to pick up speed and work the area together, staying just ahead of where the men walked.

The dogs began to circle in closer, passing and crossing in front of each other, each with his nose to the ground and following his scent.

Angelo eased his rifle around and saw his father do the same.

They walked along a creek and stopped at the edge of a ravine. The dogs disappeared into the brush with a rustling noise. From the dense thicket came the sudden, loud squeal of a boar, so shrill it drowned out the barking of the dogs.

Without warning, a huge, black boar came crashing through the thicket, closely pursued by the dogs, who were nipping at the boar's hamstrings. One of the dogs was bleeding.

Tito got off the first shot and hit the boar high on the shoulder.

The bleeding dog had the boar by the ear, and the enraged boar was shaking its head wildly, slashing with bared tusks, tossing the dog like a limp doll. There was a terrifying yelp, and they watched helplessly as the dog was hurled over the boar's back.

Angelo tried to get off another shot, but the other dog was in the way.

Giacomo, on the other side of Angelo, aimed and fired, hitting the boar in the rump.

Angelo eased around, with his back to the solid rock of the ravine. He could see that one of the dogs was dead. His father and Giacomo were trying to get in another shot, when the boar charged the other dog. Nando was trying to get around, behind the boar.

The dog was going for the boar's throat, and the boar was slashing at him with his sharp tusks. The dog wailed with pain. Angelo moved closer and tried to get the dog out, when the boar turned on him, the bristles on his neck standing out. With a squeal he lashed with his tusks. Angelo was trapped at the back of the ravine, with the boar blocking the only way out. The boar squealed again and charged. Angelo turned quickly and felt the stabbing pain in his calf, as the boar's tusks slashed open a long gash, as deep as the bone.

The boar still had Angelo against the back of the ravine, and he could feel his boot filling with blood.

The dog moved in again, distracting the boar's attention away from Angelo.

Tito and Nando eased closer, rifles raised, waiting for an opening. Nando got off a shot and hit the boar in the upper leg, just as Tito fired, hitting the boar in the back of the neck.

The boar squealed again and charged Tito.

Angelo sprang forward, shoved the barrel of his rifle in the boar's ear and fired. The *crack* echoed down the ravine, and four hundred pounds of wild, slashing boar dropped to the ground.

Angelo limped over to his father, who was sitting on a fallen log. Nando and Giacomo were rolling up Tito's pant leg. Where the boar had slashed the top of his boot, it hadn't gone through. But there was a three-inch-long cut above his boot. Thankfully, it was not deep.

Nando went to check the dogs, and Angelo reached to help his father to his feet. He felt Giacomo's hand on his arm and heard him say, "You need to sit down."

Angelo gave Tito his hand and had pulled him up, when he heard Giacomo tell him again to sit down. "Your leg is bleeding badly."

Angelo looked down and saw the tear in his pants. The blood that filled his boot was now spilling over the top. He dropped down on the log, while Giacomo and his father looked at his leg.

"It's a bad wound," Giacomo said. "He is losing much blood. We need to get him home. It will need many stitches."

They bound his leg tightly and told him to wait while they went for the horses. Giacomo had just started off, when Nando came into the clearing leading them. They helped Angelo into the saddle. Tito watched Giacomo put the wounded dog across the back of his saddle, then the two of them mounted.

"I will bury the dog and clean the boar. I will see you at the villa," Nando said.

Tito nodded, and the three men turned their horses homeward.

It wasn't the first time his mother had had to get her needle and thread out to sew up a cut for her son, but it was the first time Angelo had seen her cry after she finished.

Beatrice, on the other hand, cried during the entire event.

"I only cry when I'm not sewing," Gisella said.

"I don't think I could do what you did," Beatrice said.

"You could learn to do it the same way I did. Out of necessity. The first few times I saw my mother sew a wound, I cried worse than you."

"It isn't that bad," Angelo said, taking another big gulp of wine.

"That is because Uncle Tito gave you enough wine to fill a vat," Beatrice said. "You are beyond drunk."

"And I don't feel a thing," he said, trying to bring her face into focus.

Tito was telling Gisella how it had happened. "I would have been wounded badly if Angelo hadn't gotten off that shot in the boar's ear. It was the only place to hit him and make him drop instantly like that."

"I'm glad he was there," she said, "but I would rather the two of you left the boars alone."

"What about your flowers and your garden?" Tito asked, giving Beatrice a wink.

"I think Giacomo and Nando should be in charge of hunting," she said.

Patricia came upstairs to tell them that Nando had brought the boar home. "What shall I do with it?"

"Tell Nando to leave us a small portion and to share the rest of it with the other hands," Gisella said.

"I think Angelo needs to rest a while," Tito said.

Gisella kissed Angelo on the cheek. "I will come back later to see how you are doing."

"He will be fine," Tito said, "but tomorrow he will have a headache."

"Good," Beatrice said. "That will make him forget about the pain in his leg."

Angelo looked at Beatrice and patted the bed. "Come lay down next to me," he said.

Beatrice turned a red face toward her aunt and uncle, and said, "I will do nothing of the sort."

"Then, sit in the chair and watch me sleep."

"Stay," Gisella said as she and Tito left the room. "You might as well learn now, how pathetic men can be when they are sick or wounded."

Beatrice sat down. "I will stay for a little while," she said, "but I shan't give you any sympathy."

"Tell me you love me."

"Why should I say something like that?"

"Because it's true, and because I would tell you."

"Being in love is a mental disorder. It makes you crazy. You make silly comments. You do stupid things. You laugh when you shouldn't, and you save things that should be thrown away because the person you love touched them. You can't get anything done for thinking about the other person, and you cannot sleep. You lose your appetite. You are deliriously happy one minute and burst into tears the next.

Now, you tell me one reason why I would profess to
love you?"

"All right, then, lie to me," he said.

She reached for the glass of wine beside the bed.
"Here, drink this."

"I'm already drunk," he said, "and I am feeling
so good, I might start singing. But what I would
rather do is have you lying next to me. Are you sure
you won't reconsider?"

"I might as well make this bearable," she said,
and upending the glass, she finished off the contents.

When he had dozed off, Beatrice gave him a soft
kiss and smoothed back the damp hair around his
face. *How good he would feel,* she thought, *if he
knew how badly I want to lie down next to him, and
stay there, until I am burned by the love in those
black eyes of his.*

She straightened the sheet, kissed him again and
carried the empty wineglass downstairs.

Aunt Gisella was in the kitchen when Beatrice entered.

"Is he sleeping now?" Gisella asked.

"Like a baby," Beatrice said. "Uncle Tito?"

"The same."

"I thought so. It's too quiet."

"It's the peace that prevails in the absence of blus-
tering," Gisella said.

Beatrice laughed. "I am glad they are resting. Angelo's leg was badly cut, wasn't it?"

"Yes, but he won't know that until tomorrow,"
Gisella said. She smiled. "He is always so charmingly idiotic when he has had too much to drink."

Twelve

Beatrice was up early, and decided she would begin painting one of the four canvases she had prepared earlier. She wanted to start immediately on a portrait of Uncle Tito.

The raw canvas she had stretched and attached to the frame days ago was now ready to be sized with the gelled sizing made from animal glue. She would need a palette knife to spread it, in order to seal the interstices of the fabric.

She opened her box of supplies, intending to look for a palette knife, and saw a slim volume of Coleridge and a folded note with only her name written on it tucked inside.

She stepped closer to the candelabrum to examine the volume, and smiled when she saw that Angelo had marked several places. She put the book down and unfolded the note.

Dear Beatrice,
There is something very softening in your presence that I cannot account for. If there was time, I would ask if we could start over, to see if this time, we could get it right. But I know that would not be fair to you. My life is not my own, and I do not know how long it will be before that will change. The ground for revolt grows

green, and the future of Italy hangs in the balance. We must drive the Hapsburgs back to Austria.

And yet, I am reluctant to part from you a second time. I know if I do, I risk losing you forever. So, I hope…

What is this strange thing that has trapped us somewhere between warming the wax and making the impression?

This is only the beginning.

Angelo

P.S. You still owe me two kisses.

She tucked the note into her pocket, and, with a lighter step than normal, fetched the canvas and set to work.

It was one of those glorious days that only golden Tuscany seemed to produce, and after Beatrice finished preparing Uncle Tito's canvas, she set it aside to dry. It was simply too lovely outside to stay indoors any longer, and she decided to take her paints and easel out of doors to enjoy the perfect weather.

Since her return to Villa Mirandola, she had found herself fast falling under the spell of Italy's beautiful gates, and the Tuscan tradition of lining the drives that led to them with cypress trees only added to their beauty.

The marvelous old gate that announced a visitor's entry to Villa Mirandola land was one she had longed to paint, and today was the ideal opportunity, so she set about packing the things she would need, and carried her easel and folding chair up the driveway toward the gates.

After setting up her easel, she came back to the house for her straw hat and her paints, and went looking for Aunt Gisella, to tell her where she would be.

She found her aunt in the kitchen, telling Patricia, Lucianna and Natalina how she wanted the wild boar made into sausage.

Father Francesco was there, as well, looking as round and well-fed as he ever did. After she had greeted him, they exchanged a few words.

"I am glad to see you," Father Francesco said. "Your aunt showed me some of your paintings. I was unaware you possessed such talent. Have you ever considered doing frescoes? You know the small chapel of our church burned two years ago. We are nearing completion on the new chapel. I would like to talk with you about painting the frescoes for it."

"Oh, to paint a fresco in a church! My goodness, I never considered for a moment I had that kind of talent. Why, it should be reserved for the Caravaggios and the Michelangelos."

Father Francesco smiled and his black eyes reflected the light in the room—eyes alive with humor. "Alas, what you say may be true, but all the Caravaggios and Michelangelos seem to have died with the Renaissance. It would be a wonderful opportunity for a woman."

"Father, do not let Serena hear you say that or she will be painting the frescoes herself," Aunt Gisella said.

Beatrice smiled. "I would be honored to speak with you about it, Father."

"Wonderful," he said. "Now, may I have more biscotti?"

Aunt Gisella put the plate in front of him, which seemed to please Father Francesco, for he began to eat the biscotti with the same devotion with which he dispensed a blessing.

Her aunt asked, "Did you need to see me for something—"

Beatrice gave the chunk of meat a glance, and saw a huge, bristly boar with razor-sharp tusks. She doubted she would eat any sausage from something so frightful.

"—or have you come to help with the sausage making?"

"Hardly that. I can hardly bear a glimpse at it. Every time I do, I see black bristly hair and tusks. He must have been a dangerous-looking creature."

"An 'ugly brute' is what Tito called it, but wild boar does make the most delicious sausage. You will like it."

"If I can bring myself to try a bite. I came to tell you of my whereabouts. It is such a glorious day, I have moved my painting outside. I will be down by the big gate."

Aunt Gisella nodded. "So, you are finally going to paint it?"

"Yes, you know how long it has captured my attention, so now I will see what it does to my imagination."

"Enjoy your outing."

"If there is a paintbrush involved, you know I will."

"*Ciao,* Beatrice."

"*Ciao,* Father Francesco."

With her straw hat swinging from her arm, Beatrice returned to where she had set up her easel outside the gate. The road beyond led from Florence to Siena, and a few feet from the gate stood a shrine to the Virgin, wreathed with a climbing rose.

Beatrice removed the dead flowers surrounding the shrine and stood for a moment, looking at the serene face of the Virgin, the blessed Madonna. She bowed her head and said a short prayer for Angelo, for his safety, for his wisdom and for a cool head to temper the hot blood of patriotism that flowed in his beautiful Italian veins and fired his passion.

As she turned back to her easel, she noticed a monk coming down the road toward her. He stopped at the shrine, said a prayer and crossed himself. She saw immediately that he was a Dominican monk from the monastery of Santa Maria del Sasso near the town of Bibbiena.

"Bless you," he said, "and may God grant you the prayer you offered."

"And may He grant yours, as well," she said.

She watched him continue down the road in his sandals and a brown robe tied with a rope belt— someone who had come out of nowhere, touched her life for a moment and was gone.

She could not help wondering if Angelo, too, would touch her life just as briefly.

She pushed the thought away and thought, *Poor Angelo, with his horribly cut leg. He probably won't be able to walk for days.*

She decided today was far too lovely to fill one's head with anything save optimism, and with that she set to work.

She stared down at the canvas, and then studied the gates. Sensitive to the school of inquiry, she wanted to respond to the influences surrounding her, to paint in nature's light. Since coming to Italy, she had found herself drawn to study nature, to paint not what she saw but what she felt. The world beyond her bedroom window showed her an untouched world, a new source of material.

Often, she would carry her supplies outside and spend the afternoon making sketches that she would transfer to canvas. Later, she would paint *all'aperto* in order to give life to the drama of contrast and the force of the vivid patterns of light and shadow.

She studied the sketch of Mirandola's beautiful iron gate, anchored in stone pillars. The memory of the first time she passed through these gates flashed into her mind. Little did she know then that one day she would be sitting here, capturing their image on canvas.

She sketched with charcoal, paying close attention to line and perspective. Then she began to paint, using a rich range of blacks, whites and grays, with the cypress trees that lined the drive providing occasional touches of green and yellow ocher, all executed with the same precise accuracy and deft touch her work was known for.

The gates were magnificent in the full light, and although she was painting in the shade, the sun was high in the sky. The day grew lazy, warm and still. Even then, she could not stop. She wanted to capture the gates beneath the full influence of the sun.

Before long, she saw Lucianna coming up the drive with a basket on her arm. Lucianna waved and Beatrice waved back.

"Your aunt was afraid you would not eat." She handed Beatrice the basket.

"She is right. I would rather paint than eat."

Lucianna gazed at the painting. "Will it take you long to paint the gates?"

"I hope not, but one never knows."

"I saw your work when I cleaned your studio. You are very good."

"Do you enjoy looking at paintings?"

"Sometimes I do, but I don't understand why you want to paint something that you see every day. If you want to look at the gate, you can come out here."

"Yes, I suppose you can, but I want this painting so that when I am no longer here, I can look at it and remember this magnificent gate."

"It would be easier to stay here. Then, you would not have to do all this painting and you would not have to leave. All this coming and going. I do not understand it."

"Have you ever been to England?"

Lucianna looked completely aghast. "To England? Why would I go to England? I like it here."

Beatrice knew it would not do to laugh at Lucianna, although she was sorely tempted. "It is nice to be content."

"I will come back for the basket later."

"Tell my aunt 'thank you.'"

Lucianna nodded. "I will tell her."

Beatrice put down her brush and drew back the napkin.

Neopolitan spice cakes, prosciutto, parmesan cheese, half a loaf of bread—still warm from the oven—fresh grapes and a bottle of wine. It was enough food for half a platoon. Whatever was her aunt thinking? Before she realized it, she was speaking out loud. "Goodness, I could not eat this much food in five lunches."

"You could if you had help."

Beatrice dropped the basket with a gasp and turned around. Angelo stood there, leaning on a cane.

"Angelo Bartolini, you frightened me out of my wits. Why didn't you say something? What are you doing out of bed?"

"I did say something. I said, 'You could if you had help.' And I am out of bed because you left me alone and I can't sleep without you sitting next to me." As if those words weren't enough, he made the most pathetic attempt to look mortally wounded and leaned weakly upon his cane, to the point that she considered kicking it out from under him.

Still, he was awfully handsome, standing there with his tousled hair and his unshaven face, with an almost sleepy look that made her want to do the most unladylike things.

A smile began to tug at the corners of Beatrice's mouth. It tugged and tugged harder, until she laughed. "Why don't you have a headache?"

"Who said I didn't?"

"You don't look like you had too much to drink."

"Did I? I don't remember."

"You could not possibly feel as good as you look."

"Do I look good to you?" He raised his brows and leered at her horribly, like a satyr or, in his case, the Roman equivalent, a faun.

"That isn't what I meant." She knew he was playing with her, as if there were some sort of game going on between them, and that he teased and taunted, somehow knowing how far he could go without drawing her ire or making her blush and feel self-conscious. And he was so good at it, too, for there was no way for her to scold or reject him without appearing to have the nature of a hostile crab.

Ignoring him did no good, and neither did baiting him back. Getting mad did not work, either. She was wondering what she could say, or how she could go about getting his mind off this silly game, when he took control of the situation.

"I hope you didn't break anything when you dropped it," he said, glancing at the basket.

"I did not hear any breaking glass."

"What is in here?"

"Enough to feed a family of five for a week."

"Good, I'm starving."

She looked down at the white bandage beneath the split trouser leg. "I suppose it's been difficult for you to stay around the house, when you would rather be in the vineyards with Uncle Tito."

"I paid him a visit."

"You shouldn't be on that leg so much."

"How can I not go? He loves having me here."

"About as much as you love being there."

"Of course I love being here. It's my home."

"Then, why do you choose to live in Turin?"

"Why do you choose to paint?"

"It's my destiny, I suppose."

"And what I do is mine."

"Don't you miss all of this? The vineyards? The villa? The life you have grown accustomed to?"

"I have, but I won't be missing it much longer, now that my father has given me Villa Adriana and we are making plans to restore the vineyards."

"It is wonderful that they will be living there for a while, to help, so you can lead the life you have always wanted. How do you think Serena will feel about it? I remember her telling me how beautiful Uncle Tito's home was."

"She has always loved Villa Adriana, and I hope she will not be disappointed that father has given it to me. She will inherit Villa Mirandola from our mother, so she won't be without a home. And there is always the possibility she will marry one day."

Beatrice tried to conjure up a vision of the kind of man it would take to fall in love with Serena, and who was also the kind of man Serena would fall in love with. It was a thought as complicated as Serena herself.

He pointed to the basket. "Do you mind if I join you?"

"Please do."

"Good," he said, and reached for the basket.

"Let me carry it. How will you manage with your cane?"

She picked up the basket and carried it to a shady place beneath the lofty branches of a chestnut tree. She wasn't very hungry, so she nibbled while she watched him. She found much more pleasure in seeing him eat than in eating herself.

It made her wonder if finding pleasure in watching a man eat meant you were falling in love with him, for it did seem odd to her that she could find such heady gratification in doing so. But then, she was already in love with him, so how could she be falling in love again? And there was the fact that she had loved him all those years ago. If she loved him now, that meant she had already fallen in love with him again, which meant— She didn't know what she was trying to say. She called it supreme confusion, and since she couldn't remember where this was going, let alone where it had started, she decided to forget the whole thing.

"You did not eat much."

"I ate as much as I ever do." She began packing the leftovers into the basket. "I'm glad you joined me. This is ever so much better than eating alone.

Were you looking for me, or did you simply stumble upon me?''

''Oh, I was looking for you, all right. I wanted to see if my memory served me correctly.''

''Your memory? About what?''

''I wanted to see if your hair was as golden as I remembered it.''

She opened her mouth and then shut it.

Now he was plying her with flattery, and there was only one reason: he was doing it to frustrate her.

Well, it was working.

The problem was, she never knew where he was coming from. And that did not fit in with her plans. She had decided she needed to show him a side of her that he was not aware of—that headstrong, willful, I-can-take-care-of-myself, independent side, and she had been waiting for the opportunity to do so, but—blast him—he never provided her with an occasion to do so.

How can one rant and rave with righteous indignation against someone who is being...*nice?*

She decided to blame it on his being Italian, although it did not seem that he behaved in the manner she thought of as typically Italian. True, Aunt Gisella said he was ''charmingly idiotic'' when he drank too much. And Beatrice knew that she had, on several occasions, seen outbursts of absurdly high spirits, where he would grab her and whirl her around until she was so dizzy she thought she would get sick in front of him. And he was so verbally passionate that her face was constantly blushing. Not to mention that he was irritatingly optimistic and teeth-grindingly cheerful most of the time, which certainly grated on her staid British nerves and made it difficult to remain stoic.

With the soul of a poet, the devotion of a states-man and the compassion of a saint, he was part vag-abond, part missionary, part stage actor, and all bar-barian conquerer. And he could not understand *the English?*

Well, she asked herself, what would you expect when a country had five dozen forms of religion, and only one sauce?

He used his cane to brace himself so he could stand, and when he was on his feet, he walked closer to her canvas and began to study her work in progress. "I never gave these old gates much thought, but looking at them through your eyes, I wonder why I did not."

She wanted to throw up her hands. Now he was giving her artistic objectivity. Was there anything he did not know something about?

"I have only begun to paint them," she said, rather crossly, as she came to her feet. "I suppose that means you would like to stay a while and watch me paint. Am I right?"

If he caught on to her hostility, he did not let it show. "That depends upon how nice you are to me."

"I am always nice," she said, knowing the words came out like the snap of a dog.

"You could be nicer."

"Nicer?" she said, thinking that at last, she knew what was coming. Now he would be the epitome of humility, the loving teacher. "In what way do you mean *nice?* I am always nice," she repeated.

"Not this way," he said, and pulled her toward him. "It feels good to hold you. I have thought of little else."

This was not the response she had expected, so she decided to try something different—coyness, perhaps. Feeling enlightened, she said, "I think you must have had a very boring morning, then."

"Shh, sometimes it is better not to talk," he said. He knew she would stand here the rest of the afternoon talking about matters of little importance between two people who knew each other well and wanted to know each other even better, unless he took control.

He wondered if she had, in that stubborn head of hers, no notion of how he felt about her, or the attraction he felt to her. They had missed making their connection almost five years ago. He hoped things would head in a different direction this time, but he knew there were many obstacles for them, aside from the personal ones.

He was glad she would be coming to Villa Adriana with his family. It pleased him to think she would be so near, although part of him worried about her safety and that of his family, if things with Austria progressed to the point he feared they could.

He thought about her being close enough for him to see and touch her, after she had been gone for so very long, and he decided to save thoughts of the Austrians for when he reached Turin. He would enjoy this time they had together.

His arms went around her and he drew her to him. He could feel the flutter of her breath and knew the exact moment the awareness of what he was about registered in her mind, for he could see the affirmation in her eyes.

"I believe you owe me two kisses. I have come to collect."

"I thought you had forgotten about that."

"You do not seem to know the difference between anticipation and stupidity."

"And you don't seem to know the dumbest woman can manage the most clever man."

"I am willing to learn, *cara.* Show me." He kissed her forehead. He kissed her eyes. He kissed her mouth and had to coax her for a moment before her lips parted. With a groan, he pulled her closer, kissed her deeply and then stopped. "I like it when you kiss me back."

"I did not kiss you back. I was trying to push you away."

He drew back to take in the face he found so lovely, and wondered how she could be so comical at a moment when he was totally serious. He did not give her time to say anything or to analyze what had happened or what was about to happen. It was wise to keep her off guard, and he knew the best way to do that.

This time, the kiss was even longer and more seductive. "That's much better," he said, when he felt her relax against him. "There are worse ways to spend the afternoon, don't you think?"

She pushed him away. "That was three kisses."

"I always charge interest." He took her face in his hands and softly, gently, applied delicately placed, nibbling kisses. "You are so sweet. I wonder if I will be able to stop long enough to let you paint?"

"You might as well continue on with what you are doing," she whispered, "because Colossus is polishing off the last bit of sausage and his happily thrashing tail has just knocked over my paints."

He glanced in that direction just as the paint box fell to the ground. Blissfully unconcerned, Colossus sniffed the bottle of wine, then moved back to the basket, and after giving it one last going over, seemed satisfied that he had consumed everything edible. With a heaving sigh of contentment, the dog lay down and began to lick his paws.

"If my father were standing here, Colossus would flatten himself and crawl over here, the most penitent of spirits, to beg forgiveness."

"Would he get it?"

"I do not ever recall his being denied."

"And you? Have you been denied?"

He laughed. "More than I care to remember."

When he glanced back at her, he saw immediately that a change had come over her, one that left her distant. "What's wrong?"

"Nothing. I need to get back."

She made a move to leave, but he grabbed her arm. "What caused this change? Did I do something?"

"No. I am allowing things to go beyond my control."

"What is wrong with that?"

"I don't like being out of control. I especially don't like being out of control when that puts you in control."

"Why does either one of us have to be in control?"

"Because you are a man and a man always wants to be in command."

"This isn't the king's hussars where we need a chain of command. It's a relationship between a man and a woman—a relationship I am trying to develop into something more."

"Like what?"

"I don't know. Call it a mingling of souls."

"Then, write me a letter."

"I need to get away from here." She turned

quickly away and began gathering her spilled paints, throwing them and her brushes into her paint box.

She picked up the palette knife and was about to toss it into the paint box, too, when he took it from her. He leaned on his cane and took both of her hands in one hand, dropping the palette knife into the box. Then he lifted her fingers to his lips and kissed each one in turn.

"You would do better to forget what you think happened all those years ago. That was no routine attempt at seduction, just as this is no routine attempt at seduction."

She scoffed at that. "Why should I believe you?"

"Why shouldn't you?"

"Five years ago, I..."

"Did not stay around long enough to let me finish what I had begun."

"Oh, you mean temptation and enticement were waiting for me? How crushing to think I turned my back on all of that."

"What makes you think I was only interested in seducing you?"

"I am not a blockhead. I heard all of the stories about your liaisons—young ones, older ones, married, unmarried—it did not seem to matter. Your only criterion was that they be female."

"You are making generalities."

"You want facts? How about the Countess Elisebetta Gustavini? Or the Florentine banker's wife, Giuseppa something-or-other. Then there was the French duchess, the English poet, the American diplomat's wife... Shall I go on naming your conquests?"

"I never took liberties with a woman who did not want it, or with a woman as innocent as you, and I made it a point always to give back far more than I received. And they were all before you, *cara*."

She smacked herself on the forehead. "I cannot believe I am hearing all of this. Of all the pompous comments… Oh, that anyone could be such a braggart! Not even you. You give back more than you receive. How ridiculous. What could you possibly give?"

He burst out laughing. "One of these days, when I make love to you, you are going to feel like five kinds of fool for that comment. However, today is not that day. Now, what would it take to convince you of my serious and honorable intent?"

"You cannot, for it is impossible for someone like you to know the first thing about wooing a woman, simply because you do not know the first thing about being romantic."

"Wooing? Is that some English word for romance?"

"And if it is?"

"I should like to know, because to my ears, it sounds like something a sick dog would do."

"It means to seek, solicit and entreat the affection of a woman with the intent of romance. It means to progress to a less spiritual form of tenderness, where the seal is not yet affixed but the wax is warming."

"You missed your calling. You should have been a poet. I've never heard such a collection of words that said nothing. It would save us both a lot of time and trouble if you would say what you mean. However, that isn't the question right now. You want to turn me into Lord Byron, presenting flowers and quoting poetry?"

"You already remind me of Lord Byron. He has never spoken to a woman he hasn't bedded."

"So, you want wooing?"

"If you could put down your club long enough, that would be a nice beginning. And certainly preferable to dragging me down the lane by the hair of my head."

"All right," he said. He dropped down on his knee in front of her and took her hand in his. He kissed it gently, then looked into her eyes and spoke to her of love.

Oh, your face is much sweeter than mustard,
Fairer than turnip. A snail has pushed its vehicle
On it, and made it as it is—so lustered.
Your teeth are parsnip-white, and your sweet giggle
Would doubtless turn the Pope's heart into custard.
Your eyes are just as colorful as treacle,
Your hair is blond and white like bulbs of leeks;
Oh, make me alive! That's all my spirit seeks.

He kissed her hand again and pushed up with his cane to stand in front of her, bringing her hand to rest upon his heart. "How was that?"

"Horrid, absolutely horrid. Could you think of nothing to compare me to but food? Is that what I remind you of—a plate of vegetables?"

"You did not like it?"

"Let me put it another way, so there can be no misunderstanding. In plain terms, you are no Lord Byron. That much is now certain."

"I'll have you know that was Michelangelo I quoted."

"You defame the poor man's name."

"I speak the truth."

"Truly?"

"I said as much, did I not?"

She began to laugh. "Then, it's a good thing he switched to painting."

"Come on, I will help you pack and carry your things back to the villa."

"You are angry?"

"No, why would you think that?"

"Because I said unkind things about your poetry."

"No, you did not. You said unkind things about Michelangelo's poetry."

She watched him hobbling around trying to gather her things.

"Here," she said, snatching them away. "Let me do that before you break your fool neck."

"I love it when you talk romantically to me."

"You are impossible. You should try this approach on the Austrians. It would drive them back into Austria."

He waited patiently until her arms were full, then said, "Leave the rest of it. I will send Benito or Luciano to carry it back."

They walked along for a few minutes, each watching Colossus loping along in front of them. "Poems and flowers," he said with a shake of his head. "Wooing and romance."

"You said that like it pains you."

"It does."

She smiled. "But not for long."

He stopped. "*Mia carissima,* I would walk on hot coals if it made you think better of me."

She put her hand on his cheek. "To think better of you is impossible. Faith, I think far too much of you already."

"Do you, now?"

"Yes, and I probably will regret telling you that. I swear I am beginning to sound like an American. I tell everything I know."

"What did you say?"

"I am beginning to sound like…"

"No, before that. Did you say you thought too much of me? Do you know that leaves me feeling positively inspired?"

"Oh no, not more poetry. Spare me, please."

They reached the villa, and Beatrice led the way inside, Angelo hobbling as he followed her into her studio.

"I will put everything away later."

He waited until she had set down her paints, before he said, "Alas, fair maiden, we must part, but only for a little while."

He made a move to leave.

"Where do you go?"

He gave her a big smile. "To write poetry, of course."

"No more vegetables," she pleaded.

Thirteen

She sat in the pergola drinking her after-dinner coffee, basking in the warm, golden tones of late evening. The air was still, and occasionally she would pick up the fan to cool her face.

Beatrice was thinking she would like to paint this outdoor arbor, with the heavy clusters of grapes hanging overhead, the row of terra-cotta pots lined up along the low wall, their flowers spilling over like draperies onto the tiles.

Thinking of Angelo, she smiled. She could not help wondering why he had bothered to memorize such a terrible poem as the one he had laid at poor Michelangelo's feet. So, she decided she would ask him.

She closed her eyes to enjoy the silence and the touch of the last fading rays of sun upon her face. Heaven could not be much better than this.

At the pressure of lips upon hers, her eyes flew open. She looked into a beautiful pair of eyes: Angelo's.

He had washed his hair and it lay dark, glossy and straight, touching his collar.

He carried a bottle of Chianti and two glasses, and was walking without his cane.

"I brought us some wine."

"I was having coffee."

"The time for coffee has passed." He filled the glasses and handed one to her.

She took a sip, tasting the sunshine. "I shall miss this when I return to England."

"You are thinking of leaving?"

"I was speaking in the figurative sense. I only arrived here, you will recall. I had planned on staying in Italy for some time. Are you trying to hurry me on my way?"

"That would be like shooting myself in the foot, *cara.*"

She looked down at his bandaged leg. "It looks like you already have."

"It could not be more cumbersome if I had. I grow weary of this limping about."

"I noticed you dropped the crutch."

"I threw it away. Out my bedroom window. It landed in Mother's wisteria."

"Tell me something."

"Anything. What would you like? Love words? A serenade?"

"No, I want to know why you bothered to memorize that terrible poem you recited earlier."

"Blame my mother for that. Whenever I misbehaved, she made me memorize a poem and recite it at dinner. After a while, I decided to memorize the worst ones I could find, hoping she would find another form of torture."

"Did it work?"

"No."

"Aunt Gisella must have been a wonderful mother."

"She was…and still is. I am sorry you did not know yours."

She was sorry, as well, but she was enjoying her

time with him and did not want to sadden the moment with such thoughts. "So, did you write me a
poem while you were upstairs?"

"Of course. You wanted wooing. I said I would
write a poem. I am a man of my word."

"You are certain you wrote it?"

"I wrote it."

She gave him a skeptical look. "It isn't another
one of Michelangelo's, is it?"

"You wound me. Of course it isn't."

She leaned back and smoothed her skirts in a manner befitting a queen on her throne. "All right, let
me hear it."

"Not yet. I want the sun to go down first."

He was sitting beside her, and she had to pull her
head back to get a good look at his face. "Why?
What difference will that make?"

"Poetry is more seductive in the dark."

She smacked him on the arm with her closed fan.
"It can be as dark as a stack of Newcastle coal, but
that won't change anything."

"We shall see. What were you thinking about before I kissed you?"

"Vegetables."

"Be quiet and kiss me."

"Surely you jest..."

"I am completely serious. I do not know how it
is in England, but an Italian man does not make light
of such. I asked you to kiss me. What is wrong with
that? I know you have thought about it."

"I never..."

"You have, *cara,* so don't deny it. And why
should you? I like the idea of knowing you have
thought about kissing me again."

"And if I have?"

"Then, kiss me. What could be the harm?"

"Well, if you do not know, I shan't be the one to tell you."

"Have you never taken the initiative, or told a man you wanted to be kissed?"

"You must be on the verge of some sort of illness to speak like this."

"All right, so you have not. There is no shame in that. Everyone has a first time. It is time you did something you have never done before."

"There are plenty of things…"

"Women," he said, and leaning forward, he kissed her soundly. Then, barely lifting his mouth from hers, he kissed her again.

She eventually lost count of the number of times he kissed her, and was thinking she liked kissing him about as much as anything she had ever done, but it saddened her to think his mind would be on more grave matters once they reached Turin.

"You have the sweetest mouth."

"Tell me the poem you wrote," she said, suddenly realizing darkness surrounded them.

He picked up her glass of wine and put it to her lips.

She took a sip and then watched, mesmerized, as he drank from the same place she had. He pulled his chair closer and leaned near enough that she could feel the warm caress of his breath as he whispered against her ear.

Poems are tricky,
Flowers are sticky,
But wine that's red,
Gets you in my bed.

She brought her hand to her forehead. He was the most confounding man.

"I have never known anyone like you. You bring out the worst in me," she said, and then did something she had never done before, something no shy woman would ever do. She put her hands behind his head and pulled him toward her until their lips met.

"Ah, Beatrice, you are such a woman," he said against her mouth.

She decided that if she had gone this far and committed such a brazen act, she might as well make it last a lifetime, for she doubted she would ever do such as this again. She tightened her arms around his neck and pulled him closer, deepening the kiss.

Angelo took over from there.

When the kiss finally ended, she heard him release a ragged sigh, almost breathing the words into her mouth.

"No wonder your Lord Byron took up poetry."

Fourteen

About the time Angelo was reciting his poem to Beatrice, a captain of the Turin police arrived at Angelo's villa in Turin.

Accompanied by two privates, he knocked at the door, and when Cesare answered it, the captain informed him that the commissioner of police wanted to speak to him about the disappearance of his employer.

"But my employer has not disappeared," Cesare informed them. "He is out of town."

"You will have to explain that to the commissioner. Now, if you would accompany us to the police headquarters."

"Am I under arrest?"

"Your presence has been requested. Should you refuse, you will be placed under arrest. It would be better for you if you came voluntarily."

Cesare excused himself to get his coat.

When he returned, he locked the door, dropped the key into his coat pocket and left with the police.

Less than an hour later, two men appeared at the door of the villa, wearing the long, black coats that were very much in fashion and therefore did not make them stand out.

With Cesare's key they unlocked the door and stepped inside.

Once inside, each produced a fat candle, which he lit. One of the men held his candle aloft and surveyed their surroundings.

"You take the upstairs rooms, while I search down here. Remember, do not light any lamps, and be very careful not to move any furniture. If you open drawers, close them when you finish, and do not disturb anything. If you remove anything, remember where it was, and place it in the same place when you are finished."

"What if I find something suspicious?"

"Knock on the floor and I will come up."

The man nodded and started up the stairs, but stopped when the other called out. "Do you know what Bartolini looks like?"

"Of course."

"Then, don't forget to look for a miniature of him."

"Why?"

"I have learned that von Schisler would like a portrait of Bartolini."

"Why? He knows what he looks like."

"We are not paid to question our superiors."

"But, how can we take a portrait without Bartolini missing it?"

"You idiot! That is why I said to look for a miniature."

"Right."

There was no need to work swiftly, so they took their time to open each drawer, each armoire, in order to search the contents.

The locked drawers of Angelo's desk presented a problem, and in the end, they picked the locks. One man removed a small, leather pouch from one of the drawers, placed it on the desk and opened it. He removed a similar pouch from his pocket and withdrew a sheet of paper and a small quill, then flipped open the inkwell, dipped the quill inside and began to copy information.

When he had finished, he returned everything to the pouch and replaced it in the drawer. He did not have a key to lock the drawers, so the best he could do was hope that by the time Bartolini returned home, he would not be able to remember if he had locked the drawer before he left, or simply thought he had.

It took them less than two hours to search everything.

When they finished, they were upset over not finding something incriminating, or at least something that would make Bartolini appear guilty of suspicious activity. In fact, all they had to show for their effort were the miniature portrait of Bartolini they had found in a drawer upstairs, and the names and addresses of those listed in Bartolini's small leather notebook. They did feel some satisfaction on that account, since they recognized many of the names as Carbonari members.

The snag was, almost everyone knew who the Carbonari were and, as yet, being a member of that secret society was not a crime.

They returned to the study and library and looked over the antique guns and swords hanging on the walls. In desperation, one of them said, ''We must add these to the list.''

''Don't you think he collects these?'' the other said.

''It is only a clever way to disguise an arsenal he is gathering for a revolt. Write them down.''

The man nodded and did as instructed.

1. Suspect has six pistols, two carbines and several boxes of ammunition for these weapons.
2. Suspect has four sabers, two hunting knives and two pocketknives.
3. Suspect has mounted on wall in study and library the following:
British smoothbore musket
Old Portuguese rifle
German Wheel-lock Muzzle-Loading Rifle
Austrian flintlock short musket
A pair of 58-caliber percussion pistols, made by Charles Moore, London
Prussian Hussar cavalry model pistol, 17mm flintlock smoothbore—engraved on butt plate, Friderius Rex, King of Prussia 1740-1786
French Heavy Cavalry Battle Sword
Napoleonic French Short Saber de Mineur
Bavarian Chevauleger, Light Horsemen Officer Saber, engraved, 1788
Persian Quaddara Dagger broadsword

When they finished, they doused their candles and left by the front door, which they locked with Cesare's key.

The next morning, the commissioner of police questioned Cesare briefly. "You understand, of course, that we must follow up on reports when someone of importance disappears."

"I assure you, Commissioner, that *Signore* Bartolini is quite well and visiting his family in Tuscany."

"Accept my apologies for your inconvenience. Here are your belongings," he said, handing Cesare his money and keys. "My driver will take you home in my carriage."

Later that afternoon, while working in Angelo's bedroom, Cesare noticed several drips of candlewax in places where there had been no candles. He searched the house and found more drops of wax in places far removed from the nearest candles.

Of all the wax droppings, the ones that disturbed him most were those on the desk in Angelo's study. He checked the drawers and found them all unlocked—the *signore* always kept his desk locked.

Cesare went immediately to report his discovery to Angelo's friend, *Signore* Fossa. "Who do you suspect it was?" Cesare asked when he had finished telling Nicola about the wax.

"My first guess is the king's spies. Kings always have a lot of ears, you know. The king could have directed the police commissioner's involvement, but the Austrians could have arranged it."

"The Austrians worry me the most."

"During your questioning, was there ever any mention of or questions about anything Angelo involves himself in?"

"No. But do you think we should send a letter to him?"

"No, they may be reading his mail. There is nothing we can do at this point but wait for Angelo's return."

Fifteen

Everyone at Villa Mirandola was in the midst of a packing furor the day Serena returned home, looking like she had just come in from Kashmir, instead of Rome.

Beatrice was coming down the stairs with two hatboxes in her hands when she caught her first glimpse of the cousin she had not seen for five years.

Serena entered the house with her customary exuberance, looking very exotic in a turban and a fiery red dress, a silver dagger thrust into a colorful fringed shawl tied around her waist.

But it was the gilded cage containing the squawking parrot that made Beatrice stare in openmouthed wonder.

Where did this cousin of hers get all her unconventional ideas?

The turban on her head would have been quite outlandish upon someone like Beatrice, but with Serena's dark, exotic looks and almond-shaped eyes, it was—well, conspicuously stunning. If Serena were a building, she would have been baroque.

There was no denying that Serena had flair, which Beatrice saw as having unlimited possibilities for the theater. She wondered if Serena had ever considered such, for no one could compare with her daring, or her ability to carry off such wildness.

Beatrice hurried on down the stairs and put the hatboxes on a chair. "Serena, I am ever so happy to see you. I was most disappointed when I arrived and you were not here."

"Beatrice! If only I had known you were here, I would have rushed home. When did you arrive?"

Serena put the parrot down and the two of them hugged. Beatrice said, "I will only say I have been here long enough to miss you tremendously."

"What is going on around here?" Serena asked. "I've never seen such a commotion."

"We are all relocating to Villa Adriana for a time," Beatrice replied.

Uncle Tito had been packing in his room with his valet, but when Serena arrived, he came downstairs to greet her. "Welcome home, daughter. I suppose you heard the news?"

"Yes, and I am so happy you made this decision. I have languished in Tuscany far too long," she said.

"Languished? How can that be? You only arrived home a few minutes ago."

"I am so happy to see you, Papa." She gave her father a kiss, but the sight of the parrot suddenly distracted him.

"What are you doing with that?"

"I am teaching it to talk."

"We don't have enough squawking going on around here that you have to import more?"

"Be nice. It's a sensitive bird."

"If it's wearing those outlandish feathers, it can't be too sensitive."

Serena laughed and picked up the birdcage. "I'm off to find Mama, and then to my room to pack. There is so much to be done."

"What is your hurry? You will find someone else

to do the work for you," he said, but Serena was already too far up the stairs to hear.

Tito looked at Beatrice, who was still feeling somewhat overpowered, and said, "Every time she comes home, I expect to see bananas in her hair."

Beatrice put her hand over her mouth and turned away to muffle her laugh. By the time she turned back, Uncle Tito had noticed several of the wagons being readied to transport the heavier things, and he went outside to examine them.

It was obvious he was happy to be returning to the villa where he was born and where he grew to manhood, just as he was happy knowing that he was now turning it over to his son, as his father had done to him.

Everyone knew he was excited about the prospect of inspecting his ancestral lands once again, and being able to see for himself how well the directives he had given over the years had been carried out. Although, he already knew from Angelo that the man hired to manage things at Villa Adriana was far better at taking Tito's money than anything else.

In his room upstairs, Angelo oversaw the packing of a few things he wanted to take back to Turin. In the hallway outside, everything seemed to be in a state of utter disorder and confusion.

Serena poked her head into Angelo's room and exclaimed, "How can you stand the noise? Everything is in an uproar. It's topsy-turvy from top to bottom."

The doors to each room were open, and many pieces of furniture were being carried down the hall, along with a mirror, and a picture or two. Trunks in the rooms were still being packed, while those already full were waiting in the hall to be carried downstairs.

Bits of wrapping paper and ropes to tie bundles lay scattered here and there. The voices of servants resounded throughout the house. Uncle Tito was still bustling about the yard, looking remarkably like the red rooster who was doing his own bit of bustling not very far away.

Gisella was overseeing the packing of the things in her room.

Serena took one look at everything being done and declared, "I have a headache. I am certain it is from the grueling trip from Rome yesterday. I think I will go to my room and lie down, with a vinegar compress on my head."

This caused Beatrice to hide a smile at the great lengths her cousin would go to in order to get out of doing anything that could possibly be considered work.

For the next several days, the household continued to be abuzz with activity, for trunks were still being brought into the house and filled, not only with clothing but with various items that Gisella wanted Angelo to have, ignoring completely Tito's assurance that "Villa Adriana is full of furniture and all those nonsense objects women like to clutter up the house with."

"But I want Angelo to have some of *my* family furniture, and there are a few things at Villa Adriana I want to bring back to Villa Mirandola," Gisella said to him one day.

Tito seemed properly horrified at the thought of going through all of this again for the return trip, and started to make a hasty departure.

"Where are you going?" Gisella asked.

"To find Serena. I want to inquire about the effectiveness of the vinegar compress."

It was not until the end of the week that Tito decided things had progressed to the point that they could leave the finishing of everything yet undone to the staff. "They are perfectly capable of finishing what packing there is left, and they can come with the wagons to Turin."

Moving day had finally arrived.

Everyone was up early that day and, after breakfast, set about packing the last-minute items. The level of enthusiasm was high, and everyone was organized except for Tito, who could not seem to decide if he should supervise inside or out.

Consequently, he kept going back and forth, accomplishing what Gisella referred to as "very little, other than keeping the servants in a state of confusion. He contradicts everything I tell them."

Beatrice went about everything in her usual quiet manner, and found that since she had come to Villa Mirandola with very few belongings, so her things were quickly re-packed. She proudly announced, "I am the first one packed and ready to go."

"Don't crow overlong," Angelo said. "I have all of my last-minute packing done, as well. Why don't we sit over here, in the shade, and watch everyone else work?"

Beatrice liked that idea and joined him beneath the lofty branches of a tree.

Serena, on the other hand, seemed to treat packing as if it were a theatrical production. She shouted orders and demonstrated to the servants how they *ought* to be doing this or that. Knowing her as they did, the servants were already skeptical of anything Serena said. If she wasn't telling them a falsehood, their next assumption was that she was playing some sort of joke upon them, so their response was mostly to ignore her, which meant Serena was the last one packed and in the carriage, which did not surprise anyone but Serena.

The women rode in the family coach, while Tito and Angelo preferred to ride their horses, at least most of the time.

"But why must you ride on horseback, when the coach is much more comfortable?" Serena asked.

"When all this womanly chatter begins to seriously threaten my sanity, I must escape," replied Tito.

Beatrice had to admit she was happiest when Angelo rode inside the coach with them, and she took each moment with him to her heart. She secretly hoped the trip to Turin would be inordinately long, for she knew the moment they arrived, he would return to his villa in town and the life—and danger—that awaited him there.

Still, she could not grieve, she told herself. After all, she had beautiful memories of Angelo...and a poem.

Sixteen

Von Schisler watched the two men walk into his office like two lost members of a gaggle of geese.

"You have come from the police commissioner's office?" he asked.

In unison, they agreed that they had indeed come from the office that they considered the foundation of King Vittorio Emanuele's reign.

Von Schisler began to drum his fingers as he listened to the two Italians with their brass necks and plodding brains who called themselves spies. If this was the best the King of Sardinia had to offer, the liberals had reason to celebrate.

"So, you are telling me you found nothing to show Bartolini played a part in or is connected in any way with the publication of those inflammatory pamphlets?"

"Yes, Count, that is what we are saying."

"And you found nothing in the villa that would implicate him in any type of subversive activity, such as plotting to overthrow your king? No plans for revolts? No suspicious maps of the king's palace or public buildings? No communications with the secret societies in other cities? No stockpiling of weapons?"

As if on cue, one of the men produced a folded

paper from his pocket and placed it on von Schisler's desk. "We did find this list of weapons, Count."

Von Schisler picked up the paper and read, and the words leaped off the page, raising his irritation with the two fools to boiling rage. *Pocketknives, muskets, hundred-year-old pistols, battle sword, Persian dagger...*

"You mean to tell me that you two clownish buffoons of questionable intelligence actually think the highly intellectual members of the Carbonari are going to start a revolution using pocketknives and battle swords?"

Von Schisler stood and came around his desk, fully intending to take the two imbeciles by the scruff of their necks and physically throw them out of his office, but one of them hastily produced a velvet pouch and held it out, like a crucifix to a vampire.

"What is this?" von Schisler asked. "More of your nonsense?"

"We thought you might find this useful, Count."

Von Schisler opened the pouch and smiled at the miniature of Angelo Bartolini. "So, you have managed to save your scrawny necks in the nick of time," he said, and dropped the pouch in his pocket. "I will take care of this from now on. That will be all, gentlemen."

The two men bowed several times as they backed out of von Schisler's office, but von Schisler did not notice. He was already thinking how much this miniature would please Prince Metternich.

He returned to his desk and considered where he would go from here. He could not afford to deal with the police commissioner's office, and the sort of men Vittorio Emanuele, the King of Sardinia, had in his employ made him rethink working closely with the king in the future.

He would find his own spies.

Several days later, a Carbonari member, Luigi Codazza, met with Count von Schisler in Turin, at the *Caffè Cioccolateria Al Bicerin* in Piazza della Consolata. They were to talk over a cup of the house specialty, a hot drink made with coffee, chocolate and cream, because Count von Schisler liked chocolate and sweets, and found anything that combined the two irresistible.

At precisely the agreed hour, von Schisler walked into the *caffè* and sat at the table in the far corner. He faced out, so he could see everyone who came and went. He was determined to excel at breaking the back of these liberals, not because he really cared about them one way or the other, but because he wanted to make a name for himself. He knew Metternich was fast becoming the most powerful man in Europe, and he wanted to be there to step into his shoes when the opportunity presented itself.

He reached into his coat and removed a small leather pouch, from which he withdrew the miniature of Angelo Bartolini. He rubbed his thumb over the miniature, as if by doing so he could absorb something of his enemy's intellect and purpose.

The face in the miniature smiled up at him—a sublime fool who had no idea this small picture would elevate von Schisler considerably, at least in the eyes of Prince Metternich.

He saw Luigi Codazza come into the *caffè* and returned the miniature to his pocket.

Codazza was sweating and looking about the room in a nervous manner. When he saw von Schisler sitting alone in the back, he started toward him.

Von Schisler, not wanting him to mention his name, motioned him forward but did not introduce himself. He merely said, "Sit down."

"Thank you," Codazza said, while he removed a handkerchief and blotted his face. "It's a warm day."

"Would you like some chocolate?"

"No."

"I believe you have something you wanted to tell me."

"Someone you are interested in is returning to Turin tonight."

"And who might that be?"

"Let me simply say, you should see an increase in the proclamations written by Carbonari members in Turin, now that he is returning," Codazza said.

"Ahh, now we have something to talk about. How did you come by this information?"

"I prefer not to divulge that, but I can assure you, the information I have is quite valid. He will arrive tonight, just as I have said."

"In that case, you have my full confidence. I know you will keep me informed. You will continue to work with the Carbonari and Bartolini as long as it serves us, but bear in mind our objectives come first. He can be sacrificed in the interests of gaining our objective and, as such, is expendable. We cannot bog down in any kind of moral sensibility. Austria must come first."

"You have only to say the word, Count, and I will do your bidding."

Luigi, a small, careful man with the distracting habit of blinking, was a notary by vocation, but his true calling had been discovered when he was trained to spy upon the Austrians by his fellow Carbonari members.

That he was already in the service of the Carbonari and worked directly with their chief spy, Giuseppe Mantra, meant that not only he had access to the most secret information, but that he could be paid twice for passing along virtually the same information to Mantra that he did to von Schisler.

Codazza had seen pamphlets written by Angelo Bartolini before, and knew von Schisler would be angry to know the dissident was returning to Turin. What he did not know, but would soon learn, was that Bartolini had been sorely missed by the people of Turin—people who looked forward to his pamphlets, which kept them informed and up to date on what was happening, but, more important, kept alive their free Italy.

The pressure would be on both von Schisler and Metternich when they realized Bartolini was becoming a sort of Italian Robin Hood—not a man who robbed the rich to give to the poor, but one who gave of his time and his coin, and risked his life for a cause that would free Italy's peasants.

The last time Codazza had met with von Schisler was shortly after Bartolini left Turin, and after von Schisler's disastrous meeting with Prince Metternich in Milan. Von Schisler was in a rage for days after that meeting, and then, when Bartolini's last pamphlet hit the streets, von Schisler read it and he vowed to put an end to the man who denounced the papal government and the Bourbon tyrants in Naples, and condemned Austria's ruthless repression of Italian liberals in the north.

Immediately after reading the cursed pamphlet, von Schisler had ripped it into shreds and had sworn to have Bartolini's head on a pike for daring to insult him and his Austrian blood.

Seventeen

Church bells from Monte dei Cappuccini, with the church of Santa Maria del Monte outlined against it, were ringing as Angelo rode into Turin, and he found himself thinking he had forgotten how much noise was in the city, for today it seemed as boisterous as Rome.

Not far away, von Schisler and Codazza were concluding their talk, and shortly thereafter Codazza excused himself and departed.

Angelo rode up the straight road toward Piazza Castello. He continued on the tree-lined avenue, until he saw the somber facade of the church of San Francesco di Paola and its annexed convent, where he was to meet that beady-eyed notary, Luigi Codazza.

A warm, humid breeze blew in from the direction of Genoa, carrying the scent of orange trees. It also carried the sound of footsteps as Luigi came into view.

Their greeting was a brief one, bred of mutual dislike.

"I have gathered information for your next pamphlet and have taken the liberty of writing it out for you. It is all here," he said, handing Angelo an envelope. "There is a meeting of the 'good cousins'"—which was the way the Carbonari members referred to each other—"tomorrow night. Will you be there?"

"I will be there," Angelo said. "Any word of von Schisler or Metternich?"

"All is quiet in that regard. I have heard nothing."

"I feel certain the resumption of our pamphlets will change that. Any word from Naples?"

"They are progressing with their plans of a revolt."

"Good. That should make planning our uprising easier."

"Have you thought of a date?"

Angelo had been thinking about it, of course, but for some reason he chose not to tell Codazza. Perhaps it was because he did not care for the man— had Codazza not been a Carbonari member, Angelo would have gone so far as to say he did not trust him. "No. All we have at the present is a vision."

With nothing more than a brief nod, Codazza disappeared down one of the side streets.

It was not quite dark, so Angelo stopped by Nicola's house, but Nicola was out. He rode to his villa, feeling suddenly weary from the long journey from Tuscany. He thought about Beatrice and how difficult it had been to tell her goodbye and watch her, and his family, turn onto the road that would take them to Villa Adriana, while he took the road that led to Turin.

He reached his villa and let himself into the house. Cesare was clattering about upstairs, and Angelo called out to say he was back, then went into his study.

He took the desk key out of his pocket, and was about to put the papers from Codazza in his desk drawer, when Cesare came hurrying into the room to tell him about the night he had been taken to the police commissioner's office. He had just finished his story, when Nicola arrived.

"Nicola, this is a pleasant surprise," Angelo said, embracing his friend. "I did not expect to see you until the meeting tomorrow."

"I apologize for coming this late, but I had some urgent things to discuss with you. Did Cesare tell you he was taken in and questioned by the police?"

"Yes, I just heard."

After Cesare went upstairs, Nicola and Angelo discussed the possibility of a break-in.

"I am certain these drawers were locked before I left. And look at the scratches, and this lock is bent. It is obvious someone forced the drawers open."

"Do you think they found anything incriminating?"

"They would have if you had not removed the munitions from here." He looked at Nicola suddenly. "You did remove them, didn't you?"

Nicola smiled. "I would have to be dead to fail you," he said, "although I do wonder if I should have removed your personal guns, as well. Were any of them missing?"

"Cesare says nothing was missing, and I doubt that would have served their purpose. They obviously did not want me to know they had conducted this search. Aside from that, I see no reason to strip my home of every gun and sword I own. It isn't against the law to have arms in one's house...at least not yet. They know, I am sure, that I ride to the outskirts of town daily to practice shooting. As for the antique guns and sabers that I have collected, any imbecile could see they are just that."

"Unfortunately, we are dealing with imbeciles of the Austrian variety."

"Or the weak king who gives in to the Austrian variety."

"Have you spoken to Codazza?"

"Yes, I saw him before I stopped by your house. He gave me a packet of information he had gathered—so I could use whatever I found pertinent in the next article. Why do you ask?"

"I do not trust him. I intend to speak to Giuseppe about him."

"I don't trust him, either, but until he gives us some reason to take action, all we can do is distrust him and wait for him to betray us—although I hate to suspect him of that. He is one of the good cousins, don't forget."

"I have the feeling he is not completely devoted. And if that is true, it makes us rather like pigeons at a target practice, doesn't it?"

"Unfortunately, that is a fair analogy."

"Tell me of your suspicions about Codazza. Did anything happen while I was gone?"

"He set up a meeting for me with a priest who wants to join the Carbonari. I arrived at the inn at the edge of town, half an hour early, to meet with him. Imagine my surprise when I saw that some members of the King of Sardinia's guard were just leaving. I had no doubt that they intended to return later, while the priest and I were meeting."

"You suspect the priest?"

"These days I am suspicious of almost everyone. However, the priest is not one of them, since he supposedly committed suicide two days later."

"Do you believe it?"

"Not when those who found the body swear he was shot in the back."

"That does change things."

"I think it is time we adhered to some old advice. Never take coffee with a man who suddenly becomes your best friend. Never confide in a stranger. Never sleep with a woman whose husband is in trouble."

"That is your way of saying we need to proceed with caution."

"It is my way of saying we must exercise *extreme* caution from now on. The Austrians are not graceful losers."

Eighteen

Spring at Villa Adriana passed quietly, and an un-
hurried summer settled over Piedmont as if it intended to stay for a while.

Beatrice had never thought she would see anything
to rival Villa Mirandola, but Villa Adriana was far
grander. It was the classical palatial residence, and
had once been the site of tournaments, parties and
hunts.

The villa itself was in a spectacular setting, about
twelve miles away from Turin, and close to the little
town of Asti.

It was built more on the lines of French classicism,
with steeply pitched roofs of gray slate, numerous
skylights, columns and arches. As for stunning
views, few villas could surpass it, for almost every
window looked over the vineyards, the once magnificent gardens or the trees in the distance.

Beatrice understood immediately why Angelo
loved it here, and why he wanted to spend the rest
of his life restoring the grounds to their former gran-
deur and improving the vineyards beyond anything
they had been in the past.

The interior of the villa was well cared for, and
required only minor changes in decor, which Beatrice, Serena and Aunt Gisella were happily undertaking. Uncle Tito also seemed to be in a perpetual

state of bliss. He was back in the home where he was
born, and as Aunt Gisella described, ''He is whiling
away the hours among his beloved grapevines.''

Angelo was spending more time at the villa than
Beatrice had thought he would, although she did not
think he was completely relaxed when he was there.
He always seemed preoccupied, and each time he
left, Beatrice worried for him more. His departure
last night had been the most difficult of all.

Tonight, the family was gathered in the dining
room as they awaited Serena's arrival, although Uncle Tito was becoming a bit agitated over his daughter's tardiness.

He asked Aunt Gisella, ''Where do you suppose
she is?''

''I have no idea, Tito.''

He asked Beatrice, ''Do you know where Serena
is?''

''No, Uncle Tito, I am sorry to say I do not. The
last time I saw her was about three o'clock, when
Father Matteo came by.''

Tito bowed his head. Gisella and Beatrice exchanged glances before Gisella asked, ''Whatever
are you doing?''

''I am saying a prayer to Saint Teresa of Avila.''

''Must you pray again? We have already blessed
the meal.''

''I am not blessing the meal. I am praying to Saint
Teresa, because she is the patron saint of headaches
and your daughter is giving me one.''

In spite of Serena's absence, dinner was a pleasant
meal, and Beatrice joined the family conversation between Uncle Tito and Aunt Gisella, thinking such
interaction a fine complement for such a delicious
dinner. However, she had to admit that when she had

first seen what they were having, she'd feared *delicious* would not be the word to describe it.

Beatrice had never before eaten rabbit, which the Italians called *coniglio*. Succulent and delicious, it was roasted slowly, with herbs, garlic, red wine and balsamic vinegar, until the thick chunks of meat were juicy and tender, then it was served with tiny, roasted onions and fried potatoes.

She enjoyed two servings.

After dinner, she took a seat at a small desk near the fire to write a reply to a letter she had received. *Signora la Contessa* degli Bonacossi had written to say she would be both honored and delighted if Beatrice would consider visiting her in Milan.

Beatrice had met the *contessa* in Paris last year, and while the *contessa* had expressed some interest in having Beatrice paint her portrait, Beatrice had never expected to hear from her again. Now, several months later, the *contessa* had invited Beatrice to Milan. She was close to Beatrice's age, and quite nice.

Beatrice read the letter again.

I would consider it an honor if you would agree to visit us in Milano, and give your consent to paint my portrait and that of my two daughters.

I would like you to come as soon as it is convenient for you. If it is in the fall, bear in mind our weather in Milan is colder than Florence, so you might prefer to come when it is warmer. If you will write me of your plans and the date you can come, I will dispatch a calash and escorts for you.

I spoke very highly of you at the opera the other night, so be prepared to receive other inquiries once you are here. I do hope you will honor this request.

Beatrice replied that she would be delighted to visit the *contessa* in Milan, and would be honored to paint their portraits. Beatrice paused a moment. She had, so far, only painted Aunt Gisella's portrait, and she did not want to go traipsing off to Milan before she finished the portraits of the rest of her family.

I have several portraits I have accepted to paint, she wrote, *which will keep me busy here until after Christmas next. Should I find that I can come earlier, I will write you straightaway.*

She paused to think about Angelo again, and wondered if she would see him as much in Milan, which was eleven leagues from Turin.

"You are thinking about Angelo again. Don't bother to deny it."

Beatrice looked up to see her cousin standing in the doorway. Today, Serena looked as flamboyant as a flame-colored flamingo in a bright Spanish dress.

Serena came into the room and stood in front of the fireplace.

"Are you waiting for me to start a fire?" Beatrice asked.

Serena laughed. "A little hot for that, I fear."

"You look more windblown than hot."

"I know. It was so windy. And here, I thought March was the windy, fickle month."

"You missed dinner, and your father is quite perturbed with you."

"He loves it when I give him something to fuss about."

Beatrice was inclined to agree. "Where have you been?"

Serena rubbed her nose. "Rescuing a hungry nanny goat staked in a withered vegetable garden."

"Whose garden?"

She shrugged. "How should I know?"

"Then, whose goat was it?"

"I don't know, but it is ours now."

"You stole someone's nanny goat?"

"I did not steal it. I rescued it."

"I hope the police look at it that way."

"The police have more to concern themselves with than a missing goat," Serena said.

Beatrice smiled at the thought of Serena, dressed in a ruffled Spanish gown of saffron yellow, leading a big nanny goat out of a vegetable garden overgrown with weeds and dragging her along some country road. "Whatever shall you do with a nanny goat?"

Serena was rearranging things on Beatrice's desk. "That is your worry."

"My worry? Why is it my worry? I didn't rescue it."

"Because I am giving the goat to you for your birthday."

"You can't do that. Besides, my birthday was three weeks ago."

"It's a belated birthday present."

"Serena, I cannot have a goat."

"Why not?"

"I don't know anything about goats. I can't go traipsing all over Italy with a goat. What do they eat?"

"Everything."

"What would I do with one?"

"Anything you wanted to. Pet it. Let it pull a cart. Breed it and have a lot of little kids running around."

"Thank you for the thought, but I don't want a goat—or any of the aforementioned trimmings."

"It's too late. I've already given it to you for your birthday. You cannot return a gift."

"Yes, I can."

"Perhaps in England, but in Italy that is not done. Besides, I've already given her an English name, and I told Antonio to bathe her for you."

"What English name?"

"Fanny…Fanny the Nanny. I think it is perfect, especially when you consider I am not very good at rhyming in English."

"You aren't very good at naming pets in English, either."

"You don't like it?"

"I don't know…well, actually, I don't care for it, but perhaps it will become more likable in time."

"I certainly hope so. I am not accustomed to having people tell me they do not like my gift."

Beatrice didn't respond, for she was thinking, *I wonder why other people get civilized gifts—a muffler, a pair of mittens, a book, a new fan—but I get a nanny goat?*

"Consider yourself among the privileged few who own a goat. They are wonderful pets, you know, and quite intelligent."

"I hope it is intelligent enough to talk the police out of arresting me when they learn I am harboring a stolen goat."

"Focus on the good side of it."

"What good side? They eat everything in sight, and butt you when you least expect it."

"You will never be out of milk."

"I don't care for goat milk, thank you."

Serena glanced down at the letter Beatrice was

writing. "Are you writing to the *contessa* in Milan, or to Angelo?"

"The *contessa.*"

"And have you accepted her invitation?"

"Yes."

"When do you leave? Not right away, I hope."

"No, I cannot go until after Christmas. I want to finish the family portraits..." Suddenly, Beatrice paused. "How did you know I had had a letter from the *contessa,* and what she had said?"

"I read it."

"But, it had not been opened."

"I steamed it open and glued it back."

"Why? If you wanted to read it, all you had to do was ask and I would have let you."

"That isn't the same thing."

"I don't understand how you can find pleasure in reading someone else's mail."

"Well, your sister did."

"Maresa?"

"She was very good at steaming them open, too, but not quite as good at gluing. She kept getting the paper stuck to her fingers. Angelo kept trying to teach her how to keep from doing it, but after a while, he gave up."

"Angelo, *now* it makes sense. Still, I cannot believe you taught Maresa to steam open letters."

"That isn't all we taught her."

Beatrice did not doubt that for a moment.

The next week passed slowly, but not as slowly as it would have if she hadn't had Fanny to take care of. The goat was far worse than Colossus when it came to tearing up flower beds, and so far had eaten

Uncle Tito's pocket watch, Aunt Gisella's garden spade and two perfume bottles.

However, the biggest shock came the day Beatrice walked into the house after her morning walk and met Fanny coming down the stairs.

Nineteen

Freemasonry, long fashionable among the Italian nobility of the south, gave birth to the Carbonari in Naples, but the root of the Carbonari went back much further, to the Charbonniers, a clandestine movement in Napoleonic France whose ideals were brought to southern Italy by Napoleon's French officers.

Many of them were Sicilian, and like their fellows in Naples and in the north, they were obliged under oath to respect the rules of the Carbonari, to help one another in case of need, and not to reveal the secret, even if forced to suffer the pain of being cut into pieces and incinerated in a furnace.

Angelo had never known anyone to be incinerated, but thinking about it did give one pause, until he remembered the atrocities the Austrians committed.

It was a quiet afternoon in Turin. Angelo and Nicola were at Angelo's villa in town, discussing the state of things in Naples.

"Have you heard anything about the King of the Two Sicilies' reaction, when they asked for the new constitution?" Nicola said.

Angelo started to laugh.

Nicola looked at him oddly. "You think arrests, searches and the banning of the Carbonari is humorous?"

Angelo shook his head. "No, I was thinking of something else."

"What?"

"I was recalling how these are the same impassioned Neapolitans who imprisoned Cimarosa for his patriotic hymn and Republican sympathies, and then threw his harpsichord out the window," Angelo replied.

"Ah, the Neapolitans. No one has their passion."

"No, not even when it comes to revolt."

"You have information on it?"

"Nothing official, but I have heard rumors."

"Were they successful?"

"So far, but we both know King Ferdinand will call on Metternich to save his treacherous hide."

"Did they force Ferdinand to give them the same constitution as the Spanish received after their revolt? I understand news of the Spaniard's success is what set fire to the Neapolitans in the first place."

"Ferdinand agreed to their demands for the Spanish constitution, but that limits his royal powers and reduces his influence, and he will not tolerate that for long."

"It does not look good for our attempt to gain support for a similar revolt, then, does it?"

"We have no way of knowing. There was word of another revolt—this one in Sicily—but I understand it was brutally put down by the Austrians."

"Perhaps you should stop publishing the pamphlets for a while," Nicola said. "There is a lot of tension around town right now. There is word of new spies on the streets. Have you heard that?"

"Yes, and I know that von Schisler has opened an office in Turin and is spending a great deal of time here. Only this morning, Giuseppe informed me that

he has learned von Schisler is on his way to Vienna
to meet with Metternich.''

"You don't think he knows something that could
incriminate you, do you?''

"If they knew something, they would have arrested me. Besides, what could he know? They
searched my house and found nothing.''

It had rained all night, and the threat of rain still
hung heavily overhead as Beatrice walked along the
drive that led from Villa Adriana. She was looking
for her *capra*, that agile, ruminant mammal with
curving horns, straight hair, a short tail and an overwhelming propensity for butting, eating flowers and
escaping from every pen she was placed in.

Surely Fanny was the worst gift and the most trou-
blesome excuse for a pet Beatrice had ever seen. She
could not understand why the Greeks had wanted to
name a constellation after one.

In the distance, she saw the stone columns with
the iron gates swung wide, and remembered the day
she had walked down a similar road with her paints,
and sat in the warm, Tuscan sun...the same day Angelo had come.

But this was Piedmont, and there were no cypress
trees lining the drive.

As she passed along the road, she glanced at the
great clumps of green shrubs, so heavy with the earlier rain that they had fallen across each other in a
rather dismal way. Unfazed, the coarse summer grass
stood tall, and tiny olives still clung tightly to the
olive branches.

Suddenly, she heard a bleat, then a rustling in the
bushes beside her, and Fanny came bursting out with
her horns down, ready to butt. This aggressive goat

had butted her three times already, and Beatrice was growing weary of the experience. She picked up a nearby branch, something between the size of a log and a limb.

She looked at Fanny, who was staring back at her, and for a moment they seemed to be at a stalemate. Beatrice was wondering if they had, at last, reached some sort of truce, when Fanny charged.

Beatrice waited for the right moment. She wanted to let the goat get as close as she dared. She brought the branch down over her head with a mighty *whack*.

Fanny was unfazed, but it did seem to knock some sort of new appreciation into her thick head, because she stopped, head up, and studied Beatrice, as if seeing her in a new light. With a toss of her head, she began walking toward Beatrice, who readied the branch for a second go.

Behind her, Beatrice heard a deep, masculine laugh, and she turned with a gasp.

There sat Angelo astride his great black horse. Still laughing, he threw one leg over the saddle horn and slid to the ground. "And here I thought you were a shy English girl."

"I am…sometimes."

"A shy girl who wields a branch like one of Hippolyte's Amazons. Come here and greet me properly. I want to kiss you. I have thought of little else."

A lady would have dropped her head. A lady would have looked away. A lady would have said something like *How dare you.*

Beatrice decided she was no lady when it came to Angelo, and she rushed to him.

He kissed her as if he had missed her as much as she had missed him. "I am glad I came," he said, and kissed her again.

"As am I. How long will you be here?"

"A few days. I brought some new plans for the gardens and want to get the stonemasons working while we have such good weather."

"Good weather? It has been raining all day."

"Yes, but it will be snowing when fall comes, and that is not all that far away."

They started walking. She could hear Fanny tromping and munching her way along behind them. "Uncle Tito will be so glad to see you," she said. "I think too many women surround him. If you like, we could walk toward the olive grove. He is pruning some trees with Antonio."

"If I go now, I won't be able to spend any time alone with you."

He took her hand and led his horse as they walked down the road.

"Where are we going?"

"I will show you. Do you want to walk, or ride?"

Did he think her an idiot who preferred to walk, when she could ride and be so close to him? "I prefer to ride."

After he helped her onto his horse and mounted behind her, they rode toward the place where the casks of wine were aged. As they rode along the road edged with fields of grapevines, she tried to imagine what they would look like, blanketed with snow.

He stopped his horse in the trees near the wine cellar, which was nothing more than a man-made cave dug into the side of a hill centuries earlier. More recently, a barnlike structure had been built in front, with two huge wooden doors.

"I hope it will be cool, but not too cool, inside."

He dismounted. "Are you worried about being cold when it is this hot?"

"Yes, I am a thin-skinned English woman, and I know how chilling and damp cellars and caves can be."

"That isn't important when you have me...with all my warm Italian blood."

It was precisely all that warm Italian blood that gave her misgivings over the wisdom of coming here alone with him.

"I feel a chill already."

"I have an excellent remedy for that."

"I am certain you have a remedy for almost everything."

It was a short distance to the doors of the wine cellar, but when he opened one of the huge doors and stepped into the darkness beyond, she hesitated. She heard a scuffling sound, and, moments later, saw the soft, amber glow of a lamp.

He returned to the door, took her hand and led her inside. When he lit another lamp, she gasped. "Oh my."

She had had no idea the wine barrels were so huge, or that they were stored in such a cavernous room. "It is much larger than I thought," she said, amazed to hear the echo of her voice.

"It holds over a hundred wine barrels. We store them here because it provides the optimal humidity and temperature levels for aging wine."

"It is like a science, then."

"An ancient science affected by the soil, the climate, even the type of wood the barrels are made from."

He took a tin cup off a peg and tapped a small casket. When the cup was full, he took a drink, then brought the cup to her lips. "Here, have a taste."

She took a sip. "It's quite good."

"Of course. Do you think we produce anything that is not good?" His expression took on a pensive quality, as if he were remembering something from another time. "I have not been involved with the wine for a few years now."

"And you miss it. That much shows on your face."

"Yes, I do. My father brought me here with him when I was barely old enough to walk. Everything he knows, he taught me.

"You know why I cannot come. Things are progressing to the point in Turin, that I must remain there, at least for a little while."

She missed the softer, gentler side of him and wondered how she could get that Angelo back. Talking to him about his family's wine seemed to help. She put her hand on one of the barrels. "What kind of wood is this?"

"Most of our barrels are oak, from France. The rest are made from Italian chestnut trees."

"I would have thought you would use terra-cotta pots, since Italians seem to be so fond of them."

"We do use them for storage, but not for aging. The wood gives flavors and tannin to the wine during the aging process. The barrels are like the womb. They nurture and give birth to the wine. The coopering process—the thickness of staves, the size of the barrels, the hand-split wood, the drying in kilns, the drying over charcoal fires—all of it affects the wine."

He offered her the cup again. "Take another drink. It will warm you."

She tipped her head back to swallow and noticed two religious pictures on the wall. "Who are they?"

"Saint Morand, the patron saint of wine growers,

who fasted only on grapes during Lent. The other is Saint Vincent, the patron saint of wine.''

She began to rub her bare arms. He handed her the cup again. ''Keep drinking. It will keep you warm.''

''Wine in, wit out,'' she said, and took two swallows. Her mind was growing fuzzy, and she yawned.

''I must go. I must say hello to my father and go over the plans I've drawn up, before I go.''

''You are leaving tonight?'' she asked, noticing how the mention of Turin seemed to transform him. He was like a stranger now.

''I must be back in Turin tomorrow.''

''Can you tell me why?''

''No, I cannot.''

He made it obvious that he had another life, one that was separate from her. It caused her to wonder how there could ever be anything between them, other than this insane attraction they had for one another. Why had she thought they might have a future together?

He was already married…to Italy, and her cause.

He pulled her to her feet and walked her outside, then helped her onto his horse and mounted behind her.

When they reached the villa, he dismounted and helped her down. They walked silently to the door. ''It's getting close to dinnertime, and Mother will be worried about you.''

He was so impersonal now, and she wished again for the old Angelo to return. ''She won't worry,'' she said lightly. ''She knows I have Fanny with me.''

The old Angelo would have laughed, she thought, as she watched him walk to his horse, mount and ride away.

Twenty

Count von Schisler felt good being back in Vienna, if only for a few days.

He waited for the secretary to announce his arrival, and was surprised at how soon he returned to say, "His Majesty Prince Metternich will see you now."

As soon as von Schisler entered, Metternich said, "I hope you have brought me news of something besides the weather in Turin."

"I have, my Prince. I have." He put his hand in his pocket, withdrew the leather pouch and handed it to Metternich.

"What is this?"

"You mentioned you liked to size up the enemy and found it difficult when you had no face to put on them. I knew you had never met Bartolini, and didn't know what he looked like. I think you will be happy to put a face on the man who persists with all this Piedmontese mischief."

Metternich opened the pouch and looked at the miniature in his hand. His countenance changed and his hand closed tightly over the portrait, as if he wanted to crush it. When he spoke, his voice was full of rage.

"What kind of trick are you playing?" he said.

Von Schisler was stunned. "What? Forgive me, my Prince, but I don't know what you mean."

With barely controlled fury, Metternich opened his palm and looked at the small portrait again. "I mean this miniature—you think this is the face of the Italian radical?"

"But I assure you, it is Bartolini."

Metternich threw the miniature in von Schisler's face. "You idiot! Someone has played you for a fool! I know the man in this portrait. He is Prince Franz Ernst Ranier Klemens Kyrburg, an officer in the Imperial Army and the son of my worst enemy, Prince Kyrburg...Prince Johann Ranier Wenzel Karl Kyrburg, to be exact."

"The head of the Imperial Army in Italy?"

"The same."

"There must be some mistake."

"Obviously there is a mistake, you fool, and you are the one who made it."

Von Schisler was perspiring heavily. He bent over and picked up the miniature off the floor. He looked at Bartolini's face. "I don't understand, but I can assure you that this miniature was taken from Bartolini's villa. I have talked with Bartolini on several occasions. I know the man, and the face in this miniature is his face. If he bears a strong resemblance to Prince Kyrburg's son, I cannot help that. But the man in the portrait is Angelo Bartolini."

Metternich came around the desk and snatched the miniature out of von Schisler's hand. He looked at it for some time, thinking, *It is too strong a resemblance to be a coincidence, and yet there could be some differences. The hair perhaps, and the clothes...* He rocked back on his heels. "I wonder..."

After a long silence, von Schisler asked, "You wonder what, my Prince?"

Once again, Metternich's mood and countenance seemed to change without notice. "I wonder if it could be nothing more than a coincidence," he said, his voice suddenly mild with no hint of the previous fury.

"It must be a coincidence," von Schisler agreed.

Metternich slipped the miniature into his pocket. "Yes, that is the only explanation possible, isn't it. Well, I must say I am very pleased with your progress in Turin, Count. I trust you will continue with your exemplary work on my behalf."

Von Schisler clicked his heels together and said, "I will continue to do my utmost, my Prince."

"When do you return to Turin?"

"This afternoon, my Prince, unless you have further need of me."

"No, I need you in Turin, with your eyes and ears trained on Bartolini. This uprising in Naples, and that fool King Ferdinand giving in to their demands and granting them the Spanish constitution, is more than enough to give Bartolini and the Piedmontese ideas."

"I will keep you informed of everything he does."

"See that you do, von Schisler. See that you do."

As soon as von Schisler was gone, Metternich left his office to see his closest friend, Count Ludwig Seiffert, who, like Metternich, had once been a close friend of Prince Johann Kyrburg.

"Ah, Metternich, you finally darken my door. It is good to see you. I've been worried you were working too hard."

"I have been, and I think it is beginning to pay off. I have something to show you," he said, and reaching into his pocket, he withdrew the miniature von Schisler had given him. He handed it to Seiffert. "Tell me who that is."

Count Seiffert glanced at it briefly. "What is this, some sort of joke?"

"I do not play pranks. Who do you think that is?"

"It's Prince Kyrburg's son, Franz Ernst. He's a captain in the Imperial Army. Last I heard, he was serving with his father, in Italy."

"That's precisely who I thought it was," Metternich said.

"What do you mean, you *thought* it was?"

"What would you say if I told you this was an Italian patriot by the name of Angelo Bartolini—a liberal Carbonaro who is fast becoming a thorn in Austria's royal side?"

"I would say Franz Ernst has an Italian twin…" Seiffert stopped suddenly. "You don't suppose…that is, do you think this could be Prince Johann's son who disappeared shortly after birth?"

"The firstborn twin, who disappeared along with Johann's wife," Metternich added.

Seifert sat down, obviously shaken. "My God! This is too incredible to believe, and yet…" He looked at the tiny portrait again. "The likeness is too remarkable, even with the difference in hairstyle, the clothes."

"Think back to when Johann's wife disappeared. What do you remember about that night?"

Seifert let out a breath. "It was a long time ago."

"Twenty-nine years ago, to be exact," Metternich said.

"Johann's wife was Italian, I remember that much—quite beautiful, and miserably unhappy here in Austria."

"And miserably unhappy with her husband, too, if the gossips were right," Metternich said.

"Yes, yes, I remember that."

"And wasn't she the daughter of a duke?" Metternich asked.

"No, she was the daughter of a *marchese*...the *Marchese* di Caponi, of Parma."

"Her name was Maria Elena," Metternich said.

Seiffert shook his head. "Her name was Maria...Maria Elisa."

Metternich smiled. "I knew you would remember. I recall you fancied her yourself."

Seiffert smiled. "Yes, I did fancy her, and would have married her, if Johann hadn't pleased her father more."

"Because he was a prince."

"And I was a lowly count."

"You helped her escape, didn't you?"

Seiffert did not say anything for a long time, then with a sigh, he replied, "Yes, I helped her because she was miserable, and I loved her."

"I knew someone on the inside had to have helped her. I always suspected you were the one. Where did she go? What happened to her and the baby?"

"I arranged passage for her to go to Rome. She was to go into hiding in a convent there, until I could arrange passage for her to England. She wanted to take the twins. I tried to convince her that her chances were better if she left them. She agreed, but the night she ran away, I met her not far from their country estate. She had one of the twins with her. There was nothing I could do then. I had to take them both."

"You took her to Rome?"

"No, I took her to Trieste and put her on a boat to Venice. From there she went by coach. The arrangements were made to take her to Bologna, Florence, and then to Rome, but somewhere outside of

Florence, Johann's men caught up with her. She escaped from the inn where they were staying, the baby with her. It was in the dead of winter and there was snow on the ground. They found her two days later, frozen to death. There was no sign of the baby. It was wild country—they said the wolves could have gotten it. She was buried in Parma. I went there perhaps ten years ago. Her father had had a statue carved and placed at her grave—it was of the whitest marble, and it looked so much like her, I broke down and cried."

"That is why you never married."

"Yes."

Metternich stood and walked to where Seiffert sat. He patted him on the back. "I am sorry to stir up all these old memories."

"They are never far from me. But, tell me about the Italian—" he looked at the miniature "—the man in this picture."

Metternich told him what he knew about Angelo Bartolini.

"So, you have no proof of his heritage, other than this striking resemblance to Prince Franz Ernst?"

"No, but I hope to know more very soon. I will have my agents in Milan look into it."

"You aren't going to harm him, are you?"

"He is Austria's enemy."

"He is Maria Elisa's son."

"I give you my word I won't do anything until I talk to you."

Seiffert nodded. "I accept your word."

"You will tell me what you learn in Milan?"

"Of course. You have been a friend these many years. I must go now. I have much to do before I leave tomorrow."

"One last thing. Are you going to tell Prince Johann?"

"Johann lost that right years ago when he refused to marry the grand-niece of the King of Spain."

Seiffert nodded. "I remember."

"Until I return," Metternich said, and departed.

Later, Metternich sat behind a desk, busily composing a letter of report to the King of Austria:

The Piedmontese, Your Majesty, call for our most anxious attention, for it is in Piedmont that we find all the elements of discontent. The Turin Cabinet entertains ambitious views that can only be gratified at Austria's expense, and this requires my careful observation. For that reason, I shall depart tomorrow for Milan, where I shall spend some time and expend great effort to get to the bottom of the discontent in both Lombardy and Piedmont.

We have long known of the existence of several secret fraternities that are quite active in Milan and all of Piedmont—fraternities that foster a spirit for excitement, discontent and opposition to all we stand for.

The aspirations of their leaders and the source of their financing need scrutiny. We must estimate the danger they pose to us and our goal to repress revolts and rebellions before they occur. Seven years of observation as well as knowledge of the revolts in Naples and Sicily have shown me these sects cannot and must not be ignored. Now they count members of the Italian nobility, as well as the English poets Byron and Shelley, among their members, and they burn with the idea of Italian independence, which makes them extremely dangerous.

Your Majesty, if we are to make Austria supreme in Italy and repress the idea of a united Italy, we must continue with full aggression, with censorship, espionage and the suppression of revolutionary and nationalist movements. Like Napoleon, we must be completely and utterly ruthless in dealing with national and patriotic aspirations.

Just as the holy alliance sent French troops to Spain, we must use Austrian troops in Italy. The propaganda for a united Italy caused the rebellion against King Ferdinand in Naples. Now, the Carbonari in Turin are putting out the same propaganda and stirring the pot of rebellion with the same spoon.

At his house in Turin, Angelo was reading an account of the revolt that had broken out in Naples— a revolt that had started in the small town of Nola. Giuseppe had delivered the account—written by a Carbonaro in Naples—to him earlier.

None of this information was in the local newspapers, of course, because King Vittorio Emanuele and the Austrians did not want the Piedmontese to get ideas. Once again, it was up to Angelo to write the truth of the Naples revolt and have it printed for distribution to the people.

The revolt started on the first of July with a few garrison officers, and grew until one hundred and twenty-seven men of the king's regiment were ready to march. But it was several days before the revolt's leader, General Pepe, amassed ten thousand men in Avellino, most of them soldiers and Carbonari members. They marched to Naples and took control, miraculously, without a fight.

In King Ferdinand's private apartment, General Pepe received the king's promise to accept the Spanish constitution. A delegate was invited from each province in the Kingdom of the Two Sicilies, to enact the reforms.

The new regime would never last. Angelo knew that. They had too many enemies, and King Ferdinand had Austria on his side. The Austrians had crushed the Sicilian revolt, and now there was word that Metternich was trying to gather support for another international congress, much like the Congress of Vienna in 1815 that had given the Austrians such a foothold in Italy.

Angelo felt the pressure. If Metternich succeeded in rallying the other powers in Europe, Angelo feared, the Italian cause was doomed. They had to move and move fast. How could he reach the people, armed only with his pen?

He wished he had more information, but he knew the risks others took to get him even this much. He opened the inkwell and dipped his pen, then began his accounting of insurrections in the south.

He wrote about insurrection being instinctive, and how even a snake strikes at the foot that tries to stomp it. *It is the truest method of warfare among peoples trying to free themselves from a foreign yoke,* he wrote. *It is inevitable, and born of the same spirit as our own Roman gladiator, Spartacus.* He wrote of the victories of Spartacus, a lowly slave who had led other slaves to defeat the mighty Roman army. *We need men,* he wrote, *men who are not afraid to shed their blood, for the love of their country, for freedom from oppression.*

Angelo tried not to think about the way the Romans had crushed the slaves at last, in a battle at Lucania, where Spartacus was killed and many of his followers were crucified.

When Nicola dropped by later that night to take the article to the printer, Angelo had it ready. After a few minutes of conversation, Nicola left for Lorenzo's print shop.

Angelo stood at the window and watched his friend ride off.

He did not know that the words he had penned tonight would be like a flaming arrow shot through the Piedmontese heart, or that, emboldened by their bothers in Naples and the words of a man who would rather design gardens than fight, the people of Piedmont would begin their long, long journey toward freedom.

Twenty-One

Quiet winter settled over Villa Adriana.

Beatrice stood at the window and looked out at the frosty light of early afternoon, where an icy wind moaned and shook the tops of the trees, while the earth below was hard as iron.

It was Christmas Eve, and Angelo had not yet arrived.

She had not seen him since that day in late summer, when he seemed to turn into another person before her very eyes. How like winter his absence had been, leaving her life bare as naked woods in December. These were melancholy days, in spite of the usual excitement over the coming of Christmas and Epiphany.

She found it strange that this time of family, celebration and joy could also be the saddest time of the year. It might be the beginning of the holiday season, but for Beatrice, the joy of Christmas was missing.

She knew Angelo was busy, just as she knew he was emerging as a leader of a cause he believed in with all his heart. She knew, too, that he did not want her to worry about him. He had said as much in the letter he wrote over a month ago: "There is much to do in Turin, and my time is not my own. I will try to come home as soon as I can."

He did not mention Christmas.

He will be here, she told herself, but not even that could brighten her mood. The memory of his kiss could warm an entire winter. But in his absence, her days were as bleak and gray as January.

She studied the nativity scene, called the *presepio,* where the family would gather to pray following dinner. Aunt Gisella would then place the figure of the *bambino* in the manger, since the tradition was for the mother of the household to do so. In preparing for the coming season, everyone in the household would begin a fast from meat twenty-four hours before the big meal on Christmas Day. That was why tonight's dinner would not only be different from an English dinner, but also meatless in the Catholic tradition of penitence.

Earlier, she had asked her aunt, ''What are we having for dinner tonight?''

''Baccalà, it is the traditional Tuscan staple.''

Baccalà. The word sounded much more appetizing than the translation, for when Beatrice inquired, her aunt said, ''It is salted and dried cod.''

Cod, salted or otherwise, was not something Beatrice looked forward to eating anytime, and certainly not for Christmas Eve; however, she tried to hide her repugnance.

Aunt Gisella smiled. ''There will also be *cardoni* with Jerusalem artichokes, baked pasta with chickpeas, and boiled cabbage,'' she said, as if sensing Beatrice's despair.

Serena added the best part when she said, ''And for dessert there will be *torrone, cannoli* and *panforte di Siena.*''

All in all, Beatrice decided she must have done a poor job of hiding her revulsion, for Uncle Tito said,

"You must remember that for Catholics, this is the frugal beginning of the celebrations that end with Epiphany. There is an old Tuscan proverb to admonish those who do not rigidly keep the traditional Christmas Eve dinner, which must be fish—'He who ruins Christmas Eve has a wolf's body and the soul of a cur.'"

Properly put in her place, Beatrice vowed to try the cod, or at least put some on her plate. Perhaps she could hide it beneath the boiled cabbage.

In Italy, the holiday season started eight days before Christmas and finished after the Feast of Epiphany, which marked the official end to the Christmas season. Aunt Gisella had a better way of putting it. *"Epifania tutte le feste porta via,"* which meant, Epiphany takes away all the festivities.

In spite of the differences, Beatrice saw many similarities between England and Italy in the celebration of Christmas. The burning of the *Ceppo,* or Yule log, was one of them.

"We will light it tonight and it will burn until New Year's Eve," Serena said. "The heat and red glow symbolizes love and prosperity. Its burning is a symbol of the year that is ending and the New Year that is beginning. In England, do you eat lentils on New Year's Day?"

"No, we don't. Do you?"

"Of course."

"Why?"

"Because the lentils look like small coins, and if you eat them on New Year's Day you will have good luck and prosperity all year long."

In Beatrice's mind, lentils were far more appetizing than the feast of salted cod. No wonder Angelo stayed away.

That night, Beatrice struggled through a few bites of the salted cod, which she felt was the supreme penitence, and buried the rest beneath her pasta and chickpeas. In spite of that, dinner was a most pleasant experience, as were all meals with the Italian side of the family. She could not help remembering those awful Christmas dinners in London, before her father died, in spite of the lavish meals they had had. Now, salt cod and all, she realized the true meaning of Christmas was not in the food but in the celebration of love and family. Something she had in abundance.

"I do believe it is getting colder," Aunt Gisella said. "Do you think we might have snow?"

"Oh, I hope so," Serena said. "If only Angelo were here, we might persuade him to take us on a ride through the snow."

"A sleigh ride?" Beatrice asked.

"If I can remember where the sleigh is stored," Uncle Tito said. "There haven't been any children interested in a ride at Villa Adriana for a long time."

"I am interested now, and I do hope it snows," Serena went on. "There are so few things to do in the cold. I don't know why Christmas comes in the middle of winter."

"I believe that is because it celebrates the birth of Christ," Uncle Tito said, and everyone laughed.

After dinner, they gathered around the nativity scene and said prayers. After Aunt Gisella placed the baby in the manger, Uncle Tito poured his best wine for everyone to enjoy.

Everyone stood by the fireplace, where the Yule log burned, when a sudden draft caused the flames to leap high. Suddenly the front door slammed, and footfalls could be heard coming down the great hall.

"Who could that be?" Uncle Tito asked with a

merry voice and a wink. He sprang to his feet and started toward the door.

He had walked only a few feet before Angelo strode through the door, windblown and stiff from the cold—the most blessed Christmas present Beatrice had ever received.

She stood back a little, while the rest of the family gathered around him, bestowing hugs and kisses. She knew she was looking at him through love's eyes, but even so, she thought Angelo had never looked so good. It took all her restraint to keep from running to him and throwing her arms around him.

"I thought you were not coming," Aunt Gisella said. "Oh, look how cold you are, you poor dear. Come over here by the fire and warm yourself."

"Well, are you late for Christmas, or early for Easter?" Serena asked.

"We must count our blessings where we find them," Aunt Gisella said, "and he hasn't missed Christmas at all."

With a hearty pat to Angelo's back, Uncle Tito said, "You are home now, and I thank the blessed Virgin for that." He poured another glass of wine and handed it to Angelo, then raised his glass in a toast. "To my son, who pleases me in all things."

"Well, make me cry," Serena said, dabbing at her eyes.

Beatrice felt her own tears warm upon her cheeks, and while his family greeted him, she quietly slipped from the gathering, and went up to her room.

Later, when someone opened her door, she pretended to be asleep. As the door closed, she opened one eye just enough to see that it was Angelo.

The next morning, Beatrice awoke to an unaccustomed brightness in her room. Throwing back the covers, she got up and hurried to the window. She opened the shutters to a world of gleaming white, and felt as if she gazed upon a magic place carved by Michelangelo from Carrera marble. Silent snow came during the night, a full eight inches of light fluff.

There is something spellbinding about snow, but stepping out into the first snowfall is like entering an enchanted forest, for there it lies, as white as scattered pearls, brilliant and strange. A few minutes after waking, bundled in her cape and mittens, she stood in snow almost to the top of her boots, not minding the cold at all, for Piedmont draped in a Christmas snow was an awesome sight.

Angelo came down the steps. "There you are. I went looking for you, and when I could not find you, I thought perhaps you had come outside. Just like a child, you had to come play in the snow." He paused and stomped the snow from his boots. *"Buon Natale, cara mia!"*

The endearment cut to the heart of her, because she did not remotely feel like his beloved, but she pretended to be in the spirit of the season and said, rather halfheartedly, "Merry Christmas."

He scooped up a handful and made a snowball, then tossed it at her. She stretched her hands over her head as she tried to catch it.

He seemed surprised when she succeeded, and was even more surprised when she threw it back at him. He ducked too late, and the snowball smacked him on the head.

Laughing now, he scrambled for more snow. "No fair. You are cheating." He scooped up another handful.

"Cheating? How?" She began backing up.

He was fashioning another snowball. "How can I look at anything else, when you are standing there?"

She gave him a smile that did not convey all the feeling she carried for him, and wondered if he would even notice.

He dropped the snowball. "What is wrong? You don't seem yourself today."

"I have a headache. Perhaps I had too much wine last night."

"I noticed you disappeared quite suddenly." He started toward her.

She crossed her arms and contented herself with watching him for a moment, then wondered if she should return to the house. She decided to prolong it for a little while, because it was so very lovely out here and it wasn't often that she had the opportunity to look at a man who looked as good as he did.

"Standing there as you are—with that hood on your head and the white fur hugging your face—you look like snow is your natural element. Are you a snow fairy?"

"I feel as if I fell asleep in one world and woke up this morning in quite a different one." She closed her eyes and began to spin around, her head tilted back to feel the full impact of the sun upon her face.

She backed into Colossus, lost her balance and fell flat on her back in the snow. As far as impressions went, this was her usual fare—the grace of a goose.

He laughed and joined her, and she felt the featherlight touch of Angelo's kiss upon her lips. It traveled through her as rapidly as a jagged flash of lightning.

A distant rumble of thunder followed when he said, "I adore you."

She could have lain here all day, freezing her backside and gazing into his face. His beautiful black eyes were mere inches away. She wanted to tell him she did not believe a word of it and that actions spoke louder than words, but she did not.

He kissed her softly. "I still adore you, even if you don't have anything to say."

Oh, but her heart did. She could hear it saying with each beat, *I love you, Angelo. I feel as if I have always loved you. It's as if you were a part of me from the beginning.* But she bade her heart to keep its secret, and she said, "I'm getting wet. I need to get up."

Taking her hands, he pulled her to her feet and began dusting the snow from her clothes. "There now. Good as new."

He took her hand. "It's time to go inside. Your beautiful face is cold as ice. Your lips are turning blue."

She turned away and started toward the house.

Catching up to her, he grabbed her by the arm. "It isn't a headache, is it?"

No, she wanted to say. *It's my heart that aches, because it feels like it's broken,* but she kept her own counsel and said nothing.

He kissed her lips, not with passion but with love and understanding. "Sweet Beatrice, I cannot offer more because I do not know what the future holds. You know that. Don't make it harder on me than it already is. You don't know how it torments me to go to bed each night in Turin, knowing you are only a few miles away, sleeping in that big bed, all alone. I don't want you to think my feelings for you have changed, for they grow stronger with each passing day. I know you don't understand what I'm doing, or why I don't come home more often, but with you and my family here, I have even more reason to be cautious.''

She heard the merry ringing of bells and turned to see one of the hands, Guido, driving a one-horse sleigh toward them. She clapped her mittened hands together with a muffled sound. ''Oh, how delightful. It is just like the sleighs we have in England.''

''It is from England.''

''You brought it here?''

''My grandfather did…years ago, when my father was a child. On a visit to England, my grandmother fell in love with the sleigh rides, so my grandfather bought it and had it shipped here. Serena and I took a few sleigh rides on it when we were children, but we never came up here that much, so it has been gathering dust for years. I had Guido clean it up a little, so I could take you for a ride.''

She walked toward the sleigh and paused a moment to stroke the nose of the horse, whose breaths were coming like the steam from a teakettle. ''After my mother died, my father took his four older daughters to live in London. Only Maresa was left behind, to grow up in Yorkshire. We went back a few times at Christmas, but as Maresa grew older and began to resemble our mother more and more, he stopped taking us there. The sleigh rides at Christmas were always one of the things I missed. That, and not knowing my sister until we were both adults.''

He came to stand behind her and wrapped her in his arms. ''Perhaps that is why the two of you are so close now.''

''That and the fact that we are the two youngest and closest in age. We were both unmarried…but, of course, now Maresa has Percy.''

"And you have me."

No, not really, she thought, for she knew the only woman who held Angelo now was Italy, and it was rather difficult to fight an entire country.

After helping her into the sleigh, he took a seat beside her and wrapped a blanket around their legs. He took up the reins and, with a nod at Guido, slapped the horse's back—and they were off with a lurch. She tried to tell herself to make the most of his time here and not cause strife. If she sent him away with things not right between them, and if something happened to him, she would always see it as her fault.

It's Christmas, and you were always good at pretending. Pretend you love him without reservation. Pretend you understand this thing that always comes between you. Pretend you believe him when he says you will one day be together.

But remember and don't be fooled—pretending doesn't make it so.

The wind was cold on her face and the air was crisp and sharp. She inhaled its freshness. "Everything seems so pure, so clean."

"If only it would last."

"Perhaps that is why we cherish it so, because it does not last," she said, and thought, *just like my time with you.*

They drove through the big gates that marked the entrance to Villa Adriana, and turned down the road that meandered through valleys and traversed the hills of Piedmont on its way to Asti and Alessandria.

After they had driven for almost an hour, he turned the sleigh around, and the bell on the horse collar tinkled merrily. "We should be getting back. Mother wants us to be punctual for dinner. You know how she is about these family gatherings.''

He must have noticed she was getting cold, for he hugged her closer and pulled the blanket higher, tucking it around her. ''Better?''

''Yes, thank you,'' she said, and gave him a hesitant smile.

''Dearest of sweethearts, how can I bear the way you look at me?''

She frowned and gazed down at her mittens, and spoke with a tone of dejection. ''You seem to be doing a good job of it so far.''

His shout of laughter startled the horse and sent a tiny avalanche of snow sliding from a branch overhead. It landed on top of him.

''Serves you right,'' she said.

He turned the sleigh through the gates, and Villa Adriana rose majestically before them.

The rest of Christmas day went by too quickly, for Beatrice knew each moment that passed brought the day of Angelo's departure closer. In a way, that was probably better. It gave her less time to fall in love with him even more than she already had.

Later that night, shortly before retiring, Angelo took Beatrice by the hand and led her from the salon. As they left, Serena called out, ''Behave like a gentleman, Angelo.''

''That comes naturally around Beatrice.''

They went into the library and stood by the fire. Angelo reached into his pocket and withdrew a small box. When he opened it, she saw inside a diamond and sapphire ring.

''This belonged to your grandmother.'' He slipped it on her finger. ''Mother was right. It fits perfectly.''

"This was Aunt Gisella's. I have seen her wear it."

"She gave it to me to give to you. It was your grandmother's and rightly it should belong to you. She said Maresa has a necklace and now you have a ring. Merry Christmas."

Beatrice looked down at the magnificent piece of jewelry. "I have never seen such a large sapphire. It is so beautiful—and to think my grandmother wore it! I shall have to find the perfect thing to wear with it."

"Perhaps these will do." He handed her another box. "This time, you open it."

Her hands were shaking but she managed to do so. "Oh my. No queen has ever had anything lovelier."

She could not take her eyes off the earrings. Diamonds and sapphires sparkled in the firelight. "They match the ring."

"Yes, and there is a necklace that my mother wants to give you, but that will come later."

With Angelo, everything came later.

She was suddenly glad she would be going to Milan to paint soon, for then she would know neither when he came home, nor when he returned to the Carbonari and his life of danger and intrigue in Turin.

For now, she would enjoy the moment. She would not think about the future, for when she did, it was always with foreboding.

Twenty-Two

January, the month of Janus, had arrived. Beatrice considered the Roman god with two faces, and thought it appropriate that she was embarking upon a new adventure in the month named for the god of beginnings, the past and future. She wondered about her future, and wished that she, like Janus, were capable of looking in opposite directions with vigilance, for she had been unable to put to rest the uneasiness and uncertainty she felt about the political situation in Italy.

Toward the end of the month, a letter came by special courier. It was from Angelo. The family gathered around Uncle Tito in the great library as he read the letter to them.

Prince Metternich succeeded in gathering an international congress at Laibach. Representatives of the European powers and Italian states attended, including King Ferdinand himself. Metternich, in his customary way, was in complete control, and quite easily managed to overcome the excessively weak Anglo-French opposition, partly because of the English decision not to attend the conference. Thus, he obtained what he sought: approval for military intervention. The worst is, the congress officially proclaimed its hostility for all revolutionary regimes.

I have received word that the British and the French protested the decision, and I pray this will encourage more resistance, but the people are slow to respond.

As I write this, Austrian troops are on their way to Naples and other parts of Italy. They intend to enter Naples and reestablish the absolute government of King Ferdinand, who has officially betrayed his people.

Uncle Tito folded the letter, and no one said a word. The grave tone of Angelo's letter had hit all of them as powerfully as a declaration of war.

And in a way, Beatrice supposed that was what it was.

"With each beat of my heart, my concerns mount," she told Serena later, as she packed for her trip to Milan. "Where is my faith? Why am I such a fretful goose?"

"You are only reacting the way we are all reacting. Like you, we are worried for Angelo and his safety. How can we help it, with all the talk of revolts and revolutions? That is why we are all anxious. But Mother said this morning that she knows Angelo has the wit to take care of himself."

"I know he does," Beatrice said. "I keep recalling Maresa telling me about Angelo and his many talents."

"You mean Angelo the lock-picking escape artist, eavesdropper and mischief-maker?" Serena asked. "Everything she said is true. He has always been a master at getting himself out of scrapes as easily as he got himself into them."

Beatrice folded the dress she was holding and placed it in her trunk. "I hope you are right."

"We must trust Angelo, and we must believe in Italy." She put her hands on her hips and surveyed the stacks of clothes. "Now, can I help you pack anything? What about these painter's smocks?"

"I think I shall put them in last."

"All right, I will start with your under-things, although I don't know why you didn't let Patricia pack for you."

"I am not taking everything, and she has no way of knowing what I want to leave here, so I thought it best to do it myself. Besides, I need something to do besides worry."

The two of them spent the rest of the afternoon sorting through Beatrice's belongings. Once they had everything organized, Beatrice agreed to let Patricia do the rest of the packing, while they went down to dinner.

They met Tito, who had just returned from Turin. His expression was grave.

"Is something wrong?" Serena asked.

"There was an uprising," he said, "at the University of Turin. The first agitations were the work of some university students, which provoked several clashes with the police. It lasted two days. Several students at the university were massacred."

Everyone looked on with horror as he removed a newspaper from his coat pocket. He opened it, and with his hands shaking, he read, "'One student named Cesare Balbo saw the police were shooting the students, and he yelled, 'Stop for God, it's the blood of our brothers!' When it was over, they arrested dozens of students, and many others, as well. Now, they have closed the university.'"

"Did you see Angelo?" Beatrice asked.

"I went by his house, but he was not there. Cesare did not know where he was. He said Angelo had left early with Nicola."

Serena crossed herself. "I pray he is safe."

She turned to Beatrice. "I'm worried about you, Beatrice. Do you think you should go to Milan?"

"Of course. I am sure it is perfectly safe. Besides, I will be painting most of the time I am there, safely tucked away in the *contessa*'s villa."

It was the middle of February when the calash that carried Beatrice to Milan arrived at the home of the *contessa*, where Beatrice would live and paint for the next few months.

Contessa Teresa Bonacossi was five years older than Beatrice. She was educated, wealthy and quite beautiful, being small of stature, with lovely brown eyes and black hair. She had been living in her home in Milan since the death of her husband, who was murdered at their country villa two years ago.

The police still had no suspects and no motive.

"I am not surprised," Teresa said, "since the police are Austrians, and my husband was a member of the Carbonari and therefore their enemy. His body was found in a pasture, where he had ridden to inspect his sheep. A few feet from his body, was the body of his dog."

Beatrice had thought she left the turmoil in Piedmont, but now she realized it was just as bad in Milan.

Although only a few leagues from Turin, Milan was the capital of the imperial province of Lombardy, and under the domination of civil and military governors, which monitored the citizens for any kind of potential dissidence in every aspect of their daily lives. As the threat of revolt increased, the censorship and surveillance tightened, for the Austrians had not forgotten that this was the city where, in 1814, Count Prina, the Napoleonic finance minister, was beaten to death with umbrellas by an irate mob.

In spite of the Austrian repression, the intelligentsia and the young aristocrats were not discouraged. To the contrary, it only served to increase their number as well as their commitment. In place of outright demonstrations, the protests took the form of fervent rhetoric at Carbonari meetings, posters secretly distributed at night and pamphlets distributed to the people.

The aristocracy in Milan was both cosmopolitan and enlightened, and it attracted the Romantics of Europe. The city itself was home to some of the brightest minds in the younger generation, which included Silvio Pellico and Federico Confalonieri.

Majestic was Beatrice's first impression of her new home. Her second impression was that the owner had to be very wealthy. Villa Bianca was a wonderful old villa built on a symmetrical plan, with a central circular hall, and loggias on all three sides that connected to terraces and the surrounding grounds. At the center of the house, the two-story circular hall with overlooking balconies was roofed by a semicircular dome.

She was not surprised to learn that a prince had once lived there.

"It is a comfortable home for me and my daughters," Teresa said when she showed Beatrice around.

During her first week in Milan, Teresa insisted Beatrice accompany her to La Scala to see Rossini's beautiful opera *Bianca e Faliero*. Beatrice had attended many operas in London and Paris, but she was completely unprepared for the social life that went on inside La Scala, for it was there that Milanese society reigned, with private boxes where they played cards and talked with friends.

The second week she was taken on a tour of the city with several stops, including the *duomo* and the Ambrosiana Library.

"It is named for the patron saint of Milan. It was where your Lord Byron took a lock of Lucrezia Borgia's hair," Teresa said.

"A lock of her hair? Why would he want that?" Beatrice asked. "It was centuries old."

"I was hoping you might know. After all, he is English."

"Lord Byron is known for being drawn to unusual women."

"Well, considering how long she has been dead, I suppose Lucrezia Borgia is definitely that."

They drove along an avenue lined with plane trees with their mottled trunks, more noticeable now that the trees were bare. They passed *piazzas* filled with statues of men striking heroic poses, empty park benches and fountains that were frozen.

They passed three nuns with their heads down, walking against a wind cold enough to have blown in from Siberia, while above the street, someone braved the chill on a small balcony to hang out laundry that was sure to freeze.

"It is far lovelier than I imagined, and quite cosmopolitan."

Teresa warned Beatrice not to be caught off guard by the loveliness of the city. "You must be careful. Austrian spies are everywhere."

As proof, she instructed her driver to take them on

a tour of the notices and proclamations fly-posted on walls and buildings. The cabriolet stopped long enough for Beatrice to read a notification by the Royal Government and signed by the viceroy's chief minister, Count Strassoldo. It warned against the rapidly developing influences of the secret society known as the Carbonari, whose members were threatened with arrest and trial for high treason. Quotes from the penal code were attached as a cruel reminder of just how far the government would go to put a stop to such influences.

It was a chilling introduction that put in perspective the kind of risks Angelo was taking in Turin. Signs of repression were everywhere, and one could not live in Milan and be removed from it. Beatrice was made more conscious of the rising political tensions in the Milanese circles the *contessa* attended.

They had started to make their way back to the villa, when they turned the corner and saw a cardinal, his arms full of papers, fighting his way up the street. When he turned the corner, the wind was so strong it tore the papers from his arms and knocked the cardinal flat on what Teresa called ''his eminence.''

She and Teresa laughed so hard that they were tempted to turn around and go back, so they could personally thank the cardinal for giving them something to laugh about on a day of such abominable weather.

The wind died away during the night, and the next morning showed signs of becoming beautiful and sunny. It was still chilly enough that Teresa and Beatrice decided not to go out. Instead, the two of them sat looking onto the sun-dappled loggia with pots full of last summer's flowers, having tea and reading the newspaper—something Teresa could not do without getting angry.

"Oh, I cannot believe this is happening. The Austrians grow bolder with each passing day. Their audacity knows no bounds. They are going to shut down the newspaper *Il Conciliatore,* and its manager—poor Silvio Pellico—is being closely watched."

Beatrice recognized that name, for she had heard Uncle Tito and Angelo make reference to the articles Angelo wrote for the paper. "Why did they close it?" Beatrice asked, imagining the noose beginning to tighten around Angelo's neck.

"Because of its liberal viewpoints. The Austrians don't want us to know anything but the propaganda they think we are foolish enough to believe."

Her first month in Milan passed quickly, and Beatrice had progressed nicely with the portrait she was doing of the *contessa* and her two young daughters. At night, she would write letters to Angelo. But she was afraid to mail them, so she locked them in her letterbox, thinking perhaps there would be a time when she could give them to him. It might be foolish of her, but it made her feel closer to him, and she saw no harm in pouring out her heart in letters she would never mail.

She knew he could not correspond with her, yet she often found herself imagining that he wrote impassioned letters and dramatically smuggled them to her, under arrogant Austrian noses.

Today, Beatrice was working in her studio, putting lids on her paints, while Teresa studied the portrait.

"I think it is a very good likeness. You are exceptionally talented. Although I am delighted to have you do my portrait, something tells me you should

be doing work on a much grander scale. When I saw
your work in Paris, I knew that by the time I was
ready to have a painting done, you would be far too
famous to bother."

"You forget a female artist does not advance on
her abilities or talent. That privilege is reserved only
for men."

"I know, and it isn't right that women artists have
been ignored from the beginning. I find it quite sad
that our own Artemisia is known more for being
raped by Agostino Tassi, and having the first rape
trial ever recorded, than for her extraordinary baroque paintings. Many still feel she should have
stayed in her place and produced children instead of
art. How can you accept such treatment?"

"How can I not? I want to paint, and the only way
I can is to accept it. I have been advised by teachers
to keep my place and paint decorative art or minia-
tures or that of a sentimental nature."

"Which you obviously did not do."

"That sort of thing only serves to make me more
determined. So, I vowed to prove myself, to prove I
was better than they were."

"You know, I would like to give a formal showing
of the portrait when you finish. Once Milan's society
sees what you can do…"

"It will make no difference. If a man wrote his
name on my paintings, they would sell for four times
the amount I can sell them for. It is the same everywhere. I showed my work at the best salons in Paris.
It does not matter. Until the status of women is elevated, women artists will be secondary."

"It is despicable."

Beatrice put her hand on Teresa's arm. "My dear
friend, I could tell you instances of women artists

being looked over and ignored that would infuriate you. Of all the injustices, the worst in my eyes is being excluded from life drawing classes, and being directed instead to paint bowls of fruit.''

"Life drawing classes? Is that what you call painting live models?''

"Live, nude models. Do you know that men are allowed to paint male and female nudes, but women are forbidden to paint even the female anatomy?''

"I had no idea.''

"So, now you know,'' Beatrice said, putting away the linseed oil. She looked at Teresa's exquisite face and saw the anger that sparked in her velvet-brown eyes. "Time is what we have in our favor. Time changes all things.''

"You are so patient.''

"You get it by having tribulation.''

A few days later, Beatrice was surprised to see the young composer Andrea Romanelli call on Teresa. She remembered Teresa had introduced her to him the night they attended the opera, but Teresa had not mentioned she knew him so well.

Beatrice was painting in the salon, so Teresa received him in the drawing room across the hall. Naturally Beatrice could not help overhearing at least part of what they said.

There were moments of conversation, bursts of laughter, the intimacy of softly spoken words, and distracting occasional silences. It was the quiet periods that Beatrice found disturbing. Much more so than if she had been in the room with them—for at least then, she would know why they were being so quiet.

The handsome composer stayed for almost two

hours, and Teresa smiled for at least four after his departure.

"I was beginning to think we should charge him for room and board," Beatrice said.

Teresa laughed and said, "Tell me you like him."

"I like him very much. Where did the two of you meet?"

"At a reception after the opera, a few weeks before you came. He has asked several times to call upon me, but I always declined."

"Why?"

"He is younger than I am."

"Posh! What difference does that make? If you like him, if you are compatible, those should be your criteria for deciding to see him or not."

Teresa sighed. "You have no idea how relieved I am to hear you say that. I needed someone to confide in. Someone who understands."

"It is obvious you like him."

"Like him? I am completely infatuated. I have never felt like this before. My dear husband, the count, was twenty years older than I. I loved him, but not in this way."

"There was no passion."

"No. He was very understanding."

"He was probably relieved."

Teresa gave her a stunned look, and laughing, they dropped to the sofa with a rustle of skirts. When they had sufficiently exhausted themselves, they decided a good laugh was exactly what both of them had needed.

"Tell me about Angelo. How did you first meet? Was it love at first sight?"

"Hardly. The first time I came to Italy, I was so reserved and quiet. He was handsome and worldly—

a man who was equally at ease riding a wildly galloping horse, dueling with a saber, dancing at the balls of the titled nobles of the oldest houses in Florence, or seducing the beautiful Florentine women in their boudoirs. He was charming, dashing and adored by every woman he met.''

"Did he manage to liberate you?''

"No, although he did come close a time or two. I began to second-guess him and his motives.''

"Oh dear, that never does help the course of true love run smooth.''

"No, it didn't, and I returned to England.''

"One of you must have changed a great deal by the time you returned.''

"We both changed, and I soon fell in love with him all over again. He has such a deep love of his country, and his passion for life is unequaled. His charisma, his devotion to his principles, his honesty, his kindness, his delightful ways…truly, he has enchanted my very soul. I think you will like him very much.''

Teresa laughed. "Of course I will! I have never met a handsome man I did not like.''

Twenty-Three

Von Schisler read the dispatch from Metternich and felt quite satisfied. Apparently the miniature he had given the prince had elevated his position, for now Metternich was asking for his help in learning more about Bartolini.

"Rest assured, Count, that if we know about what goes on in Bartolini's life, then he knows what *we* are doing. The last thing you want to do is underestimate him. At this point I do not want him jailed, but if you were to find a way to place him in enough danger that he might begin to fear for his life, it would be beneficial to our cause. I want you to find out all you can about him and his family. I want to know his weakness."

Pacing back and forth in his office, von Schisler crossed the room in three long strides, turned and spoke of Angelo to the head of his secret police in Turin, Filippo Cadornai. "Tell me what you know of him, his background."

Filippo recounted the circumstances of Angelo's unknown parentage and his adoption into the family of Tito Bartolini. "His father is quite wealthy, and although not a member of the nobility, they are a family with a long history of wealth and respectability. His mother comes from the noble house of Antonari."

"And Angelo?"

"He came to Turin shortly after he graduated from the University of Bologna, and fell in with several members of the Carbonari. One of his best friends in Bologna was a fellow student by the name of Nicola Fossa. The two of them, along with several others, developed moderately radical beliefs. Bartolini wrote many articles for the school paper—articles that were against foreign domination and portrayed Austria as a threat to national unity. Because he is wealthy, he gives generously to support Carbonari activities. We have been monitoring his mail for some time, but I suspect that he knows this and has taken precautions to communicate by other means."

"Other than that, his personal life is clean?"

"He was quite a womanizer, but that seems to have changed since his affiliation with the Carbonari. Now, he uses his considerable charm and handsome face to gain support for his cause. He is a natural-born leader, capable of moving with the same ease among the highest social classes as he does with the peasants. His brand of liberal patriotism is especially appealing to the young university students, who see him as one of their own."

The developing romance between Teresa and Andrea showed all the signs of blossoming into much more. It was so obvious they were both completely in love. Beatrice was happy for Teresa, and she liked Andrea very much, but seeing the two of them together was difficult, for it made her separation from Angelo all the more painful.

For two hours one morning, Beatrice worked on the portraits of Teresa's daughters, Angelina and Cecilia. Once they went upstairs with their nanny, she set to work on Teresa's painting. After a few minutes she threw down her brush.

"It's all wrong!"

She turned away and walked a few feet, intending to leave the room, but then she glanced at Teresa and suddenly something struck her. She went back to the painting and studied Teresa's face, then she turned back to look at Teresa.

"What is it?" Teresa asked, looking stunned.

"Something has changed. Your face is different."

"My face is different? How can that be?"

Beatrice threw up her arms. "I don't know. Something is different about your face. Your expression...it isn't the same as when we first began."

"That's impossible."

"No, it's true. You are different. Your expression... That's it! How can I say it? There is a softness that was not there before, and the eyes...they have a luminous quality that is new—almost as if you are spellbound and transported with joy."

"You make me sound like I've been possessed."

"No, not possessed, but someone has had a powerful emotional effect upon you."

"That is certainly no secret." Teresa's face colored. "Well, what is wrong with having a painting with an enraptured look?"

"You would soon grow tired of it and begin to blame the artist."

"I would never blame you, Beatrice."

"Tides turn."

"I am too much in love to pay that any mind. Do you think Andrea is handsome?"

"Yes, and I have answered these questions several times already." She picked up the paintbrush again and began painting over the areas that were not right.

"I think I truly am in love with him. I know I am, because when he is absent, I am sad. Do you feel that way about Angelo?"

"Yes, whenever I am away from him, there is a dull ache inside of me that never goes away—which means I have a bellyache all the time." She dipped the brush into yellow ochre and smeared it with a touch of raw umber.

"In that case, you will be most happy to hear what I have to tell you. Andrea's opera is being performed in Turin. He has asked me to come. I would like you to accompany me."

"As your friend, or your chaperone?"

She laughed. "As my chaperone when I am not with Andrea. As my friend when I am."

"When do you leave?"

"Day after tomorrow."

"How long do you plan to stay?"

Teresa hugged herself and spun around dreamily. "Forever…as long as it takes to produce an opera… I don't know. Darling Andrea will take a house for us in town. Sophia will follow us next week with the rest of the luggage and the girls."

"You mean we are going to *live* there?"

"Of course, at least until the opera closes, which won't be for some time."

"Hmm. I should pack my paints, then."

"Leave them here. I shall buy you new paints in Turin."

"It is no trouble to pack them. In truth, I would be lost without them."

"Then, bring them. We've plenty of room."

Beatrice could barely contain herself. She was going to live in Turin! Suddenly she realized she was becoming as dreamily infatuated as Teresa looked.

Still, she could not stop Angelo's name from reso-
nating in her mind—the sound prolonged, subtle and
filled with yearning.

Her heart hammering, she was too excited to paint.
"I'm sorry. All of this talk of going to Turin...I
cannot concentrate." She shoved the brush into a
bottle of turpentine.

"Good, for I cannot sit still another minute. We
can continue this once we are in Turin."

"The paints are still wet. They need to dry. I don't
think we should move it."

Teresa put her hands on her hips in a thoughtful
pose. "Very well. Leave it here. While we are in
Turin, you shall paint my portrait...as a gift for me
to give Andrea."

"And this one?"

"We will finish it when we return. Surely the paint
will be dry by then."

Beatrice returned Teresa's teasing smile. "That
depends on how long we stay."

"A lifetime, if need be."

"You *are* in love with him, aren't you?"

"Desperately. Passionately. I cannot live without
him."

"I think he feels the same."

"Do you?"

"Yes. I see it in his eyes...the way he gazes at
you." Beatrice glanced down, remembering a similar
look she had seen in Angelo's eyes before she began
to distance herself from him. She wished with all her
heart to have the kind of happiness and togetherness
Andrea and Teresa had, but she feared more and
more that sort of happiness would never come
her way.

"I am dying to meet your Angelo. I do hope he likes me."

"You are my friend. He will like you."

She glanced at the clock. "Goodness, look at the hour. I need to spend some time with the children. It is a good thing we called an end to this for today. I will see you at dinner."

After Teresa was gone, Beatrice began to put away her paints and go through the usual routine of cleaning up. Visions of Angelo's haunting face began to swim before her eyes. She was going to Turin. She began to wonder how she would get word to him that she was coming, for there was not enough time to have a letter delivered.

Joy coursed through her as she realized she would simply have to surprise him, which led her to wonder what he would say when he saw her. Similar thoughts occupied her consciousness for the next two days, until the morning they departed.

By then, Andrea had been in Turin over a week, and had written to Teresa that he had found the perfect villa for them in the heart of the city, with a lovely view of the river Po.

Teresa had informed her earlier that the two of them would make the journey to Turin alone, since she definitely had decided to settle into the house— which the maids had been working to prepare for three days—before the nanny arrived with the children a week later.

Now, while Teresa hugged and kissed her daughters and gave the nanny the same last-minute instructions she had given her four times previously, Beatrice settled herself comfortably in the deep seats of the calash, pulled by sleek horses with their tails braided and tied up. Beatrice stood for a moment staring absently at the well-oiled harnesses,

"Thanks be to God!" she said with a satisfied sigh. "Hopefully I can see Angelo soon, and put an end to this distance that has grown between us."

Finding herself in a restless frame of mind, Beatrice took pleasure in fidgeting and arranging herself for the journey. With her beautiful artist's hands, she opened her little black bag, took out a small pillow and placed it behind her back before she settled herself comfortably once again.

Teresa soon joined her and, like Beatrice, took great care to make herself comfortable. They exchanged only a few words. Their minds each occupied with other thoughts, they did not find any true degree of entertainment from the conversation, and soon let it die away quite naturally. Teresa fell asleep, her small hands still clutching the brown leather bag on her lap.

Beatrice found herself unable to think of much of anything save Angelo and, as a diversion, opened her little black bag again and removed a novel. She began to read, but soon found she was making no progress; she kept losing her place and having to start over. The excitement of the trip and the anticipation of being in the same city as Angelo was more than she could bear.

Teresa awoke at half past one, when the right rear wheel of the calash hit a pothole and tossed the two occupants with a violent jerk. The driver stopped and opened the door to inquire after their safety.

"We are fine, Giancarlo. A little shaken, but fine."

"*Bene, bene,*" he said, then asked about their preference for lunch.

"No, we do not wish to stop. I want to reach Turin

as early as possible. Hand down the hamper. We shall partake of a little cheese and bread while you drive.''

He retrieved the hamper and placed it on the floor between the two seats.

He was about to close the door, when Teresa said, "Wait a moment.'' She handed him a large wedge of cheese and a round of bread. "We can wait long enough for you to have something to eat.''

"Grazie, signora. Grazie,'' he said, and with a nod he took the proffered food.

They were soon on their way again, and found they could now settle comfortably into conversation, so they talked about England, about Teresa's children, and about Andrea and Angelo.

As they left Lombardy and crossed into Piedmont, Beatrice was overcome with emotion at the prospect of seeing Angelo again, and worry over the political situation and his safety.

When they arrived at the villa, Beatrice stepped out of the calash and ran up the stairs into the cool interior of the villa. She could not suppress her eagerness to embark immediately upon a quest to send word to the man she loved.

Soon the villa was filled with porters and footmen carrying trunks. Inside, the maids were working in the kitchen, and when Teresa and Beatrice entered, they saw cupboard doors flung wide open for cleaning.

Beatrice left Teresa in the kitchen to speak with the maids, and followed the porters with their trunks up the stairs and down the hall to the large corner bedroom she would occupy, next to Teresa's suite of rooms.

As soon as she gave the maid instructions for unpacking her belongings, she hastily wrote a note to Angelo and dispatched a courier to deliver it to his villa.

Throwing open the shutters of her bedroom window, she watched the courier ride down the street. Below, several gardeners were talking softly as they busied themselves with the grooming of the gardens, in spite of the chill in the air. Dear Andrea. He was so thoughtful, for truly he had taken complete care of everything, even the stocking of the kitchen.

After closing the window, she turned back to the room. Her gaze settled upon her paint box, and she tried to focus on how she would approach a new portrait of Teresa. After a few minutes she gave up. She could not think about art when her thoughts were with a dark-haired patriot.

Twenty-Four

Early that morning, Angelo had ridden into the country to exercise his horse, and he had taken Tiberius along for a little exercise, as well.

Upon his return, Cesare handed him a note.

He recognized Beatrice's writing, and after reading her tender words and knowing the love and emotion that had inspired them, he was conscious of nothing and no one save her. How was it possible that a few heartfelt words could make him forget for a while the turmoil going on around him? Not that he believed he was deserving of her affections or her love, but simply because the very thought of her made him happy.

He folded her note and put it in the desk drawer, then said to Cesare, "I am going out for a little while." He considered taking the cabriolet, but it was such a beautiful evening and not too cold, and her house was only a few blocks away, so he opted to walk instead.

As he walked, he kept thinking of the last time he had seen her at Villa Adriana, and wondered again at the change that had come over her.

He turned the corner and came face-to-face with Count von Schisler.

He could tell by the shocked expression on von Schisler's face that this was not a prearranged meeting, for the count looked as surprised as Angelo. Before von Schisler could react, Angelo looked at him with displeasure, as if vaguely recalling who he was—something he knew would infuriate the count. And he was right, for a red rage seemed to explode on von Schisler's face.

It was a good feeling, for Angelo could see his composure and self-confidence had struck like crossed sabers upon the cold confidence of his enemy.

"Count," said Angelo, "have you moved to Turin?"

"Your confidence overwhelms me as much as your impertinence, especially when one considers your not-so-secret, secret activities," he said, articulating syllables, as though each were a separate knife he was pressing into Angelo's flesh. "Are you on your way to the lodge, *buon cousine?*" He presented the question in such a way as to let Angelo know he knew of the Carbonari schedule for their meetings.

"No, but if you are on your way there, I can save you the trouble. Today's meeting was moved to tomorrow."

"Your days are numbered."

"As are yours," Angelo replied, and with a curt nod, he dismissed the Austrian count and continued on down the street, knowing he was foolish to draw attention to himself or to anger von Schisler any further.

Angelo decided he would have to postpone seeing Beatrice for a while. Instead, he went to Nicola's house and told him about von Schisler.

"You should have passed on by without saying anything to him."

"Why should I? He knows who I am, just as he knows what I do. What angers him is that he cannot find any proof."

"Why draw attention to yourself unnecessarily? Anger him, and he will find a way to get even. Remember, he does not need proof to arrest you. Have you forgotten about all the patriots they arrested when they shut down *Il Conciliatore?* They know each article you wrote for that paper, believe me. That alone gives them grounds to arrest you."

"Then, why don't they?"

"To be honest, I am surprised they haven't done so. You must exercise extreme caution from now on."

"He is capable of much, but he is not vindictive. He is too politically oriented for that, and smart enough to know it does not pay to carry a grudge in politics. He acts with harsh certainty, but he also recognizes that he is a human being and therefore fallible."

"I still say you are too well known and he will not be able to resist clamping down on you."

Angelo shrugged. "He will do what he must in order to achieve what he wants."

"And if he arrests you? He could even have you killed. Have you thought about that?"

"Of course I've thought about it. He could easily do a number of things, but I do not think he would go so far as to have me killed. Right now, he does not need a martyr, or a reason for the Piedmontese to unite in revolt. If he arrests me, it will be to make an example of me. Arrest and then clemency."

"He would never do that."

"Oh, but he would, but not at the cost of his goals and ideas. His oppression is strongest when protecting these. That is when he resorts to his system of spies and secret police and strict censorship, which enables him to control the whole country. He will not be happy until Italy sinks to the level of a Hapsburg province in the most desperate of economic straits.''

''Do you think his coming to Turin is coincidence, or does he know of our plans?''

''I doubt he knows anything specific, but I think he has his suspicions. I am certain he has his spies working around the clock to find out the degree of dissatisfaction of the Italian states. He has always been on a mission to collect data. Remember a few years back, when he had Count Diego Guicciardi and Count Tito Manzi doing the same thing, and how energetically he took measures against the dissidents they turned up?''

''I remember their going from town to town. I was not aware they were working for von Schisler until a year ago. Still, I cannot help worrying for you.''

''What will happen will happen. Worry changes nothing.''

''No, but it gives me something to do in the meantime.''

Angelo laughed and clapped Nicola on the back. ''Go find Fioriana. In the meantime, I must pay a call upon Beatrice. She is residing in Turin for a time with the countess from Milan. Perhaps we can meet for coffee at the *cafè* later. I am anxious for you to meet her.''

''I will walk part of the way with you,'' Nicola said, and the two of them started out.

They had gone no more than five blocks when they passed a narrow street. Angelo noticed out of the corner of his eye that someone was standing there, but he did not pay any attention until he saw the man reach inside his coat.

Angelo had only enough time to shove Nicola out of the way before he saw the white flash of gunfire.

A red-hot, searing pain tore across Angelo's left shoulder. He gave a slight moan and staggered.

The man disappeared down an alley.

Nicola started after him, but Angelo called him back. "Let him go. You will never catch him. He probably has a horse waiting around the corner."

Angelo was leaning against a building, holding his shoulder. Blood was running down his arm. He reached in his pocket with his other hand and withdrew a handkerchief, which he handed to Nicola to place over the bullet hole.

Nicola folded the handkerchief. "You are fortunate, my friend. The bullet hit high in the shoulder. Thankfully, it missed your heart."

"Did you see who it was?"

"I only saw the coward's back as he was running away. With that black coat, he could have been anyone. Do you think you can make it home?"

"I can make it."

"Here, lean on me." Nicola put his arm around Angelo to steady him as they walked. "We are closer to my house. I will take you there. My housekeeper will see to your wound until we can get a doctor."

Angelo could see the blood dripping from his fingers. Already he was beginning to lose strength. They reached the horses, but came up against a barricade set up in the street.

"What is this?" Angelo asked.

"I don't know," Nicola said. "They are Austrian soldiers. It looks like they are checking everyone coming and going. Perhaps they are looking for someone."

"They are probably doing it to remind us that they can do whatever they like."

"We will have to take the long way around," Nicola said. "It wouldn't look too good for us to go there with you bleeding like you are."

"I don't think I can make it that far. Take me to the convent. The nuns will care for me."

Nicola took him to the convent, but the nuns would not let Nicola stay.

"You can come back tomorrow," Sister Annamaria said to Nicola, and then shut the convent door.

When Nicola returned to see Angelo the next day, Angelo vaguely remembered arriving there the day before.

"You look much better than you did yesterday," Nicola said.

"I feel much better."

"It was a good thing we got here when we did. Sister Rosetta said you wouldn't have had any blood left if we had taken much longer. How are you feeling?"

"Weak as water."

"You are pale as a moonbeam. The sisters say you must stay here for at least a week. You must rest to regain your strength."

"I cannot stay. I must get back home."

"But not today."

Angelo smiled weakly. "No, not today. Right now, I don't think I could pull myself onto my horse. Any news about the roadblock last night?"

"The Austrians are saying it was only a routine check."

Angelo put his hand under his pillow and withdrew a sheet of paper. "I have finished the preliminary plans for the uprising. See that copies of it get to those who need it."

"You cannot rest even when you have only one good arm. Where did you get the paper, by the way?"

"Sister Maria Teresa. I appealed to her patriotic side."

Nicola laughed and put the paper in his coat. "I will see that it gets distributed."

Sister Rosetta came and announced Nicola would have to leave.

"I will come back tomorrow," he said.

Nicola had just left when Angelo remembered he had meant to ask his friend to get word to Beatrice. He hated to have her thinking he had callously ignored her note.

Angelo got out of bed, found his clothes and placed them on the chair. He was about to dress, when Sister Maria Teresa came in, took one look at the fresh blood on his bandage and said, "You cannot leave until the bleeding has stopped." She scooped up his clothes and departed with them. Sister Rosetta came in then, and gave him a serious scolding.

When Nicola arrived the next day, Angelo asked him to get a message to Beatrice. "Tell her I will come as soon as I can get out of here. I feel like a prisoner. They have taken my clothes."

Nicola laughed. "I will deliver your message. I am sure she will want to come see you."

"Tell her not to come. The sisters won't let her stay more than five minutes and, besides, it is too dangerous."

"I will tell her. Before I forget, we've got several

of our spies looking for information on your would-be assassin, but no suspects yet.''

"We may never know who it was.''

Sister Annamaria poked her head in the room. "You will have to leave now.''

"See what I mean?'' Angelo said.

"Well, at least you are safe from the Austrians.''

"Yes, for now, at least.''

Not long after Nicola left, Angelo decided he was ready to leave, with or without his clothes. He got out of bed and pulled the sheet with him.

When Sister Rosetta came into his room, he was standing beside the bed, wrapping a sheet around his naked body in a rather pitiful attempt to look like a monk.

"What do you think you are doing?''

"I have to get home.''

Sister Rosetta was almost as tall as Angelo and outweighed him by about thirty pounds. *Formidable* would have been a kind description of her. She yanked the sheet from him. "If you go, you will go as God created you. Now, back into that bed with you.''

Naked as a stalk, Angelo did as he was told, but he did grumble to the Sister's retreating back, "I should have gone to Nicola's.''

Twenty-Five

The next day, Angelo managed to convince the Sisters that he was well enough to arm wrestle, and after much pleading, a reluctant Sister Annamaria brought him his clothes.

"They have been washed and the bullet hole mended," she said, and placed them at the foot of his bed. She placed a piece of paper on the pile of clothes. "This note was in your pocket."

He wasted no time in dressing, and after giving the Sisters his gratitude and a large donation, he departed.

Captain Karl Rohan, a spy of the Austrian government, stood in the window on the upper level of a building across the street, watching Angelo Bartolini leave the convent. His expression was cold, his handsome face marred by a dueling scar that cut across one cheek.

Next to the building, in the *piazza*, two priests sat on a bench and talked, but they, too, watched Angelo Bartolini with impassive expressions, as he left the convent that afternoon.

Not far away, Filippo Cadornai walked into the building that housed Count von Schisler's office, and he passed Luigi Codazza, who was coming out.

Neither man spoke.

Filippo continued up the stairs to the second floor

and entered von Schisler's office. The secretary recognized him and said, "I will tell the Count you are here." Filippo watched the secretary leave his desk. He did not care for the secretary any more than he cared for von Schisler.

The secretary returned. "You may go in now."

Filippo walked into von Schisler's office. "You sent for me?"

"Yes, sit down."

Filippo dropped into a chair in front of von Schisler's desk. "I passed Codazza on my way in. You aren't too particular who you hire to work for you."

"I hire the man who brings me information. And speaking of information, what have you got for me?"

Filippo removed an envelope from his pocket. "The information you wanted on Bartolini. It is all in this envelope."

"Excellent. Now, I have something else for you to do."

"Involving Bartolini?"

"Yes. I am thinking a few days in jail might dampen his enthusiasm."

"He is just now recovering from a gunshot. Don't you think it would be a good idea to let him think about that threat for a while?"

"I want to worry him, and make him think about saving his hide instead of planning revolts."

"There is a revolt planned, and not just hearsay? In Turin?"

"Oh yes. It has been in the making for some time, but Bartolini has managed to put the finishing touches on it even while he recuperated in the convent."

"How did you—" He caught himself. "Of

course…Codazza. It would make sense. He is one of the Carbonari.''

Von Schisler smiled. ''A Carbonaro, but not one of the 'good cousins'. Now, back to Bartolini. He has left the convent. I want you to find him.''

''And when I do?''

''Find him and arrest him. If he is distributing his pamphlets, that is good. If he is plotting a revolt, even better.''

''I do not mean to appear disagreeable, but in my opinion, to take such action against him would only have the opposite effect. Any losses he suffered would only serve to add kindling to a fire that is already burning out of control. It would serve to make him more determined than ever.''

Ignoring Filippo's warning, von Schisler said, ''Arrest him and tell me of those closest to him. Find his Achilles' heel. I want to hit him where it will benefit us the most.''

Filippo nodded. ''It will be done as you requested.''

By the time Filippo left von Schisler's office, Angelo had hired a cab and was on his way to the address Beatrice had sent in her note.

When he arrived, the iron gates were thrown back, so he walked up the gravel drive. There he saw a gardener turning the earth around the roses with a spade, and stopped to ask, ''Are the ladies at home?''

The gardener dug the spade into the dirt, then said, ''The *contessa* is out. *Signora* Fairweather is home. If you will go to the front door, one of the servants will answer and announce you.''

Angelo took the sandy pathway that led to the house, barely taking notice of the colorful flowers being planted along the way. His mind was filled with thoughts of Beatrice and the anticipation of seeing her again.

When he knocked at the door, a maidservant answered and led him to a parlor where he could wait. "I will find the *signora,*" she said.

Before long, he heard the sound of footsteps coming quickly down the corridor. He watched the door, hungry for a glimpse of her, his face incapable of expressing the emotions he was feeling inside.

The door opened. With intense joy, he gazed at the figure of his Beatrice and slowly rose to his feet, his heart hammering out the rhythm of her name.

She had only a few moments ago returned from a short walk, and was still wearing a knitted scarf around her neck and shoulders. She entered the room with that erect bearing he had come to equate with her, and as she approached him, she moved with a swift, resolute step that was at the same time light. It was a step peculiar to her, and it distinguished her from other women of her class.

"Hello, love."

She bestowed upon him a most glorious smile that filled the room and made it brighter, like a lamp being lit. "You cannot know how pleased I am to see you. I was beginning to fear my note to you had gone astray, or you did not wish to see me. Thank you for sending your nice friend, Nicola." She glanced at his shoulder. "How do you feel?"

"Much better now that I'm away from those Sisters. They had me feeling like I was some sort of hostage. Forgive me for not getting word to you sooner."

"You are here now. That is all that matters."

"I am glad to hear you say that. Unless my memory fails me, you were rather distant the last few times I saw you.''

''I thought it best. You seemed to have so much on your mind. I did not want to add to your responsibilities.''

''You are all that matters to me.'' He went to her and put his arm around her. ''I need to touch you.''

''I am glad you came. Truly.''

''Do you not know that you are all my life? Can you not understand that I know no peace when I am away from you? I can no longer visualize us as two separate beings. I cannot think of us apart. I know this situation is difficult for you, because it is the same for me.''

''I have missed you so much,'' she said. ''More than you can imagine.'' She placed her head against his chest and thought she could remain there indefinitely while he let his hand travel up and down her spine. She put her arms around him and allowed herself to measure the width of his back, to feel the play of muscles there. She was no longer shy around him, but since their time apart, she did not feel comfortable enough to play the role of initiator.

''I have missed you, and have found it difficult to concentrate on any of the things that needed my attention. I want to take you home with me. I want to see you in my bed. I want to make love to you so much, I can think of little else,'' he whispered with his lips pressed lightly against hers.

She made no reply, but that did not stop him from thinking, *She is mine. I never knew there could be a woman like her for me, and now I have found her, and the best part is, she belongs to me as much as I belong to her.* She held within her delicate hands his future, for with her he could accomplish anything. He could not imagine life without her.

"Teresa will be home before long. I do hope you can stay until she returns. I want you to meet her. Perhaps you could stay for dinner, and you could meet Andrea, as well. Do you think you could stay?"

"I would prefer to have you all to myself. As for dinner, I think we should postpone it a bit. I took a big risk for all of you in coming here, but I had to see you."

He knew she was disappointed, but it could not be helped. He did not want to involve her and her friends in this. He wanted to prevent their names from showing up on the Austrians' roster.

She would have spoken at that moment, but he was faster. "Try to understand what I am saying, love. I want nothing more than to be with you every moment of the day, but I cannot risk your safety. Metternich has moved his head man, Count von Schisler, to Turin. I know I am being watched. For you to be seen with me would be dangerous."

He took a few steps away from her. "There can be no correspondence between us until I find a safer way to get messages to you."

A lone lamp burned in the room. It cast lengthy shadows across the parquet floor. A small desk in front of the window displayed the pretty sort of feminine knickknacks women admired. Two small frames bore the images of a man and a woman—faces Angelo did not know.

Beatrice consumed his thoughts, and he wondered how it was that this calm and quiet English woman had changed his life and filled it with dreams of a future with her at his side. She was the desire of his life, but not the only desire, and he was at a loss as to how he could explain that to her.

He stood only a few feet away from her, feeling completely absorbed in his passion for her. She was his in an emotional way that was not part of his external life—a life which was taken up with the cause of liberty and freedom. To make her part of all of that, would be to place her in the gravest danger. And yet, withholding part of his life from her was not what he wanted, either.

There was another reason, too—a reason why he could not draw her into his external life. The Carbonari played an important role in what he saw as his personal calling. His fellow members respected him and his abilities. They looked to him for leadership, something their cause for freedom in Italy lacked.

There were many followers devoted to the cause. What they lacked were leaders.

Italy, with all her faults, he must put above everything, even her, even himself.

He came back to her, wanting her to see his love for her in his eyes. "I wish I had the words to speak more clearly of my feelings and my duty. I grapple with a way to make you understand."

"Perhaps I understand more than you give me credit for. I know you love me, and I also know you love Italy—for what it is now, for what it can someday be."

"I pray you do, and that you understand what this kind of love means. I do not know the origin of my birth, but I know my heart is Italian. I would die for Italy, but I will not let Italy die because of me, because I was weak or put other things before her. I want to leave Italy better than I found her. Does any of this make sense? Can you still love me, knowing my heart must be with Italy until this is finished?''

"How could I love you if I did not understand you? How could I despise a patriot—a man who would gladly lay down his life for a country he loves and believes in? I know Italy is your life now, that the concept of what Italy can be consumes you. I remember asking Maresa's husband how Napoleon managed all that he did. Percy told me that it was because Napoleon believed in one thing and one thing only—'France before everything.'''

Taking the corners of her scarf in his hands, he drew her to him and kissed her with a quiet sort of passion born of love and understanding. "How wise of me to fall in love with you. No other woman exists that could partner me as do you. You are truly my mate in all that I do, all that I believe in. Our future is Italy."

The clock on the mantel chimed the hour. The front door opened and then closed. The sound of rapidly approaching footsteps echoed down the corridor.

"I think Teresa is home."

"And I have stayed here longer than I intended. It is so hard to leave you."

Teresa came into the room and, seeing the two of them, stopped. "Oh dear. I am sorry. I had no idea..."

Beatrice smiled warmly at her friend to put her at ease. "Angelo was just leaving, but come, you know I have been dying for you to meet him. This is Angelo Bartolini, and this is my dear friend, *Contessa* Teresa Bonacossi."

Angelo bowed. *"Contessa,"* he said, and taking her hand, he kissed it.

"I am sorry to hear about your accident. Are you feeling better?"

"Much better now that I am away from those nuns."

She smiled. "Yes, they do have a will of iron. Any word on your would-be assassin?"

"No, I am not optimistic that we will ever learn his identity. It is safe to assume he is on the payroll of Austria. That is enough. I am glad I overstayed my welcome, for it gave me the opportunity to meet you at last. Beatrice has spoken fondly of you, and I am grateful to you for bringing her to Turin with you."

"I dare not go anywhere without her. She is like a sister to me. The first time I saw her in Paris, I knew she was extraordinary."

"Then, we have something in common," he said, "for I fell the same way."

Angelo made his farewells and departed with a promise to see Beatrice as soon as possible.

"You did not tell me he was so charming or so handsome," Teresa said after he was gone.

"I think the element of surprise can be nice."

"Very nice. Do invite him to dinner. I want him to meet Andrea."

"I don't know if that will be possible. The Austrians are watching him very carefully. I would not want to do anything to implicate you or Andrea in any way."

"He is one of the liberals and a Carbonaro—both of which my husband believed in. The Austrians have known about me, and my hatred of them, for a long time. It is my deepest desire to see them crushed. I hate those Austrian bastards. Forgive me for putting it that way, but that is the only word I can find that illustrates the way I feel about them. My husband was a good man. He did not deserve to die alone in a muddy field. I hope Angelo and the others succeed in driving them back to Austria where they belong.''

''At present, it seems they can do little more than confound the Austrians' politics and frustrate their carefully laid plans. Angelo's biggest obstacle is the lack of leadership and organization.''

''The people are slow to respond.''

''I did not mean to remind you of such unpleasant things.''

''It only serves to make me more determined to do what I can to further the cause. I have been thinking of playing hostess to a political salon.''

''You must be careful, Teresa.''

''Yes, but patriotism is highly contagious. Be careful, or it will consume you, too.''

''I think one idealistic patriot in this relationship is enough.''

''There was never a patriot born who wasn't a fool about something else. It is obvious that he loves you very much.''

''I know he does, but for now, I must accept that Italy comes first.'' She began to pick at a loop of scarf yarn that was caught on her sleeve. ''There is so much to be done, and he is only one man.''

''A country's history begins in the heart of one man and it grows from the seeds he plants in the minds of others.'' Teresa came to her and gave her a hug. ''Do not worry. He will be safe, and one day you will be married and all of this will fade into the past.''

''I hope you are right—and now you had better change your clothes.''

"Goodness, look at the time. You are right. I must change. I'm glad you remembered Andrea is coming to dine with us tonight."

"How could I forget such an important occasion?"

After Teresa departed, Beatrice went to the window to see if she could catch a glimpse of Angelo. She saw him leaving through the iron gate. A moment later, he turned the corner and disappeared. She was reminded of the lonely road he traveled—one where only great men had walked before.

Twenty-Six

Angelo entered the gates of his villa, and when he reached the front door, removed the key from his pocket.

He put the key in the lock, opened the door and stepped inside.

He did not have a chance to close the door before he was tackled from behind. His hands were tied behind him, and he was pushed out the door and shoved into a calash with shuttered windows.

Once inside, he was blindfolded and shoved back against the seat. A sharp pain shot through his shoulder. "I don't suppose it would do any good to tell you I've got a bullet wound in my shoulder, seeing as how it was probably one of you who put it there."

His reply was a cold laugh.

"Where are you taking me?"

"You will know soon enough. Ask any more questions and you will be gagged, as well."

It was a rough ride through the streets of Turin, and he figured they were not taking the direct route, wherever they were going. When they stopped, he was pulled from the carriage and led up several steps, through a door and down what he supposed was a long hallway. Someone put a hand on his head and shoved him down, and then he passed through what seemed to be a low doorway.

"Circular steps, going down. Watch your step." That attempt at levity was followed by another cold laugh.

He inched his way down a circular stairwell, until someone said, "Stop."

He heard the creaking of a heavy door and felt the ropes cut from his wrists. Before he could rub the stiffness from his arms, two strong hands spread themselves across his back and shoved him through the door.

The scarf was yanked from his eyes, and he saw he was in a small cell, dark and barren of furniture. Only a tiny window high above him admitted a meager sliver of moonlight. "Where am I?"

The door creaked, then closed with a hollow *clang*. Keys rattled. He heard the turn of the lock.

The sound of the tread of boots upon stone was his last connection with something alive, but all too soon even that grew faint. He watched the light coming through the small opening in the door, but it began to grow dim, and dimmer still, to the point of almost fading completely.

Surrounded by silence, he was left to huddle in the murky darkness, a solitary being with nothing to do but fight the battles of his spirit in the obscure cell of an unknown prison.

Outside, hunched in the shadows of an old wall, a beggar pulled a bottle out of the pocket of his ragged coat and staggered up the street. He wandered around the city for several hours, digging in trash and asking those who passed by if they could spare some change.

It was past midnight when he stumbled into a

stable and found an empty stall where he could sleep. His loud snoring cut into the silence of the night.

At half-past five in the morning, a smartly dressed man in expensive riding clothes rode out of the stables on a chestnut horse with an obviously superior bloodline. As the man rode he tipped his hat to two women who crossed the street.

At five-thirty, he knocked on the door of Nicola Fossa's house.

Nicola's housekeeper answered the door. "Come in, *Signore* Mantra. I will call *Signore* Fossa."

Nicola came into the room a few minutes later. "Giuseppe, this is an early-morning surprise." He stopped and looked Giuseppe over. "My, that is a very smart riding outfit."

"A few hours ago you wouldn't have let me into your house. In any case, I have news of Angelo."

"What's happened now?"

"The Hapsburg police have arrested him."

"I was afraid of that. Where have they taken him?"

"To the Citadel."

After Giuseppe left, Nicola went to see Beatrice. It was six o'clock in the morning when Nicola arrived at the *contessa*'s. The villa was dark. He walked around to the back, where he saw a light on in the kitchen. He knocked and bid the cook a good morning.

"Forgive the early hour, but I must speak with *Signora* Fairweather."

"She is not up."

"I understand, but I would not be here at this hour if it were not important. I must speak with her about something of the gravest urgency. Would you please wake her? Tell her Nicola Fossa is here."

She stepped back and held the door open. "Please, come in. I will get you some coffee."

He saw the pot on the stove. "I'll get it."

"I will awaken the *signora*."

Nicola poured a cup of coffee. It was hot and strong—exactly what he needed. He poured a second cup for Beatrice, knowing that she would need it as much as he, and wished all the while that there was more he could do to offer her comfort than hand her a cup of hot coffee.

Several minutes passed before Beatrice rushed into the kitchen, tying the sash on her dressing gown as she did. Her eyes were bright with alarm, her face pale. "Nicola, what is wrong? What has happened? Is it Angelo? Has something happened to him?"

"He was arrested last night by the secret police." He handed her the cup of coffee. "Sit down and drink this. I don't have much to tell you at this point. I only received the information a few minutes ago."

"What have they done with him? They aren't taking him to Austria, are they?"

"No, he has been taken to the Citadel...at least, for now."

She brought one hand up to her stomach, the other to her forehead. She stared down at the floor as if searching for an answer as to how to proceed. "What can we do to help him, to get him released?"

"Angelo will probably be released after a few days. I think this is how Metternich acts when he wants to make someone an example. I will pay a call to my attorney as soon as he opens his office."

He finished the last of his coffee. "I wrestled with the idea of coming here. I did not want to alarm you, but I was afraid you would find out some other way."

"What can I do?"

"The best thing you can do is to act perfectly normal. Don't try to see him. Don't discuss it with anyone, don't change your normal routine. It is likely they are watching this house and all who come and go. If you don't act alarmed, it will reinforce the fact that Angelo has done nothing, broken no laws."

For the rest of the day, Beatrice tried to do as Nicola had said, but it was impossible. How could she act normal when the whole world seemed upside down? She worried about Angelo's family at Villa Adriana, but she did not dare try to get word to them. And truly, she did not want to worry them unnecessarily.

Oh, Angelo, she thought. *You are too much in my thoughts and in my life for me to sit idly by and wring my hands.* "How am I supposed go about a normal routine, when there is nothing normal about any of this?" she asked herself.

"Don't try to expel him from your thoughts," Teresa said. "That's just like a man to suggest such, as if we can brush aside someone we love as easily as we change our dress. My advice is to stay busy. Why don't I sit for my portrait?"

"I don't think I can paint today."

"You can always paint."

Painting was a good idea, and soon Beatrice found herself immersed in what she was doing. By three o'clock she had the preliminary sketch on the canvas and had laid the background color. When she saw Teresa put her hand to her back, she realized how long her friend had been posing. "I'm sorry I kept you so long. That's enough for today. Tomorrow I shall be more considerate."

"It's a good time to stop. I think I've got a crick

in my neck and I *know* I've got one in my back.''
She stood up and began to massage her neck. "We
have a date for the opera tonight, don't forget."

"I don't..."

"You cannot miss tonight. You do not need to be
here alone, and this is Andrea's most important night
yet. He is expecting both of us to be there. It will be
a terrible disappointment to him if you do not attend."

Teresa was right. She did not need to be alone
tonight. "I wouldn't do that to Andrea. Of course
I'm going. I shall wear blue."

"Light blue or dark?"

"Dark."

"I'm wearing red."

"You should. It is your best color."

"I'm so nervous."

"Don't be," Beatrice said. "The *Contessa di
Romigiana* is a delightful opera, and I think the music equals any of the comic operas Rossini has
done.''

"I don't say this because I care for him, but because I truly believe he is a master of the opéra
bouffe," Teresa said. "I am so happy he decided not
to do *La Mascherata.* This is definitely not the time
for opéra seria. I don't think you could cope with a
tragedy right now."

"No, a comic opera is much better, and a laugh
or two will be most welcome...for both of us." She
turned away, feeling the burn of rising tears, and buried her face in her hands. "I don't think I can do
this. My heart is breaking. I am so afraid they may
keep him incarcerated in some dark hole forever.
How can I laugh when he suffers so?"

Teresa put her arms around Beatrice. "You can

because you are a strong woman and you know that is what he would want you to do. Remember what Nicola said. They will be watching you. If you go to the opera, if you laugh, you will show them that Angelo has done nothing to cause even you, the woman who loves him, the slightest concern."

Beatrice wiped her eyes. "You are right, of course. I'm sorry for being so sensitive. I know Angelo would be the first to laugh at my behavior." *Patience and control,* she thought. "It is so hard to remain passive when I want to throw something or hit someone."

Teresa picked up a porcelain figurine of a shepherdess, dainty in her blue dress with her staff in her hand, the ribbons from her bonnet tied in a perfect bow beneath her chin. "Here, throw this."

Beatrice was so startled that she stared mutely at the figurine.

"Go ahead. Throw it. It's Austrian."

"No, I couldn't."

"Of course you can. Throw it. You will feel better."

"You're sure it's Austrian?"

Teresa nodded. "I regret to say I purchased it in Vienna, myself. Here, do us both a favor. Throw it!"

Beatrice tentatively put out her hand, and Teresa thrust the figurine toward her. She turned it upside down and read the signature on the bottom:

Friedrich von Harrach
Austria

She took a few steps to the fireplace and hurled the figurine, which shattered into a hundred dusty pieces. Exhilaration—a sudden rush of blood to her

head. The room suddenly seemed too brilliant, and
it took on a dull, white cast that seemed to turn Teresa's figure to porcelain.

"Are you all right?"

The room whirled. Teresa's face came into focus.
The brilliance faded and the room stood still. "Yes.
I feel as if everything inside me went rushing some-
place else. I felt dizzy for a moment."

"Euphoric joy! It's like too many carriages entering the intersection at the same time."

"Yes, that's exactly the way I feel. You obviously
have experienced it, too."

"Every time Andrea looks at me. You know, it
has occurred to me this very moment that you should
wear my red dress tonight."

"Don't be silly."

"It's perfect. I shall wear your blue and you will
wear my red. Flaunt it. One cannot wear anything
more confident than red. Red is the color of the mata-
dor's cape that he waves in front of the bull. I wonder
how Metternich will react when his lowly spies report to him. I can almost hear it now. *The grieving
sweetheart wore red.*"

Beatrice cringed inwardly at the thought of wearing something as conspicuous as a red ball gown,
and one with a plunging décolletage at that. On the
other hand, if she wanted to portray confident boldness, red would do it, and the thought of throwing a
challenge to Metternich fired her blood.

"Red for courage, red for love." Tonight she
would be as fierce as the color—undaunted and un-
afraid. For Angelo, she could do anything, be anyone.

"Come, we haven't much time. Andrea is sending
a cabriolet for us so we can join him an hour before

the performance. There will be a grand reception afterward.''

They climbed the stairs side by side. "Did you love opera this much before you met Andrea?"

"I've always loved it, but we did not attend very much. My husband did not enjoy it. He could not comprehend why a French opera was written by an English composer, sung by a Spanish tenor, in Italian, to a Swiss audience that could not understand."

"Although I do love opera, I can see his point. I think it is one of those things in life that one cannot dissect."

They arrived at Beatrice's room. "Come in and I will give you the blue dress."

While Teresa waited, she picked up a book Beatrice had been reading. "Ugo Foscolo? I had no idea you enjoyed reading his books."

"That is my first."

Teresa examined the book a moment longer. "I am a bit curious, though, as to why you chose this book. *Lettere di Jacopo Ortis* shows Foscolo's fiery spirit and his loathing of the Austrians."

"I am reading it to better understand the strong patriotic feelings that leave Angelo burning with enthusiasm and clamoring for reform. I want to understand the feelings that inspire his thirst for intellectual liberty and emancipation for Italy. Of course, we have patriots and patriotic feelings in England—but whose history can compare with yours? I am ashamed of England's role in the Congress of Vienna, which gave the Austrians the major share of Italy's plunder. How does Austria feel justified in forcing Italy to accept their rule and rigidly repressing Italy and her people? Now the burden falls upon the bourgeoisie to plan, to lead and to fight, for the royals and the priests are worthless—as inert as the stone columns that adorn St. Peter's.''

Teresa placed the book back on the table. ''It does appear that you have tapped the vein of the liberal and lofty ideals that motivate Angelo and others like him.''

''Angelo said unification will take years. I know that men like him are only the first to take up the banner.''

''There will always be others who follow,'' Teresa said. ''The burden rests upon the shoulders of men like Angelo, those ready to sacrifice everything in order to stir deeper feelings in those who come later. Metternich, fool that he is, does not realize that he is sewing dragon's teeth. For every patriot killed, a hundred others will rise up to take his place.''

''I must confess my woman's heart only wants this over quickly and Angelo safe,'' Beatrice said. ''I worry that he will continue until he brings about his own downfall.''

''Andrea said Angelo knows what he is doing. He said everyone calls Angelo a natural-born leader.''

''I pray that is so. I want to understand him, and stand by him, but I cannot watch him give up his life. I know him. I know his spirit. I don't want him to end up like Silvio Pellico.''

''What happened to him? I have not heard.''

''It was in the paper two days ago. They closed the paper, and he was arrested. They also accused him of Carbonarism. He was confined to the prison of St. Margaret for a time, and then he was moved to Piombi, on the Isle of San Michele in Venice.''

''That distresses me. He is such a gentle soul—a young man, guilty of nothing.''

Beatrice wrapped her arms around her waist. ''I

fear for Angelo. I want him alive. I do not want him to be glorified in death…a martyr. And yet, I cannot encourage him to do anything less, for to do so would break him." Her eyes filled with tears. "I lose either way."

"Focus on your love for one another."

"I try, but it is so difficult, with him where he is now. When shall I see him again? Will *I* see him again? Will prison bars always come between us?"

"I don't know what to say," Teresa said. "Truly, I don't."

Beatrice regained control. "I must be strong for him. I must. Hand me the red dress."

The next morning, Teresa sat for her painting until eleven o'clock. "Do you think we could stop now? Andrea is coming to take me to lunch."

"Of course. Go change your dress. That is enough for today."

Punctuality was only one of Andrea's good qualities, and at half-past eleven he arrived and was on his way to the salon, when Beatrice came down the hall, still wearing her painter's smock.

"Hello, Andrea. Teresa should be right down."

"You are not coming with us?"

"No, not today."

"I didn't come for Teresa only," Andrea said. "I want you to join us."

She looked at Andrea's kind and gentle eyes and thought him the perfect man for Teresa. "Thank you, Andrea, but I insist the two of you dine alone."

"I told her it was nonsense, but she won't listen," Teresa said as she descended the stairs in dark green silk that did wonderful things to her eyes and skin.

"Nicola said he might drop by this afternoon," Beatrice said. "He was going to see his lawyer."

After they were gone, Beatrice returned to the studio and painted wildly, as she sometimes did when her need to paint came over her in a kind of rage. Every so often it happened like that, and if she didn't pour out her heart in slashes of color, she felt she would go mad.

Later would come the time for her more tempered moments at the easel, but it was when she felt the urge to paint as one tormented—felt that she had to exorcise her demons or die—that she knew she did her best work.

Twenty-Seven

On a fine spring morning, in another part of Italy, the British poet, Lord Byron, sat at his desk composing a letter he would soon post to England.

"The affairs of this part of Italy are simplifying; the liberals have delayed till it is too late for them to do anything to the purpose. If the scoundrels of Troppau decide on a massacre (as is probable) the Barbarians will march in by one frontier, and the Neapolitans by the other. They have both asked permission of his Holiness so to do, which is equivalent to asking a man's permission to give him a kick on the a-se; if he grants it, it is a sign he can't return it.

"The worst of all is, that this devoted country will become, for the six thousandth time, since God made man in his own image, the seat of war. Here all is suspicion and terrorism, bullying, arming, and disarming; the priests scared, the people gloomy, and the merchants buying up corn to supply the armies. I am so pleased with the last piece of Italic patriotism, that I have underlined it for your remark.

"They have taken it into their heads that I am popular (which no one ever was in Italy but an opera singer, or ever will be till the resurrection of Romulus), and are trying by all kinds of petty vexations to disgust and make me retire. This I should hardly believe, it seems so absurd, if some of their priests did not avow it. They try to fix squabbles upon my servants, to involve me in scrapes (no difficult matter), and lastly they (the governing party) menace to shut *Madame* Guiccioli up in a convent. The last piece of policy springs from two motives; the one because her family are suspected of liberal principles, and the second because mine (although I do not preach them) are known, and were known when it was far less reputable to be a friend to liberty than it is now..."

Yours,
Byron

Angelo Bartolini sat on the floor of his cell and scratched the words of Tacticus, *Imperium et Libertas,* on the wall with a broken piece of nail he had worked out of the door. His hand was bleeding by the time he finished, and he tossed the piece of nail into the corner.

Empire and Liberty. The words of the ancient Roman lived on.

He worried about Beatrice, and hoped Nicola had gone to see her, to press her to remain calm and to do nothing foolish. He knew her British "take charge" nature emerged when calamity struck. He reached for his watch, and then remembered they had taken it from him, along with his money—everything in his pockets, actually—which, the jailer had assured, would be returned upon his release.

The jailer had sounded more optimistic than Angelo felt.

Angelo had undergone a long examination during the past two days, and now exhaustion and a weariness of spirit had crept over him. In the beginning, he had tried to look out the small opening in the door and the high window, but all he could see through the door were more cells like his in this dank, dark dungeon, and the tiny window overhead was but a tormenting reminder of the life that went on around him. Outside, he could hear the comings and goings of the jailers, the occasional jingle of keys or the melodious trill of a bird.

He rolled to the side, stretched out on the thin pallet and closed his eyes. It was long after midnight when he heard the *secondini*, the under-jailers, come on duty. He dozed off again, and slept until he heard the key turning in the door and a cup of coffee being placed on the floor.

The morning light coming through the narrow window was thin, but he was thankful for the assurance that he had survived another night. He drank the coffee and found he was beginning to fear that he would never be released and that the Austrians would use him as a frightening example to deter other patriots—condemning him to death or to life in some hellhole prison.

That day passed, and night brought his only relief in the form of sleep. He had no idea how long he had slept, when he was awakened by the noise of chains and keys. He opened his eyes and saw the door to his cell open.

Two men stood in the hallway—one holding the door open, the other holding a lantern aloft.

He raised his hand to shield his eyes from the brightness.

He was wondering if this was the execution squad come to fetch him, when a small, slight man, well dressed and with a noble carriage, stepped out of the shadows. Angelo recognized him as the commissioner of police.

"Come with me."

With a feeling of despair, Angelo wearily climbed to his feet and followed the commissioner through the bowels of the dungeon, up two flights of stairs and through a doorway, which, he was surprised to see, opened onto the main floor.

Outside, Angelo could see the first hint of morning light rising over the city. With a look of confusion, he glanced at the commissioner.

"You are free to go."

Angelo hesitated, wondering whether, if he took a step, he would be shot and accused of trying to escape. Then he saw Nicola coming toward him, and Angelo hurried to him.

Nicola embraced him. "I am heartily glad to see you, my friend."

"I apologize for my filthy state. I have never been half so happy to see anyone as I am to see you. How did you manage?"

"Come, let us be away from this place. I will tell you on the way to your house."

As they drove through the streets of Turin, Nicola related all that had transpired, and how his attorney had confessed it was not of his doing, but a miracle, that von Schisler had been persuaded to appear magnanimous by releasing Angelo.

"One I will pay for later, more than likely," Angelo said.

"You must be careful. You will be watched even more closely now, and if they get you a second time, it will be worse for you. I have a suspicion that the secret police feel they can learn more by watching you than by keeping you under lock and key. You must be cautious with every step you take, every word you utter. They are like vultures…waiting. Your life depends on it.''

''I'll be careful.''

''Come to my house at five o'clock. I have some new developments to tell you about.''

''Tell me now.''

''It can wait. Go see Beatrice. She is a strong woman and puts up a good front, but inside, she grieves. I am off for a turn along the river with Fioriana, whom I have much neglected these past few days.''

''Thank you, my friend. When are you two getting married?''

''In three months, if Fioriana can stand the life I lead for that long.''

The cabriolet stopped in front of Angelo's house. He embraced his friend again and climbed out. ''I will see you later. Thank you for what you have done.''

''You would have done the same for me. I will drop by later, after you have had time to rest and pay a call upon your lady.''

Teresa and Beatrice had spent the morning in the studio. The portrait was coming along nicely, partly due to Teresa's stillness while sitting—something Beatrice attributed to the state of love, which seemed to have a calming effect upon her friend.

The nanny would be arriving with the children tomorrow, and the time Teresa could spare to pose would be severely diminished.

After lunch, Teresa took a drive with Andrea, while Beatrice went to sit on the terrace with a sketchbook. She did not draw anything magnificently displayed by Mother Nature, preferring, instead, to sketch, from memory, a dozen or so images of Angelo's face.

Having been shown into the house and told Beatrice was on the terrace, Angelo approached her, his heart swelling with the delight in seeing her sitting with the full blessing of the sun. She wore a gown as yellow as a field of sunflowers, intricately embroidered with white thread, and the effect of the sun upon it, at first glance, made her appear more sun goddess than woman. She sat on a garden chair big enough for two, near a large terra-cotta pot containing a lemon tree in full bloom.

He paused in the doorway, as she picked a blossom and brought it to her nose, neither seeing nor hearing him.

She bent her golden head and stroked her face with the bloom, and the beauty of her lovely, artist's hands struck him. He stood silently, trying to absorb the gracefulness of her whole figure, her head, her neck, her hands. He was love-struck, smitten, enraptured, and each time he saw her, it was like falling in love all over again.

He walked quietly toward her and, leaning over, placed a kiss at the nape of her neck, where soft, fragrant curls lay. Almost instantly, she was in his arms, her cheeks wet with tears as she scattered kisses over his face.

"My love...my love...my love..." It was all she could say.

Angelo returned her kisses with one filled with love and longing and the agony resulting from their painful separation. "I love you, and I missed you more than I can say, darling Beatrice. My love. My life. My everything."

"I have dreamed of this moment over and again,

and now that you are here, I cannot think of anything save the need to take your face in my hands and to kiss your dear mouth.''

"Shh. Don't speak. Just let me hold you." The scent of turpentine and rosemary clung to her, his little artist, and when he picked up her hand to kiss it, he saw the traces of oil paints around her nails. "My beloved."

She turned away from him and withdrew a handkerchief. But, in spite of her efforts to be calm, her lips were quivering.

"Forgive me for surprising you this way and not sending word I was free, but I couldn't go a moment longer without seeing you," he said, softly breathing the words in Italian.

"Forgive you? Can you not see how happy I am to see you?"

"I saw the worry, the grief that gripped you," he said, not releasing her. "What were you thinking of when you held that flower?"

"You. Always you," she replied.

They sat together on the garden chair. She asked him about his imprisonment, and if he had been tortured. Had they fed him? Had they interrogated him long into the night? Had he been afraid of dying? Had he thought of her?

He answered her questions and, seeing that she grieved still, he tried to reassure her with calm tones as he told her they had only wanted to ask him a few questions. He knew that is what she wanted to hear— even though she would not believe it.

She did not say anything, and, bending her head slightly, she gave him a look of inquiry from beneath her knitted brow. For a moment, her long eyelashes distracted him, and then he watched how her hand shook as she picked another bloom from the lemon tree.

"Don't cry."

"I'm not crying. I am so angry at you."

"Why? What did I do?"

"Oh, I know you think you were strong and brave, and that all the wonderful things you have done out of your deep patriotism and love for Italy somehow justified it in the end, but I want you to know that I don't see you as brave at all. I see you as a man who has completely lost every drop of common sense. How could you be so careless and have such little regard for your own life? How could you imagine yourself a patriot, when you were only walking a fine line between bravery and stupidity, not unlike the narrow difference between genius and idiocy? You make me so angry, I want to punch you."

He could not help himself. He began to laugh. "I think I love you most when you are like this, because I know your anger is born of love. Do not fret for me. You are reason enough for any man to survive. We will be together. I promise."

"And we will invite Metternich to our wedding…"

"Don't worry. We will be together, just as I said."

"But how, Angelo? Tell me how."

She spoke in a tone that lingered somewhere between mockery and melancholy, overshadowed with a hint of hopelessness, and he realized that she was serious.

"Is there a place for us, a time when things will be normal for us?" she asked.

"Have you never heard there is a time for everything?"

"I've heard there is even a time for dying, but I don't want that. I want to live first."

"Love, don't torture yourself over this. It is done, and I am here with you."

"Yes, you are here with me for now," she said, "but what about tomorrow? What about next time?"

He kissed her because he longed to do it, and because it was the only way to shut her up.

She drew back and looked at him with disbelief. "That doesn't change anything. I am still angry."

"And I still adore you. What would you like to do with the rest of the afternoon?"

Her face colored and she lowered her head. He knew exactly what she was thinking, and could not help laughing. It was one of the things he loved about her—that inability to hide her feelings. He held her close, not in a passionate way but in a way that bespoke of love and security, of well-being and permanence. "God only knows it is what I would like to do, as well. All I think about of late is making love to you. This is a first for me, you know."

"You don't expect me to believe that, do you?"

"I meant it is the first time I have found myself wanting a woman and not having her."

"I don't want to hear any more. I only want to be with you, for as long as I can, without interruption, without Austrians, or causes, or revolutions, or any of the other things that come between us."

He knew she was thinking that if you love someone and want to spend the rest of your life with that person, it should begin now, as soon as possible.

"Have dinner with me tonight?"

"Do you think we should be seen in public?"

"*Cara,* they had me in jail. They are watching me as if stalking a lion. I think it is safe to assume they know of my presence here. I want to take you to dinner tonight in a nice restaurant, and I want you to wear your loveliest dress, so I can spend the evening looking at you."

She laid her head against his chest, and he took that for a yes.

"I will come for you at seven."

Twenty-Eight

Nicola arrived half an hour late. *"Scusa,"* he said, apologizing.

"Meglio tardi che mai," Angelo replied. Better late than never.

"I had a meeting of the Council of Bridges and Roads. It ran late, as usual."

Angelo clapped him on the back. "Sit down. You've got your hands full with friends locked up by the Austrians, a fiancée, a grandmother to check on and a job."

"You are as bad as I, now that you've fallen in love. Only difference is, I'm not a rich man and able to devote myself to the cause full time. What did you do after I left you? Have you been to see Beatrice? By the way, I meant to tell you that she had remarkable strength and reserve during all of this."

Angelo chuckled at that. "Well, if she did, she lost it the moment she saw me."

"Ah, well, we wouldn't want our women as strong as Scythian warriors, would we?" Nicola said.

"Did you stop by the lodge?" Angelo asked.

"No. I ran out of time."

"I just received a bit of news from Pinerolo. Tonight the government and its party mean to strike a blow for freedom," Angelo said. "It seems the cardinal here has orders to make several arrests immediately, and our liberal brothers are arming themselves. Patrols have been posted in the streets, ready to sound the alarm and the call to fight.''

''What do you make of it?'' Nicola asked.

''It may come to nothing, or it could be put down before it has a chance to go anywhere. Or, it could spill over to ignite the fuse here in Turin.''

''Are we ready if that happens?''

''We are ready.''

''What should we do?''

''Nothing, unless fighting occurs here. If any of our good cousins are in immediate danger of arrest, I will take any I can into my house. I've plenty of guns, and with the help of my servants, I can defend them.''

''It may come to nothing, as you said.'' Nicola sounded the chimes on his watch. ''I must go. Fioriana is waiting for me, and I want to get her safely home, just in case. Not a good night to go out, under the circumstances.''

Angelo did not tell him he was taking his lady to dinner tonight.

After Nicola left, Angelo went to see Beatrice, in hopes of arriving before she started to dress for dinner.

Andrea and Teresa were there, and planning to go out, as well, but after Angelo told them of the situation in Pinerolo, they decided to stay in.

''We can dine here,'' Teresa said, and hurried to the kitchen to make arrangements for dinner.

It turned out to be a good choice, for a fierce thunderstorm blew in. Outside, the night was black as hell, and the wind blew the rain against the windows with much noise. When dinner was done, they gathered by the fire and played Briscola, and after win-ning two games, Andrea and Angelo made their departures.

By the time he arrived back home, Angelo decided to wait up for a while, in case there was some sort of disturbance in Turin that night. It was easier to remain awake than to be roused from a deep sleep and find himself unable to think clearly. He used the time to sit in his study and read the newspaper, half expecting to hear the roll of a drum or the firing of a gun. After two hours, however, he saw only the rain pelting the window and heard only the gusts of wind coming down the chimney.

He was not overly concerned. The Carbonari were strong enough to beat back the king's troops, and many of those troops, he knew, were sympathetic to the Carbonari's cause.

At two o'clock he went to bed.

Nicola came at half past nine the next morning. Angelo was still in his apartments. "What news?" he asked, when Nicola entered.

"I don't know how accurate this is, but first reports are that the government did not issue orders for any arrests in Turin, and the uprising in Pinerolo never occurred."

"Let me dress, and we can go for coffee. Perhaps we can gather more news on the street."

"I find it a bit strange that nothing happened last night, don't you?"

"Yes, the secret police never miss a chance to arrest someone, or worse. Making an example at the expense of some poor wretch is their favorite pastime. It makes me wonder what they decided to do in lieu of the arrests."

Once he was dressed, they took the cabriolet into town. Before they reached the center of the city and

Piazza Castello, the cabriolet slowed due to a gathering throng of people. To make better time, Angelo made arrangements to meet the driver later, and then he and Nicola got out and started in the direction of the *piazza*.

"I wonder what is going on—" Nicola said. He and Angelo had the breath sucked from their lungs when they saw the horror.

Hanging from the swaying branches of a lofty chestnut tree was the body of a man.

"Gesu," Nicola said, and made the sign of the cross.

Angelo was, at first, too stunned to do more than stare, and then he got control of himself. He walked closer, stood for a moment looking into the vacant, staring eyes of the man, and then made the sign of the cross. He withdrew his pocketknife.

Nicola grabbed his hand. "I know you want to, but don't. They are watching. If you cut him down, they will hang you in his place."

"I don't care. He doesn't deserve this."

"No, and you don't deserve this, either," Nicola said, and picking up one of the iron weights used to tether horses, he confronted Angelo. "Touch him and I'll put you to sleep for two days. You have my word on it. Think of the cause, the useless sacrifice of your life. Is it worth it? The man is dead. You can do more to honor his memory and the memory of those who will follow him than simply dying. Where is the glory in that? Think of Beatrice. Doesn't she deserve more than to spend the rest of her life mourning your pointless death?"

Angelo burned with the desire to knock Nicola senseless, the Austrians be damned, but reason took over. He knew Nicola was right.

Nicola touched his arm. "We can't stay here. Let's go."

The two of them walked away, leaving the man to look out upon the *piazza* with his lifeless stare.

Later, at a meeting at the Carbonari lodge, they discussed the revolt and how support was rising, and they laid out their plan for action. They learned the man hung in the *piazza* was a patriot from Pinerolo. No one knew exactly when he was hung, but it was said that his body was there, in Piazza Castello, when dawn announced itself and rose over the Alps and the first horse-drawn carts came down the street to make early-morning deliveries.

It was said the secret police hung him in the *piazza* to serve as a warning to all who saw him—a warning as to what would happen to those who opposed the Austrian regime.

It had the opposite effect. It was only one more injustice to fire the patriotic blood of the Piedmontese.

Twenty-Nine

Angelo had been working on the motions for a new constitution, and when it was finished, he gave it to a young Piedmontese, *Conte* Santorre di Santarosa, who had been working closely with the Carbonari. Santarosa wanted to establish a constitutional monarchy under prince Carl Alberto di Savoia, heir to the throne of Sardinia.

"I have met with the prince, Charles Albert," Santarosa said. "He is sympathetic to our cause. If we can get him on the throne, he will work with us."

"I don't trust any of the Savoys," Angelo said.

Nicola agreed. "Neither do I."

"We have no choice but to trust him. The Piedmontese army is set to join the revolt if our demands are not met. Everything is set for the sixth of March, when we will petition the king."

"That is too soon," Angelo said. "We need more time. We aren't organized enough. We have no real plan of attack. We can't make demands with nothing more than a patriotic mob. We planned this for the end of April."

"It is already set. There is no going back now."

"You should have stayed with our original plan. However, I will inform the Carbonari."

"Tell them to be ready," Santarosa said. "We will go to war with Austria if it comes to that."

"We are ready to die for Italy," Angelo said, "but not to be cut down senselessly by Austrian troops. We aren't ready. We should wait. Now, I fear we will not succeed as well as the Neapolitans did, and theirs was a small victory at best."

The plan was in motion. Angelo, Nicola and a few others met with Prince Charles Albert.

The prince listened to their demands and encouraged them with words of rebellion, sympathizing with them. "You have my full support," he said.

He watched the delegation leave, and then he turned his aide. "Send for the Minister of War. I need to alert him to a conspiracy."

The revolt began on a sunny March morning in Alessandria, led by the king's own dragoons. It spread quickly to neighboring towns, and reached Turin on the morning of March eleventh. Angelo, Nicola and the other Carbonari members met them at the outskirts of the city and joined the march. The Citadel was taken after the king ordered his guards to intercede and they refused.

The city was in turmoil.

Bands of men roamed the streets. In order to avoid bloodshed, King Vittorio Emanuele abdicated in favor of his brother Charles Felix, who was in Modena. In his absence, Prince Charles Albert became Regent.

Angelo, Nicola, Santarosa and several others met with the traitorous Charles Albert who granted the new constitution. "Only on the condition that it must be approved by the king," he said.

The city was jubilant, but Angelo and Nicola remained out of the melee, preferring to observe the celebration from a block away. Angelo had been surprised at himself all day, at the lack of adrenalin and excitement he felt. He was anticipating something

other than what was happening. The Turinese celebrated a victory that was not yet theirs, for in truth,
they had gained nothing. Everything granted them
was contingent upon the approval of the new king,
Carl Felix.

"Something isn't right," Angelo said at last. "It
was too easy."

"Too easy?" Nicola repeated. "Why do you think
that?"

"I don't know why. I only know it was too easy,
and we need to be on guard. I must see Beatrice, to
warn her to keep away from the center of town until
this thing has ended—whenever that is. You should
go to Fioriana."

"Are you sure?"

"Nicola, I have never been more certain of anything in my life."

Angelo spent only an hour with Beatrice and Teresa, and gave them a briefing on what had transpired.

"I am worried about Andrea," Teresa said. "I
wish he were here."

"I will get word to him," Angelo said. "In the
meantime, stay inside. Keep your servants inside. Do
not send out for anything. Keep your shutters locked.
Do nothing to draw attention to you or this house.
There are bands of restless people out there. The king
has abdicated, and we have a traitor temporarily sitting on the throne. The new king is in Modena. The
city is a hotbed of lawlessness. It's like a powder keg
waiting to be lit."

"Do you think they will come here?"

"We have no way of knowing. Anything is possible when you have a large number of people gathered, and nothing to tell them. They think they have

won a victory, but it does not feel like a victory. Not even those celebrating in the *piazzas* are doing so with any jubilation. It's as if they all know they are sitting on a volcano that is about to erupt.''

''Bu, I thought you had this all planned,'' Beatrice said.

''We did, but the military got anxious and started everything before we had our plans well laid.''

''I think I will go upstairs and get things organized,'' Teresa said, and excused herself, giving Angelo a few precious minutes alone with Beatrice.

''I wish I could ask you not to go, and that you would listen to me for once,'' she said.

He put a finger against her lips. ''I don't want to waste what little time we have together talking.'' He wrapped her in his arms, and she pressed urgently against him. His mouth covered hers with a kiss, but he did not feel he was kissing her. It was more like being swept down a river by a raging current, and he was filled both with exhilaration and anticipation, while in the background resided the dreaded fear of drowning.

He broke the kiss but did not let her go. ''My love, my love, my only love. Why does Italy keep coming between us? I have to go, but I want to remain here, with you.''

She pulled away then, and lifted his hand to her lips and kissed it. ''Go on. They will need your level head. Everything at its appointed hour, as the scripture says. This is the time for Italy. We shall have to wait for ours. Be careful. I love you.''

He kissed her quickly. ''I will be careful, and don't forget what I told you. I love you.''

''I can hear Teresa and the servants closing the shutters upstairs now.''

Angelo left and went to Andrea's. Thankfully Andrea was at home, hunched over his piano and picking out the notes of a new composition.

Angelo walked into the room. "I swear you could miss a cannon going off in your own backyard. Have you had no word of the trouble that is brewing?"

"I thought it was all settled, that Carl Albert gave in to all the demands," Andrea said.

"Carl Albert is a fool, and has no more power than I do," Angelo said. "The minute Carl Felix gets word of this, he will send Albert running with his tail tucked between his legs."

When Angelo finished giving Andrea the update, he said, "I think you should lock up your house and secure all the shutters, then go to Teresa's. The women will be frightened if there is gunplay."

Andrea said, "I will go to Teresa's straightaway. I will take my male servants with me. We can defend the villa, if need be."

"I pray it won't come to that. Take care of my lady."

"I will, and take care of yourself."

On the sixteenth of March, new developments were taking place in Modena, after the arrival of Carl Albert's ambassador, who delivered news of the situation in Turin to the new king. Carl Felix immediately assumed power.

"I hereby declare Carl Albert's rule illegitimate," he said, "and you, *Signore Ambasciatore,* can run as fast as your short little legs will carry you back to Turin with a message to Carl Albert to abandon the throne, or face the consequences."

The ambassador hurried away, believing every word Carl Felix had said.

In Turin, Santarosa assumed the role of Minister of War, and, shortly after that, Carl Albert, receiving the news his uncle had sent via the ambassador, fled to Novara with a faithful contingent.

"It looks bad for Santarosa," Angelo said. "The king will not tolerate him now that he has been named Minister of War."

"Should we warn him?" Nicola asked.

"I will go," Angelo said.

Angelo found Santarosa and tried to convince him to leave the city. "If you remain, your life is in danger."

"There is no danger. I know we can rally the people behind us to go to war against the Austrians."

"They might rally, but they will bolt at the sight of the first Austrian dragoon. Get out now, before it's too late. Go to France, or Switzerland—anywhere, as long as you are out of Italy. They won't let you get away with this, Santarosa. Believe what I say."

In truth, it did not even take the Austrian dragoons to put an end to the revolt in Turin, for things began to fall apart shortly after Carl Albert abandoned the throne and fled to Novara.

Angelo went to Teresa's and found everyone there, anxious to hear what was happening. "The news isn't good. The revolt will fail. It is as good as over," he said.

"But why?" Teresa asked. "What happened? What caused it to fail?"

"There are a lot of reasons, not one weighty alone, but when you put them all together they are enough to topple the hopes and dreams of the people," Angelo said. "Carl Albert's actions were a contributing factor, not to mention that the Church gave aid to the Austrians against us.''

"The Church turned against its own people?" Beatrice asked. "How can it?"

"The Church serves itself," Nicola said.

"Tell us more," Teresa said.

"The revolt was too soon, before we were completely organized," Angelo said. "Too many different groups tried to participate and lead, without any true sense of direction."

"Everyone wants independence," Nicola said, "but they want someone else to carry the burden. At the first sign of trouble, they abandoned the cause."

"At least the peasants were honest about their reluctance to fight. They said they preferred bread to freedom."

On April second, the Austrian troops were returning from restoring King Ferdinand to the throne in Naples, when they received a call for help from the new King of Sardinia, Carl Felix. When Metternich heard Carl Felix had asked for the Austrians to intervene, he was only too happy to send the Imperial troops to the aid of Piedmont.

Angelo went out the next morning, and when he returned he reported to those still gathered at Teresa's. "Carl Felix has signed an edict declaring that all soldiers who participated in the revolution are declared traitors, and that severe repressions are officially enacted."

Three days later, courts were convened, and the first sentences of death by hanging were to be carried out on June the nineteenth. The official end to the revolt came on April eighth, when the Austrians put down the last remnant of the Piedmontese revolutionaries at Novara—the same way they had done in Naples.

Conte Santorre di Santarosa knew his days were numbered, and he fled into exile. All of his assets were confiscated.

Like Lord Byron, he died fighting for Greek independence four years later.

Thirty

Beatrice was sitting in the morning room, having her coffee as she read the account of the uprising in the Turin newspaper, *Gazzetta Piedmontese*. She had not seen Angelo in two days, although Andrea had said Angelo had gotten word to him that he was safe.

Teresa walked in and sat down while her coffee was served. "Anything new we haven't heard about?"

"Carl Felix has returned to Turin. Death sentences have been issued."

"I suppose it is finished," Teresa said. "I shouldn't be surprised. Angelo said they were doomed to fail before they started. You know, of all the reasons I heard him give, it was what he said two days ago that really hit me."

"What was that?"

"I don't think you were in the room when he told Andrea that one reason for their failure was that they were isolated from the rest of the population." Teresa rubbed her arms. "Even now, it gives me chills."

"I don't understand," Beatrice said. "What do you mean 'isolated from the rest of the population'?"

"I asked Angelo the same question. He said we cannot drive the Austrians out of Italy with just the aristocratic and educated liberals. He said we need the common people, the bourgeoisie, but they simply are not prepared or inspired for revolt. They were involved only marginally, and most of them were completely indifferent. One peasant farmer was quoted as saying 'I don't care who rules us, as long as we eat.'"

"There will be even more severe repercussions than those the king enacted," Beatrice said. "The Austrians are coming, and they will not let us off lightly."

Teresa nodded. "Andrea said there was already talk that almost all public rights which free men prize are banned. Newspapers will be forbidden. The printing presses are to be shackled. Freedom of speech will be a crime, and those guilty of it will meet instant punishment."

"So, what it amounts to is, if you are educated, outspoken and believe in independence or freedom of opinions and views, you will be suspect."

"Precisely," Teresa said.

"That is incorrigible. No one can live under such tyranny."

Teresa sighed. "Italy can. We have been conquered, sacked, ruled, overrun, occupied, subjugated, dominated, controlled, defeated, liberated and reconquered so many times—most of us are beginning to feel as does that peasant farmer."

"And yet, in spite of all the warfare, terror, murder, bloodshed and conquering, you have produced Michelangelo, Leonardo and the Renaissance."

Teresa smiled wanly. "You always have another way of looking at things."

"I like to remind myself that a hundred years from now, none of this will matter."

"You sit there with the greatest sangfroid," Teresa said. "How can you be so calm under such pressure? If I had not seen Andrea in two days, I would be having a screaming fit."

"No, you wouldn't, because Angelina and Cecilia would start crying. And speaking of your darling daughters, here they come in their matching dressing gowns."

Angelina clambered into her mother's lap and Cecilia climbed into Beatrice's. All talk of revolts and uprisings was put away in preference for more pleasant things, but thoughts of Angelo never completely left Beatrice's mind.

Shortly after midnight that same night, Beatrice was awakened and told Angelo waited for her downstairs.

In minutes, she was out of bed and rushing down the stairs as she struggled into her dressing gown. She stopped for a moment to take in the sight of him, looking better than she could remember in a long, double-breasted redingote that flared below the waist.

But he looked tired.

She hurried to him, needing his nearness, his warmth and the assurance of his loving arms. Warm, solid, comforting, loyal, devoted. He was all of these things and more. Kisses, not words, seemed to express what they both felt, and it was some time before either of them said anything.

At last she pulled away. "You are going away, aren't you."

"The Hapsburgs have two guards posted at my front door, and in case you haven't read today's paper, my name is on the list of political suspects wanted for questioning, which is a polite way of saying 'imprisonment.'"

"Oh, Angelo, what are we going to do?"

He brushed his lips across her forehead. "*Amore mio, we* aren't going to do anything. I must go away for a while. They are trying to stop us from the top down. If they get rid of the liberals, the thinkers, the motivators, the planners, the instigators, they have stopped us. I will stay away until it is time to regroup and try again."

"Where? Where will you go?"

"Switzerland or France."

"I'm coming with you."

"No, you aren't."

"Then, I shall follow you every step of the way."

"Sweet love, I cannot take you with me. If I am caught, you will be imprisoned along with me."

"They wouldn't imprison a woman."

"Never underestimate the Hapsburgs. They are beating women in the *piazza* and forcing them to watch the killing of their loved ones."

"And you think I am going to wait around for that? When are we leaving?"

"Nicola is coming here shortly with the arrangements. I must be out of Turin well before daylight."

A servant made his excuses, and announced, "*Signore* Fossa has arrived."

"Show him in please," Beatrice replied.

Nicola entered the room. Teresa, who, like Beatrice, was wearing her dressing gown, followed him.

"What have I missed?" she asked.

Beatrice said, "They are after Angelo. He is going into exile."

"Oh *Gesu,*" Teresa said, and made the sign of the cross.

"What would I do without you, Nicola?" Angelo said, rising to greet his friend.

"We have problems," Nicola said. "Earthquake-size."

"What kind of problems?"

Nicola removed a Hapsburg poster from his vest pocket and handed it to Angelo. Angelo skimmed the page and stopped.

"Beatrice? For the love of God, why is her name on this list?"

"I wondered about that myself," Nicola said, "especially when one considers *my* name isn't on the list, and I'm seen with you much more in public than she is."

"They're using her as a pawn," Teresa said. "They found the weakest link in your chain, Angelo, and they are going to yank it until you are no longer a threat to them."

"Of course," Nicola agreed. "What better way to get a man than by using the woman he loves. The question is, what are we going to do? I could try getting her to your family at Villa Adriana."

"No, I don't want to involve Aunt Gisella and Uncle Tito in any of this," Beatrice said.

"They will look for us at Villa Adriana and Villa Mirandola," Angelo said. "You can count on it."

"This is my problem," Beatrice said. "I will solve it. I suppose a return to England is out of the question."

"It is *our* problem," Angelo said, "and we will solve it together. Returning to England isn't the answer. To consider such would be to grossly underestimate the secret police. It is the first thing they would suspect. They would pick you up before you got within twenty leagues of a seaport."

"Perhaps I could go to France or Switzerland, and

go to England from there." Beatrice studied Angelo's face, waiting for his reaction.

"We don't have time to decide right now, and a hasty decision could be a regretful one. There is nothing else to do. You will have to come with me. Once we are safely away from here, we can decide the best way to get you out of the country."

"I think going with Angelo is best," Teresa said, and gave Beatrice's hand a squeeze.

"You will not be able to bring anything with you other than a change of clothes," Angelo said. "I am sorry, but we must travel by horseback, fast and light."

"I've got our horses tied in the trees," Nicola said. "Beatrice can have my horse."

"There is no need for that," Teresa said. "She can have one of the horses in the stable."

"Go upstairs and gather a change of clothes, while Nicola and I saddle a horse for you," Angelo said. "You do know how to ride, don't you?"

"Of course."

"You are in love with her, and you do not know if she can ride a horse?" Teresa asked in amazement.

"The topic never came up," Angelo said, and everyone laughed.

Beatrice left the room smiling. A little humor was a good beginning for a journey into the unknown. Heaven only knew when they might have something to laugh at again.

Before she reached the stairs, the sporadic sound of gunfire rang out. She whirled around and ran to the window. By the time she reached it, Angelo and Nicola were peering through the shutters.

"What is it?" Teresa asked, standing on her toes behind them and trying to see.

"Someone has been shot. He is lying in the street," Nicola said.

Beatrice found a place to look out, and saw the man lying there, about three hundred paces from the front door.

"Can you see who it is?" Teresa asked.

"It's awfully dark," Beatrice said.

"I would bet you fifty *scudi* he is Austrian," Nicola said.

"Who would have shot him?" Teresa asked.

"Any number of ten thousand people," Nicola replied. "There have been groups wandering all over the city."

"No matter who he is, we cannot leave him out there to bleed to death," Beatrice said.

"No, we can't," Angelo said. "I suppose the poor bastard deserves better than that, although I doubt he would offer the same consideration toward any of us."

"I will go after him," Nicola said.

"You can't go alone," Angelo said.

"Someone might see you," Teresa said.

"We'll have to take that chance" was Angelo's reply.

Several servants came hurrying into the room at that moment, and Teresa directed two of the men to bring the wounded soldier into the house. They went out, and grasping the man under the arms, they dragged him toward the house and through the door.

By the time they had him inside, all the other servants were up, and scampering to and fro in readiness, as Teresa told them what to do.

Nicola stood looking down at the man. "It is Filippo Cardonai."

"Who is that?" Beatrice asked.

"The head of the Hapsburg police here in Turin."

"Shall I send for a doctor?" Teresa asked.

"He won't be needing a doctor," Angelo said, examining him. "He's got three nicely placed bullet holes in his chest. It's my guess that one of them went through his heart. At any rate, he is stone dead."

"*Madonna mia!*" Teresa said, and turned to one of the male servants. "Hurry to Dr. Romanelli's and tell him I need him here as soon as possible."

"No, don't send for the doctor," Angelo said.

They all stood around staring at the dead man, no one seeming to know what to do. The servants were wringing their hands and whimpering "Santa Maria, Madonna, and Oh *Gesu*," as well as an assortment of saints' names.

"I suppose we will have to become accustomed to this sort of thing," Teresa said, "for I think we will be seeing a lot of it from now on."

Not wanting to stare at the dead man any longer, Beatrice covered his face with her shawl and excused herself to pack a change of clothes.

It did not take long to have everything ready, and she carried her belongings—including her sketch pad and charcoal—downstairs. When she rejoined the others in the salon, everything was much as it had been before.

"Are you certain I shouldn't send for the doctor?" Teresa asked. "I know the man is dead, but perhaps the doctor will know what to do. I am at a loss. I can't very well toss him into the street, but neither do I relish having him bleeding on my rug for the rest of the day."

"Send for the doctor," Angelo said. "We'll slip away in the meantime. It is black as a lump of coal out there, and there's lots of confusion still. It could prove to be a good distraction.''

Teresa sent a servant with instructions to bring Dr. Romanelli. ''And tell him an Austrian has been shot. That should put a little kindling in his fire.''

''Shouldn't you call a priest, as well?'' Beatrice asked.

''Of course I should. I only hope I have enough servants to go around,'' Teresa said as she dispatched another one to fetch Father Ignatius.

Angelo handed Beatrice a pistol.

''I don't need that.''

''You might. Do you know how to shoot?''

''Yes, I've hunted before, but I've never shot a person.''

''There isn't much difference,'' he said. ''Either way, you aim and pull the trigger.''

Beatrice handed the gun back to him. ''I don't think I could shoot a person,'' she said.

He pushed the gun back toward her. ''You could if they were going to kill you.''

She dropped the pistol into the deep pocket of her cape.

Then, in the midst of all the confusion, Beatrice and Angelo slipped quietly away.

Thirty-One

The lilac bushes were in flower and their scent filled the night air with a sweet fragrance, as Beatrice and Angelo rode out the gates and disappeared down the street, covered by the blanket of early-morning darkness.

The air was cool, and they would be riding north into the Italian Alps, so Beatrice had her warmest cape thrown over her shoulders. Next to her, Angelo still wore his long black coat.

They kept to the side streets where there were few lampposts, and crossed the river Po. Once they were away from the city, they would ride toward St. Vincent, keeping to the valleys and following the fast-flowing Dora Baltea River.

They did not make it that far.

They had barely crossed the river, when they heard the thundering report of hoofbeats coming across the bridge behind them, moving at a fast pace.

Angelo turned in the saddle and looked behind them. A second later, he shouted, "Ride!"

Beatrice dug her heels into the sides of her horse, and the gelding leaped forward.

She could see Angelo racing along beside her. She had no clue who was behind them—whether it was the king's dragoons, the Hapsburg secret police or the Austrian Imperial troops. Not that it mattered, for any of them were capable of killing.

She had no idea where they were going or even where this road led, but Angelo seemed to know, and she trusted him.

She heard the *crack* of rifle fire and felt the bullet whiz between them. "Get off the road," Angelo shouted. "Head for those trees."

She jerked the reins to the right, and the gelding left the road. They went flying over some farmer's plowed field, the horse tearing out great clods of dirt that flew behind them.

She heard another shot and another, and when she looked, she couldn't see Angelo. Suddenly she was terrified.

Oh God, what if they had killed him?

Don't think that, she told herself. *Have more faith in him than that. Keep your mind on what he told you. Head for the trees. He will find you. Head for the trees.*

The trees weren't far away now. She could still hear gunshots behind her. Angelo was nowhere in sight.

She ducked under a low tree branch just in time, and felt a burn in her scalp when a good-size piece of her hair caught and was torn out. She could feel blood running over her ear, and wondered if she had been scalped. But she could still feel her hair billowing out behind her, and she felt no pain.

The trees were growing denser now, and she slowed her horse to a walk. The animal was winded and breathing heavily, and she could feel his sides heaving. She could not hear anything—not gunshots, not shouts, not even the sound of a horse running.

She prayed earnestly that they had not captured Angelo.

After riding for some time and still hearing no sounds, she decided to stop. She had no idea where she was or where she was going. She thought about dismounting, but feared the horse might run away, so she rode beneath a large tree and eased the horse close to the trunk, then waited.

It was a still night, and the earlier clouds had all but disappeared, leaving a full moon floating in the blackness overhead.

Suddenly, she saw the horse's ears prick forward, and he snorted and shook his head. She listened, and could just make out the muffled sound of a horse approaching at a walk.

She wanted to call out, but that could bring the enemy. If it was safe to call out, she knew Angelo would have called her name by now.

She stroked the horse's neck to calm him, and searched the darkness ahead. She saw a horse and rider come into the clearing and was about to say *Angelo, over here,* when she saw the gleam of a helmet and recognized the uniform of an Austrian lancer.

Her heart began to pound. She did not know if he had seen her, and prayed her horse would not give her away. The lancer came closer, and then he stopped and looked straight at her, and she knew she had been spotted.

Slowly, she eased her hand into the pocket of her cape and withdrew the pistol Angelo had given her.

She kept the gun close to the horse's neck, half hidden in the black mane. When the lancer was no more than three feet away, she heard the *swish* of his sword as it left the scabbard.

"Tonight we take no prisoners," he said, and holding the saber in a charge position, he kicked his horse.

Beatrice aimed the gun and fired.

Blinding smoke rose up in front of her, at the same instant her horse bolted.

They hadn't gone far before she brought him under control and slowed him to a trot. She knew the gunshot was likely to bring the other soldiers, and she had to save her horse in case they needed to flee. She had no idea if she had killed the lancer, or if she had even come close to hitting him, but at least there was no one behind her—she was relieved that something was going her way at last.

She saw another rider coming across the field toward her, and wondered if the gun Angelo had given her had more than one shot.

She decided there was one way to find out. Pulling her horse to a stop, she readied the pistol.

"Don't shoot," Angelo said.

Relief washed over her, and she was so overcome with emotion, everything in her head seemed to shut down. She couldn't say a word, and had no idea if she should stay on her horse, dismount or just sit there and cry.

Before she could decide, he rode up beside her and dismounted. A second later, he pulled her from her horse and into his arms.

"My little English grenadier," he said, and kissed the top of her head.

He looked at the blood on his hand.

"You're bleeding."

"It's nothing. I caught my hair on a branch— I shot a man," she added, "or, at least, I shot *at* one. I don't know if I hit him or not."

"Oh, you hit him, all right."

"You saw me?"

"No, but I found the evidence."

"He isn't dead, is he?"

"Quite dead, with a bullet through the heart."

"Oh God, I didn't mean it."

"Shh. His saber was drawn. He would have cut you down. You didn't have a choice. I'm sorry I wasn't there. I tried to draw them away from you. I guess our friend must have seen you get away."

"I'm just glad we made it. Do you think they are gone?"

"They will realize I tricked them and they will be back. We need to be well away from here before sunup. Can you ride?"

"I can, if you can."

He chuckled. "Let's be off, then."

He helped her mount, and once again, they turned their horses toward the Alps.

The sunrise was accompanied by clouds, which the sun seemed content to slip in and out of, until it banished the clouds altogether and blessed those below with a beautiful spring day. Beyond, the ragged peaks of the Alps rose like sharp teeth, their prominent peaks often wreathed in the white mists that lurked there throughout the day.

The Dora Baltea River flowed from the slopes of Monte Bianco and ran along a deep furrow between the mountains, into a narrow valley about a mile wide. It was not a meandering river, but a violent flow born of melting snow and ice glaciers that rushed through chasms and flowed into the Aosta Valley in a thundering torrent of pale blue that foamed and swirled on its way to join the Po.

They rode with the river on their right, passing into

the higher altitudes, which provided homes to wonderful little creatures, like marmots and ermine, Beatrice was wholly unfamiliar with. And when they reached the Alpine pasturelands, the sight of a rather confident Steinbock, with his long, curved horns, captivated her, as he scampered over the steep mountainside.

"It is so beautiful here. I had no idea the Alps were so magnificent."

"Magnificent, treacherous, and in use since ancient times. It was through these passes that Napoleon first entered Italy when he made his famous march through the St. Bernard Pass and entered the Po Valley."

"I remember that story. The Italians held him off."

"At the Fortress of Bard. It dominates the narrowest point in the valley, and when Napoleon invaded, the defenders fought so strongly, they held the French there for fifteen days. The French were victorious in the end, but Napoleon was so angered, he ordered the fortress torn down before he continued on."

"To defeat the Austrians at the Battle of Marengo."

"You have been reading Italian history."

"We English fought Napoleon, too, if you will recollect."

Neither of them spoke for some time, until Angelo said, "There were only two generals besides Napoleon who made this crossing—Charlemagne and Hannibal."

"Hannibal and his elephants," she mused. "It seems far superior to Napoleon's crossing on a donkey, although the paintings depicting the scene have him on a magnificent white horse.''

"You have seen the paintings?''

"Yes, in Paris.''

Once an old Roman outpost, the Aosta Valley was an area of small hamlets and feudal castles that had been there for centuries—since the earliest travelers had used the Mont Cenis and Mont Genèvre passes through the Alps—and consequently had influenced greatly not only the history of the Piedmontese, but their culture.

Because the area was a route through the Alps into Italy from Switzerland and France, the tiny valley was for many years under the rule of France. Throughout history it had been a place of frequent conquests and battles, which explained why there were so many castles, strongholds and watchtowers in the area.

Now it was mostly mountain people and shepherds, clinging to their old traditions, who lived in the sparsely populated valley. Although part of Italy for many years now, most of the inhabitants still spoke the French language and retained their French surnames.

Consequently, it did not surprise Beatrice when they came upon a French-speaking shepherd moving his herd. She was surprised, however, to discover that Angelo spoke enough French to inquire about the best route to take over the Alps.

"That depends,'' the man said. "Take St. Bernard or Mont Cenis if you don't mind the Austrians.''

"And if we do?''

"Then, I would go back where I came from, because the Austrians control all the passes and they are looking for Piedmontese revolutionaries escaping into France and Switzerland.''

"Thank you, good friend, for that bit of information.''

The man nodded. ''If you need a place to abide for a while, there is an abandoned castle not far from St. Vincent. Castello di Fenis, it is called.''

They rode on, and after a while came to St. Vincent, tucked among the Mount Zerbion foothills. They stopped there long enough to get something to eat at a small inn, while the hostler fed the horses.

After they'd left the inn, Angelo stopped an old man driving a small wooden cart and asked for directions to Fenis Castle. Beatrice knew Angelo had not asked at the inn as a precaution, for they had no way of knowing if any of the other travelers present were Austrian sympathizers.

The man told them to continue on up the road, which they did. They followed the river for several miles, until they came to a bridge and crossed over. From there, the road was nothing more than a cart trail, and even this eventually gave way to a weeded path used by sheep. The path led up a hill to the castle.

There it stood—Fenis Castle, golden in the afternoon sun, as if proclaiming its resistance to the harsh weather of the valley, with its solid, rectangular towers thrusting heavenward. From the moment Beatrice first caught a glimpse of it she was captivated, and found it remarkable that she, being from a country where castles flourished, would be impressed with this tiny medieval jewel.

As they drew near, she could see the sculpted apotropaic heads projecting from the walls, as if announcing their intent to ward off evil and bad luck.

"Loopholes," she said, pointing toward towers with narrow slits for shooting arrows. "They are corbeled, and when under siege, the inhabitants would hurl down all manner of projectiles through the embrasures—at least, that's what they did in England."

"It was the same here," he said.

She caught the way he was looking at her. She felt a shy blush warm her face. "I don't know why I am telling you this. I suppose you learned it all when you were younger."

"My interests lay more in the direction of charming girls than in learning the ancient art of castle warfare."

Amused, she turned back to look at the castle. Obviously built for warfare, for it possessed all the defensive apparatus of a stronghold—surrounded by a double line of curtain walls, with watchtowers connected by battlements and parapets. "This is every child's image of a fairy tale castle."

"And now it has you for a fairy tale princess."

They dismounted and led their horses through a gateway surmounted by a barbican and defended by a portcullis that led to the inner ward.

"It must have been quite princely at one time," Beatrice said, and that much was true, for it possessed a quaint and picturesque courtyard with a semicircular stairway and wooden loggia.

"Hello," Angelo called out as they entered the castle.

"It does not look as if anyone has been here for a long time," Beatrice said.

In the courtyard and many of the interior rooms, they found magnificent and remarkably well-preserved frescoes. "Some of these look to be the work of Giacomo Jaquerio, or at least inspired by his

work, which would date them in the early fourteen
hundreds.''

"How do you know that?''

"I once went with Andrea and Teresa to Saluzzo,
and we visited Castello della Manta. The cycle of
frescoes there are ranked among the most beautiful
of the gothic style of the European court. The frescoes there are of nine heroes and nine heroines
dressed in the fashion of the Court of France in the
fifteenth century. They resemble these a great deal.''

The stables were quite dilapidated, but Angelo
managed to secure them enough to unsaddle the
horses. Sadly, the castle was not in much better
shape. It must have been abandoned for some time,
for the courtyard was now invaded with weeds, and
the chapel was strewn with moldy hay.

Once they entered the central residential block,
which was shaped like an irregular pentagon, Angelo
took her hand and the two of them went from room
to room, like children in search of a hidden treasure.

Most of the furniture was long removed, but there
were a few three-legged tables and wobbly chairs,
which would suffice, since their needs were simple
and this was not a permanent home.

"How long do you think we will be here?''

"You won't be here long. I shall try to arrange
passage for you to France or Switzerland as soon as
possible. It won't be safe for you to return to Turin,
at least for the time being.''

They found the kitchen, with a huge fireplace and
even a few battered utensils. "I will find a farmhouse
and see if I can purchase something for us to eat.''

"I will look for firewood while you are gone.''

"Be careful. After years of abandonment and neglect, I would not place too much trust in all the wood stairs and such.''

"I will exercise extreme caution,'' she said, and lifting her skirts, she demonstrated, by tiptoeing across the kitchen.

He came from behind and grabbed her, then began to spin her around the room, with her shrieking and laughing. Then he stopped and kissed her soundly. "If I didn't know we were both in need of food, I would forgo dinner and make love to you, instead. How about the kitchen table?''

"Oh my,'' she said, suddenly realizing that the two of them sleeping alone in this big castle was quite different than the two of them sleeping by a campfire as they had done on the journey from Turin. And it presented an entirely new set of circumstances.

Unable to hide her embarrassment, she said, "I will look for firewood now,'' and hurried from the room, wincing when she heard the musical notes of his laughter.

After Angelo left, Beatrice wandered out of the courtyard, and found the castle rather like a labyrinth. She came upon a few sticks of firewood, which she placed at the bottom of the courtyard steps that led up to the first level. That done, she realized how hungry she was and went inside to ready things in the kitchen, for she knew Angelo would return, hungry as a hunter.

Thirty-Two

He returned with six eggs, a round of cheese, two bottles of wine, a loaf of bread and eight candles. And he carried everything into the kitchen with the confident polish of a man who knew all about grand entrances.

"I cannot believe you were able to get so much."

"I found a farm nearby, with a very accommodating widow."

"How accommodating?"

"You've nothing to worry about. I only complimented her."

"You got all of this for a simple compliment? At this rate, you'll end up with the whole farm in a week's time."

"The thought does have some merit."

"Go bring in the firewood. I left some by the courtyard steps. There is more stacked near the stables."

"Whatever you say, my little grenadier." He gave her a salute, and whistled on his way out.

Angelo, she decided, was one of those rare individuals who aged in years only. He always regarded life as something to be enjoyed to the fullest, and saw it in the most relative terms. Faith! She would swear he was born old and growing younger.

She busied herself with putting away the things he

had brought, and decided they could simply boil the eggs in the small cooking pot that hung on a hook in the fireplace.

Angelo came in with an armload of wood, which he dropped on the floor next to the enormous fireplace. "One would have to chop down an entire forest to fill this hearth."

She looked the firewood over. "That should be enough to boil six eggs. Can you light it?"

"You think I carried this wood all this way to leave it like this?"

She crossed her arms and watched him strike flint several times before he coaxed some dry grass into a humble flame. She lowered her head to prevent his seeing her smile.

"What are you doing?" he asked.

"I am praying that you can have that ready before winter sets in."

It took half an hour, but at last he had a respectable flame going and the wood stacked around it. He made a satisfied sound and came to his feet, in that proud way men sometimes have when they are pleased with themselves—and his face bore exactly the kind of expression she would have painted on Sir Lancelot after he slayed the dragon.

"Why are you looking at me with that oddly amused expression?"

"I am trying to decide if the ape from which you descended was on your mother's side or your father's."

It took an inordinate amount of time for the eggs to boil, and at one point, she said, "I hope it starts to boil in my lifetime," and then began to slice the cheese. "It would have been nice to have a cup of coffee before I die of old age."

"This mountain air has sharpened your wit." He reached into his pocket and withdrew a kerchief, which he handed to her. "I didn't forget the coffee. I forgot to give it to you."

"We have no coffeepot."

"We can boil it and strain the grounds with the kerchief."

He picked up a piece of cheese and placed it on a slice of bread, then walked over to the cooking pot and peered at the eggs. "What say you, we have them for breakfast?"

"This week, or next?"

"What I would like is some nice hot polenta, sweetened with a little bit of sugar."

"Wishes are nice, but not very filling."

He came back to her and offered her a bite.

She eyed the cheese. "Is this some sort of trap?"

"What do you think? Are you afraid to partake?"

"Only a trifling bite," she said, and took a nibble.

"I was right. This mountain air *does* agree with you. It puts an edge on your speech."

She knew she had been rather caustic with her wit, which was not normally her way. Try as she might, she could not discern the reason for it.

He obviously had no trouble in that area, for he said, "Make them laugh, make them cry, make them wait. It won't work, *amore mio*. Give way."

She must have had a perfectly horrified expression, for he laughed heartily.

By the time the eggs were finally done and they sat down, they both were looking forward to the meal. They were hungry, and ate with little conversation. When they finished their humble fare, Angelo went to the stables to feed the horses and rub them down. While he was gone, Beatrice walked to the cistern and drew a bucket of water to heat for a bath.

She put the water on to heat over the fire, and busied herself pulling a dented laundry tub closer to the hearth.

"Are you taking a bath?" he asked upon his return.

"Yes, and you are not invited."

"You're a hard-hearted woman."

"A necessity, if one wants to protect her virtue."

"That particular ploy never worked with me."

"Yes, so I have heard."

"Serena tells everything she knows."

"And here, I thought she made most of it up."

The water was boiling now, and she picked up her skirt to use as a pot holder.

He crossed the room quickly, and took out his handkerchief to lift the pot from the hook. "Using your skirt like that is a good way to catch yourself on fire."

"Well, I am sorry if I was not raised a rustic."

He poured the boiling water into the laundry pot, and she added the rest of the cold water from the bucket. Using her finger, she tested the temperature.

"Perfect," she said.

"It would be, if only you had some soap."

She put her hand in her pocket and withdrew a small bar of soap. "I packed this in with my clean clothes."

"Don't undress just yet," he said, and picked up the empty bucket. "I'll bring in some more water to heat."

"I don't need any more hot water."

"This is for my bath," he said, and carried the pail out of the kitchen.

She was standing beside the tub with her arms folded when he returned.

"This won't take long," he said, and filled the cooking pot with fresh water. He pushed it over the flame and added another piece of wood. "I will let that heat while you bathe."

"Where will you be?"

"I thought I'd sit over here and watch." Before she could reply, he laughed and said, "I was teasing."

"I will call you when I am finished. Where will you be?"

"Checking upstairs to decide what room would be the best to sleep in."

There were several bedrooms on the first floor, which were part of the residence for the lord of the manor, which also included the great hall which contained a beautifully frescoed chapel and several rooms of state, where the overlord once heard the pleading of cases and decided on the punishment for his vassals' crimes. The second floor contained the servants' quarters, the guest rooms and the granary.

After exploring, he decided the largest bedroom on the first floor to be the best situated. It also had a big window with a stone seat beneath and a handsome fireplace—though he doubted they would need it.

He went back downstairs and carried the bedding he had purchased up to the bedroom. There was no bed in the room—only a carved chest along one wall. He put the bedding on the chest because he knew it did not matter where he put the bed—a woman would always think it best to put it someplace else.

From the window, he surveyed the land beyond

the castle, confident that this was the best place to observe anyone who might approach from the direction of the river.

"I am through with my bath. Although I must say it is the first time I bathed in an inch of water. I left the soap for you."

She stood in the doorway wearing a long, white gown.

"Where did you find a nightgown?"

She glanced at the gown and back at him. "This is my gown. I packed it with my change of clothes."

That seemed to amuse him. "What else did you bring?"

"My sketch pad and charcoal." She walked over to the chest and looked at the bedding. "Where did you find this?"

"It is amazing what people will part with if you offer them enough coin."

"Oh, the widow? Are you sure coin is all you offered?"

He laughed and said nothing.

"Well, it is much better than sleeping on my cloak." She surveyed the room. "It is a lovely room. Do you think it belonged to the castle's owner?"

"That is my guess. It is the largest bedroom and it has a good view in case of intruders."

"Then, I think you should have this room. I will take one of the others."

"I think it best if we stay in the same room."

"I know it best if I stay elsewhere."

He started to argue the point, but she quickly said, "Do take your bath before the water grows cold."

"A bath it is," he said, and went below.

Downstairs, Angelo passed an hour of absolute tranquil pleasure and, after bathing, allowed himself to remain in the water a bit longer, while he lit one of his little cigars and enjoyed the pure luxury of a fine smoke.

He noticed Beatrice had washed her clothes and draped them over the chair near the fire. He looked at his own dirty clothes and decided a little water wouldn't hurt them, either. Though tempted to smoke another cigar, he decided washing his clothes was more important. He put on clean garments before he washed the dirty ones in the tub and hung them over the other chair to dry. Then he emptied the water, lit a candle and went upstairs to see where Beatrice had chosen to spend the night.

He stopped by the large bedroom and was disappointed to find she was not there, in spite of his hopes that she would change her mind. Her cape and one of the blankets was gone. He went in search of her and found her in the room nearest his. It brought a smile to his lips to know that though her sense of propriety wouldn't allow her to sleep in the same room with him, it wasn't so strict as to prevent her from sleeping close by.

The door was open, and he saw that she was lying on the floor, near the window. "Are you asleep?"

"No. The castle is full of strange noises."

He went to her and dropped to his knees. He could see by her wide-eyed expression that she was uncertain about his purpose for being here. He took her face in his hands. "You know I love you."

"Yes."

"I know you love me."

She smiled. "I think you have always known that."

"You know I want nothing more than to make love to you."

"Yes."

"I assume the feeling is mutual."

"Yes."

"So, what happens when two people love each other, want each other and can think of little else?"

He saw a blush rise to her face. "I suppose they end up making love," she said.

"Wrong. They get married."

A light came into her eyes. "Are you asking me to marry you?"

"It sounds that way to me. Are you going to say yes? Give me your answer...or are you going to be one of those coy women who says she has to think about it?"

"I've been *thinking* about it since the first time I saw you. Now is the time for action."

"Oh?" He screwed up his face in a most lecherous manner. He twisted an imaginary mustache. "Ready for action, are you?"

She laughed and pushed him. "Stop that. You know what I meant."

"You still haven't answered my question. Beatrice Fairweather, will you marry me?"

"Yes. A thousand times yes," she said, and threw her arms around him. "But I think it had better be soon."

"Love, it cannot be soon enough to suit me."

"It's been hard on both of us," she said.

"If only you knew," he said. "Now, get some sleep. We will work on the details as soon as we are safely out of here. Leave the door open. If you're afraid, or need anything, just call out my name."

"I will."

"Good night, then," he said, and kissed her softly.

Her arms went around his neck and the kiss deepened. "You make it hard for me to leave you."

"I know. I feel the same way."

He gave her another quick kiss and rose to his feet, before he had a chance to reconsider.

Thirty-Three

Many days passed, and the Austrians were still checking the mountain passes. Only a week ago Angelo had attempted to get Beatrice into France via the St. Bernard Pass. They had dressed in the manner of the residents of the Italian Alps. Angelo had thought it best to pass themselves off as French speaking. Chances were that most of the Austrian guards would not speak the language.

"I thought most Austrians could speak French," Beatrice said.

"The upper class does, but the guards at the pass will be soldiers from the lower classes."

For his part, Angelo carried out his French-speaking *duplicité* without incident.

Beatrice was not so fortunate.

There happened to be one Austrian soldier that day who did speak French, and chose to ask Beatrice a question. Naturally, she could not answer. When Angelo tried to respond for her, the guard called out for them to be arrested.

They narrowly escaped with their lives, and only because Angelo managed—with one well-placed slash of his saber—to cut the latch on a wagon-load of pigs, sending the animals spilling out into the narrow road, squealing and tripping the guards who gave chase.

"I don't want to try going over the pass," Beatrice said when they reached safety.

"No, especially not now, for they will double the guard and be on the lookout for us."

"Do you think they knew it was us?"

"Perhaps not, but they obviously know we were trying to pass ourselves off as something we were not, and since the Austrians seem to have invented suspicion, that is enough."

As it turned out, they had to forgo any excursions into the countryside or the village for over a week, due to the sudden appearance of several detachments of soldiers combing the area.

Angelo knew he had to get Beatrice away from here, and the pressure to do so was mounting. Some time ago, he had dispatched a letter to Andrea, asking him to get a message to Nicola, since it was probable that the Austrians were intercepting Nicola's mail.

With each passing day, Angelo knew he was pressing their luck, for sooner or later, the Austrians would find them. Metternich was flawlessly persistent. Yet something told Angelo that the Austrian prince had another motivation for chasing him down. It was as if there were an age-old enmity between them, as if they both sprang from the fatal loins of warring ancestors. They were political enemies, to be sure, but this pursuit went deeper, cutting into the bone of hate.

"But, what could make him hate you?" Beatrice asked one day as they sat discussing the Austrians. "You have never even seen the man."

"I wish I knew."

"Perhaps you are wrong."

"I pray to God that I am, but do not forget he issued orders for your arrest."

"You think that came from Metternich?"

Angelo laughed. "*Cara, everything* comes from Metternich. His underlings don't change clothes without him dictating what they shall wear."

One day he stood, as he often did, at the window of his bedroom, searching the land beyond for any sign of a military patrol. Everything was quiet now. He saw no patrols, and Beatrice was off somewhere in the castle with her sketchbook, making drawings of the frescoes that were in almost every room. His little artist, his little English grenadier, his Gentiana, his Mouse...

She was all of these things and more.

He lit one of his cigars as he pondered their situation. To have Beatrice so close and yet to not touch her was becoming more difficult with each day that passed. Although he had been raised to be a gentleman, he would have pressed his case long before now, save for the fact that without the option of marriage available to them, he would be a fool to risk getting her with child.

If that were to occur and something happened to him, her life would be ruined. He knew that his love for her, his ever increasing desire for her, and his obligation to protect her were at odds, and he worried that the result would be that he would make a small mistake—enough to send the Austrians swooping down upon them.

Several times they had discussed having a local priest marry them, but Angelo's greatest concern was that the papacy supported the Austrians. He was reluctant to trust the loyalty of a priest he did not know. He was aware firsthand of what treachery the papacy in Piedmont and Lombardy were capable of.

Beatrice would prefer to marry at Villa Adriana or

Villa Mirandola, with the family present, and he would prefer that, as well. But Angelo knew their situation was precarious. He was a wanted man. If they should marry and the Austrians caught him, what then? She could end up a widow, or married to a man spending the rest of his life in prison.

But loving her as he did, and wanting her and having her so close rode heavily on his mind. And this, of all times, was when he needed his mind sharply focused on outguessing the Austrians and saving their lives.

Simply put, the time was not right to marry, and he had to get her out of here. They both knew it.

He crushed the cigar. All this thinking and he was right back where he had started. He could only hope that Nicola had received his letter and would arrive soon to take Beatrice home. If that did not happen, Angelo would be forced to take her back himself, at a great risk to both their lives.

Once she was safe, he could decide the best course of action for himself.

Angelo went downstairs and outside, to feed the horses, at the same time taking a turn about the castle, checking doors and gates. He climbed the steps up to the battlement and looked out over the land in all directions, much as the original lord of the castle must have done. Angelo had a new understanding now, of those men who had built this castle five hundred years ago, and of men like Metternich who had been out to destroy them, forcing them to build such impregnable keeps.

He remained there for a long time and, once, he saw her come out to look for him. When she saw where he was she turned around and went back inside. Returning to the castle, Angelo found Beatrice in the kitchen. She was banging pans and chopping carrots and literally throwing the vegetables into the pot over the fire.

"Are you angry about something?"

"You have to ask? You—with all your experience—cannot tell when a woman is angry? Well, let me help you." She picked up a piece of crockery and hurled it across the room. She picked up another and did the same.

"All right, you're angry. I can see that. There is no need to break every dish in the room. We may need them before this is over."

"We wouldn't have needed any of these things, just like we wouldn't have needed to come here in the first place, if it hadn't been for you."

"Well, this is a fine time to start thinking about that. I wouldn't have brought you here if there had been any other way to protect you."

"Ha! If you cared about protecting me you wouldn't have placed me in jeopardy to begin with."

"Bea, you knew what my life was like from the moment you came back to Italy."

"Oh, and what was I supposed to do? Turn around and go back to Paris?"

"So, what is the point of all of this?"

"The point? You want to know the point? The point is, you expect me to give up everything to be with you. Your life comes first. Your politics come first. Italy comes first. I'm beginning to wonder just where I fit in."

"I didn't mean for you to be pulled into all of this. I did my best to—"

"Your best? The Austrians have me on their list, and you call that your best? Well, it isn't good enough for me. I have a life, too. I have dreams. I am an artist. I want to paint. Not hide out in some moldering old castle, fearful to poke my head out of doors. I'm tired of wearing the same dress every day, and I'm sick of soup, and cooking…*I hate* to cook, by the way, and I'm sick of sleeping on the floor, and taking a bath in a soup pot."

"If you could just be patient a little longer."

She caught him off guard when she threw the next piece of crockery, and it thumped him on the shoulder.

"Stop telling me what to do. You have done nothing but give me orders and endanger my life. I was almost run through by that bloody lancer, and had to shoot him because of you. You make me pretend to be some French-speaking simpleton, and almost get me arrested. I jump at my own shadow. I see Austrian faces in my sleep. Even the clouds overhead are beginning to look like canons firing at me and mounted dragoons charging me. I want to be in charge for a while."

She picked up the knife and began chopping carrots.

"All right. You are in charge."

"Don't be condescending. I hate that, too."

"Fine, just tell me what you want me to do."

"You make the bloody soup," she said, and hurled the knife down with such force, it stuck in the tabletop with the handle vibrating to and fro.

Before he could say anything, she left the room.

Angelo went to the table and picked up the knife. From upstairs came the sound of Beatrice banging and slamming things.

He cleaned up all the broken pottery, and then began to chop the carrots. The onions came next. He sliced one sausage, and dumped all of it into the pot.

When the vegetables were almost tender, Angelo dropped in dried *conchiglie,* which looked like little shells. When it was all done, he ladled it into two bowls and put finely diced tomatoes on top. After putting two spoons beside the bowls, he went upstairs to find Beatrice.

He heard her coughing, and found her standing at his window, smoking one of his cigars.

She choked again and began to fan the smoke.

"What are you doing?"

"I am smoking, as you can see."

"I didn't know you liked to smoke."

"I don't, and this is my first time. I only tried it because you seem to do it when you are under pressure."

"And you thought if it worked for me, it would work for you?"

"Yes."

"I'm sorry you didn't find it to your liking."

"You should be glad. This way, the cigars will last longer." She turned around and handed him the cigar. "You finish it."

"Do you feel better?"

"Somewhat."

"Dinner is served in the kitchen."

"Are you being smart?"

"No. Dinner is ready. How else can I put it... *Signora,* your gastronomical delight humbly awaits your appetite in the food workshop below?"

"You can be so irritating," she said, walking around him and down the stairs.

He followed her down to the kitchen, where he found her staring at the two bowls.

"You did this on purpose," she said. "You made your dinner look better than all the ones I've made."

"Truly, I did not. I just dumped whatever I could find in the pot."

"So, what is it?"

"Humble pie," he said, and she began to laugh.

At last, he thought, and pulled out her chair. They ate in silence, and when she finished, she said, "I'm going to bed now."

He nodded and began cleaning the kitchen. Afterward, he went upstairs. There was no light coming from her room now, and he knew that she had snuffed her candle.

Angelo went to bed but he did not sleep, for his mind was still occupied, long after the rest of him had claimed exhaustion. At last, sleep overcame him.

A thunderstorm blew in during the night. He was awakened briefly, but a vague sort of consciousness allowed him only to identify the intrusion as unthreatening and he went back to sleep.

He had no way of knowing how much later it was when he heard Beatrice scream.

He sprang to his feet and ran into her room. She was sitting up in the early-morning light, slapping herself, the way a crazy person would do.

Then he saw the spiders.

They were everywhere, crawling over the bedding, on her gown, in her hair.

He grabbed her, pulled her to her feet and began brushing the spiders off. When he was satisfied they were gone, he carried her into his room and put her down on his bed. "Stay here."

Returning to her room, he looked up at the ceiling. "They're harmless," he called out. "We call them cellar spiders."

She shuddered. "I know what they are, but harmless or not, I don't want to sleep with them. What I don't understand is how they got into my bed, or why. There are so many of them.''

''They live in houses and make their webs in the corner of a wall or a ceiling. I can still see some up there.''

He came back into his room. ''They hang upside down, and when they sense danger, they vibrate—whether from fear or to ward off danger, I don't know.''

''Why did they crawl all over me?''

''The ceiling was wet. I think the storm loosened a tile on the roof and moisture leaked through. Perhaps that caused them to fall on top of you.''

She shuddered again and rubbed her arms. ''I won't be able to sleep now. I know the moment I close my eyes, I will feel things crawling on me.''

''It is too early to get up. Do you want me to move your bed to another room?''

''No. I don't want another room.''

''Take my bed. I'll go to another room.''

''I don't want you to leave.''

''Bea...''

She threw her arms around his neck. ''I don't care. I don't want to hear what you are going to say. I know all the reasons why you are going to say that isn't a good idea. I know it's wrong. I know we may come to regret it. But I simply cannot go another night like this. I am tired of thinking about the Austrians. I am tired of being afraid of what might happen to us, of hiding and pretending I don't want to make love with you. I am tired of being proper and thinking about propriety and of what I should do, instead of what I want. I wish I could dump propriety down the cistern and leave it there. None of these things matter, because in my heart I am already mar-

ried to you. I have been for some time now. I want
you. I want you with or without marriage. I want you
in spite of the revolts and the Austrians and the
Church and my reputation and even these creeping
spiders. I don't care about any of it anymore, because
if I go another day like this I will go raving mad."

"You're…" He stopped, because he could not believe this wonderful woman who had been through
so much and had shown him day by day how strong
and determined she was, had started to cry.

Tears rolled down her cheeks and dripped onto the
bodice of her gown.

"You're going to get the floor wet and the spiders
on the ceiling downstairs are going to fall into the
cooking pot."

"I don't care."

He started to ask her what was wrong but stopped
himself, because he knew. Deep down inside, he
knew. They had been living in a dangerous situation,
but it was also one that combined the ultimate temptation with maximum opportunity.

And opportunity was a strong seducer.

Their love was pure and devoted, from the heart,
and meant for marriage in all the proper ways—with
loved ones and friends gathering, with flowers and
vows whispered and true—but sometimes you have
to make sacrifices, or substitutions, or changes, and
marriage is not a choice open to you, for times are
trying, and life fleeting, and you find yourself filled
with love in the most desolate of places.

And yet, love must go on.

He took her in his arms and rubbed her back, but
that only made her cry harder. Placing his hands on
each side of her head, he lifted her face to his, and

as he did, he began to kiss the tears, first on one side and then the other, softly, gently, and with love.

Beatrice stopped crying and looked at him through watery eyes that were big and bright and filled with wonder.

She placed her lips on his and managed to say "love," before they found themselves on the bed.

He kissed her and touched her, tenderly releasing all that had been held back for so long into the passion of each lingering kiss. Consumed with hunger and desperation, they could not stop the kisses or the warm words of endearment.

He held himself back, wanting to move slowly because this was her first time, but it wasn't easy. As he kissed her and teased her, he knew he was driving her wild, and still he waited, until at last, breathlessly, she said, "Angelo, are you ever going to do this, or shall I?"

What man could resist an offer like that? he wondered, so he said, "Go ahead."

She sat up and pulled her gown over her head. Her breasts were small, firm and round.

"Beautiful," he said.

She crossed her arms over her breasts. "They are awfully small."

He moved her hands, and placed his over her breasts. "They fit perfectly. Any more would go to waste."

She smiled. "Aren't you going to remove your clothes?"

He had to stand up to do that. She did not look away, but watched him with great interest as he joined her on the bed.

She was lying on her back, the sheet drawn over

her hips. He slid the sheet back and said, "I'll take over now."

Her body was lovely, and he taught her a few things about it. In turn he learned a few things himself—that the pleasure of making love to a woman you loved far surpassed the pleasure of making love to one you did not.

He found her mouth and put his hand on the flat recess of her stomach. His hand slipped lower, and she cried out. He waited, and when he knew she was ready he positioned himself above her, holding himself back until he heard her helpless little sounds. "I love you," he said, and forged an unbreakable bond. She was a woman now. But he knew it was not complete—nor would it ever be, until she was his wife.

"And to think," she said later, "that we owe all of this to spiders."

Thirty-Four

They were lovers now, in every sense of the word, and there was for them no happier state than to love and be loved. It was all-encompassing—a time when the most unexpected sparks kindled the brightest blazes.

Beatrice knew that nothing in life was constant, and such bliss could not last. She knew one only had moments and, if one were fortunate enough, one would remember them throughout life.

But for now, she could not dwell upon that. She was young and in love, and for now being close to one another was all that mattered for either of them.

Happiness was something she wanted to understand, to take apart and put back together, in order to grasp its magic. If she could find the secret, if she could hold on to it and make it last longer, perhaps she could make it stay forever.

They were lovers—joyously, drunkenly, serenely, divinely in love—but the heart has its wisdom, and no human heart could contain so much love forever.

It had to end. They both knew it.

They just didn't know when.

It ended the day Nicola arrived at Fenis Castle.

They were standing upon the battlements when they saw Nicola riding toward the castle, and were both surprised and delighted to see Fioriana was with him. A moment later, they were running down the stairs and across the courtyard, to meet him at the gate.

"Thank God you are here," Angelo said.

Nicola's brows went up. "Tired of her already?" he asked.

"Never," Angelo replied, hugging Beatrice to his side.

Nicola dismounted and embraced his friend, and then the four of them greeted one another. Beatrice was especially happy.

"I am ecstatic over having a woman to talk to. I cannot thank you enough for coming."

"I know it was hard for you," Fioriana said to her.

"It was harder on the crockery," Angelo said, but only he and Beatrice laughed. "I will explain it to you later," he added.

"No need," Nicola said. "Fioriana has been known to throw a fit and a few pieces of crockery along with it."

Everyone laughed, but Angelo could see Nicola was tired—mentally tired.

"I am happy to see both of you, and regret having to call upon you for such a journey. I was afraid you would not get my message."

"Andrea saved the day. He presented us with box seats to his new opera, and gave me your letter that night. Fioriana and I left right away. It wasn't until we were halfway here that we wondered what would happen if we came all this way, only to find you gone."

"No chance of that," Angelo said. "They have us bottled up here, you might say."

"Have you had many problems?"

"More than we wanted. Ironically, our closest encounter happened right after we crossed the Po, the night we left Turin. We tried to cross the border into France at the St. Bernard Pass, and barely evaded capture. Another time we were chased for several miles by a patrol, but managed to lose them."

"Please come inside," Beatrice said. "It is cooler there and you can sit down. We are anxious for news from Turin."

"We are starved for any kind of news. The locals here don't seem to care if the rest of Italy is in turmoil or not," Angelo added.

They walked inside, but Beatrice and Fioriana lagged behind in womanly fashion, their heads together as they talked.

"I am sorry it took us so long to arrive," Nicola said. "As a precaution I did not choose a route that would bring us directly here. Anyone following us would have thought I was drunk as a friar, for I was weaving my way across Piedmont by the most unorthodox route possible."

Angelo clapped him on the back. "At least you are here now."

"You were surprised to see Fioriana?" Nicola asked.

"Somewhat, but I knew you were married by now—I am sorry to have missed that event, by the way, but you know I would have been there if at all possible."

"Yes, I know," Nicola said. "I think it will be easier on Beatrice, having Fioriana along."

"I hope to procure a carriage so the women will be more comfortable on the journey back. As man and wife, Fioriana and I should draw no suspicion, and Beatrice will be Fioriana's cousin, visiting from England.''

"A good plan, and it will give you more practice in playing the role of husband."

Nicola laughed. "I've had plenty of that," he said. "It has been easier on both of us—being married, I mean. Nothing in life is certain, save the fact that we love each other. It makes us stronger knowing we face the wrath of Austria together, rather than separately."

"Do things seem to be settling in for a long duration?"

"I think it will be a long time before our dreams of a free and independent Italy are realized. I doubt either of us will be alive by then. There is little doubt in my mind that the powers in Europe mean to war with the Italian people until *freedom* is no longer a word in our vocabulary. Lord Byron keeps the hope alive for many of us who are Carbonari. He has said, 'King times are fast finishing, and blood will be shed like water, and tears like mist; but the people will conquer in the end.' He also feels it will be a long time coming. 'I shall not live to see it, but I foresee it' were his exact words."

"How are things in Piedmont?"

"The Austrians put down another revolt in Piedmont not long after you left. Already they are setting in place a policy of fierce persecution of all liberals and Carbonari. Lombardy and Venetia are under severely oppressive rule. German has been declared the official language, and the army is everywhere, ready to suppress anything they deem to be of a hostile nature. Newspapers are being closed, activities restricted and Italian history has been banned in schools to prevent the children from hearing about Rome's glorious past.''

Angelo shook his head. ''They want not only to annihilate us, but to wipe out our history.''

''It is a good thing you are not there to see these things happening. There are many men fleeing to England and France. Some are going all the way to America. Many of them are Carbonari.''

''It's worse than I thought.''

''Why don't you marry Beatrice now, and the four of us can go to France?''

''Is that what you are going to do?''

''We have talked about it, but have not decided. I want to start a family and feel a part of something besides danger. I am torn between loyalty to the future of Italy and loyalty to my own future.''

''You cannot have a future if Italy is not free.''

''Not in Italy, but there are other places.''

''I am Italian and I will not leave.''

''And Beatrice?''

''We cannot marry now. Once she is safe with my family, I will return to Italy and we will marry at home. Do you know where my parents are? Are they still at Villa Adriana?''

''Yes, I went to the villa after I received your letter. I told your father I was coming here to get Beatrice. He said they would return to Tuscany immediately, that he thought it would be safer for her there.''

''That is such a long journey for you to make to Tuscany.''

''Fioriana and I actually look forward to it. Traveling is definitely preferable to being in the midst of turmoil in Turin.''

The women entered and began preparations for

dinner. Angelo and Nicola went into town to see about the prospects of purchasing a carriage.

When they returned the women were still in the kitchen, and dinner was ready.

"Did you find a carriage?" Beatrice asked, as they walked in.

"No, nothing," Nicola replied. "We shall have to settle for the diligence that runs weekly."

The four of them ate and drank wine, laughing and remembering old times, forgetting for a while the dark cloud that had come out of the north and had settled over the future.

After dinner, the men smoked their small cigars, while Beatrice and Fioriana put the food away. "Will we have to wait a week for the diligence?" Fioriana asked.

"No," Angelo said, "it comes through here to-morrow."

Beatrice dropped her tin cup and it rolled across the floor with a solemn echo. After that, no one felt much like talking. A few minutes of silence passed before they said good night and went upstairs, Nicola and Fioriana talking softly, Beatrice and Angelo quietly holding hands.

Beatrice waited until Angelo had shut the door, before she said, "I did not anticipate I would be leaving so soon."

He came to stand behind her and wrapped her in his arms. "None of us did. Perhaps this way is better. It will shorten the wait, and lessen the time for grieving."

"Quick and final, like the slice of a knife." She turned toward him and put her arms around him. "I cannot bear the thought of not seeing you each day."

"It is the same with me. Once you are gone, this

castle will be a prison of torment. Your face, your memory will be everywhere.''

They lay together after making love. Beatrice sensed a deep desperation in the way Angelo held her that made her think he was afraid to let her go, as if in doing so she would be lost to him forever.

He fell asleep, but sleep would not come to Beatrice. She lay silently beside him, studying with an artist's eye the superlative male beauty and magnificent physique of a body that seemed more the result of mathematical excellence and scientific daring, than the ritual of breeding and childbirth.

How perfect, how beautiful was a man's nakedness. She understood now, why the masters had so often painted it.

For some time, she had been searching for a way to hold on to the memory of their time here. Now she had the perfect way.

With slow, easy movements, she withdrew carefully from the bed, so as not to disturb him. She lit two more candles and placed them on the floor near him, to give better light and to highlight shadow and dimension. When she finished, she went for her sketchbook and pencils.

She sat with her back against the wall and began to sketch. Later, when she was home, she would transfer the drawings to canvas, and then she would give proof to this moment by painting it into existence.

There was no doubt that Beatrice knew what she was doing was forbidden. It did not matter that she did not agree with the theories of the male-dominated arts or the attitude toward women like herself—artists forbidden to capture the beauty of the naked body of either sex.

She knew discovery meant she would be ostracized, or worse. She also knew times were changing, and she was changing along with it. That made her think of Serena, and she smiled, wondering what that flamboyant cousin of hers was wearing now, and what cause had captured her mercurial attention.

Beatrice sketched quickly, afraid Angelo might waken and she would lose the moment. Her hand moved swiftly and surely, to detail the play of relaxed muscles that so enhanced the mood and posture of slumber. She was aware of the difficulty in duplicating the exact coil of tense expectation, the pent-up energy and muscular tension in contrast with such a casual pose.

She marveled at the human body, and sketched many views to depict the way one part of the anatomy glides imperceptibly into another, with the subtle transition between tone and shape. She sketched the entire figure first, and then, on a separate paper, drew smaller sketches to give detail—of long, tapering fingers, his head, his foot, and then the bend of his knee.

When finished, she turned back to the first drawing. By using the Renaissance technique of *sfumato,* she blurred and softened the sharp outlines by a gradual, subtle blending of one tone into the other. This gave a smoky haziness to the shading, heightening the candle glow upon his skin, the subtle modulation of light into shadow, and the almost luminous glossiness of his flesh—a still-life, without movement, but suggestive of life instead.

She studied the twist of bedding, the shadows upon closed eyes, the tranquil expression of sleep—

and saw not her simple sketch, but the adoration that would produce the finished painting. The mere concept of painting him thus, moved her profoundly.

As quietly as she had begun, she put everything away, returned to lie beside him and joined him in sleep.

Morning came softly. Her eyes fluttered; she mumbled something in her sleep and opened her eyes. Awake now, Angelo leaned on one arm to watch her. The sight of him and her abiding love for him held her captive. Yet, at her most contented moment, she knew such joy was not something she could grasp and hold in her hand, for beneath the sweet disguise, joy had a bitter taste. It was everywhere; it was nowhere. You could not keep it out when it wanted in. You could not find it if you looked for it.

She felt the touch of his hand as it stroked her face, her throat and the curve of her breast.

"What are you thinking?" he asked.

"That you don't find happiness by looking for it." She moved closer to him and put her head on his shoulder. "I don't want to leave you, Angelo. I'm afraid if I leave…"

"Nothing will ever come between us. Nothing will keep us apart. No matter what happens, hold on to that, Beatrice. We might be separated by lies, cruelty, fate or war, but in the end, I will find you. Go to my family, my love, and plan our wedding. I want you to have the most beautiful dress any bride ever had. Make the wedding as big or as small as you like. My only request is that you love me for the rest of my life. Everything else I leave to you. I love you. Now, and forever. Nothing will ever change that. I will come to you as soon as I can."

She believed him because she wanted to believe

him, but deep inside she knew happiness parallels
life, and love is born perishable.

Morning gave them no quarter. The sun climbed
higher in the sky, and the hour of her departure came
too soon—as swift and sharp as an arrow's piercing.

Suddenly, they were in the village, standing beside
the diligence.

One last caress, one last kiss...

Nicola held the door open. Fioriana climbed inside. Nicola looked at Beatrice.

She clung to Angelo, until he had to push her up
the steps.

"I love you." He whispered the words with a kiss
against her ear.

She paused on the top step. "I love you," she said
softly, and tried to keep the tears back.

"You are the beating of my heart. Don't cry,
amore mio. I will come to you as soon as I can. Be
strong, and always remember I love you."

She took her seat. The door slammed. The *crack*
of a whip, and the carriage rolled away.

When she poked her head out the window, he was
standing there, his hand raised to wave. She did not
move her gaze from him until the towers of Fenis
Castle bled into the distant landscape, and her tears
began to bleed into a blur against the sun.

Thirty-Five

Prince Metternich was writing a dispatch in his Vienna office when his aide entered.

"My Prince, this letter has just arrived from Count von Schisler." He placed the pouch containing the letter on Metternich's desk.

Metternich nodded and put his pen down. Opening the pouch and removing von Schisler's letter, he signalled the aide to leave the room.

"I wonder what he has bungled now," the prince said as he unfolded the letter.

Your Majesty,

I regret to inform you that we have not, as yet, been able to find Angelo Bartolini, or the English woman, Beatrice Fairweather.

We have questioned Bartolini's household, and have sent troops to his villa in the country, where we found his parents and sister in residence. They claimed to have no knowledge that Bartolini had left Turin, or where he might have gone. None of Bartolini's friends claim any knowledge of his whereabouts.

We have also questioned the English woman's friends, with much the same results. After searching the city and all the places Bartolini is known to frequent, I am of the opinion

that he has fled the area and that he may have
taken the English woman with him. I say this
because our lancers saw a man and a woman
leaving Turin during the dead hours of the night.
This occurred shortly after the revolt was put
down. The lancers gave chase, but lost the trail.
The following morning, one of our lancers was
found shot through the heart.

Rest assured that we are continuing our surveillance of their haunts, and have placed
posters, with large rewards for information on
them, about town. I will keep you abreast of all
that is happening.

Until then,
I am your most devoted servant,

von Schisler

"'Devoted servant.' I am surrounded by devoted
servants. I don't need more servants. I need a man
who thinks." Metternich stood, knocking over his
chair. "Fool! I am surrounded by fools! If I had one
man...one single man with Bartolini's intelligence,
devotion and finesse, I could conquer Italy in less
than a month."

He went to the door and jerked it open. "Come
inside," he said to his aide. "I want you to write a
letter to von Schisler. I want it dispatched immediately, and tell the rider he is to stop and change
horses frequently. I want this letter in motion until it
reaches Turin. I want it to go straight through, do
you understand? Straight through, without delay."

"Yes, my Prince."

A moment later, the aide was scribbling away as
Metternich dictated the letter while he paced back
and forth in front of the windows.

"You must learn to anticipate the enemy, von Schisler. I do not want reports of your failures. I do not want to hear a summation of transpired events. I want you to think like an Italian, and this means putting yourself in Bartolini's place and asking, where would he go? In case it has not occurred to you, he would head for the Alps and, like countless others before him, would attempt to cross into Switzerland or France. I have done part of your job for you by learning our guards at the St. Bernard Pass did have an encounter with a man and woman trying to cross into France. But, like you, they bungled their attempt to capture them.

"You have the entire Austrian army at your disposal, and yet you cannot find one man and one woman. I tire of reminding you of your job, and of instructing you on how to think ahead. I want Bartolini and the English woman. I do not want any more excuses."

Metternich paused, rocking back and forth on his heels. "Read it back to me."

He listened and made a few changes, then signed the letter. "You know what to do," he said.

"Yes, my Prince. I will see the letter gets off immediately."

Metternich watched his aide rush from the room, then returned to the window.

Less than five minutes later, a courier rode to the steps below his window and dismounted. His aide hurried down the steps, exchanging a few words with the courier, and then handed him the pouch.

The courier nodded, tucked the pouch in his breast pocket and mounted. With a salute, he spurred his horse, scattering bits of gravel with the force of his departure.

At last, he witnessed someone who acted responsibly.

Metternich smiled. He wondered how his aide would fare if he gave him von Schisler's job.

Thirty-Six

Villa Mirandola. *Beloved house, you still look the same,* she thought.

From the moment of her first glance at the stately old villa, Beatrice was comforted with the knowledge that some things never changed. Everyone needed some sort of permanence in their life, an anchor that held them to their place on earth, and Villa Mirandola was hers.

Aunt Gisella and Serena were in Florence on the day Beatrice arrived, but Uncle Tito was there, and he insisted that Nicola and Fioriana stay a few days to rest after "an episode of such travels," as he put it.

At first they declined, but Uncle Tito insisted, and when he insisted on something, he almost always got his way.

They accepted his invitation. "But for only one night," Nicola said. "I must get back to my work in Turin before they realize they can get along without me."

Later, after everyone had rested and had the luxury of taking a bath, they relaxed in the garden. Fioriana and Beatrice took a stroll, while Nicola and Uncle Tito sat among pots of basil and rosemary and discussed the political situation in the north over a glass of wine.

As Fioriana and Beatrice approached the garden, Nicola was saying, "We were stopped once by a patrol near Bologna. It was at night, and we could see the bayonets of the soldiers some time before we came upon their barricade in the road. We did not have any trouble passing through, thankfully."

"All of us owe you a great deal, and I am pleased to know he has a man of such caliber as a friend. Of course, that does nothing to relieve my distress over the fact that Angelo kept Beatrice with him all that time, without a chaperone. I would expect such from an imbecile, but not my only son. In my day, such was unheard of."

"The situation was unavoidable, considering the circumstances."

"They should have married as soon as they arrived in the Alps," Tito said.

"Angelo said they discussed it."

"Discussed it? He should have done more than discuss it. Did he give any reason why he acted so unwisely?"

"His primary concern was having a priest he did not know perform the marriage. He did not know the priests there. He thought it foolish to go to them, considering their loyalty lies with the pope, and the pope's sympathies are with the Austrians."

"Everything is changing," Tito said. "Nothing is as it was. Sometimes I don't know what is happening in the world. I feel lost in my own country."

Tito placed his wineglass on the table and, with a scowl, glanced at the front of his shirt where a drop of wine had had the audacity to land.

Colossus thrust his nose forward and sniffed the stain. "Down!"

A flock of startled birds flew out of the tree, and

Colossus, massive though he was, lay down immediately. Tito gazed around in a satisfied manner,
proud that such evidence gave testimony to his au-
thority over all.

He took in the red clay pots, and the perfect shapes
of the pruned shrubs and the myrtle hedges recently
trimmed. He gazed for a moment at the fountain
against the back wall, with a statue of Aphrodite—
the bronze mottled and blackened with age—and the
row of cedar trees standing at attention in a straight
line. *Everything is orderly,* he thought, with a sigh
of satisfaction.

He sniffed at the scent of wood smoke that put a
haze in the air, fueled by dozens of small fires that
dotted the hillside, where the branches pruned from
trees burned. His contented gaze came to rest upon
kitchen gardens where Colossus had laid waste to the
straight rows of herbs and vegetables his wife had
planted the month before: carrots dug up, onions
hauled off, tomato plants trampled, bean lattices destroyed and the wood chewed to pulp.

Tito's scowl landed on Colossus again.

Colossus gave a pitiful moan and inched his way
forward, dragging himself by his front paws. When
he was close enough, he shoved his nose against
Tito's hand.

In a manner befitting the Emperor of Rome, he
dispensed a pat to the head, and with one solitary
stroke, forgave the dog's transgressions.

When he realized Nicola's wineglass was empty,
he picked up the bottle of wine and refilled the glass.
Tito's gaze rolled in the direction of his own glass,
which was also empty. A moment of indecision hovered over him.

He thought about his promise to Gisella to have

only one glass, then decided a woman who always got her way would soon want the upper hand. He filled his glass to the brim.

Nicola sipped his wine and sighed. "I can see why Beatrice loves it here."

"This old villa has been in Beatrice's family for centuries. Her mother and my wife were both raised here—they were twins, did you know that?"

"No, I did not."

"Well, they were, but I suppose she could tell you all of this, since she is listening to everything over the garden wall."

There was a rustling in the bougainvillea that poured over the trellis like robes of priestly brocade. "I only heard the last part."

With red faces, Fioriana and Beatrice came through the gate and joined them.

"It's all Angelo's fault," Uncle Tito said. "He taught her how to be a snoop. He also taught his sister Serena, and he taught Beatrice's sister, Maresa."

Nicola laughed. "It is a skill he has found useful at times."

Aunt Gisella and Serena returned and there was much excitement over Beatrice's return, which was celebrated with a grand dinner, served in the garden beneath the gentle sway of lanterns, and marred by only a pesky insect or two.

Fioriana and Nicola left the next morning, but not before Beatrice had given them a letter for Teresa.

Beatrice spent some time with Aunt Gisella and Serena, telling them about her life and the events in Piedmont during her time away.

"You have been through so much," Serena said.

"How could you cope with such circumstances? Weren't you afraid?"

"No. Angelo was always nearby. That is the hardest thing to adjust to, now. I miss him."

"The best remedy is to stay busy," Aunt Gisella said. "We could all use something to occupy our time—and what better way than to make plans for your wedding."

"We don't know when it will be. How can we make plans now?" Serena asked.

"We should be prepared. We never know when Angelo might suddenly appear and want the wedding to take place immediately. With a little forethought we can have all the preparations made. We can plan the events—the menu, the guest list, decorations, even Beatrice's dress."

"I shall wear the darkest blue," Serena said, "unless it is in the summer—then I shall wear green. And you, Beatrice? What shall you wear?"

"I have not given it much thought, but perhaps a dress in the Florentine style from the Renaissance period."

"Lovely," Aunt Gisella said.

"We shall go to Florence to the Uffizi…to all the museums to view the paintings of the period," Serena said. "You could pattern your dress after that of the daughter of Florence, Catherine de' Medici."

"I don't know," Aunt Gisella said. "Catherine de' Medici wore an elaborate golden silk gown, opulent with lace. Opulent is not how I would describe Beatrice's taste."

"I do not see myself as opulent, that is true. If only I had my mother's dress…"

"I have your grandmother's wedding dress. Would you like to see it?"

"Oh yes."

The dress was exquisitely lovely and touchingly old-fashioned, in a way that appealed strongly to Beatrice. She lifted the sleeve, feeling the texture of Belgian lace.

"Try it on," Aunt Gisella said.

"Grandmother had big hips," Serena said, when the dress slid down over Beatrice's head.

"Good for child bearing," Gisella said, "but the dress can be altered. The important thing is, the rest of it fits to perfection, and the rose color is lovely with your hair and skin. I shall have Patricia take it to the green bedroom and hang it there for a few days. You can try it on again, after you have given it some thought."

Beatrice spent the rest of the afternoon in her studio, which had been sorely neglected after her hasty departure to Milan. Aunt Gisella had had strict instructions: "Touch nothing in this room."

She surveyed the jugs and bottles filled with powders and dye; bowls, melting pots, shelves of fabrics, bolts of white linen for drapes, the bloodred, deep blue and emerald-green velvets stacked on trestle tables.

She picked up a terra-cotta pot, the bottom lined with lead, and saw the residue of oil inside. The urge to paint pressed upon her, and she got a piece of paper and began to take an inventory of her supplies.

The sole force driving her now was the need to express herself on canvas. There was no joy, no excitement, no anticipation in the things she did. It was too soon for that. She was too recently torn from the one who held her heart in safekeeping, and the pain of separation cut into her still.

She told herself that she must try, that she must

make an effort each day to find joy in something she did, and find some way to give joy to those she was with. She recalled something Maresa had once said. *"I start each morning reminding myself that each day is a gift."*

She would use her days wisely. She might not be happy, but she could be content.

Thirty-Seven

A life spent in hiding was no life.

Not long after Beatrice's departure, Angelo began to make preparations for his own journey to Tuscany. He anticipated returning to Villa Mirandola to marry the woman he loved, and felt that once she was his wife and they could be together, surely everything else would fall into place.

He was up with the sun one morning, exactly two weeks to the day after Beatrice left. He rode from Fenis Castle and headed south. To avoid patrols, he kept away from the main roads, often riding through forests and along rocky riverbanks, and sometimes through a farmer's cornfield.

He rode his horse and led the horse Beatrice had ridden, often stopping and changing mounts, which rested the horses and allowed him to make better time. He only went into small villages when he could not find a farmer willing to sell him some food.

Angelo made his way across the Aosta Valley and down into the Po Valley, then across Piedmont and into Tuscany, keeping away from the mountainous coastline that would have slowed his pace.

He traveled mile after mile, through unfamiliar Italian countryside, through sunlit mornings and coal-dark nights, until one morning, during his second week, he encountered stormy weather, not far from the little town of Zocca, between Modena and Pistoia.

Thunder rocked across the valley. Tiles were flying off the rooftops, and tormented poplars bent over so far it seemed they would break. A farmer's hat came bouncing and rolling down the road.

He continued on, until jagged flashes of lightning ripped across the sky. His horses were becoming skittish. It had started to rain so hard, he could barely see the road ahead of him.

He stopped at a run-down farmhouse and took shelter in the barn, hoping to wait out the storm before starting out again. The place looked deserted, but he knew it best to make certain. He did not want to risk being shot for a thief by some angry farmer.

He rubbed the horses down and found a few handfuls of hay and a bit of feed for them. It was still raining hard when he made the dash from the barn to the house. After several loud knocks, no answer, so he tried the door. It was open. He stepped inside and stood dripping all over the floor. The room was sparsely furnished. The fireplace was full of ashes— cold ashes that looked as if they had been there for a long time.

He waited and listened, not picking up another human sound.

At last, he thought, *I cannot stand here until tomorrow,* and began to inch his way forward, careful and quiet until he reached the bottom of a staircase. He put his hand on the banister and stepped up to the first step. He began his ascent with great caution, pausing to listen every now and then.

When he reached the top of the landing, he saw that it opened onto a narrow hall, dark and dingy, with only two doors, both of them open. He stopped and listened, hearing nothing but the wind. He made his way down the hall until he reached the first door, and peered inside. It was filled with junk, bits of old broken furniture, baskets, a spinning wheel, a churn turned on its side and a portrait of someone's ancestors looking at him with stern expressions that seemed to tell him they knew what he was about.

Angelo continued on, heading toward the second door. He had taken no more than four or five steps when what sounded like a woman's painful moan cut through the silence. He stopped, frozen in place. Had he heard a woman, or was it simply the wind?

The second time he heard a cry, he knew it came from the next room. He kicked a broken stool out of the way and followed the sound.

A woman lay on a small bed, drenched in sweat and in the throes of labor. He had no knowledge of such things, but he had seen enough horses foal to know a birthing scene when he saw it.

He stood looking down at the woman, thinking, *She is someone's daughter—some unknown man's wife or sweetheart.* He had no idea what he should do—only that he had to try. He put his hand on the woman's forehead. She was hot, and the bedding beneath her was wet from perspiration, making him think she had been in this condition for some time.

He wondered if there was some problem with the baby. The woman would lie so still, like a dead person, and then quite suddenly she would come alive, to moan and writhe as if in excruciating pain.

He went downstairs and found the kitchen. There he filled a basin with water and picked up a towel, both of which he carried upstairs.

He did what he could, but knew bathing her face and hands was accomplishing little. He wondered what to do. Instinct and self-preservation told him to get his horses and ride away from here, but his human side told him he had to offer whatever assistance he could.

She needed help—and not the kind of help he was giving her. She required a doctor, and doctors lived in towns, and towns were places he was trying to avoid. If he risked riding into town, he knew the chances were quite good that there would be a policeman or military man who would wonder about him.

He continued bathing her face and, after a while, that seemed to soothe her, for she opened her eyes and looked at him.

"It's all right," he said. "I'm not going to hurt you. I'm here to help, if I can. My name is Angelo. Are you alone?" he asked.

"Yes."

"Your husband? Where is he?"

She shook her head. "No."

"I think he should be here. Tell me where to find him."

She slammed the bed with her fist. "No husband. My Fabrizio…is dead. The Austrians…Napoli."

"How far to the nearest town?"

"Zocca," she panted. "Not far."

He started to leave, but she grabbed his arm. "Don't leave…I'm afraid."

"I will come back. You need a doctor or a midwife…someone to help you."

She nodded. Her lips were parched, and he put the wet cloth to her mouth, then held her head up so she could drink water from a tin cup.

"I am dying," she said. "Get me a priest."

He nodded and gave her hand a squeeze. "I will hurry."

There was no doctor in Zocca, but there was a woman, *Senora* Zira Lodeserto, who assisted with many of the village births. She agreed to accompany him and, thankfully, she knew how to ride.

"A necessity in my business," she said.

"A priest," he said. "I need a priest."

She directed him to the tiny village church, where he found Father Sertino Pierantoni. Soon the three of them were on their way back to the farmhouse.

When they arrived and had checked on the pregnant woman, Zira ran Angelo and Father Sertino out of the room. "I will call you if I need you."

In the kitchen, Angelo found some coffee, and was about to put water on to boil when Zira appeared.

"It is very bad. She has lost too much blood. I can do nothing."

"The baby?" Father Sertino asked.

"Perhaps I can save the baby, I don't know. You must come now, Father, to administer last rites."

"Do you know her name? What about her husband? Where is he?"

"Her name is Lisetta Ferrelli. She is unwed. The Austrians in Naples killed the man she was to marry three months ago. She is from Biella and she was on her way there, hoping to find someone in her family willing to take her in. Then the baby started to come—she has been like this for three days. Hurry, Father, there isn't much time."

Father Sertino went in first and closed the door. Angelo paced the hallway.

After a while the door opened and Father Sertino came out.

Angelo asked. "Is she…"

"No, not yet. I cannot get her to give me her confession, yet she is afraid of dying in a state of sin. She seems to think she should be married first."

"Well, that is obviously impossible," Angelo said. "What about the baby?"

"I think it is for the baby she fears the most. I have reminded her that the baby is innocent, but she does not seem to trust that."

"Why are you telling me all of this?"

"She has asked for you. I thought perhaps you might persuade her to let me hear her confession."

"I can try, Father, but I don't know what help I can be."

Angelo followed Father Sertino into the room. When they reached Lisetta's side, Father Sertino took her hand and whispered to her.

Angelo stepped closer. He had never seen anyone who looked closer to death but was alive. Her entire body seemed to be in pain, and still she strained, pushing her muscles beyond what was humanly possible.

"Let me hear your confession," Father Sertino whispered again.

"No."

Angelo tucked the sheet up under her neck and was about to pull his hand away, when her icy hand seized his and clamped around his wrist with inhuman strength.

"Please, *signore,* let the priest marry us so my baby will not be born a bastard. It will mean nothing to you. I am dying. Please, *signore.* Please, care for my baby."

Angelo opened his mouth to say no, but Lisetta began to beg him.

"It is nothing to you. I will be dead in an hour's

time. Give my baby a name and a home. Why should
an innocent baby suffer for my sin? Help my orphaned baby, *signore*. Please, say you will help my
baby. Help my little orphan.''

When she said the word *orphan,* Angelo felt as if
a cold shadow had passed over him, and his next
thoughts were about his own mother—not Gisella,
but the woman who gave birth to him. Was this what
had happened to her? Was he like this baby, born
into a world of sin—a bastard born? He thought how
easily his own life could have been one of ignorance,
pain and suffering if the Bartolinis had turned their
back on the tiny orphaned baby left at their door.

"You must hurry, Father," Zira said. "She is losing too much blood."

Father Sertino looked at Angelo, as if reminding
him the choice was his.

"I must give last rites," Father Sertino said again.

Lisetta began to writhe and pant more heavily.

"Do it quickly, Father," Zira said.

"The marriage. Is what she asks possible, Father?"

"In a situation like this, it is possible. But I must
hear her confession first. The choice is yours."

"All right," Angelo said. "Marry us, but do it
quickly."

"I must hear her confession and administer last
rites before I can perform a marriage. You will have
to leave the room."

Angelo and Zira left the room. As they waited on
the other side of the door Zira took a rosary from her
pocket and began praying. Angelo walked to the
front door and opened it, to get some fresh air. He
stepped outside and lit a cigar.

He was about to be married, and not to the woman he loved.

He thought of Beatrice, and somehow knew that Beatrice, if she were here, would tell him to help this woman. It seemed so strange to him—but then, life was strange. *I suppose it cannot hurt anything,* he thought, *and it will be one less orphan tossed out into the world.*

Father Sertino came to the door. "Come quickly."

When he first entered the room and looked at her, Angelo thought Lisetta was dead. Her face was pale with a waxy green tint. It glistened with sweat. Her lips were turning blue.

"*Gesu,*" she whispered.

Angelo approached the bed and nodded at Father Sertino.

And there, in a short ceremony, in an abandoned farmhouse, Angelo Bartolini took a wife.

Afterward, Zira said, "I will do what I can to save the baby."

Angelo and Father Sertino returned to the kitchen, and Angelo poured them a cup of coffee. They sat there for a long time talking, until Father Sertino began to nod off.

When the first rays of morning came through the windows, Father Sertino was still asleep in the chair. Angelo got to his feet and walked outside. The sun was as yellow as straw, climbing higher in the sky. The birds were out, singing in the trees. The storm had passed and it looked like the beginning of a beautiful day.

That image was shattered a few minutes later when Zira came outside to find him.

She was drying her hands on her apron and shaking her head. "I am sorry. I did everything I could, but the baby is dead. I am sorry. There was nothing I could do.''

"The mother?"

"It is a miracle, *signore*. I have stopped the bleeding. She is weak, but I think she will live."

The world around Angelo turned blindingly white. A sharp pain pierced his heart. He dropped down to his knees. His head thrown back, he released a tormented cry. "Dear God, what have I done?"

"Signore…"

"Leave me alone."

"Signore, please…''

"I said, get away from me."

Zira turned away and returned to the house.

Some time passed before Father Sertino came outside and found Angelo sitting under a tree, his head in his hands.

"Sometimes it is difficult to understand why things happen."

"I want no sermons, Father. I want no prayers, no counsel, no scriptures and no conversation, because there is nothing in this world or the next that can comfort me. I am damned. My soul has departed. I am nothing inside."

"What will you do now? In spite of the tragedy, she is your wife."

"Do you think that I don't know it? Do you think I will ever forget it for even a moment for the rest of my cursed life? Take the midwife and go back to your church and leave me be. I don't need your comforting words. God has turned His back on me. I am alone. Go say your prayers for someone else, for I am already lost."

"Do not be angry at God. He did not cause this."

"No, but neither did he prevent it."

"I—"

Angelo sprang to his feet. "Forgive me, Father. I cannot talk of this. Not now, anyway."

He started walking, with no destination in mind.

For hours he walked, not caring where he went, cutting across pastures and down ravines, and finally crossing a stream and stopping for a drink.

What was the cost of a mistake? Not even cutting out his faithless heart would undo the wrong he had done. There could be nothing human left in a heart that bore such pain and emptiness. He was lost...to love, to happiness, to life itself—hopelessly ensnared having betrayed the trust of the woman he loved and had promised to marry. He saw what he had done as the vilest betrayal of love possible.

He was less than the dirt beneath the worst sinner's feet, less than the weeds that lined the road, less than a man. His life was damned. He was nothing. Faithless as the wind, he had committed the worst sin against love, and, in one brief moment, had destroyed both their lives.

It was almost dark when he returned, walking down the same road he had taken earlier in the day. He saw Father Sertino was still waiting.

"We must make arrangements to bury the baby."

"You take care of it, Father," he said, and handed money to the priest.

Angelo hired Zira to care for Lisetta. He spent most of his time in town, and found that if he drank enough, he could forget...for a time.

When she was well enough to travel, he decided, he would take her to Villa Mirandola. His parents would look after her, but more important, he had to see Beatrice. He had to try to explain the unexplainable—just how it was that he had come to destroy both their lives.

Thirty-Eight

It is amazing what the human body is capable of, and during a two-week frenzy of painting—a period in which Beatrice slept little and ate little—she thought about nothing, save giving life to the sketches of Angelo she had drawn that morning at Fenis Castle.

When she finished and had placed the painting where it could dry, she thought it was possibly the best work she had ever done. She left her studio, locking the door behind her, and she did not return until one morning, a week later, when she decided it was time. The painting would be dry.

Taking the key from her pocket, she stepped inside the studio.

Without making a sound, she stood looking at the painting, awed by what she had created. She saw not a painting but Angelo himself as he had been that morning when she had first awakened and seen him lying beside her.

She could feel the warmth and the weight of him, and recall the gloomy thought of separation that hung, heavy and grievous, over their last hours together. She lit a candle and held it close to the painting, and saw him come to life: the proud and perfect head, the strong column of his neck, the tenderness of his face and the emotion it evoked. She touched the sensitive mouth, and looked at the fragile lids of his closed eyes, recalling the power of the gaze that lay beneath.

She traced her finger across the reclining figure. She loved the scent of his skin, the feel of his body, which she wanted, even now, to caress. She would never have need to speak of her feeling for him again, for it was all here, written with the strokes of a brush, expressed in the colors of living flesh—the acknowledgment of her love and her desire for him.

Always him.

With one last look, she locked the door, and after breakfast with her aunt and Serena, she returned to her room to write letters to her sisters in England.

She seated herself at her desk, but instead of writing letters, she gazed out the window, her mind paralyzed. She willed her life to move forward, but thoughts of Angelo kept getting in the way. Why could she not release him and be comforted with the knowledge that he loved her, wanted her, and that they would, as soon as he arrived, be blessed in the union of marriage? Didn't her grandmother's wedding gown hang in the room upstairs?

In the distance, she watched the approach of what looked to be a coach. As it steadily grew nearer, she became aware that it was indeed a coach, and it was coming to a stop right below her window.

She felt no curiosity and gave the arrival no thought. Her hand moved to the inkwell, and she flipped back the lid, then picked up her pen. She was about to dip the pen into the ink, when she heard the sound of footsteps hurrying first in the hall below, then up the stairs.

"Beatrice, come quick."

It was Serena's voice, and the tone of urgency in

it made Beatrice leave what she was doing to rush downstairs. She could hear a commotion, the scraping of baggage and the sound of voices as servants called out to one another.

She was almost to the entryway when she glanced up and her heart leaped at the sight of Angelo. A smile spread across her face, and she was about to call out his name, when suddenly, Serena clamped a hand around her wrist and yanked her aside.

"Brace yourself, Beatrice. Something terrible has happened."

Aunt Gisella came hurrying toward them, and Beatrice noticed an expression on her aunt's face she had never seen before.

"Serena, show Lisetta to the blue bedroom," she said. "I have sent for your father."

"But, I wanted—"

"Serena, please do as I said." Her words were calm and cold, and so unlike Aunt Gisella that Beatrice stared at her in amazement.

Confused, Beatrice asked, "Who is Lisetta?"

"She is my wife."

Beatrice's head jerked around. Angelo stood in the doorway, looking tired, old and haggard.

Beatrice felt trapped—caught momentarily in that lost period of time between perception and comprehension, when nothing is understood. Her right hand came up between her breasts. Her mouth parted, but no words came out. If blood had oozed from his pores, Angelo couldn't have shown more suffering and pain than he did at that moment when he looked at her with pleading eyes.

"It is not as you think." He turned to Gisella. "Let me have a few minutes with her, Mother."

Gisella looked on the verge of tears herself, but

she held herself together. "Yes, I think that is certainly called for. Go into your father's study. It is quieter there."

"I..."

"Go with him, Beatrice. God knows, the two of you need to talk."

They walked in silence down the hall. Part of her wanted to take his hand, to throw her arms around his neck and tell him she didn't care what had happened. He could take a hundred wives, and still she would feel the same. But the other part of her wanted to scratch his eyes out, to hurt him as badly as she was hurting.

He opened the door and stepped aside for her to enter. As she walked into the room, she caught a glimpse of her face in the mirror, white and frozen.

The door closed behind her.

She turned, unable to think of anything to say. There was no expression on her face, she knew, save the question in her eyes.

Angelo shoved his hands deep into his pockets. "I have never done anything that hurts me as much as having to say what I just said—when I want nothing more than to take you in my arms."

"Don't."

He looked at her with pleading eyes, and when she said nothing, he walked to the window and gazed out. "I cannot explain what happened, or how it happened, or even why it happened. I can only relate the course of events that somehow turned a good deed into a nightmare."

She said nothing.

"After you left, everything changed. I felt lost and miserable without you. I regretted my cautious behavior and wished with all my being that we had

thrown caution to the wind and married in the Alps.
I left Fenis earlier than I had planned, anxious to be
home, so I could marry you.''

Mute, she listened to his telling of a story too horrible to believe, and yet she knew every word of it
was true. Trembling, she listened, at first so angry
with him that she wanted to hurt him until blood ran
in rivulets from the room—but even then, she knew
she could not come close to easing the pain she felt.

And then, somewhere in the telling of his story,
she began to see she was not the only one affected,
and she understood that his life, his goals, his future,
his very happiness were as lost as hers.

There is nothing sadder, she decided, than to see
the man you love humbled, broken and hurting inside, and yet desperately trying to find a way to di-
minish the pain he has caused.

He is trying to be strong for me, she thought, *like
a wounded and bleeding artillery officer who shouts
encouragement to his dead comrades, not knowing
the battle is already lost.*

She heard the woman's name—Lisetta, the woman
who was now his wife. *I should hate her,* she
thought, *for she has stolen the only thing I ever
wanted—she has stepped into my place, to be Angelo's wife.*

''Why, Angelo? Why?''

He talked, pouring out his heart in words of agony,
until the words began to hum like great, grinding
wheels in her head.

''It wasn't supposed to end this way,'' he said.

You did not do this, her mind screamed. *Tell me
it is only a dream. Tell me it isn't true.* Only then
was she aware the room had fallen silent; only then

did she see the slump of his shoulders, his head lowered in defeat.

She realized there is something in the way you love a person that is all-encompassing, that enables one lover to see the other's pain. There welled up within her a sympathy beyond telling, hidden in her heart that loved.

She realized there was nothing he could ever do that would make her stop loving him.

She would never be his. They would live their lives apart. He would live with this woman until the day he died. Beatrice would never see him again. He had broken her heart and stolen the rest of her life.

But she would never stop loving him.

She went to him and placed her cheek against his back, feeling his warmth through his coat. Her arms went around his waist. "I love you too much to cause you more pain. Ease yourself of the burden of hurting me, for I know now, your pain is even greater than mine."

He turned toward her, and she saw something more painful than the tears on his face. She knew that her understanding, her compassion, had hurt him as no hurtful words could ever do.

With tears in her eyes and a sad smile on her lips, she took his beloved face in her hands for the last time and placed a kiss on his forehead. "Above all, even my own happiness, I wish you to be happy."

He threw back his head with an anguished cry. "I cannot be happy with anyone but you. Ask anything of me, but not this. I love you. I adore you. My heart has been ripped out. Say you won't leave me. There must be some way out of this. Promise me you will stay."

"I cannot stay. You know I cannot. I must leave,

for both of us," she said, for she felt herself weakening, wanting, yes, *needing* to be held in his arms and kissed with passion one last time.

As she reached the door and opened it, she turned and saw he stood with his back to her, his forehead pressed against the window as if he could not bear to watch her walk out of his life.

"You know, the best part and the worst part of all of this is that neither one of us is to blame. So here we stand, each apart from the other—blameless. Yet our eternal punishment has been decreed: You will never again feel the touch of my kiss, and I will never bear your name."

Thirty-Nine

Beatrice had dinner in her room that night, and when Patricia carried in her tray, she exclaimed, "Everyone is eating in their room tonight. No one wants to join the *Senora* and Serena for dinner."

Beatrice was surprised to hear this. "Uncle Tito is not there?"

"No, he is taking dinner in the library with Angelo."

"And Angelo's wife?"

"She is resting, and also taking dinner in her room."

"What is she like, Patricia?"

"She is quiet, and has not said much. I don't think she really understands what has happened. It is easy to tell she is in love with him."

Of course, Beatrice thought. *What woman wouldn't be?* "How do you mean?" she asked.

"Whenever he is around, she never takes her eyes off him," Patricia said. "She said he had been very kind, but I have the feeling she wants more than kindness from him. I pity her, for he will never love her."

"Perhaps that will come in time."

"I know it will not. I have known Angelo since he was a baby. He will not blame her, but he will never love her."

Before retiring for the evening, Angelo surprised almost everyone by announcing he would be leaving for Turin the next morning. It was something that did not surprise Beatrice, however, for she had known he would go back, with even less regard for his life now than he had had before.

Serena and Beatrice talked together in Serena's room after everyone had gone to bed. When Serena yawned, Beatrice looked at the clock on the mantel. "Goodness, look at the time."

She jumped out of the chair and hurried to the bed to give Serena a quick kiss on the cheek. "Good night, dear cousin."

"Will you come downstairs in the morning to see Angelo off? I know how much that would mean to him."

"You know that I cannot."

Serena sighed. "Yes, I know, but I was hoping."

"Set your hopes on something more realistic. There can never be anything between us now. You know that."

Beatrice left Serena and walked quietly down the hall to her room. When she opened the door and stepped inside, Angelo was waiting for her.

"What are you doing in my room? Get out. What if someone saw you?"

"Everyone is asleep."

"You cannot do this. Please, leave. This will accomplish nothing."

"I only came to tell you goodbye. I am returning to Turin in the morning. I know you will not come downstairs to see me off. This is the only way I could see you alone, one last time."

He came to her and took her by the hand, saying softly, "Beatrice, if there was any way I could undo this, any way I could make up to you for what I have done, I would do it.''

She did not say anything.

"Talk to me," he pleaded.

"I do not wish to be a burden, a stone around your neck. I don't want to make you wretched, I don't want to cause you more pain. I cannot talk to you because I am so bloody angry at you for your stupidity, I could kill you with my bare hands. Now, does that shock you? I hope it does. I hope it shocks you enough that you will leave me alone forever.''

"Love, I do not mean to distress you." He took her hand and kissed it.

She jerked back as if burned. "Don't. That is blasphemy.''

"I cannot live without you. If that is blasphemy, so be it.''

The same tenderness she remembered was in his face, and she heard the pain in his voice. Her heart went out to him, knowing his burden was far greater than hers. She put her arms round him, and covered his head, his neck, even his hands with kisses.

Suddenly she caught herself and pulled back. Her hands came up to cover her face. "Oh God, what is happening to me?''

He took her in his arms and held her. "You have done nothing but love me, as I love you. That is both our sin and our punishment." He took her face in his hands and kissed her, tenderly at first, but it soon blossomed into something more.

She pushed away from him. "I cannot," she said. "You know I cannot." But the words held no meaning for him, and his mouth was upon hers, in a kiss born of love and desperation, and before she knew what was happening she wanted him as much as he wanted her.

She was terrified now, because she loved him so much and feared she did not have the strength to stop him. God help her, but she wanted him—wanted him to touch her, to make love to her, to stay with her and never leave.

Passion had gone beyond control, and she felt herself giving in, felt him undoing the buttons of her dress and his mouth upon her breast.

She shoved him back. "You dishonor me."

"It is only because I want you so much I cannot think. Your name is burned into my head. Don't worry, love. I have hurt you enough. I will never put you in such a position again. Don't think I regret coming here, because you have given me something I shall carry always. Goodbye, my love."

He loves me, that I know, she thought. *He is married to another woman, and there is no changing that. I want love and marriage, and he cannot give it to me. It is finished. There is no going back.* She had to leave here.

She tried to direct her thoughts to where she would go, what she would do. She could not return to Teresa as long as her friend remained in Turin. Even Milan was too close to where he would be. She could go back to Paris, or return to London, but neither held any appeal. She loved Italy. She was sympathetic to its cause. She cared what happened. She wanted to paint here.

Early the next morning, she heard the sound of his footsteps on the stairs. He had asked for his horse to be brought around. She went to the window and watched him take the reins to his horse, with only a nod of thanks. He put his feet in the stirrups, and turned to gaze at the window of her room.

Her first instinct was to draw back and not let him see her—but to what purpose? Why would she purposefully hurt the one she most loved in the world? *I do not have much that I can give him, but I cannot send him off so cruelly.*

She stepped into the sunlight coming through her window, touched her fingers to her lips and pressed them to the glass. "Go with God, my love," she whispered. She saw the expression on his face, and knew in her heart she had done the right thing.

He brought his fingers up to his hat as a salute to her. And then he was riding away. Out of sight. Out of her life. But not out of her heart.

"He has gone," she whispered. "It is over."

Tears ran down her face. *No! It cannot be!*

It had been the spring of their greatest happiness, but now, spring had given way to winter's dread.

Everyone managed to make it through the stress of the next few days. Uncle Tito had his farming and vineyards to attend to, which left Gisella to orchestrate things concerning Lisetta becoming part of the family. It was a role Gisella handled beautifully, and Beatrice did all she could to make it easier on her aunt.

Beatrice could not be angry with Lisetta. She was kindhearted and soft-spoken, and it was obvious from the beginning that she wanted to make Angelo a good wife. It was also apparent that she had no idea as to the relationship between Angelo and Beatrice, or what she had done to them.

"I truly hope she never finds out," Beatrice told Serena.

"Secrets are hard to keep."

"I know that, but I want us to try. There has been enough hurt to last us all a lifetime."

Strange though it was, Serena was the one who had the most difficulty accepting Lisetta. "I'm sorry, Beatrice. I don't know how you do it. Every time I look at her, I see someone I despise. I want to like her, but the truth is, I despise her. How can you overlook the fact that she is married to Angelo?"

"We can't control the things that happen to us. We can only control the way we react to them. She is as much a victim of this as are Angelo and myself. How can I blame her?"

"Do you think she was truly dying?"

"I cannot pass judgment on that. Angelo believed her. The midwife thought she was dying, and so did the priest. I don't want to dwell on those things, and it would be better if you didn't, either."

"I will try not to, but you know I do not have your even disposition or your understanding nature."

"That is why we are such good friends. If there were two of me, or two of you, we would fight like the wild cats at the Roman ruins."

Beatrice and Gisella made every effort to welcome Lisetta into the family, and after a while they saw signs that even Serena was coming around. For her part, Beatrice was especially kind to Angelo's wife, and even offered to paint her portrait.

One especially lovely morning, the four of them—Beatrice, Serena, Gisella and Lisetta—were in the garden, sitting among pots of bright flowers and brilliant green foliage. Aunt Gisella was napping, with a book lying tentlike in her lap. Serena was reading Mary Shelley. Lisetta, determined to learn how to knit, was unraveling her knitting for the fourth time.

Beatrice had her sketchbook in her lap, but she had paused in her sketching and fallen into introspection, a frequent occurrence of late. In the beginning there were always thoughts of Angelo and love lost, but gradually her thoughts had moved on. She was learning a great deal about herself, for she had not known she was so open-minded, or that her capacity for understanding and compassion was so great. She had always thought of herself as a rather shallow person, too sheltered to have much of interest to offer others, too timid to reach out, too shy to respond to those who reached out to her. She was beginning to see herself in a new light.

She had learned, too, that the body and the mind have their own ways of dealing with grief, and that time does heal. Life does go on. The pain was lessening now.

Her love for Angelo was not.

It was about this time that Lisetta, in spite of the family's many kindnesses to her, became curious about the relationship between Angelo and Beatrice. One day, she even went so far as to ask Beatrice if she ever had made love to Angelo.

Beatrice did not answer her, but she had a feeling Lisetta knew the truth.

In spite of all the careful orchestrating by the family, they were only human, and slip-ups and mistakes inevitably occurred. The first incident came one evening as the family gathered after dinner. Conversing lightly, they were discussing a range of subjects, and someone mentioned Beatrice's sister, Maresa, and how Angelo had taught her to pick locks.

"Did he teach you when you first came?" Lisetta asked Beatrice.

Serena, forgetting herself, laughed and said, "No,

he kissed Beatrice at a Carnevale ball and frightened
her so much, she stayed in her room for two days. It
was five years before she mustered the courage to
pay us another visit. It wasn't long before Angelo
tried to—'' She stopped abruptly, obviously realizing
what she had almost said.

Thankfully, Aunt Gisella spoke up. ''Angelo tried
to tease her about it for years. Is that what you were
going to say?''

Serena nodded. ''I don't know what happened. I
simply lost my direction of thought.''

Beatrice stole a glance at Lisetta, and saw her head
tilted to one side as she looked at Serena with deep
contemplation. A moment later, Beatrice felt
Lisetta's glance in her direction.

''This is not going to work,'' Aunt Gisella said to
Beatrice the next day. ''We cannot go on this way,
afraid to speak for fear of mentioning something that
will alert her to the truth about you and Angelo. I
think we should tell her.''

''No, don't tell her. I will be leaving soon. I have
received a letter from Teresa. She is back in Milan
and she wants me to join her so I can finish her
portrait.''

''Even so, I think we should tell her.''

''If you must, Aunt, please wait and tell her after
I have gone.''

In the end, however, it was Beatrice who gave the
truth all away.

She was ready to transfer one of her sketches to
canvas, when she remembered she had worked on
the sketch in bed the night before. Beatrice returned
to her room for it, and since she was coming right
back, she left the studio door open.

About that time, Lisetta came down the hall. When

she saw the open door and all the paintings stacked along the wall, she was curious to see Beatrice's work, and stepped inside.

When Beatrice returned only a few minutes later, she found Lisetta standing beside the trestle table with a pale face. One of Beatrice's sketchbooks was in her hands.

Beatrice knew, even before she glanced down, that Lisetta was looking at the sketchbook from Fenis Castle. She knew, too, that the only sketches that could produce such a reaction were those of Angelo that she had completed that last morning they were together.

Beatrice reached out to take the sketchbook from Lisetta's hands. "I am sorry you saw that. Truly. It was never meant for anyone's eyes. Not even Angelo has seen it. He never knew I sketched it."

To her credit, Lisetta appeared perfectly calm. Other than the tremor in her voice and the pale face, she seemed perfectly composed when she spoke. "It's true, isn't it. You and Angelo. It is true, isn't it."

Beatrice put her arms around Lisetta, distressed to be the one to tell her the truth. "It doesn't matter, Lisetta. Believe me, it does not matter now. Whatever there was between us is over. It is in the past. You are his wife, and you are the one he will come home to. That is all you need to know. Don't stop loving him because of something that does not exist."

She jerked away. "I want to know. I have to know. I deserve to know. Did Angelo ask you to marry him?"

Beatrice did not say anything.

"Did he?" Her voice was shrill and high. "Tell me!" She slammed her hand down on the table.

"Yes, but..."

"Did you accept?"

"Yes."

"*Dio!* How you must hate me."

"I don't hate you. How could I? You had no way of knowing. There are not guilty persons in this— only innocent ones. We cannot go back, only forward. Don't think about it."

"I can't help it!" Lisetta raked her hand across the table, and the sketchbook and other drawings crashed to the floor. Tears ran down her face and dropped to her dress. "Why do you have to be so kind to me? Why don't you blame me? Hate me? Curse my name to perdition? I ruined your life. Don't you see? I ruined both of your lives, and the worst of it is, I fell in love with him, and I never understood why he could not bear to be around me. I thought it was me. Now I understand. He will never love me. There is not room for both of us in his heart. There never will be."

Before Beatrice could speak, Lisetta ran from the room.

Forty

Angelo was not far from Turin when he saw smoke rising over the next hill.

He turned his horse in that direction and rode to the rise. A battle scene unfolded before him, looking very much like a scene from a painting. Everything was so still.

As he kicked his horse and rode down, he could see bodies everywhere. There must have been some skirmish between the patriots of a nearby town and the Austrians, for many of the dead he passed wore Austrian uniforms.

Angelo stopped and tied his horse to the wheel of a cannon. A dead man lay a few feet away. A peasant woman was going through his pockets. Angelo turned away.

He had never seen a scene like this, and was deeply moved by the pointlessness of it. He had no knowledge of what had led to this battle, but that did not seem to matter much right now.

Walking among the dead, he checked both the patriots and the Austrians for signs of life. He saw two men and a young boy, their arms full of rifles, one of them dragging a powder keg.

Angelo wondered if there had been any victor here, or if everyone was dead. He continued to walk until he came upon a uniform he recognized as that of a captain in the hussars. The man's uniform looked as if he had been the kind to take particular pains with his appearance, and he was wearing several medals on his once proud chest. He looked every inch the noble, and Angelo was curious about the face of such a man, for his face was turned away.

"Help me."

Angelo was surprised when the man spoke, since he had thought him dead. He was also surprised that in spite of being Austrian, the man spoke Italian.

Angelo stepped over him and dropped down on one knee. He pushed the helmet back, and stared into his own face.

The same shock that must have registered on Angelo's face was upon the hussar's face, and for a moment they stared at the other, each of them wondering how something like this could happen in such a place.

"Who are you?" the hussar asked. "How is it you have stolen my face?"

"I was about to ask the same of you," Angelo said, "for it is my face you seem to have taken."

The man coughed, and Angelo saw the bright red stain on his chest grow larger. He heard the gurgle in the man's throat and knew he was bleeding in his lungs. The hussar would soon drown in his own blood.

"What is your name?" the man asked again.

"Angelo. Angelo Bartolini. Why do you ask?"

"I am Prince Franz Ernst Ranier Klemens Kyrburg, and I think you are my lost twin brother."

Angelo was stunned. "What…"

"I do not have much time. I know I am dying, but I want to relate a story, and if it has any meaning for you, please tell me. I have just finished my twenty-eighth year. I was born in Vienna, the second born, my twin brother having come first. My mother was unhappy. After giving birth, she took the firstborn twin and ran away. My father's men tracked her as far as the countryside near Florence before they lost her trail. When they found her a few days later, she was dead, frozen in a field, but she was alone. There was no trace of the baby.''

''I—''

''Please. I must finish. When I am gone, you must look in my pocket. Inside, you will find a notebook with my father's name and address inside. If what I have told you fits within the framework of your past, you must contact my father. He can answer the questions that I will not live long enough to hear. I only ask one thing—that you bury me, so the wolves will not carry me away.''

Angelo nodded. ''I will see to it.''

''If you would like to know—and I think you would—your name is Prince Karl Rudolf Lothar Johann Kyrburg.''

''Where is your father now?'' Angelo asked. ''Is there anything you want me to tell him?''

But Prince Kyrburg had already passed on, and left Angelo to wonder if all that he had learned was true.

He looked in the man's pocket and found the small leather notebook. Inside was the name Prince Johann Ranier Wenzel Karl Kyrburg, and underneath his name was the address for Prince Kyrburg, Commander of the Imperial Austrian Army in Italy.

Angelo put the notebook in his pocket. Then he picked up the body of the man who claimed to be his brother and buried him beneath a plane tree—so he could remember, if he ever again passed this way.

Forty-One

Beatrice knew it was time to go, and she sat down to compose a letter to Teresa, telling her she would be joining her in Milan before the month was out. She was addressing the envelope when Aunt Gisella came into her room.

"I am worried about Lisetta. She is quite despondent and seems so very sick at heart. She is afraid to think overlong upon what she has done, and yet she cannot do anything else. It haunts her."

"Have you spoken with her?"

"Yes, as has Tito, but our words go over her like water."

"She should talk about it. It would do her good."

"She refuses all our attempts to get her to do so. She says the same thing over and over. She is consumed with the fact that Angelo married her out of the goodness of his heart. She said she knew he did it to help her, to ease her mind. She apologizes for living. She always ends by saying, 'If it weren't for me, two people who love each other would be married by now. I have done nothing but repay the kindness and goodness of this family by giving you all loss and pain. I cannot bear to speak of it.'"

"I think it will get better as soon as I am gone." Beatrice glanced down at the envelope she was addressing. "I have finished my letter to Teresa. I told her I am coming as soon as possible. Things will be better then. For Lisetta…for all of you.''

''You will paint?''

''Yes. A musician must make music. A poet must write. An artist must paint if he is to be at peace with himself at the end of each day. What one can be, one must be. A happy person must find a way to be happy.''

Gisella took her in her arms. ''Child of my only sister, life is short and you must do what you can to be happy. Go with God and my blessings, but I shall miss seeing your sweet, loving face.''

''And I shall always remember yours.''

Three days later, Beatrice left for Milan and the life that awaited her there, believing that God never closed one door that He did not open another.

As the diligence traversed the roads between Florence and Milan, Beatrice passed the time by posting her thoughts in her journal, and by the time the coach was on the outskirts of Milan, she had made her last entry.

Forty-Two

Angelo arrived in Turin, still in turmoil over the startling events of the past few days.

Was he really Prince Karl Rudolf Lothar Johann Kyrburg of Austria?

The name alone was so preposterous that Angelo threw back his head and laughed. A name like that represented everything wrong in the world. It did not help that the only Austrian prince Angelo was familiar with was Prince Metternich.

Prince Karl Rudolf...now, that was about the heaviest stone a parent could hang around a child's neck, and if it was his true name, it was a demon that would follow him for the rest of his life.

Prince Karl Rudolf... Was that his true identity, or not? The idea began to haunt him.

There was no possible room for doubt that the dead hussar had had his face—the likeness was eerily identical.

And the fact that the snatches of background the captain had given him meshed perfectly with Angelo's unknown past was undeniable. How could he argue with it, when he had no past beyond the day Gisella opened her door and found him swaddled there?

There were other things, too, like their identical ages. True, Angelo did not know the exact date of his birth, but he knew Gisella had said he was not more than three or four weeks old when she found him.

The most decisive factor was the captain's dead mother. It was the one detail Angelo could not ignore: she had been found near Florence. She was dead, her body frozen during a winter snow. Her baby was never found.

Those details were a perfect match with the circumstances under which he was found. Villa Mirandola was near Florence, and many, many times as a child, Angelo had crawled upon Gisella's lap and asked her to tell him the story about the day she found him at her door during a snowstorm. "The wind carried you there, so I would find you and bring you in out of the cold," she would say. "You are my little snowman. A gift of the wind."

Put together, the stories seemed interwoven beyond denial. His mother could have been Italian— unhappily married to an Austrian prince—who, after giving birth to twin sons, took the firstborn twin and left Vienna.

It was likely she had returned to Italy, and likelier still that her husband's men had pursued her. Once it became apparent she could not outrun them, she would have been faced with two choices: let herself and the baby be captured, or perish with the child in the cold. If captured, she would face a life more miserable than the one she had run away from. True, she might choose death over capture for herself, but a mother's instinct would be to protect her baby. Last, a titled woman would be more likely to leave her baby at the door of a beautiful villa than at the door of a peasant's hovel.

Her last act to protect her child from discovery

would have been to continue on, to lead her captors away from her baby.

He had to admit it was not very likely that within that one-month time frame—between the time Angelo was born and time Gisella found him—there could have been *two* misplaced infants near Florence.

Once he had analyzed the facts one by one, he asked himself—was it chilling coincidence, or undeniable truth?

In the end, he decided the story probably was true. He was quick to add that it did not change anything. His father might be Austrian, but he, Angelo Bartolini, was not.

He would go to Prince Kyrburg and tell him where his son was buried. He had promised the dead captain he would do so, and he had to admit he had a certain amount of curiosity about the man who had, in all likelihood, fathered him.

Angelo went to Milan, to the military headquarters for the Austrian Imperial Army, in Palazzo Borromeo. Once inside, he stopped at the desk of an officer who seemed to be some sort of clerk, for he was dispensing information.

"I would like to see Prince Johann Kyrburg."

The officer looked at him strangely. "Why are you out of uniform?"

"I am not a soldier."

The officer was obviously confused. "Oh, I see. That is, for a moment, I thought you...well, never mind. His Majesty is in Vienna."

"When do you expect him back?" Angelo asked, aware that the officer was still looking at him in a wary manner.

The officer began to sort through a pile of papers on his desk. "Today is Tuesday," he said. "This schedule shows Prince Kyrburg will be back in Milan on Thursday.''

"May I leave this envelope for him? It contains something he will want.''

The officer nodded and took the envelope. "I will see that he gets it.''

The envelope contained an explanation describing how Angelo had found the hussar captain, as well as the notebook he had taken from the captain's pocket. He also left directions to the place where the man was buried. Angelo did not mention anything else.

Angelo intended to return to Turin, but as he made his departure, it was his unfortunate circumstance to meet, face-to-face, someone who not only knew him, but also knew he was wanted by the Austrians. He stepped through the door and almost bumped into Count von Schisler coming into the building, accompanied by two Austrian officers.

Von Schisler said in a clipped, authoritarian voice, "Arrest him.''

Angelo tried to dart around the guards by the door, but he was caught by one of them. A moment later, the brawny arms of the other guard came around his chest and nearly squeezed the breath from him.

Everything from that moment on passed with impressive swiftness.

Someone said, "Take him downstairs,'' and he was almost lifted off his feet, for he had a memory of his boots barely skimming the floor.

"Who is he?'' he heard someone ask.

"A liberal bastard from Turin,'' was the reply.

As the guards hauled him away, Angelo noticed von Schisler talking to the clerk who had said "His Majesty is in Vienna.''

With a guard on each arm, Angelo was hauled

downstairs into the bowels of the building. He did not know if the cell into which he was thrown was an official prison cell or not. He only knew it was very small and very dark.

Angelo sat on a bunk against one wall, his elbows resting on his knees. There was no window in the room—only a perpendicular slit, high overhead in the wall. He stretched out and folded his hands behind his head, thinking this all seemed to be one more episode in a life that was suddenly cursed at every turn.

An altogether ironic set of circumstances for "a liberal bastard from Turin."

Forty-Three

"Lisetta dear, come and join us for dinner," Gisella said, when Lisetta came into the house from her walk.

"I am not hungry. Perhaps I will take dinner in my room later," she said, which soon became her reply each time she was invited to dine with the family.

As the days passed, and filled with mounting hopelessness, Lisetta spent her time reading Shakespeare.

"This week it is *Hamlet,*" Serena said to her mother.

"I am beyond concerned. Dr. Barzini said her mind has slipped to the point where she is not stable. I have written to your brother. Angelo needs to be here."

Gisella went to find Lisetta. It wasn't difficult, for she was usually in her room. The door was open when Gisella arrived, and she saw Lisetta sitting in a chair next to a lamp, a book in her lap—but she wasn't reading.

Gisella knocked and stepped into the room. "I wanted to come and visit with you. You seem so unhappy. Is there nothing any of us can do?"

Lisetta quickly dried her eyes and took up her book, composing herself. "What? Oh, I didn't hear you come in."

Gisella stepped closer and repeated what she had said. "Please give us a chance to know you…give yourself a chance to know us. All is not as hopeless as it seems. Things will get better. Beatrice is out of our house now. Angelo is gone, but he will return. All is not lost. You must not give up."

"There is nothing wrong. I simply prefer to stay in my room."

Time passed, and Lisetta continued to withdraw into her world of books. Frequently, she would be heard wandering through the house, quoting passages. With growing concern, Tito sent for Father Francesco, who spent several hours with her.

At the end of the fourth hour, Father Francesco came out of the room and asked to speak to Tito. "She does not want help. Without her willingness to cooperate, there is little I can do, except pray for her."

The next afternoon found Serena and Gisella sitting in the garden, where the fragrant scent of rosemary filled the air.

"Look," Serena said, "Lisetta is coming out to join us."

They watched her approach in a lovely, white embroidered dress Gisella had made for her. "I am so happy to see her in that dress. She must like it, for she has even woven flowers into her hair."

"She looks lovely," Serena said. "She should do her hair that way more often."

The two of them watched as Lisetta walked on by and continued down the pathway that led from the garden.

Gisella glanced in question toward Serena, then back at Lisetta and said, "Lisetta, where are you going? Why don't you join us?"

"I am going for a walk."

"Serena and I were admiring your hair. The orange blossoms are lovely. You should wear it like that more often."

Lisetta did not say anything, nor did she pet Colossus when he ran after her.

"She has always loved Colossus, but now she hardly notices him," Serena said.

"I will be glad when Angelo arrives," Gisella said. "I think this has been too much for her…losing the man she loved, then her child, and then finding out it was Beatrice whom Angelo loved. It has not been easy for her, I know, to find herself thrust among strangers. Angelo should have stayed longer."

"We should not give all our pity to Lisetta," Serena said. "Angelo and Beatrice have suffered greatly."

Gisella agreed. "I know. Angelo has done so much to help her already. At some point, she must learn to carry some of her burden herself."

"I know, you always say, 'It is not what we are given, but what we do with it, that matters.'" Drumming her fingers on the arm of her chair, Serena added, "You know, I don't think it is a good idea to allow her to read so much Shakespeare…the last thing she needs is more tragedy. I think she needs to read something uplifting, not something like *Hamlet*. I think we should hide Shakespeare. I would hate to see her end up as poor Ophelia did."

"I never thought about that, but now that you mention it, I do see reason for concern. Today, she even braided orange blossoms into her hair."

Gisella had no more finished these words than she gasped and said, "Just like Ophelia!"

"Madonna mia!" Serena said. "You don't suppose..."

Suddenly, Gisella and Serena were running down the path Lisetta had taken, calling for help.

Workers rushed out of the vineyards and the gardens to see what had sent the *signora* and *signorina* dashing off—calling with such fear in their voices. They reached the river in time to see Serena's hands come up to her face.

"Orange blossoms," she said, when she saw a few petals come drifting by.

Frantic, everyone started to run along the riverbank, until they came to the place where Colossus sat as if waiting for someone.

"We're too late," Gisella said. "If only we had realized sooner."

Serena came to her, and the two of them stood with their arms around each other. "There was nothing we could do, Mother. When someone wants to end her life, she will find a way to do it. I think it was too late for Lisetta a long time ago...before she even came here."

Someone had gone to find Tito, and when he arrived, he organized the men to search along the river for Lisetta's body. They found nothing, so several of the younger men began to dive into the river.

It was almost an hour later that Matteo surfaced with the words they dreaded to hear. "I found her. I found the *signora.*"

They carried Lisetta's body out of the water and placed her upon the grass. Serena broke into tears. "She looks so peaceful, more like she is asleep than dead."

Gisella dropped to the ground beside Lisetta and pushed the wet strands of hair back from her face.

"Dear, tormented child, this is the first look of peace I have seen upon your sad face."

Lisetta was buried in the family cemetery, after Gisella insisted that no one in the family tell Father Francesco that they knew Lisetta's death was a suicide. "She has suffered enough. She deserves to be buried on consecrated ground."

"But that is lying, Mama," Serena said. "We know it was not an accident."

"No, it isn't. We are simply withholding our observations. You must learn, Serena, that sometimes a little inexactness is necessary."

The days after Lisetta's death turned into weeks, and still there was no word from Angelo.

"This is so unlike him," Gisella said. "He has always come home when notified of a crisis. I am beginning to fear something has happened."

"I imagine he must have serious commitments and cannot leave just yet," Tito said.

"Or perhaps the letters you've sent him have gone astray or, more likely, been confiscated by the Austrians."

The family continued to wait for him, and then one day they received a letter from Nicola. After Tito read the letter through, he relayed the heartbreaking news to Gisella and Serena.

"The Austrians arrested Angelo in Milan four weeks ago. He has been moved to the Piombi in Venice."

"But why Venice?" Gisella asked.

"I do not know," Tito said, "but I shall find out. I have been to the Piombi." Pain lodged in his throat like a choking fist, making the next words difficult to say. "It is a notorious and dreaded place."

Gisella's head dropped to her chest as she made the sign of the cross and began to pray.

Serena began to cry softly. "Why?" she asked, looking at her father through tear-filled eyes. "Why are they doing this?"

"Because they want to break him," Tito said sadly. "They want to break us all."

Forty-Four

The Milanese villa of *Contessa* Teresa Bonacossi was becoming quite a political salon, where guests would mingle and talk about Metternich or the Hapsburg police, or the latest string of injustices aimed at the liberals being jailed in growing numbers.

Some of the salons were less formal, but on a few occasions, guests would be treated to the music of the brilliant young composer Andrea Romanelli, played on the piano by none other than Andrea himself. Teresa would frequently accompany him on the spinet. At other times Andrea would play and Teresa would sing.

That the two of them were in love was obvious, and they were becoming quite the talk of Milanese society.

Lord Byron, who attended many of the salons, frequently accompanied by his lover, *Contessa* Teresa Guiccioli, inquired one evening, "Have the two of you set a date? You are getting married, I understand."

"Yes," Andrea said, "Teresa has greatly honored me by agreeing to become my wife. We are planning on the end of the month."

During this period, Beatrice finished the portrait she had started the year before, of Teresa and her two daughters. Teresa thought it exceptional and far

beyond what she had hoped for. To show her gratitude, she hung it in the most prominent place in the
villa, so all those who attended her salons would see
it.

Beatrice also finished Teresa's portrait, but she did
not show it to Teresa or Andrea, in order to surprise
them with it as a wedding present.

Beatrice was making a name for herself in Milan,
and several of those attending the salons commis-
sioned her to paint portraits for them. On numerous
occasions she even demonstrated her painting tech-
niques by working on a portrait during a salon, to
entertain the guests. Now her canvases were beginning to hang in the salons of the Milanese nobility
and the private chapels of cardinals.

One place they did not hang were the homes of
Austrians and Austrian sympathizers.

Beatrice soon became too busy to drop in during
the salons, and would isolate herself among the pots
of varnish and paints, often entertained by the distant
gay laughter and lovely melodies that came to life
beneath the magic of Andrea's fingers as they danced
over the keys of the piano.

Beatrice had never known any two people more in
love than Teresa and Andrea. It was difficult to be
in the villa with them, for she would walk into a
room and catch them in an embrace, or kissing. At
night, she would sometimes lay in bed and hear
sounds of their lovemaking coming from Teresa's
room.

Although not a day had passed that Angelo was
not on her mind, Teresa's approaching wedding
seemed to bring his image to the forefront of her
mind. She would recall the happy times in Tuscany,
just before he broke her heart, when she had planned

her wedding and danced around the house in her grandmother's wedding dress.

Oh, she knew there would never be anything between them, but that did not matter. She was still hungry for news of him.

One afternoon, while she was working on a painting, Teresa came into the room.

"This letter just came for you. It bears the crest of the *Marchese* di Varese. His home is in Lombardy, near Lake Maggiore. He is extremely wealthy, and more importantly, very, very powerful."

Beatrice opened the letter and read it twice.

"What does he say?"

"He wants me to be a guest at his villa, and listen to this—he wants me to paint frescoes! I am to name my fee and simply advise him as to when I can be ready to leave here. He will arrange everything and send his personal coach for me."

"I am so happy for you. I knew something would come along. I knew it. You must go, of course...but not before the wedding. Please stay for that, at least."

"It is only a week away. I doubt I could pack before then."

"You should write him immediately. Oh, Beatrice, think what this means. You will be famous."

That evening as Beatrice penned her letter to the *marchese,* she knew she was doing the right thing. Teresa and Andrea would be married soon. It was time for her to find other lodgings and other work. But her main reason for accepting the position was that it would take her away from Turin. She had always been concerned about being so close to Turin, and that Angelo knew where Teresa lived. Once he

learned where she was, he might pay her a visit—
and when it came to Angelo, she was as weak as
water.

For the next week, Beatrice had no time to think
about herself, for the house was bustling with plans
for the upcoming wedding. And when the day finally
arrived, Beatrice was certain she was more nervous
than Teresa.

Their wedding was a small, private affair, held in
the garden of Teresa's villa. The bride was beautiful,
the groom handsome, and Beatrice cried during the
entire event. She cried out of love for Andrea and
Teresa, and joy that such a perfect love had ended
this way, but her most profound tears were selfishly
for herself and the love that was lost forever.

As Beatrice listened to the priest conduct the marriage vows, she was torn in two—happy for Teresa,
but heartbroken that she was not blessed with the
same happiness. The pain of losing Angelo was still
acute, and having to participate in a wedding so soon
was agonizing for her. It was so difficult to act happy
when she was dying inside.

For the ball following the ceremony the villa was
beautifully decorated, but not even that could lift Beatrice's spirits.

"There you are, you wonderful, talented woman.
I simply adore the portrait you did of *Signora* Giacomo's daughter. Tell me that you will do a similar
one for my Antonella."

"Ah, *Signora* Pirrone, you always make me feel
like another Michelangelo with your praise. I regret
to say, I will be unable to do a portrait for you at
this time. I am leaving at first light for…" She realized suddenly that she should not tell anyone where
she was going, so she said, "…home, and a much

needed rest. I fear I have overextended myself, of late.''

"Oh, my dear, of course you should. But, you must promise me that you will let me know the minute you return.''

"I promise you shall be the first to know.''

Appeased, *Signora* Pirrone faded into the room of people.

As for Beatrice, she remained at the ball only an hour, then slipped upstairs in order to retire early. As she was walking down the hall toward her room, she caught a glimpse of Andrea and Teresa going into their apartments and, as she passed, saw them kissing passionately in the doorway.

For a moment she froze, staring at them, reliving her own moments of passion with Angelo, until she realized what she was doing and hurried on down the hall.

She fell across her bed, unable to hold back the tears of loss. "I cannot do it,'' she cried. "I cannot go through each day as if I was the same person I was before. I'm not the same anymore. Angelo has changed my life. Loving him has changed me. I cannot go back. I haven't the heart to go forward. Dear God, what am I going to do? How can I live without him? Help me. Help me, please. I cannot do this alone. I can't.''

What happened to those blissful days of love, when she had felt no burden, had thought nothing of trouble, had found strength in joy, and had seen nothing as impossible? Where had it all gone? It had left when he did, and all she had now were the memories and thoughts of what might have been.

If only. If only she could turn back the clock. If only she could change history. If only he had not seen fit to do a good deed. If only the very sound of his name did not catch like a dry cinder in her throat. *There is nothing worse that the loss of love,* she thought. *Whomever it was that said death is worse, lied.*

Oh, she would go on. She would not be defeated.

Early the next morning, a coach bearing the crest of the *Marchese* di Varese arrived. Beatrice stood at the door and supervised the loading of her luggage, and when it was all done, she bid Teresa and Andrea goodbye.

She climbed into the carriage, and turned her face toward Lake Maggiore, a woman stronger than even she knew—a woman learning to live with a broken heart.

"I want something Michelangelo could have painted—a Botticelli, a Caravaggio, a da Vinci, a throwback to the Renaissance. Nothing religious, mind you. I find that everywhere I go," the *marchese* said.

Beatrice began by sketching rough outlines on the walls with graphite, and the villa echoed with the sound of scratching and scraping, until it was quite commonplace. She spent hours boiling oil and sizing canvases, applying the ground and grinding colors, until at last she was ready to paint.

From the moment she entered the *marchese*'s employ, her mode of dress became the voluminous painter's smock she wore to protect her clothes while working. It was loose and paint-spattered, wrinkled and old. With her hair up in a turban and streaks of paint on her face, she was altogether sexless, a far cry from the woman with the Botticelli face and the body of an angel.

Absorbed in her work now, she had no notion of the world beyond the villa's walls, no inkling the country was in a state of proscription, no idea of the oppression, the arrest of over a thousand in Romagna. She had not been told of those exiled or imprisoned, many without trial or representation, nor was she cognizant of the countless names of so many friends that were missing.

She only knew that the sun came up on a new day each morning, that the walls were her world and her paintbrush her only line of communication. She wielded her brush with a dip to the palette and a stroke across canvas, often toiling long into the night, her eyes straining to see by dim candlelight. She lost weight. The long hours smelling paint fumes left her head aching. Exhaustion caused her arm to tremble, and yet she would not stop.

It was as if her body and the arm that held the brush were disconnected, as if the arm were something apart from her that painted incessantly, possessed, until her legs gave way beneath her. She would lay the brush aside and return to her room, fatigue driving her to fall across the bed, asleep before her head touched the pillow, her only blanket the cloak of night that covered her when the candle beside the bed sputtered and went out.

One afternoon as she was painting, the *marchesa* and two of her children walked by. "Look, Mama, she moves the brush so fast, it looks as if she is fencing."

"Indeed, Alfredo, it does look that way."

Like a woman obsessed, Beatrice painted in a frenzy, for it was the only way she could keep her mind off the pain—a reminder of the love she had lost. Work was her cure, and she devoted herself to it to the point that even the *marchese* asked her to slow down and spare her health.

When she departed from Lake Maggiore nine months later, she left the *marchese* happy, his villa filled with angels and saints, cherubs and bare-breasted women. She promised to stay in touch, but she did not tell anyone where she was going.

She had been thinking about Angelo, focusing not only on her love for him, but upon his love of Italy, and the people he loved. Losing him made her feel closer to the cause he was devoted to, and she felt some deep need to be a part of something connected with him, however remote it was.

It occurred to her that she could serve the cause of liberty through her painting. More than once she had witnessed Austrian cruelties, and many times she had gone so far as to make sketches of them, but she had never painted those scenes.

That now became her goal. She decided she would travel south, perhaps as far as Naples, and whenever she came upon the poor, mistreated peasants, or examples of their severe treatment by the Austrians, she would record the scene in her sketchbook.

She went first to Bellagio, and took a lovely little villa on the lake. This would be her home, where she would live and paint during the cold, snowbound winter months. In the spring and summer, she would travel and sketch, then return late in the fall to Bellagio.

She hired a man and his wife to be the caretakers of her villa when she was away, and she gave him several of her paintings to take into the larger towns to sell. The money was not what mattered. What was important was to get the patriotic paintings into the hands of the people.

When she left Bellagio, she stopped in the first town long enough to post several letters: one to her family in England, one to those at Villa Mirandola, and one to Teresa. ''I depart this day upon a journey to the place where I hope to find healing for a broken heart, peace for a troubled mind.''

And so, she began a new portrait in her book of life, painted in the colors of loss and resignation.

Forty-Five

There is no glory in prison.

Angelo lay on his narrow bed, beneath the window of his cell, surrounded by nothing but oppressive solitude, his body damp with sweat. He was asleep but the dream was real, and he lived the nightmare again—the inquisitor, reading with a cold heart and defiant eye, "Angelo Bartolini, condemned to death. The imperial decree is that the sentence has been commuted to ten years' imprisonment in Spielberg Prison."

He heard the chiming of the bells of San Marco, while the flap of pigeons' wings reminded him that they were free and he was not.

And then one morning, four months after he was arrested, he was awakened by the sound of someone approaching—someone who walked with a step different from the shuffle of his jailers. He listened, because it was almost unheard of that a person would pay a visit to someone here, and he thought of the other souls incarcerated here, wondering which of them this visitor would stop to see.

He was totally unprepared for his door to open, but it did, and a tall, slender man ducked his white head as he stepped into Angelo's cell. The jailer stood to one side and held the lantern aloft. For a man accustomed to darkness, the brilliant light made it almost impossible for Angelo to see.

"Bring the lamp closer," the man said as he approached Angelo, placing his hand under his chin and lifting his face into the light.

"It very well could be," he said, and Angelo recognized the thick Austrian accent. "I want this man bathed, shaved and put into decent clothes, and then bring him to me. I will be waiting upstairs."

Angelo was taken upstairs, where a bath waited. A barber was brought in to shave him and cut his hair. The clothes were as fine as, if not superior to, his own, and the size was perfect. Even the boots, which had obviously been worn a few times, were custom made, supple, and his exact size.

When dressed he was taken, under guard, up to the second floor, and placed in a small room with a table and four chairs. Two guards stood outside the door. After a few minutes, he heard brisk footsteps approaching. The door opened and the tall Austrian entered the room.

The minute his gaze fell upon Angelo's face, he said, "So, it is true. I have lost one and found the other."

"Who are you?" Angelo asked.

"Apparently, I am your father, Prince Johann Kyrburg. And you, I understand, happened upon my son, Franz Ernst, shortly before he died. I have the map to the place where you buried him."

"I did bury him, that much is true, but as for being your son, there is no proof of that."

"The proof is in your face."

Angelo studied the man whose bearing displayed considerable vigor. He seemed too young to have white hair. "That could be a coincidence," Angelo

said. "It is said that everyone has a double somewhere."

"But not to this degree. Your size, your carriage,
your mannerisms…it is too much to consider coincidence. The clothes you are wearing belonged to
Franz Ernst, and I apologize for having you wear
them if you find wearing the clothes of a dead man
offensive."

"Why am I wearing his clothes?"

"I wanted to see you in them. Aside from improving your appearance, it is obvious you and Franz
Ernst were the same size."

"I don't know why you are wasting your time
with all of this. I will be on my way to Spielberg
Prison soon, and even if I am your son, there is nothing I can do to change that. What purpose does this
serve? Were you curious? Is that why you came
here?"

"I never gave up on finding you. I always knew
that someday I would."

"You talk as though you are convinced I am your
son."

"I know more about the circumstances of your
past than you do, but the details of how you came
to be raised by the Bartolinis were the pieces of the
puzzle that were missing. You are my son. Of that,
I have no doubt."

"And so you have found your son, a criminal on
his way to Spielberg Prison. What satisfaction can
you find in that?"

"None, but it is my hope that now that you know
the true origin of your birth, you will be willing to
renounce your liberal past and—"

"Betray Italy and my countrymen?"

"If you choose to put it that way."

"That is something I will never do. Tell them I am ready to go back to my cell. I am finished talking to you."

Angelo saw the anger flare up in the Austrian's eyes, just before he said, "You cannot escape who you are. You are Austrian, like it or not."

"I am half Italian, and that is the half I lay claim to."

"I was warned that you would be difficult."

"Imprisoned men are never at their best."

"And if I could change that for you?"

"You would have my gratitude, nothing more."

"For now, that is enough," he said.

The full impact of his words did not strike Angelo until after he had been returned to his cell.

Prince Johann Kyrburg waited near the Ponte di Rialto, one of the bridges that crossed Venice's Grand Canal. He was dressed as a commoner, in clothing oddly out of fashion. His wig was brown and tied back in that old, peculiar way, and his shoes had higher heels than men now wore with queer square buckles that said this was someone from another time.

He saw the Italian approach, and waited until he was close enough to whisper, "This way."

The man followed him through several Venetian alleys, narrow and confining, where their shadows stretched before them, as if leading the way. He turned up an alleyway, through which they had to walk single file, until they reached a door. He opened it, and the man followed him inside.

"You have made the arrangements?" he asked.

The man nodded. "Everything is set."

"You have explained to your fellow liberals who the prisoner is, so they know he is one of them?"

"Yes, some do not know him, but they all know of him."

"Good." He removed a fat pouch from his coat pocket. "I trust you will put this contribution to good use."

"Very good use."

The prince removed another pouch from his pocket, this one smaller than the first. "Give him this once you arrive in Arona."

"As you wish."

Angelo passed the next few days in his cell, still uncertain about the date of his transfer to Spielberg.

The time came when he least expected it—late one night. He was asleep when he heard the key shoved into his cell door. By the time he was on his feet the door was open, and two men came in and placed a hood over his head before they led him away.

"Where are you taking me?"

"To Spielberg. What did you think? That we were going to let you go?"

Angelo listened to their laughter as his hands were shackled behind him and he was placed in a coach. He heard the slam of the door and the *crack* of the driver's whip. The coach lurched forward.

So this is the way it is to be, he thought—ignominiously secreted away to Spielberg, hooded, and in the dark.

As the coach rocked and rolled along, covering mile after country mile, Angelo had no concept of time, or even of when days changed into night. The hood was removed only long enough for him to eat. He was conscious that the coach stopped several times, but only for short periods when the horses were changed.

He found this puzzling, and he could not help wondering just why the Austrians wanted to get him to Spielberg at such a fast pace.

Metternich paced the length of his office, his face twisted in a rage. He could not understand how something like this could have happened—how this prisoner, of all prisoners, had managed to disappear.

He was still wondering how those idiots who had transported Bartolini from Venice to Spielberg, who swore they had left his head covered during the entire way, except to eat, had not noticed, until they reached their destination, that the man in the coach was not the same man they had removed from the cell in Venice.

Bartolini had cleverly managed to disappear, and a prisoner who was due to be hanged was in his place in Spielberg Prison.

Somewhere there was someone who knew something. His best spies were working on it, but after two weeks, they still had no clues. They only knew Bartolini was not in Venice, or Milan, or Turin, and he was not at his family home in Tuscany.

Bartolini may have disappeared into thin air but he was out there somewhere, Metternich knew, and he would not rest until he found him.

Forty-Six

Angelo walked along the shores of Lake Maggiore and looked across the water to the Lombardy side. He was restless, and tired of killing time in Arona— picturesque though it was—when there was so much to be done in Turin.

Still, he knew his compatriots were right—they had released him and given him the pouch of money and the letter from his father warning him not to return to Turin until he received word that it was safe.

He wasn't fool enough to think the secret police and the military would not be combing Milan and Turin looking for him. He suspected his friends had all been questioned, and probably his family, too.

He shoved his hands deep into his pockets. It was cooler here, with the wind blowing off a lake filled with melted Alpine snow. He thought it such a waste that he was in this romantic spot, one that Beatrice would have loved, and yet, he was here without her.

He imagined her safely ensconced with his family at Villa Mirandola—and then he remembered Lisetta and all the pain he had caused Beatrice because of one small kindness he had performed. He felt like a prisoner here. He had no family, no friends. He was afraid to socialize for fear of meeting an Austrian sympathizer, so he kept to himself. He was beginning to wonder what good could come from a life spent in this manner. His life had lost its purpose—in fact, he had no life. He simply existed.

He heard music and walked past the shops by the lake. Then he visited an outdoor market and wandered through the vendors' stalls, stopping for a time to appreciate the local art.

There was one artist whose work he much admired—one he did not think local, since the landscapes were not from around here. They were signed *Vérité*, which he knew was the French word for "truth." An odd name for an artist, he thought, but then artists could often be the odd sort.

He imagined saying such to Beatrice, and had a clear vision of the kind of face she would make in reply. Content to keep his thoughts on her for a while, he wandered away from the art and walked slowly back to the boardinghouse where he had taken a room.

He spent three months in Arona before deciding he could not sit there any longer, letting life pass him by. A life being chased by the Austrians was preferable to wasting away. He was still a prisoner— behind bars of his own making—what did it matter anyway? He was restless, and needed something to do. At least running for his life would keep him busy. And if he was captured, or even killed, so be it. He didn't have anything to lose now—except his sanity.

He began to grow a moustache and, when it was long enough, he had his horse groomed and saddled for the journey to Turin.

Because he had only a few belongings to pack, he rolled them up in a blanket, and lashed them to the back of his saddle.

As he rode out of Arona, he calculated that even if he took his time, he would be in Turin tomorrow.

Making good time, he reached the outskirts of Turin before nightfall the following day. He tethered his horse and took a nap, preferring to enter the city under cover of darkness. He crossed into Turin later by a less traveled bridge, and took a zigzag route to Nicola's house.

"I am glad to see you, my friend, but worried that you have returned," Nicola said when he greeted Angelo. "You know you cannot stay, though. It is not safe for you here. The secret police are everywhere, and dozens are arrested daily. The hangings in the square are a daily ritual. If you stay, you will be in hiding. You cannot work. You cannot even show your face around here—moustache or no moustache. It is far too risky. You should go into France, where we both have many friends."

"I have been considering it," Angelo said.

"So have I, my friend. So have I." He put his hand on Angelo's shoulder. "Come into my study. I think we could both use a glass of wine."

"Have you heard anything from my family...from Beatrice?"

"Fioriana wrote Beatrice a letter several months ago, but it was Serena who wrote her back. She said Beatrice had left Villa Mirandola not too long after you did. She went to Milan to finish the paintings she was doing for Teresa. It was about the time that Teresa and Andrea were married. Beatrice left shortly after the wedding and it seems she has virtually disappeared. I saw Teresa and Andrea at the opera not long ago. Teresa said Beatrice did not want to be found. She speculated that if she were still in Italy, she would not be using her real name."

"She would do that because she knows I would look for her. She would never forgive herself if anything happened between us, now that I am married to Lisetta. I decided, on my way here, that as soon as I find a safe place I am going to have the marriage annulled—or divorce her, if need be. I cannot live this way.''

Nicola had a strange look on his face. ''You don't know about Lisetta, do you.''

''What about her?''

''Serena said she drowned, and implied it was not an accident.''

For a moment, Angelo was so stunned he could not say anything. He only knew that now he was free to marry Beatrice but, ironically, he did not know where she was.

Still, he was not happy over Lisetta's death. ''No, I did not know about her death. It is a tremendous shock. I did not wish to be married to her, true, but I never wished for her death—not even in my moments of deepest despair.''

''I know that,'' Nicola said. ''You sacrificed much to help her. No one could ever accuse you of not wishing her well.''

Angelo barely heard the words. His heart was racing far ahead of his mind, and he could feel only a bittersweet sort of pain—knowing he was free to marry Bea, but had no inkling as to where she was. And even if he found her, he was an escaped felon, hunted like a wild boar by the Austrians. He had nothing to offer her but himself.

''I'm sorry to be the bearer of such bad news,'' Nicola said. ''I couldn't think of a kinder way to tell you.''

''When you lose the woman you love, there is no kind way,'' Angelo said.

''Do you think she would have gone back to Paris?'' Nicola asked.

"No, but either way, it won't be difficult to validate."

"What are you going to do now?"

"I am going to find her. With her name on her paintings, it shouldn't be too difficult to track her down."

"Perhaps, but you cannot afford to be seen about town, visiting art galleries, can you?"

"Not in Turin or Milan, but there are other towns."

"You are welcome to stay here as long as you like."

"I know, and I thank you, but like you said, Turin is too dangerous for me to remain here."

"That is true, but where will you go?"

"I have been thinking about Naples."

"Naples would be a good idea…if you stay away from the Carbonari."

Angelo grinned, and left for Naples that night.

He took a nomad's route to Naples, wandering in and out of hilltop villages and seaside towns, never remaining in one place long enough to earn a reputation or attract suspicion.

As for art, he had seen enough of it to know what he liked. He was not surprised to discover that the art he identified with most depicted the harshness of Austrian brutality and the manner in which the Austrians repressed the Italian people. He supposed this was due partly to the fact he was now cut off from active participation in something that once had been his life.

Ironically, these paintings were all signed by the same artist—the one he had come across in Arona, who called himself *Vérité*.

In Lucca, Angelo went so far as to purchase one of them—an oil on canvas entitled *Italy on the*

Graves of Patriots, with its depiction of a woman standing with her breasts bared, a sea of bodies beneath her feet, a saber in one hand and a tattered banner that read *Liberty* in the other.

The more he traveled, the more paintings he encountered, and not only oils. There were also watercolors, drawings and even a few lithographs. This artist, he knew, was a man who had suffered, and suffered greatly.

He began to find *Vérité*'s work with such frequency that he wondered if one man could have painted them all. Smoke rose from burned homes, women cried over their dead husbands by the front door, a baby wailed over a mother lying with her throat cut—all sufferings, all horrible, and all too real.

The paintings were always the same in their incredibly true rendering of what the artist had to have witnessed firsthand, for the desolation, the bloody massacres, the horrible fires and the rubble of destruction were all too representative of inhumane horrors—a testimony to the barbarity of civilized man.

He pondered over the man who had painted these, and how the artist must travel from place to place, following the Austrian troops as they stamped out human lives along with rebellion. For a moment, Angelo almost found that humorous, for his own life seemed to parallel that of this artist with his obvious passion for Italy and her freedom.

He began to make inquiries about the artist, but no one had ever seen him. Angelo wondered about this mysterious man who did more to turn the hearts of the Italian people than a hundred revolts could have done.

One day, while he was looking at art in Parma, he

had a conversation with Count Vero de Gambaloto, who seemed to be as impressed as Angelo was with the artist.

"I own six of *Vérité*'s paintings and I am quite eager to obtain more. I would be delighted if you would join my family and me for dinner tonight. Afterward, it would be a great honor to show you my collection."

"I have never been known to turn down dinner or the opportunity to view art."

Count Vero laughed. "Shall we say, dinner at seven?"

In many ways the family of the count reminded Angelo of his own family, and he found sitting at the table with them sadly mindful of the life he had misplaced. He was actually glad when dinner was over.

After they had smoked a cigar, the count showed Angelo his collection of art.

Angelo was most interested in his *Vérité*s, of course, but there was one that sucked the very breath from his lungs. He was talking amiably one minute, then rendered speechless the next.

There on the wall, not more than two feet in front of him, were the ancient gates at Villa Mirandola— the same gates Beatrice had painted that day so long ago.

Trying to hide his shock as best he could, he went to the painting for a closer look, and saw the misty presence of Villa Mirandola at the end of the long, curving drive. And there, in the lower right corner, the painting was signed *Vérité*.

Beatrice… At long last, he had found her.

Now, it was only a matter of time.

Forty-Seven

It surprised him how very easy it actually was to find her.

He had written his mother to inquire if they had any news of Beatrice's whereabouts. Gisella replied they had received several letters from Bea, but added that she never revealed where she lived. "I did notice, however, that her last letter was mailed in Como. I hope this small bit of information will help you in your search. Find her, Angelo. Do not give up until you do. All of our prayers are with you."

Como. It was the break he had been waiting for.

He left Parma immediately, not caring that it was bitterly cold. He had suffered so much pain and loneliness apart from her, he would have walked there barefoot if need be. It would take more than cold weather to hold him back now.

He arrived in Como late one afternoon, and wasted no time asking questions. After three days and dozens of inquiries, he located a man who said his brother Carlo frequently mailed letters for an English lady—an artist who lived not very far away.

"Where?" Angelo asked. "How far away? What town?"

"In Bellagio, *signore*...on the other side of the lake. Carlo and his wife work for the *signora*," he said.

"Do you know if the *signora* is in Bellagio now?"

"*Sí,* she is there. She is always there in the wintertime. She travels to make sketches in the warm months, then returns to her villa in Bellagio to paint during the winter."

"This villa—do you know where it is?"

"Of course I know. My brother has told me many times. It is called Villa Giuliana. I can draw you a map if you like."

Map in hand, Angelo hired a boat to take him to Bellagio on the edge of Lake Como, not far from the Swiss border. The wind blowing across the lake was cold, but it had stopped snowing by the time Angelo reached his destination.

Poised at the far end of a promontory that divided the two branches of the lake, the village was surrounded by blue glacier waters, rugged Alpine mountains and green woods, dusted with snow. It was very quaint, nestled along the edge of the lake and covered in a thick blanket of snow. Bellagio glistened like a priceless pearl, and Angelo could not help thinking this was a good omen.

As he climbed the cobbled steps up from the harbor, the bells rang out from the belfry of the ancient Basilica di San Giacomo. He felt the bells were calling him to the church and, accordingly, he went inside. He saw the priest standing just inside the door, as if he were waiting for him. Angelo spoke briefly with Father Marcus before continuing on his way, anxious to find his love at last.

Villa Giuliana occupied a tranquil setting on the shores of the lake, near the point where the lake divided in two. It was an imposing structure that seemed far too large for the small woman who occupied it, and he wondered if she tried to lose herself in its massive rooms.

Carlo's wife, Lucianna, answered the door and, after a brief conversation, she invited him inside while she went to find her husband. "Please, give me your coat and warm yourself by the fire," she said, "while I go to find Carlo."

The cold numbness was leaving the tips of Angelo's fingers by the time Lucianna returned with her husband. Carlo was a small, wiry man with sharp, black eyes, full of suspicion. They missed nothing. Angelo knew immediately that this was not a man to be easily persuaded, or one who would accept anything but the truth. He did not know how much about her past Beatrice had revealed to them, but the protective manner both Lucianna and Carlo exhibited made him think they were more to Beatrice than mere servants.

He knew he would get nowhere with them unless he was completely honest, and so he said, "My name is Angelo Bartolini. I would like to see Beatrice, and I know she would want to hear what I have to tell her."

"I am sure you would like to see her," Carlo said, "but you see, the problem is the *signora* would not like to see you."

"She has told you about me?"

He nodded. "Enough to know you are not welcome here, *signore*."

"I have news that Beatrice will welcome," Angelo said, and then told Carlo and his wife why he had come.

Carlo considered Angelo's words for a moment before he and Lucianna moved to a corner of the room, where they discussed it between themselves.

Several minutes later they returned to where Angelo waited by the fireplace.

"If what you are saying is true, and you are free, I know it would be pleasing to the *signora*'s ears. However, if you are not telling the truth, and you hurt her, I will cut out your heart."

"Fair enough," Angelo said, believing that Carlo would do exactly as he said. Still, it was obvious they were true romantics at heart, for Lucianna gently told him Beatrice had finished breakfast and would be working in her studio.

Carlo said, "I will take you there, *signore*."

Lucianna gave Carlo a stern look and said, "He can find her studio by himself, Carlo. You and I have some shopping to do."

"I did the shopping yesterday," Carlo said.

Lucianna gave him an exasperated look. "I want to do *more* shopping." Then to Angelo she said, "The studio is easy to find, *signore*. It is up the stairs—the third door on the right."

"Follow your nose, *signore*. The smell of turpentine is strongest there," Carlo said, and the two of them put on their coats and scarves and left. Before closing the door, Carlo winked and said they would return in two hours.

As soon as they were gone, Angelo hurried up the stairs, but when he found the studio, Beatrice was not there.

There were many rooms going down the hallway in both directions, and Angelo made his rounds, checking each room until he came to one door that he knew instinctively was the door to her room. He paused and heard the sound of someone moving about inside. He opened the door slowly and saw her.

She stood at the window, holding the drapery aside. She looked both beautiful and sad.

He stood motionless, unable to take his gaze from her. It had been so long. Seeing her now released a flow of throbbing awareness, long suppressed. Every nerve ending in his body seemed acutely aware of her and the attraction, the love he had for her. Relief and desire flooded his brain and he fought the strong urgings, the yearning desire and craving need. Her. Always her. He found it almost impossible to conquer his body's reflexive response. It had waited so very long for this moment.

Timing, they say, is everything, and at the exact moment he pushed the door open and stepped into the room, Beatrice dropped the curtain and unbuttoned her gown. Angelo watched with a dry mouth and pounding heart as she let it slide from her body. She turned to reach for her clothes and saw him. As if frozen in time, she opened her mouth but no sound came forth. She did not move, but stood as still and pale as a snow-covered statue.

She stood before him in perfect and complete nudity, her body warmed by the golden glow of early morning light filtering through the draperies—lovely, solitary and alone.

He had never wanted to make love to her more than he did at this moment, the urge flowing through his veins like the spiraling sweetness of an opium pipe, seductive and sweet. Everything became dreamlike.

He heard her breathless whisper. "Angelo…"

Sanity returned and he went to her. A moment later she was in his arms.

He had no recollection of taking his clothes off, or moving with her to the bed. The only sobering point came when she said, "Angelo, you are married. We cannot."

"We can, love. I am free, Bea, and unless I die making love to you, which I plan to do in two seconds, I will explain everything later."

"I don't believe you. You are only telling me that."

"No, *cara*, I am telling the truth. You know I would do nothing to ruin things between us now. We have a lot of unfinished things between us and a lifetime to work them out—but right now all I can think about is making love to you. Trust me, Bea, and stop asking questions. I have loved you for so long, I can no longer remember a time when thoughts of you did not crowd my consciousness and fill my heart with love."

His gaze wandered over her face and paused a moment at her lips, then dropped lower, past the wild fluttering in her throat, to the swell of her breasts. It was arousing, but it was the words he spoke with his eyes—the pain, the regret, the despair, the almost hopeless desolation of loving and not being loved in return—that moved her. "I love you, Angelo. Nothing could ever change that. Nothing."

The sound of her name was a litany playing over and over in his brain, but it was not enough. No matter how close he was to her, it was never close enough. Already, when he thought of her, it was difficult to imagine the place where he stopped and she began. She was part of him, the center of his being, something as necessary to his survival as the air he breathed.

"The memory of you is all that kept me going," he whispered hoarsely, as his mouth covered hers with a kiss of assurance, and she knew this wonderful, honorable, gentle man loved and adored her. She did not know what had happened to change things between them, nor how it was that he was free, but she knew more than anything that she could trust him.

Nothing is as capable of betrayal as the human body, and Beatrice felt everything within her rush outward, acutely aware of him with every fiber of her being. She wanted him with a fierceness that was almost frightening. The heat of his skin warmed her and she was conscious of the tugging feeling inside.

She moved beneath the hands passing over her with tender inquiry and she felt her arms go around his neck to pull him even closer. She began kissing him, across the forehead, along his jaw, down to his throat where she could feel his pounding pulse. She nipped his shoulder as her hand slipped lower to close around him, feeling his body jerk.

"I love you more than life," he said. "I want to spend eternity with you. I want to see our children and pray they will all be like you. I want to give you the world. You have only to ask."

She smiled against the warm flesh of his neck. "You have spent almost the entire time I've known you trying to get me into bed, and now that I am here, you want to talk?"

She felt the vibration of his laugh and she pressed her hips against him. His breath mingled with hers, and his mouth covered hers with a swirling warmth. His chest pressed against her breasts and she felt a ripple of desire coil low in her stomach, spinning faster and faster still. He turned her palm and pressed a kiss in it and his breath came hot against her ear. His body quivered with excitement and his mouth sought the warmth of hers with another kiss.

His breathing was faster now, and he said something soft and liquid in Italian and she felt the hard press of him when he came into her. She raised her knees, drawing him deeper as he began to move with sure, slow strokes. Her hands spread over his back, touching the taut muscles. She moved against him in unconscious passion, washed by strong rhythms of love and desire, each one stronger and more intense, until her body took complete control.

Her body moved of its own accord now, and drove her to a point of insanity and she cried out his name. Still, he did not stop until she felt the muscles of his legs grow tense, and his buttocks clench tight in the fulfillment of passion.

They lay together in pure, quiet stillness, and from somewhere deep inside her she felt a small flickering light of perfect peace. He held her close, his body like hers, exquisitely at rest. She knew the moment had been so much more than a joining of flesh, or lovemaking between a man and a woman. This was real. This was love. This was belonging. It was the end of Angelo and Beatrice as separate entities, and the beginning of two people who become one. This was the point when each of them lost their solitude, their privacy and their aloneness. They belonged to each other now and welcomed the bonds that would hold them fast from now on.

"Why are you here?" she asked.

"Because I love you and cannot live without you. Isn't that obvious to you by now?"

"Yes, my love, it is, but I mean, what happened? I know you would not come here and tell me to trust you and then dishonor us both. What about Lisetta?"

"Lisetta is dead."

She felt a stabbing pain to her heart. "I am sorry.

I never wished for this, not even at the moment when I wanted you the most, when I thought I would die at the thought of never seeing you again.''

He kissed her shoulder. ''I know. Strangely enough, I never blamed her for what happened. It was an unfortunate set of circumstances—a good deed gone wrong. I hated her coming between us, but I did not hate her. Like you, I never wished for her death.''

He rolled over and he cradled her against him. Her hand was on his chest. ''That is one of the things I have always admired about you. You are so wonderfully, terribly male, yet you have this beautiful, compassionate, gentle side. It is rare to find the two together.''

''You bring out the gentleness in me, Bea, with your own calm nature and loving ways.''

''How did she die?''

He stroked her arm as he told her about his mother's letter and her explanation of Lisetta's death. ''There will be time enough to speak of it later, if you like, but now we have so much between us to talk about.''

''How did you find me?''

''I became interested in the work of a certain artist called Vérité. While in Parma, I met Count Vero de Gambaloto who was also an admirer of Vérité. He invited me to dinner and offered to show me his paintings. Imagine my surprise when I saw one of the paintings was of the gates at Villa Mirandola.''

''That seems so long ago.''

''To me, as well. Every day apart from you was like eternity.''

''So you knew I was Vérité, but how did you know I was here, in Bellagio?''

He told her about the letter his mother received. "It was mailed in Como."

"And you went there."

He nodded. "After asking a lot of questions, I found Carlo's brother."

"Ahh," she said. "And I thought I had everything so well planned. I did not think you would be able to find me so easily."

"It was meant to be, just as you and I are meant to be. As much as I would like to stay here and make love to you again, we cannot. We must get dressed now, or we will be late."

"Late for what?"

"Our wedding. I stopped by the church on my way here. Father Marcus is waiting for us. I have invited Carlo and Lucianna."

"We are to be married?"

"Love, with the things that have come between us in the past, do you think I would let one more second pass without making you my wife? I will not risk losing you again."

"I cannot help thinking about that wedding gown at Villa Mirandola."

"Bea, I cannot take any more uncertainty. We do this now. If you like, we can do it again at Villa Mirandola, but I won't risk anything else coming between us. It is enough."

"Yes," she said, kissing him. "It is more than enough and I find I am as anxious as you."

He watched her leave the bed, thinking he was the most fortunate of men.

He had loved her shyness all those years ago when she first came to Italy; he had loved her lovely nakedness when standing by a castle window in the Alps; he had loved her paint-smeared fingers and the scent of turpentine she always wore; he had even loved her the day he married another woman; but there was nothing to compare to a love forged by danger and mistakes, by hurt and suffering, by wanderlust and terrible loss, and the joy of finding her again.

ELAINE COFFMAN

66842	THE FIFTH DAUGHTER	___ $6.99 U.S.	___ $8.50 CAN.
66596	THE BRIDE OF BLACK DOUGLAS	___ $6.99 U.S.	___ $8.50 CAN.

(limited quantities available)

TOTAL AMOUNT	$_____
POSTAGE & HANDLING	$_____
($1.00 for one book; 50¢ for each additional)	
APPLICABLE TAXES*	$_____
TOTAL PAYABLE	$_____
(check or money order—please do not send cash)	

To order, complete this form and send it, along with a check or money order for the total above, payable to MIRA Books®, to: **In the U.S.:** 3010 Walden Avenue, P.O. Box 9077, Buffalo, NY 14269-9077; **In Canada:** P.O. Box 636, Fort Erie, Ontario, L2A 5X3.

Name:_____

Address:_____ City:_____

State/Prov.:_____ Zip/Postal Code:_____

Account Number (if applicable):_____

075 CSAS

*New York residents remit applicable sales taxes.
 Canadian residents remit applicable GST and provincial taxes.

MIRA®

Visit us at www.mirabooks.com   MEC1102BL